An Incomparable Woman

She moved into the room slowly, without speaking. Grayson went to her. Her hair was like skeins of silk through his fingers. He rubbed the back of his hand against her cheek. Her skin made him think of satin and delicate lace and French perfume. He took her hand and touched his lips to the inside of her wrist. Nothing existed but the two of them, alone in the cool dimness. His mouth brushed her temple, her cheekbone, the tender hollow at the base of her throat. Then he tipped her chin up with his forefinger until her eyes looked up into his.

"I want you, Cassandra."

It wasn't what he'd meant to say. She trembled so violently he had to hold her. She didn't answer, but let him press her body against his. Her shivering ceased. He swept her up into his arms.

Also by Marianne Willman

Yesterday's Shadows

**Available from
HarperPaperbacks**

SILVER SHADOWS

MARIANNE WILLMAN

HarperPaperbacks
A Division of HarperCollinsPublishers

This is a work of fiction. The characters, incidents, and dialogues are products of the author's imagination and are not to be construed as real. Any resemblance to actual events or persons, living or dead, is entirely coincidental.

HarperPaperbacks *A Division of* HarperCollins*Publishers*
10 East 53rd Street, New York, N.Y. 10022

Copyright © 1993 by Marianne Willman

Cover illustration by Elaine Gignilliat

First printing: March 1993

Printed in the United States of America

HarperPaperbacks, HarperMonogram, and colophon are trademarks of HarperCollins*Publishers*

10 9 8 7 6 5 4 3 2 1

To my son, Scott, one of the most courageous and gallant persons I have ever known—with pride and love. Stay off those motorcycles! To his beautiful new daughter, Jozi Lea, and her beautiful big sister, Amber (my little mermaid), with love.

And to the dedicated nurses and doctors, physical therapists and cast technicians of Mt. Clemens General Hospital and Henry Ford Hospital, who saw Scott through his many operations—especially Dr. Peter Ajluni, Dr. Jim Jamieson, Dr. Ditmars, Dr. Watson, and the incomparable Dr. Bertran Moed. My deepest gratitude.

Finally, to Karen Solem, editor-in-chief of Harper-Paperbacks, and my editor, Carolyn Marino, for seeing me through these trying months with understanding and compassion.

Prologue

Colorado, 1860

The silence was uncanny.

Unnatural.

The man who was called Grayson Howard among the white men and Gray Wolf among the Cheyenne rode warily toward their encampment. There was no breeze to ruffle the fringe of his buckskin shirt or fan his long hair away from his neck. There was not even bird song or the scurrying of small animals to break the stillness. He rode the half mile up the steep slope in growing dread.

A glint of metal caught his eye and he dismounted to pick it up. It was a piece of decorative metal in the curious wagon wheel symbol of the Fortuna Investment Company. The hated emblem of the men who were trying to chase the Cheyenne and their allies from their hunting grounds, so they might rip and gouge the earth in search of gold.

At the top of the rise he caught the sharp, coppery scent of blood even before his horse smelled it, and was ready when the gelding reared in fear. There had been no circling of buzzards overhead to prepare him. They were too busy feasting.

The peaceful camp along the line of willows was gone and devastation was everywhere. At first he had only seen the ruins of the burned lodges. Then he saw the pitiful, tattered heaps of bodies, streaked black with dried blood and flies. Somewhere among the dead he would find the lifeless bodies of his young wife and son.

He knew it without hope or doubt.

His search among the bodies was short and agonizing. Uncles, cousins, aunts, friends . . . children. Grayson slashed his arms with the razor-sharp edge of his knife in mourning and respect. The blood dripped down over his hands until they were slick and red with it. She Laughs was facedown at the edge of the creek, still clasping the boy against her breast. Her head had been nearly severed from her body. He touched their beloved faces. Cold . . . so cold.

The unearthly silence was rent by anguished cries. They seemed to come from a distance, although Grayson was dimly aware that he was their source. He prayed and fasted and ministered to his dead. For two days he did not sleep, but still he dreamed. Grayson saw the Fortuna wagon wheel rolling west across the land. West toward the sea. Blood welled up in the furrow of its passing.

All around him voices cried out for vengeance. Out of his grief and agony he forged an iron purpose and consecrated it with a vow: He would find those responsible for this foul deed and make them suffer for it—at any cost.

Even to himself.

1

San Francisco, 1870

Grayson awakened, drenched with sweat, to the sound of thunder. It echoed in his ears like a barrage of gunfire. Instinctively he reached for his rifle. Instead his hand closed on the bone-handled butt of his Navy Colt. His eyes opened, not to the Cheyenne lodge he'd expected but to a high-ceilinged bedroom of elegant proportions. Instead of translucent hide walls hung with utensils and weapons, he saw crimson wallpaper, heavily flocked, and the frosted globes of the unlit gas lamps.

His racing heartbeat slowed as Grayson recognized his surroundings. A hotel in San Francisco, not the summer camp the Cheyenne called Bitter Creek. Relief came, warm and reassuring, followed by the cold pain of loss. He ached with it. He'd been dreaming again, reliving the moments that had shattered his life into a thousand bloody pieces. *Goddammit, it had seemed so real! He had been so sure that this time he would turn the tide . . . change the outcome . . .*

He threw back the covers, the cold sweat already drying on his bronzed and sinewy frame. He was naked except for the beaded medallion that hung from a gold chain about his neck. Old and worn, fashioned from elk hide and hundreds of tiny blue and white glass beads, worked into the Cheyenne symbol of the Morning Star, it served as both talisman and symbol of what Grayson had lost. He wore it always.

Sitting on the edge of the ornate bed, he took a deep, shuddering breath in and slowly let it flow out again. The very air seemed saturated with the smell of blood.

Lightning flared. The nightmare retreated but the memories remained. Voices from the violent past murmured in the shadows of his mind. How long would it take to subdue them?

The answer was always the same: We will be silent when vengeance is taken.

Grayson smiled grimly. Not much longer, then.

He rose and drew on his robe. The brocade was cool at first but warmed quickly to his skin. He still preferred cambric and buckskin. It had taken him a long time to make his way from the bloody massacre on the high plains to the best hotel in San Francisco. Lean and haunted years. And tonight he'd be the honored guest of one of California's wealthiest and most influential men.

The smell of cigar smoke drifted in from the adjoining room. Jaime was early. Grayson dressed and went through to the parlor. The draperies were open with a view to the bay. The fog was fading, melting away in pearly layers. Thunder boomed again, rattling the tall windows. Suddenly the rain came down in silver sheets against the glass, casting the room into luminous darkness relieved only by the glow from the hearth.

Jaime McFee, who served as agent for Grayson's mining interests, lounged in the comfortable chair drawn up before the fire. His feet were propped up on the fringed hassock and a glass of whiskey was in his hand. He had the carrot-red hair of his Scots father, and the pale blue eyes of his English mother.

Grayson leaned against the doorjamb and spoke over the rain. "Getting a head start on the day?"

Jaime jumped up and set the crystal glass on the side table. Christ, the man was as silent as a ghost! Or an Indian. He cleared his throat. "Since you decided to sleep away the morning, I thought I'd make myself comfortable while I waited."

"So I see." Grayson crossed the carpet to his unofficial aide-de-camp. "A little early for whiskey, isn't it?"

The other man's eyes crinkled at the corners. "Not for a McFee. We were weaned on it. And it would be a sin not to avail myself of a wee bit when it's here for the taking. Damn good whiskey, too. It would be even more a sin if it went to waste."

He eyed Grayson in his well-tailored suit and vest. "I don't think I'll ever get used to seeing you in city clothes."

"I don't think I'll ever get used to wearing them. These collars are damned uncomfortable." Grayson's smile faded. He was too impatient for small talk today. "Were you able to get the picture I asked for?"

"Yes, and everything else on your list." Jaime unwrapped the contents of the parcel from their various layers, setting some papers on the table.

"Excellent." Grayson's changeable eyes darkened, went suddenly from the sheen of tarnished silver to dull, hard slate. He leaned his arm along the mantelpiece. "My enemies . . . tell me about them."

Jaime sat back. "Tyler Lucton is everything you imagined. Perhaps worse. His wife, Cassandra, is the granddaughter of an English lord. A certified beauty, with blood bluer than the queen's."

A bitter smile curved Grayson's mouth. "The perfect ornament for a man who means to rise in the world—whatever the cost."

"Yes. Nothing but the best for Tyler Lucton. As to the girl, her name is Catherine but she's called Kitty. An orphaned niece of Mrs. Lucton taken in as a young child. Young and bidding fair to be pretty one day—but you can judge for yourself."

Carefully, Jaime extracted a rectangle of scalloped-edged paperboard from his packet and held it out. "I told the parlor maid that I was a journalist doing a story and that I only wanted to borrow the photographs for a day."

Grayson took the sepia-toned picture. He turned it toward the light and caught his breath in surprise. Pretty? Why she was beautiful! Masses of shining hair framing an oval face. A graceful throat, lovely shoulders, and a high, round bosom. There was something in the lift of her chin, the light that the photographer had captured in her eyes, that intrigued him. Thick lashes framed eyes—blue or green, he imagined—that were large and clear. There was sorrow in their depths, masked by her smile. Intriguing.

His heart beat a little faster. So this was Kitty Hamilton. She was more than he'd expected—quite frankly, more than he wanted. That part of his life had died at

Bitter Creek. If he began to think of her as a person rather than Tyler Lucton's niece, it would be his undoing. Grayson's determination wavered. Then he looked again and frowned.

"I was told that Lucton's niece was barely of marriageable age."

Jaime sprang up to look at the sepia tint in Grayson's hand, and swore. "Damn it, that's the wrong one. That's his wife. Cassandra."

Grayson reached inside the envelope and removed the others. One was a formal pose of Cassandra against a backdrop of fake Grecian pillars and artificial roses, done in a local studio. Almost reluctantly, he focused on her face. She had changed since the earlier portrait had been taken. Her features were more finely chiseled and her lips were pressed together tightly; but it was her eyes that had changed most of all. They were as bright and clear as polished glass, and just as empty of life. All the vibrant emotion of her youth was gone, dead or shuttered away. He set it aside.

The third was a double pose of Cassandra with a young girl. Jaime peered over his shoulder. "There. That's the niece."

In this joint portrait, Cassandra Lucton's features were animated with genuine warmth. Grayson wondered what made her change from picture to picture. Which was the real woman? He glanced at Kitty beside her, and experienced an unexpected—and very unwelcome—pang of disappointment. There was a mild family resemblance between the two, mostly in the shape of nose and mouth, but very little else.

A pity.

But, he reminded himself sharply, this was business, not pleasure.

Jaime found it difficult to guess at what emotions raged behind Grayson's controlled features. But then, few knew what Grayson thought or felt at any given time—unless he wanted them to. Then there was no doubt at all. He'd never known anyone to stay as completely motionless as Grayson, either. Must be the Cheyenne blood, he thought, scratching his chin.

He shifted restlessly. "What do you think?"

Grayson shrugged and concentrated on Kitty's likeness. "I can't tell much with so rigid a pose. This appears to have been taken a few years ago. I suppose the girl has changed since this sitting. Have you actually seen her?"

"Once or twice. Pretty, in an unformed sort of way, but can't hold a candle to the flame-haired Cassandra."

Once again Grayson's eyes sought Cassandra's portrait. "No, I don't imagine she would." He forced himself to look away. "Are there any serious suitors for the girl's hand?"

"Not that I could discover. She's been ill. Had the scarlatina or some such thing. She'll make her debut to society next week at a fancy ball the Luctons are giving. All the high muckety-mucks will be there."

Jaime picked up his glass and downed the whiskey at a gulp. "You've been mighty closelipped about all this. What have you got up your sleeve?"

"I don't mean the girl any harm. It's her uncle I'm after."

Grayson stood the photographs in a row along the mantelpiece. "Everyone seems to think that Tyler Lucton has been coining gold hand over fist through his shipping concerns. I know differently. In the past three months Lucton's been borrowing secretly—and heavily. If he thinks he's about to make a wealthy marriage for his niece with a hefty marriage settlement, he'll plunge even deeper. And when he's in so far over his head that he can't climb out again, I'll see that he buries himself!"

Jaime whistled in surprise. He poured out another finger of whiskey and swirled the honey-colored liquid in the heavy glass. "How do you know all this?"

Frost glittered in Grayson's eyes. "I'm the man he's been borrowing from."

"Christ! Are you insane?" Jaime couldn't believe his ears. "You're liable to lose everything you've worked for, Grayson! Get out, before it's too late."

"It already is."

There would be no turning back now. Grayson had waited for this day for many years. And it was only the beginning.

It had taken planning, hard work, and more than a little luck. He'd succeeded, spurred on by his private Furies. He'd never doubted that he would. He tried not to think of the two women in the photographs. Vengeance was a two-edged sword. Sometimes it struck the innocent as well as the guilty. Just as it had at Bitter Creek.

Today marked the true beginning of his atonement. The vows he had made so long ago would finally be redeemed. A slight smile played about Grayson's mouth. "Tonight, when you're drinking rum with the dancing girls at the Blue Parrot, think of me suffering in evening dress at the Lorenzes' fancy soiree."

Jaime didn't laugh. He knew some of Grayson's past. The rest, he'd painted in from bits and pieces he learned —and the picture they made was a terrible one, bright with tears and dark with blood and savagery. "The Irish have a saying, you know: 'Revenge is a dish best eaten cold.'"

Grayson smiled again. This time the effect was decidedly unpleasant. "You're wrong, Jaime. Vengeance, like passion, is far more satisfying when the blood runs hot!"

Jaime shook his head. It must be hell to be driven as Grayson was. He could almost feel sorry for him. Almost, but not quite. From the day he was born Jaime had struggled to pull himself up from poverty. He found it impossible to have sympathy for a man who had everything that he himself most coveted—and who was ready to throw it away in his quest for revenge. He would have cheerfully changed places with Grayson at the drop of the proverbial hat.

When Jaime had taken his leave, Grayson went to the glass parlor doors of his expensive suite. The rain had passed and the fog was vanishing beneath a benevolent sun. It would be a beautiful day. He gazed past the mansions perched on the heights until he picked out the twin towers of Tyler Lucton's grand home. It was less a mansion than a castle.

Parts of it had come over from England in the holds of the Lucton ships and been reconstructed here, panel by panel and stone by stone. "Lucton's Folly," it had been called by the town wags, for its expense and unfashionable location. Now, as the city sprawled up the hills toward it, the place was referred to by its proper name: Stoneleigh. The home of Grayson's mortal enemy.

His fingertips touched the medallion that hung around his throat. It clashed with his elegant, gilded surroundings, yet it was his most prized possession. The truest thing, he thought, in the entire room. His fingers slid over the rows of beads tenderly, as if they were caressing a woman's skin.

"I will remember my vow," he whispered through clenched teeth. *"I will remember."*

But the moment he turned back to the room his eye was caught by the photograph of the Lucton women. He took it to the window to examine it in the better light. Cassandra's face mesmerized him.

Did she, too, know the pain and emptiness that echoed inside him, or was it merely a trick of the light? He traced one finger along the pale scar that zigzagged across his wrist like a lightning bolt.

Something stirred inside him. An interest, an excitement of anticipation that he hadn't felt in years. He shook it away with a shrug of his wide shoulders. He must not think of Cassandra Lucton or her niece as anything but pawns in his deadly game. There was no room in his heart for pity or regret. Nor for desire.

It was already filled with vengeance.

High on the hills above the bay, the Lucton household was just beginning to stir. Belowstairs the servants yawned and went about their early morning duties; abovestairs only one member of the family was awake to greet the dawn. Cassandra Lucton, lying still beneath the blue silk coverlet, had no presentiment that this day, which began like every other day, would change her life forever.

She was surrounded on every side by all the luxuries a woman of her age and status could want; inside she was filled with an aching restlessness.

Her dressing room was lined with built-in wardrobes to house her clothes: morning dresses, day dresses, evening gowns, ball gowns, riding habits; shoes and shawls, hats and gloves and scarves. More than she had ever dreamed of owning before she married Tyler Lucton. Her jewel cases were well stocked with ropes of pearls, with suites of garnet and topaz, diamond and sapphire and aquamarine. But somewhere among the many possessions, she seemed to have lost herself.

It wasn't the boredom that comes too often with ease and aimlessness. She had Kitty, her beloved niece, to look after. There were several charitable committees that she chaired: they had raised enough money to endow an orphanage and a home for unfortunate young women. There were parties and balls to organize or attend, her gardens and her music. Why did she feel so useless?

She stared up at the ornate plaster ceiling, where gilt-trimmed cupids frolicked amid swirls of ribbons and bows, seeing nothing. Today was her birthday. Twenty-nine. A milestone of sorts for a woman. The dividing line between blossoming young womanhood and the ripeness of maturity. A time to settle back in contentment and count one's blessings.

All her life she had greeted each morning with a certain eagerness, believing that somewhere ahead—if not today, then surely tomorrow or the next—a marvelous surprise, a special destiny awaited just around the corner. Today she had turned that corner, and there was nothing there. Only halls that led to doors that did not open.

In the small dressing room next door, Cassandra could hear her maid moving about, lighting the spirit lamp beneath the small pot to make her morning cup of chocolate and keep it at the perfect drinking temperature. Povey, poor thing, would begin to fret soon. Cassandra had told her maid that she would be up early this morning. Instead she remained in her silk-hung bed.

She was filled with rebellion against the life that society ordained for a woman of her age and station. She was unwilling to leave the rapid mainstream of youth for quieter backwaters. Unwilling to wait docilely while silver settled in her hair and rheumatism in her bones. To sit upon the sidelines while life passed her by.

Yet she knew that the course of her life, like so many others of her station, had been set from cradle to grave. Each day would be exactly like the one before it, and the one to follow. The knowledge of it was like a door slamming shut.

The only shining spots were the secret hours when she poured her feelings into her music, playing and composing at the pianoforte, and her relationship with Kitty.

Cassandra rubbed her temples. She had slept deeply, but not well. She felt weighted down by the gossamer coverlet and the heavy velvet draperies that shut out the morning light. The room was suddenly stifling. She threw back the covers and got out of bed. The chamber was dim, but as she crossed the thick carpet, the dull day beyond her windows suddenly blossomed with brilliant golden light.

A glory of morning sun spilled around the edges of the draperies and where the center panels met. Stray beams slanted across the room, shattering rainbows from the crystal perfume bottles and gilded fitments of her ornate dressing table. Then the brilliance dimmed again, as a cloud passed over the sun. The room was returned to a shadowy undersea cavern, crisscrossed by the thin beams of light that entered around the edges of the hangings.

Cassandra was entranced. The walls and floor and ceiling, her very person, were netted with incandescent bars of light. But as she turned she once again caught her reflection in the triple mirror, and gasped at the eerie illusion. Cassandra's image shimmered in the glass, blurred and insubstantial.

A shadow woman, imprisoned in a golden cage.

She held her breath, then reached for the tasseled bell cord and pulled it sharply.

The door of the dressing room opened. Povey, a spare woman dressed in the subdued garments of a lady's maid, entered silently bearing a white lacquer tray. Halfway through the door she paused with a sound of surprise, sharing the uncanny illusion.

In an instant she recovered herself. Pursing her wide mouth, she set her burden down on an inlaid ivory table, and crossed briskly to one of the long windows. Povey was a sensible woman, not one to be intimidated by tricks of light and shadow. With a practiced motion she threw back the hangings and the illusion was swept away by the fierce tide of light.

Cassandra blinked, as if emerging from a spell, and straightened her slim shoulders. There was no use in repining over what could not be changed. "Good morning, Povey."

"Good morning, my lady."

The day had officially begun. Everything was just the same as it had always been. Cassandra saw her life stretching out to some infinite horizon, unchanged. Suddenly she wished fiercely that something would happen to transform the regimented orderliness of her life. Something that would shake her out of her growing apathy.

Like most idle wishes, hers would soon be granted, but, of course, not at all in the way that she had hoped.

* * *

Cassandra went down the magnificent, carved gothic stairway, her gown of jonquil silk whispering with her descent. The case clock struck eight as she reached the bottom step. While more fashionable wives lingered in bed until well past noon, breakfasting from trays, she usually came down for this one informal meal of the day. Often it was the only chance she had to talk to Tyler, without twenty feet of snowy damask separating their place settings and a platoon of liveried servants listening to every word.

The front door burst open and her niece came in, dressed in a habit of dark blue twill. Kitty's cheeks, usually pale, bloomed with becoming color and her gray eyes sparkled. Someday, when her fine bone structure emerged from its childhood roundness, she would be a great beauty, Cassandra thought. "Good morning, Kitty," she called out cheerfully.

Kitty jumped. "Oh! How you startled me!" She set her gloves and crop down on the console table and gave Cassandra a kiss on her cheek. "Happy birthday, dearest aunt."

"Thank you." Cassandra tilted her head. "You look as lovely and fresh as a summer rose. I think these morning rides of yours are an excellent idea."

Kitty flushed redly. "D-do you think so?"

Cassandra wished that her niece would be more comfortable accepting compliments. It irritated Tyler. "I do indeed," she said. "And you will become used to hearing such things once you make your formal come-out in society this season."

It was an unfortunate topic. Kitty dreaded her debut. "I'd better hurry and change," she said quickly. "I am meeting Helene Pettigrew at ten." She rushed up the stairs without a backward glance.

Cassandra watched until she was out of sight. If only Kitty weren't so shy! She turned down the left corridor toward the breakfast room and paused on the threshold. Her husband was so deep in thought he didn't even notice. At times she was sure that he forgot her existence.

At forty-five Tyler Lucton was handsome and vigorous. He was tall and heavy-featured, the kind of man who seemed habitually out of place indoors. In a large drawing room he managed to overwhelm his surroundings with raw energy and sheer physical presence. In this small, intimate parlor, with its delicate chinoiserie and fine-scaled furnishings, the phenomenon was accentuated. Behind his broad shoulders the dainty traceries of the hand-blocked wallpaper seemed faded, the furnishings effeminate and frail.

Tyler had been sitting quietly for some time, Cassandra realized. Juno, his aged and nearly blind spaniel, dreamed contentedly with her chin resting across the toe of her master's boot. It was strange to find someone of his energy sitting so still. The gold-rimmed plate, of the same jade as the room's decor, held the congealed remnants of breakfast, barely disturbed.

He might be worried or merely distracted. She couldn't guess from his expression. After fourteen years of marriage she could no more read his face than she could the Chinese scroll that hung between the long windows overlooking the rose garden. How very odd, she thought, to live intimately with a man for so many years and yet not know him. They dwelled beneath the same roof like polite strangers, thrown together by circumstance.

Cassandra moved quietly toward the sideboard that

held chafing dishes filled with scrambled eggs, deviled kidneys, country ham, and rare beef. She selected a hot roll and went toward the table. Morton, the ever efficient butler, deftly filled a china cup with coffee from the ornate silver urn and carried it to her accustomed place.

"Thank you, Morton."

At her murmur Tyler looked up and his brown eyes focused upon her with their usual intensity. "Ah, there you are!" He nodded dismissal and the butler vanished discreetly. "I have something of great importance to discuss with you."

Cassandra's heart leapt with anxiety. "Oh, Tyler, is it news of the *Lady*?" The *Lady Cassandra*, flagship of the Lucton Line, was six weeks overdue in port.

"No," he said curtly. "No word on her yet. It concerns your niece. I've decided to arrange a match for Kitty."

Disbelief was Cassandra's first reaction. Surely she had misheard him. But Tyler repeated his statement. "We'll announce it at our ball," he added smugly, as if the matter were already settled.

Cassandra was shocked. "But—but Kitty is a child. Only fifteen. She has not even made her formal come-out."

"What of it? You were fifteen years old when you and I married."

"But she is so young, far younger for her years than I was."

"Nonsense! There's nothing like marriage to settle a girl, give her a little backbone." Tyler was very annoyed. "You may rest assured that I'll find her a suitable match."

"Your idea of what is suitable in a husband might

differ quite widely from mine," she retorted. "Certainly from Kitty's!"

He fixed her with a sharp look. "Need I remind you that she has nothing but birth and breeding to recommend her? Everyone knows her parents left her penniless, and that any settlements she brings to a husband rest solely on my generosity. If she refuses to listen to my advice, I will cut her off without a red cent!"

Cassandra was stunned to silence. She struggled to gather her scattered thoughts. Kitty had been born with a biddable temperament, a romantic outlook, and an almost excruciating willingness to please. At Stoneleigh, alone with her aunt and uncle, Kitty was sweetly charming. In the presence of others she retreated into a protective shell. She tiptoed through life more observer than participant.

Cassandra pointed out the obvious to her husband. "There are no suitors for her hand."

"Once word gets out that I'm ready to marry the chit off, they'll line up at the door. I have two or three in mind . . ." He paused and favored her with a rather sly look. "Clayton Everett, for one."

Everett was old enough to be Kitty's grandfather. A blank despair rolled over Cassandra. She clenched her hands in her lap and tried to find the proper words. There weren't any.

Tyler scowled and slapped his palm down upon the table impatiently. The silver and china clattered in protest. "Well? Have you nothing further to say? I would think that you'd be pleased to know I have the girl's best interests at heart."

Although she was panicked, Cassandra forced herself to answer calmly: opposition only hardened Tyler's resolve. "This is all rather sudden. I hadn't expected to lose Kitty so soon."

The lines on his forehead merged into a single deep groove. "The sooner the better, I say. Kitty, for all her quiet ways, is her mother's daughter—and you know what happened to Margaret. Is that what you want for her?"

"Of course not!"

Cassandra stirred her coffee, trying to gain time. Trying to see the future in its clouded ripples. There was no help to be found there. "Kitty is deeply aware of what she owes to you, Tyler. But, please, don't use her gratitude to force her into an unhappy marriage."

Seeing the firm set of his wife's full mouth, Tyler switched tactics. Although Cassandra was usually accommodating, at times she proved as stubborn as an Irishman. That would not do. Especially now. It might be disastrous to his schemes. He softened his bullying tone.

"How could she be unhappy married to one of the wealthiest men in all of California?"

Cassandra's heart sank. If only it were so easy.

Tyler pressed on. "I have never once raised my hand to Kitty, and I have showered her with all the advantages any girl could want. She has a duty to oblige me in this. After all, I am her legal guardian."

He pushed back his chair as if the conversation were concluded, but Cassandra stopped him from rising with the gentle pressure of her fingers upon his sleeve. In all other matters she conceded to Tyler's wishes—initially out of gratitude, later because it was easiest to do so. But when it came to Kitty, she would face his wrath and stand firm.

She faced him resolutely, two flags of high color on

her cheeks. "I am not one of those ambitious match-makers whose only aim is to arrange a splendid marriage. Kitty's happiness must be considered. If she takes a dislike to any would-be suitors, neither the man's wealth nor your anger will sway me into coercing her."

His face grew ruddy. "What kind of sentimental female twaddle is this? Kitty has no choice. Nor do you. Marriage for a girl of her class is not a Romeo and Juliet affair. This is business. Surely *you* should understand that."

Cassandra gasped. Tyler was not usually so crude, although he often said aloud what ordinary civility would have left unspoken. For a moment he glared at her, the cords of his neck standing out sharply. "Come, let us speak plainly for once, Cassandra. Your mother was in dire straits when I came on the scene. She needed money to pay her overwhelming debts and I wanted entree to society to further my shipping concerns. We struck a bargain. It made good sound business sense from both sides. She knew what she had to do—and so did you."

Cassandra glanced involuntarily toward the door and he lowered his voice against eavesdropping servants. "Things would have been different if your father had lived to inherit the earldom, instead of its passing on to your cousin. And I'm not saying that you haven't kept your side of the bargain, and kept it well. If you had provided me with sons, I could not fault you on anything. But you've done nicely for yourself, Cassandra. I should not have to remind you of that."

His blunt words landed on her ears like blows, but she retained her outward composure. She'd had sufficient practice in the fourteen years she had been his wife.

And, of course, what he said was true. If not for his

timely proposal her mother would have been ruined. There had been no other choice open to either of them. The only cost had been her innocence and pride. At times like this, when Tyler threw out the fact that he had purchased her as he might some high-stepping mare, it seemed too much to have sacrificed.

That strange restlessness echoed inside her again. She did not want Kitty to know this same emptiness. She couldn't bear it. Cassandra's blue-green eyes lost their luster, becoming as pale and colorless as unpolished pebbles.

Tyler's impatience was tempered with bafflement. He didn't understand Cassandra. Never had, and never would. Where did she go at times like this, when her face went still and empty? It was like talking to a statue. And it was happening more frequently of late. He felt uneasy. Perhaps she was going mad. They were all in-bred, these blue-blooded English families!

"Cassandra?"

She gazed at him coolly. Her eyes had not changed. "I will speak to Kitty."

"Good. Then that's settled." He sat back in his chair and smiled with relief. "Ah, I almost forgot." Reaching into his coat pocket, he pulled out a long black velvet box, banded with gold.

"A little remembrance to celebrate your birthday."

Cassandra took the box with hidden reluctance. It was light in her hands but pressed heavily on her spirit: she knew it for what it was. Another link in the chain. Another brick in the wall. She was in no hurry to open it.

He was. Reaching across her, Tyler swung the lid up and turned the hinged case toward the light. The bright sun struck its contents, dazzling her momentarily. Inside, on midnight velvet, lay an antique choker of enormous tear-shaped rubies, encrusted with diamonds. Willow wisps of prismed light flickered and danced across her face and throat.

"The Fayne Rubies!" she exclaimed in astonishment. There was no mistaking their unique cut, size, and color. They held a special depth and glow, like burgundy in fine lead crystal. Cassandra had recognized them at once, although she'd seen them only in portraits of her great-grandmother. They had been sold long before she was born to pay her late father's gaming debts.

Slipping her hand beneath, she let the jewels stain the whiteness of her skin with rich color. She realized she hadn't thanked him. "You are extremely generous, Tyler. I expected the necklace had been broken up and sold long ago."

"I've been trying to track it down for years, without results. Then, when I'd almost given up, I ran into the very man who owned it at, ah, at a private party. He experienced some reverses lately and was forced to sell it."

The memory lifted Tyler's spirits. What an evening that had been! The cards had run in his favor all night and by dawn the fabled Lucton Luck had vanquished all challengers. And the timing, he thought, could not have been better. He had not had such a winning streak since, but no matter. The actual necklace was worth a fortune, its symbolic value far greater. It had stifled the whispers before they had spread too far: a man on the verge of ruin didn't buy extravagantly expensive baubles for his wife.

But he had always been a gambler. It would be all or nothing.

Tyler smiled. With the latest loan from Grayson Howard, he'd speculated in the stock market. His investments were steadily gaining and once he sold out, there would be more than enough to tide them over until September. And by then the *Lady Cassandra* would be returned safely from her long voyage, bursting with profitable cargo. He was sure of it. Wasn't he known as "Lucky" Lucton?

He surveyed his wife with the pride of ownership. Cassandra was acknowledged to be the most beautiful woman in San Francisco. She would be sensational in the Fayne Rubies. "Wear the necklace tonight for the Lorenzes' reception."

Cassandra was startled. "This necklace is something to be worn at a grand ball, not a small reception."

"Nevertheless," he said emphatically, "you *will* wear it. And don't lift your chin at me like that. I've had enough of your airs and graces today."

She looked down at her hands without replying. Tyler wasn't through. He scowled. "This isn't England, you know. These Yankees don't care for form or polite restraint. They are raw and half-civilized, like this country. Their royalty is not a matter of heredity, but of wealth and power. It's the only thing they understand."

The glittering gems slipped through Cassandra's fingers and a protruding prong snagged her skin. Blood welled up, first a minute dot, then a growing crimson bead. She stared blindly at the necklace, oblivious of the injury. Tyler expected her to strut about like a peacock tonight, displaying a fortune in jewels. He didn't understand the unwritten rules of etiquette and he didn't understand her. They were opposites in every way.

Her finger throbbed and she dabbed absently at the tear with her lace-edged handkerchief. Tyler took the necklace and hefted it across his palm. "Isn't there some legend associated with the Fayne Rubies?"

She didn't look up. "I believe there is. However I can't recall it at the moment."

He gave a grunt of disappointment. "Well, perhaps you'll think of it before the reception. Try the necklace on. No need to wait."

Picking the glittering band of gems up, he wound them around Cassandra's neck and hooked the clasp in back. It clamped about her throat like an icy hand. She couldn't get her breath.

"Please. It's—it's too tight," she said in a thready voice, fumbling to undo the catch.

"No, hold still! You've snagged a bit of lace on it and that's what is pulling." He fiddled with the ruffle at her throat and the constriction eased. She still couldn't breathe.

"What is it, Cassandra? You've gone so pale."

"Nothing . . . I didn't sleep well last night."

He examined her closely. Cassandra was touched by his unaccustomed solicitousness. Then she realized that Tyler was merely admiring the Fayne Rubies once again.

"You look magnificent," he said. "Like a queen!"

He picked up his newspaper and went out. Cassandra pushed back her chair. Her appetite was gone. She wanted to take the necklace off, but couldn't manage the catch. Povey would help her. She left the breakfast room with the fabulous jeweled band still ringing her throat.

Tyler's last words echoed in her head. "Like a queen!"

As Cassandra ascended the gothic staircase, reassembled from its original home at Castle Fayne, the trailing hem of her gown whispered behind her. From the deeply carved panels opposite the entwined balusters, a procession of stoic saints and grim apostles followed her progress from step to step. Cassandra had the sudden impression that the whispering sound came from them, that they were alive and watching her with grave disapproval.

She hurried up the staircase as if pursued, wondering what impulse had made her withhold the truth from her husband. Perhaps it was to shield him: Tyler was terribly superstitious. It would be foolish to upset him with a myth—for Cassandra did indeed remember the legend of the fabled Fayne necklace.

It had come into the family in the Tudor Era, during the reign of Henry VIII. Over the centuries the Fayne Rubies had gathered stories in the way that ruins gather moss. They were said to bring great misfortune to their owner. The original setting had been commissioned by the king as a wedding gift to Anne Boleyn—the queen he had later beheaded.

She shivered and hurried up to the landing. At the top of it, Cassandra paused where the stairway branched, startled. The large pier glass on the wall trapped her reflection. She saw herself, wide-eyed and pale, the ruby necklace ringing her throat like a raw and bloody gash.

It seemed it was not a day for looking into mirrors.

2

Grayson left his hotel in Portsmouth Square early and rode away from the other fine hotels and the high-class bordellos along Washington Street. Although it was still early, the streets were clogged with horses and wagons, the sidewalks with servants bound for market, with sailors and loiterers and drifters conning for a mark.

His first stop of the morning was a small printing shop. He could hear the thunk and thump of the press before he opened the door. Inside the air was thick with noise and the smell of wet ink. A man in a smudged apron and cap came from the back. He smiled, recognizing Grayson, and wiped the ink from his stained fingers with a grimy rag.

"Yer order's ready, sir. Second one on the right, next to the circus flyers. I'd git it for ye but I'd just git me prints all over everything."

There were four stacks on the end of the counter: a political broadside, a wanted poster of a bearded desperado, an expensive flyer for Ryan's, and the one Grayson had ordered made up. It was eye-catching, with bold lettering and an excellent reproduction of the photograph. Bronco would be pleased, he thought. Not that it would do him much good. His foreman's missing sister was surely long dead or they would have heard something of her by now.

The reproduced photograph showed a woman in her thirties standing between a rangy blond youth on the verge of manhood, and a girl of perhaps twelve years. The picture was blurred, as if the original had faded with years and been creased by too much handling.

HAVE YOU SEEN HER?
ANNETTE MASON
Golden hair, Blue eyes, Slight build
Would be approx. 23 years old
$500 REWARD

The printer was ready to show sympathy. "Pretty lass. Relation o' yers?"

"No. She's the half sister of my ranch foreman back in Colorado."

"Hope ye find her."

Grayson gave him a generous bonus for the rush job and went out into the bright, bustling morning. Twenty years before this had been a city of tar and sheet-metal shacks, awash in a sea of oozing mud with every rain. Now it climbed halfway up the hills, as fresh and new looking as if it had been built yesterday.

Some of it had.

San Francisco was in a class by itself. It burned its

past with startling regularity. The greater part of the city's buildings had been razed by flames as often as three times in a single year. Candles, open fires, and kerosene lamps caused the frequent fires. Whipped by wind, the flames roared through the close-packed wooden buildings, reducing them to cinder and ash.

The city always rose again, like the fabled phoenix. Now fine mansions on the heights and abundant night life had gained it the title "The Paris of the West." And highest of all was the Lucton mansion. Grayson caught a glimpse of it, washed in golden light. He would meet the fair Cassandra at the Lorenzes' reception on Nob Hill tonight. He wondered if she could really be as beautiful in real life as in the photographs.

He wondered why her face seemed to dominate his thoughts.

With an oath he resolutely turned away and unhitched the roan. The breeze was fresh with a tang of salt. Below, the waters of the Golden Gate danced in the sunlight. A white-sailed vessel of the China trade appeared on the horizon, looking like a ghost ship through the shimmer of distance. Closer in two steamships passed each other, trailing ruffles of lace through the sapphire water.

A beautiful scene. But Grayson ached for the freedom of the sweeping plains, and the plateaus and peaks of the high country. The ceaseless bustle of the city strangled his spirit. On the high Colorado plateau, he'd traveled often for weeks without seeing another soul. Never once had he known this bone-deep ache of loneliness. But the choice to follow this path had been his, and he must suffer the consequences of it.

*　　*　　*

Arguing voices floated from an open window. Italian, he thought. The shop on the opposite corner sold German sausage and cheese, next to the Lunquist dry goods store. It was said, and rightly so, that a man could walk twenty paces in San Francisco and hear as many different tongues. It drew people from the four corners of the earth. Some had made their fortunes and lost their souls. Many had lost their lives, as well.

Grayson left his horse at a livery stable and made his way on foot to Chinatown. The streets were even more crowded. Racks of dried fish and golden roast ducklings hung over the sidewalks. Vendors sold rice and dumplings on the street and the tea shops were full. Women bargained over the price of vegetables and young men diced in the alleyways. He stood out like a cowboy at a quilting bee. Strangely, he felt less alien among the merchants' stalls than he did inside the turreted mansions and fancy hotels.

Grayson's goal was a certain small shop, lacquered red with gold Chinese characters. Curtains of colored beads and a screen of translucent rice paper prevented passersby from looking inside. It sold joss sticks and incense, and small statues in porcelain, fired clay, and jade. In the back room fortunes were told, horoscopes cast, and marriages arranged between the young women of the ancient country and the men who had emigrated to this raw and barely civilized place called California.

He pushed his way inside and was surrounded by a rich variety of smells: amber and sandalwood, cedar oil and exotic perfumes, green leaf tea and boiled noodles with pork. Bells tinkled as the door swung shut, rousing the old woman dozing in the corner. He kept his face in shadow and held out a pierced coin, the accepted signal. The woman gestured toward the back of the place.

He went through another beaded curtain into the dim back room. A wooden door led into a narrow courtyard, then up an open stairway to another door. He opened it and went in without knocking.

A young Chinese in a blue robe was napping with his feet up on the scarred wooden table. The opening of the door woke him with a start and he almost fell off the chair. As he reached for the knife hidden in his robe, Grayson leaned forward and caught his wrist. "Getting careless, old friend?"

Ling Cheung looked exceedingly relieved when he identified his visitor. "If I were a cat," he chided, "I would only have eight lives left."

"If you were a cat, you'd have heard me coming." Grayson straddled a chair. "What if, instead of myself, it had been some enemy from another tong? I'd hate to take news like that back to your mother."

The young man was fully awake now. "Ah, do not speak of such things. They bring bad luck." He opened a drawer and pulled out a sheaf of papers. "And so far, fortune has favored both of us in obtaining that which you sought."

Grayson took the papers he was handed and scanned them quickly. "Very interesting."

"Indeed. In the past year Tyler Lucton has been directly or indirectly responsible for the failure of three of his business rivals. One of them, Jim Hoeker, hung himself from a lamppost."

"You are a man of your word, Ling Cheung. This confirms my suspicions." Grayson folded the papers and tucked them inside his jacket. "I congratulate you on your ingenuity."

"It was not difficult," the other man said wryly. "You were wise to send me as your agent rather than Mr.

McFee. Before I went to mingle with the workers on the pier I became invisible—a cotton smock and hat and sandals of woven straw such as you are wearing, and I became just another coolie in their view. And in those of your friend, Mr. Lucton."

Grayson's eyes darkened. "He is no friend of mine. But you have been, Ling Cheung. Many thanks. If there is ever anything I can do for you, you have only to ask."

His words were genuine. Their bond of friendship was strong and went back many years. Ling Cheung hesitated as if about to speak, then changed his mind. He glanced at the stack of bundled flyers that Grayson had set down. "This is the other job of which you spoke?"

"Yes. I want these plastered everywhere." Grayson produced a handful of gold and silver coins to pay the young boys who would have them posted. "Personally, I think it's a lost cause, but you know Bronco. He can't give up until he knows—either way."

Ling Cheung picked up the top flyer and examined it. The information on who to contact was listed below but Ling Cheung agreed with Grayson. Bronco was wasting his money. Annette had run away from a cruel stepfather just before her thirteenth birthday and vanished near Sacramento. Her mother had been sure Annette was headed straight for the Thunder Ranch and had sent word to Bronco in care of Grayson. If Annette had set out for the ranch, she had either changed her mind or had it changed for her. There had been no word and she was probably long dead. Ling Cheung shook his head.

"A comely maid, with the promise of beauty in her fine bones. But I fear that you are right. Is there anything else?"

"Yes. Check with your contacts. I intend to find the

soft spot in Tyler Lucton's underbelly—because that is where I'll strike."

The look on Grayson's face was frightening. Ling Cheung watched the familiar features turn to stone, the eyes he knew so well turn cold as death. There was more to this business than he'd guessed. "You mean to ruin this man?"

Grayson's smile was a grim rictus that sent a chill through his companion. "I intend to destroy Tyler Lucton. Body and soul."

Cassandra went along the sunny corridor in search of her niece. A meeting with the housekeeper had taken up most of her morning and Kitty's drive with Helena Petti-grew had prevented them from having their talk earlier. She was afraid that Tyler would blurt out his plans be-fore she had a chance to forewarn Kitty.

Knowing her niece's habits, she headed for the yellow sitting room that ran the entire width of the south wing, to take full advantage of the natural warmth and light in winter. Unlike the rest of the house, grandly done to Tyler's specifications, this chamber was furnished with comfortable sofas and chairs suitable for reading or cozy conversation. Long windows were flanked by built-in cabinets housing books and a collection of porcelain fig-urines, and the fireplaces at each end ensured a snug retreat in cold weather.

It also housed Cassandra's piano, a homelier version of the one that graced the music room, and a small desk where she wrote her music.

Until recently Kitty could usually be found curled up in one of the window seats, reading. Cassandra knew it was only natural that Kitty should outgrow her youthful habits, and that someday she would marry and set up her own home. But, she thought wistfully, neither of them was quite ready for that day to arrive.

Kitty must not be forced into a disastrous marriage as her mother had been. Cassandra sighed. Dear Margaret, so lovely and loving. So vivacious and full of life. Margaret, who could charm the birds from the trees and their grandfather, the crusty and ailing Earl of Fayne, from his dark moods. It seemed only yesterday that she had laughed and waved a kiss to Cassandra and her infant daughter and then driven off in a spanking-new town carriage for a private dinner.

That was the last time they had seen Margaret alive. Now her sister had been dead and buried these twelve years. How quickly the time had passed! Kitty had been a child of only three.

Not many men would have taken in an orphan surrounded by such scandal. Cassandra had always been grateful to Tyler for that, and for agreeing to become Kitty's legal guardian. He had supplied his ward with toys and dresses, nurses and governesses, watching her progress with benign indifference. In his eyes, finding Kitty a wealthy husband was merely an extension of his responsibilities. And that was what made everything so very difficult.

Cassandra was deeply troubled. She couldn't very well sell her jewels and flee with Kitty into the night, as if Tyler were some terrible ogre and they, the heroines of a bad melodrama. Still, there must be some way to combine Tyler's ambitions with Kitty's happiness.

There simply had to be.

* * *

Unaware that she was the center of a brewing storm, Kitty was curled up in the yellow sitting room with a book. She turned another page. It was a novel she'd borrowed from her best friend, Helena Pettigrew. On the ledge beside her, Mrs. Alcott's *Little Women* was stacked atop two volumes of tales from the Brothers Grimm and Charles Perrault. Kitty had forgotten their very existence. Romance and carriage rides without adult chaperons had superseded them. And Madame Fortescue's novel was a further step in her education.

She turned another page. Although Helena had recommended it highly, the novel wasn't much to Kitty's taste. The fair Sophia got herself from one silly scrape into another, each more dire than the one before it—and always right where the chapter ended. It was rather infuriating.

But Kitty meant to discover how the virtuous heroine eventually escaped disaster to find happiness at last with her one true love.

She had just reached the part where Count Berringer, the evil villain, had cornered the heroine in his dungeon. The lovely and virtuous Sophia, her gossamer gown in shreds about her heaving bosom, was holding the wicked count at bay by sheer hysteria and a veritable flood of tears.

If Sophia was silly, the hero was prosy and dull. In the previous chapter, instead of challenging the count to a duel, the noble Sigmund had arrived in the nick of time, seemingly determined to overcome the villain by boring the man to death with long-winded speeches. Now Sophia was chained in the dungeon of the crumbling chateau for refusing to let the villain have his way with her. Whatever that might mean.

Kitty sighed. Why Sophia was so stupid as to flee

Sherringham Manor in the dead of winter, clad in nothing but her nightdress, was more than she could understand. But she did understand Sophia's dread of her grandfather's temper. Kitty loved Uncle Tyler, but when he gave her one of his scoldings, she always ended up with a headache. She knew she was a severe disappointment to him. He liked lively, pretty girls like Helena, who knew how to talk to men in just the way they liked.

She turned the page and tried to concentrate. Would Sigmund arrive in time to save Sophia's honor from the lustful count? And, Kitty wondered, why would being found alone with the count damage Sophia's honor, when she'd done nothing wrong? It was quite confusing. Kitty was at a difficult time in life, her ripening body responding to signals she neither recognized nor understood. There were times when she was sure there was some great secret that everyone but she knew.

She put the book down in her lap. Sigmund would pale beside Jake. He was the new young groom whom Tomms had taken on a few weeks ago. Jake was handsome and dashing. Kitty was sure that he would never stand around making speeches while a damsel was left in distress. Not that she knew him well. But her recent interest in riding stemmed directly from his arrival.

Kitty lost herself in pretty daydreams. Images of the handsome Jake figured largely in them, coupled with visions of moonlit strolls with whispered words of love and smoldering glances accompanied by furtive brushing of his hands against hers. The first was imaginary. The second was not.

Kitty flushed thinking of it. No one had ever looked at her in the way that Jake did. It made her feel hot and cold inside, and completely grown-up. And more than a little frightened.

The sound of footsteps yanked her rudely out of her fantasies of the handsome stable lad. Kitty jumped and dislodged the book from her lap. Cassandra entered as the book fell, and bent gracefully to retrieve it. *"The Kidnapped Heiress, or: The Missing Princess of Castle d'Or."*

She handed the book back, a thoughtful expression on her face. Kitty took it and blushed guiltily, relieved that Cassandra hadn't said anything about the novel. But then, perhaps she didn't know it was a love story. Her aunt was still beautiful, but getting rather old for such things.

Cassandra smiled. "May I interrupt your reading awhile? There is something I need to discuss with you."

Kitty quailed inside. Had Tomms reported that she'd been flirting with Jake? She couldn't face the prospect now. She looked at the porcelain clock. "Oh, dear! Is it so late already? Helena is coming for me in a quarter hour. We're to dine with her grandmother this evening."

"I'd forgotten you were to see Mrs. Champion today." Cassandra was almost relieved. "We'll have our talk in the morning, then."

When Cassandra left, Kitty turned back to the book. She might be able to finish it if she read quickly. She buried her head in the novel along with her prickling conscience. The evil count was threatening the heroine with a fate worse than death. Whatever *that* might be.

Just as Sophia's white bosom was laid bare for Count Berringer's knife, the noble Sigmund burst into the room. After vanquishing the villain, he threw his cloak over Sophia to preserve her modesty. With a promise of tender love, he carried her away to safety.

Kitty shivered. Of course, no one did such things in real life. Jake hadn't even really held her hand yet; but yesterday, when helping her to dismount, he'd kept his hand on hers lingeringly, and the warm look in his eyes had thrown her into confusion. There had been no opportunity for them to exchange words, with Tomms hovering over them like a hen with one chick.

That was why Jake had been forced to send a note. The paper crackled in the pocket of her skirt. It was written on the back of a piece of paper torn from a religious tract. It was her first love letter, the ill-formed words more precious than pearls. Jake must have written them in a terrible hurry.

What would Jake say when she slipped away to meet him this afternoon? Would he, like the noble Sigmund, drop to his knees to declare his undying love? Would he try to kiss her? Her face grew rosy as eager waves of anticipation danced through her. She felt hot and cold . . .

Cassandra dressed for the Lorenzes' reception with care. Povey was shocked when she said that she would wear the Fayne Rubies. She stared at her mistress, appalled.

"But . . . but, madam . . ."

She stopped and pursed her thin lips. In all the years she'd been with Madam, Povey had never known her to make a mistake in matters of fashion or etiquette. *Not* the mistress's idea, she decided quickly, but the master's. Why, if he had his way he'd force her to wear every jewel she had at the same time, just to puff off his wealth! He was nothing but a jumped-up mushroom, with no sense of what was fitting.

Cassandra finished her toilette with a touch of the rose and lavender perfume that had been made specially for her. Then she started down to join Tyler. As she

reached the top of the staircase she heard the unmistakable sounds of an arrival. She peered over the railing and
saw Morton open the door for an older man, gray-
haired and running to fat despite his well-cut clothes.
Clayton Everett.

She stepped back so that he wouldn't see her. It was
certainly an odd hour to come to ask for permission to
court. Perhaps he had come on some other errand, connected with Tyler's business affairs.

Raised voices floated up the staircase, but too garbled
for Cassandra to make out. She hovered on the upper
landing until she heard the door slam and saw the carriage driving away.

Cassandra couldn't stand the suspense a moment
longer. She ran lightly down to Tyler's study, and
stopped dead on the threshold. A stranger was standing
near the desk, his head bowed and his back to the fireplace. The lamp had been extinguished and the glow
from the hearth tinged the weary contours of his face.

Then a log crackled and the flames leapt higher. Cassandra laughed at her fanciful imagination. It was only
Tyler. He turned toward her, as vital and vigorous as
ever. "I've ordered the carriage."

"Did—did Everett ask permission to court Kitty?"

"Is that why you rushed down here, my dear?" His
mouth twisted in a skewed smile. "Your congratulations
would have been premature. My meeting with Everett
tonight was strictly business."

He escorted her into the vestibule and took his hat
and gloves from Morton, while Cassandra said a silent
prayer of thanks.

*   *   *

The tall house on Nob Hill glittered like a jewel, every leaded window ablaze with light. It was the third built high on California Street, and the most extravagant. The silver doorknobs throughout the house were polished three times a day and the stables were paneled in mahogany. Judging by the familiar carriages lining up before their door, the cream of San Francisco society would be present.

As Cassandra stepped down from the carriage, the Fayne Rubies caught the lantern light and trapped it deep in their glowing hearts. The diamonds sent it back in darts of fire. Tyler stopped to look at her.

"You will do me proud tonight," he murmured. "Every woman in the room will envy you"—his eyes shone as he looked at her—"that necklace."

Cassandra flinched. The jeweled band seemed to tighten about her throat. She was choking in the blood of rubies.

Strangling in her golden cage.

They reached the portico and waited their turn to enter. Cassandra suddenly had the feeling that she was under intense scrutiny. She glanced around from behind her fan, but none of the guests waiting to enter appeared to be so much as looking her way.

Then she saw him, standing in the floor-to-ceiling bow window that gave onto the portico. Tall. Dark-haired and wide-shouldered. His face was half in shadow but she noted high cheekbones and a strong, determined jaw. Cassandra's color rose. He was definitely staring at her.

Or at her necklace. Yes, that was it, surely.

She lifted her head proudly, pretending that she hadn't noticed. It made her think of her honeymoon in Paris. She had visited a jeweler's shop with Tyler. Across the way she'd noticed a lovely young woman with dark auburn hair and clear gray eyes, wearing a sapphire and diamond tiara. It had been so out of place in the middle of the day that Cassandra had found herself staring.

It had taken her a moment to realize that it was not a real woman, but a display bust—a beautiful wax creation whose only reason for being was to display the wealth of gems around her throat. Cassandra felt a sudden kinship with it now. Her husband did not think of her as a living, breathing woman, but as a mere prop to display his success.

She swallowed past a sudden constriction in her throat. It had been many years since she'd ceased hoping to be something more to him than that. The line moved again, carrying Cassandra with it.

Grayson remained at the window, examining her profile through the glass. She was even lovelier than her photographs. He'd caught a glimpse of blue-green eyes, fringed by dark lashes. Her skin was as delicate as porcelain, her hair a rich, deep auburn. A spoiled beauty, used to receiving homage. He'd been wrong about her photographs. There was no sign of warmth or vulnerability now, and she wore a fortune in rubies and diamonds around her throat as casually as another woman might wear a satin ribbon.

Then she turned toward the window and their eyes locked. The sudden surge of mingled anger and desire that swept through him caught Grayson off guard. It hit him like a mule's kick to the midsection, and was just as welcome.

He made his hands into fists and turned away abruptly, schooling his face against his inner fury. She was his enemy's wife. He wanted nothing that belonged to Tyler Lucton. He only wanted to bring about his enemy's ruin.

And God help anyone who stood in his way.

Cassandra's face was averted but she knew the exact moment that he left the window. A most disturbing man. She hoped no one would offer an introduction.

"Watch your step, my dear," Tyler said affably as they entered the marble foyer and went up the ornate staircase where their host and hostess awaited them. Cassandra—and the Fayne Rubies—would be a great success. By morning everyone would be talking about them.

Alfred Lorenz took Cassandra's hand. He was a dignified man in his mid-sixties. He had a neatly trimmed white beard, a thick German accent, and impeccable manners. "I am charmed that you grace my home again, Mrs. Lucton."

Mae Belle Lorenz was some twenty years her husband's junior. She had a kiss on the cheek for Cassandra and a wink and a smile for Tyler. There was not a shred of pretense or snobbery in Mae Belle's character and she had a lively sense of humor that occasionally got out of hand. She had created a *cause célèbre* at a dinner party she'd given in London by seating a royal duke beside a chimney sweep whom she'd decked out in full evening regalia. The duke had not been amused. Only the power of her great wealth and Alfred's connections to the royal family had enabled her to come about after that escapade.

Tonight she was dressed in a garish gown of parrot-green, which she mistakenly thought set off her high color and red hair to advantage. Since her first appearance as the wife of the widowed financier, rumors about her background abounded. It was said that, in her long

and checkered career, Mae Belle Lorenz had been everything from a lumber camp cook and laundress to a
dance hall girl, before ending up a wealthy widow. Her
second marriage to Alfred Lorenz had at first shocked,
then amused his peers. Cassandra liked her immensely.

Mae Belle leaned down to whisper in her ear. "Didn't
invite any young women to this little soiree. Too much
competition at our age."

At our age. Cassandra smiled and went into the
drawing room on Tyler's arm. She suddenly felt the
weight of her birthday. She felt time slipping through
her fingers, taking her bloom of youth with it. Life was
moving too quickly, sweeping Kitty away on its tides,
and leaving Cassandra stranded and alone.

The room was already crowded. Hundreds of candles
burned in the chandeliers overhead. Alfred Lorenz
thought gas lamps were a ridiculous fad and refused to
have them in his house. It didn't take long for heads to
turn and tongues to wag once Cassandra's necklace was
spotted. "A family heirloom, missing these past fifty
years," she replied to a false compliment from Mrs.
Merrivale. "My husband located and presented it to me
this morning as a birthday gift."

The spiteful light in the matron's eyes died. She examined the jewels through her lorgnette with new appreciation. What she had seen as a vulgar display of wealth
had become something else entirely, as an heirloom of a
noble family. She swept off to share this interesting tid-
bit with her cronies.

Cassandra tried to join in the conversations. Frumpy
Mrs. Spencer spoke excitedly to Cassandra of Sarah
Bernhardt's success playing Cordelia in *King Lear,* and
the possibility of her bringing the role to San Francisco.
Mrs. Froman was more excited over the Clay Street

Railroad Company's trolley car line, and others chatted of the Boston fire that had raged for three days, causing terrible destruction. There was nothing that chilled San Franciscans' hearts more than the sound of the firebells.

The men's conversation revolved around horse racing, the stock market, and the expansion of the railroads. Like President Grant, half the men in the room had invested in the company that furnished the rails for the Union Pacific. Some, like Leland Stanford and C. P. Huntington, were major shareholders. Kings of the railroad.

The room was growing hotter by the minute, and Cassandra was growing increasingly bored. The same people, the same topics, and the same weary conversations were, week after week, rehashed and served up as new. Everyone else seemed to be enjoying the reception. Something was wrong with her, she thought. She was not like them. She would rather be home with Kitty or at her piano, composing. Her fellow guests laughed and talked and moved about, but they seemed unreal to Cassandra, like actors speaking lines from a play to which she hadn't been given a script.

She overheard Becca St. Claire accost their hostess. "The story came to me from a very creditable source, Mae Belle, that you have invited a red Indian to this reception to entertain us."

Mae Belle grinned. "If anything, I hoped that we might entertain him!"

Miss Dorrington looked pained. Her withered lips pursed together. Was this one of Mae Belle's famous jokes? "Do you mean that butler of yours? I always figured him for a man of color."

Cassandra moved on. The heat of myriad candles and the heavy scent of the massed flowers were overpowering. She felt as if she were melting like one of the bees-wax tapers. She moved toward the glass doors that opened to the terrace. Fifteen feet away she noticed the stranger lounging against the wall beside the doors.

He fit in even less than she did, Cassandra thought. She eyed him warily, as if she'd stepped out into a formal rose garden and discovered a panther prowling the paths. He was dark and intense, with an aura of danger. His face was deeply bronzed by sun and wind, and his eyes looked mocking and amused. Even motionless, Cassandra thought suddenly, he is more animated and alive than anyone else in this room. More alive than I have ever been.

She glanced around. The other men were like empty husks compared to this man's fierce vitality. The gilded reception room, the great banks of hothouse blooms, and the glittering gowns and jewels seemed colorless in comparison.

His eyes raked the room, yet he didn't seem to search for any particular person. Cassandra stepped next to a pillar, hoping to evade him. Too late. Her heart skipped a beat when his probing gaze reached her. For a split second his dark eyes held hers, then he looked purposely away. Cassandra felt unaccountably diminished, somehow. It was as if she had been noted and dismissed, as being of no value to him. There was only one way to save face. She pretended not to have seen him at all and turned back the way she had come and joined the nearest group.

Cassandra had exceptional hearing. There were times when she overheard things she had no desire to know, and this was one of them. ". . . not really interested in meeting Mrs. Lucton," she heard a man say in a low voice behind her. She knew exactly who he was.

"Nonsense," Mae Belle retorted from the same direction. "Every man wants to meet the most beautiful woman in the room."

Cassandra took a few quick steps and tried to lose herself in the throng. It was too late. Mae Belle grabbed her arm. "Where have you been hiding all evening?"

There was no avoiding the introduction that followed. The stranger was even more commanding at close range. She was surprised to see a beaded medallion against the crisp white of his shirt. Was this Mae Belle's Indian guest? He certainly didn't fit the mental image she had formed. His eyes were a striking combination of gray and brown, with a silvery sheen. They made Cassandra think of autumn leaves sealed beneath a thin layer of ice.

"It's a pleasure to meet you, Mrs. Lucton," he said easily. He kissed her gloved fingertips, inhaling her haunting perfume. "Your husband and I have had some recent business dealings."

His manner was smooth and practiced with just the proper air. Cassandra felt the heat of his hand radiating through her glove. With it came an intimation of danger once more. She suddenly feared this handsome stranger, with the cynical smile and mocking eyes. It was all she could do to keep from snatching her hand away.

Grayson's mouth twisted wryly. His eyes held heat but no warmth. So, she didn't like him? Well, the feeling was definitely mutual. Cassandra Lucton was not at all the type of woman he admired. She was far too haughty and controlled. But perhaps his first impression was wrong. A woman with a mouth like that was made for kissing. And he was sure he'd seen a flare of temper before her sea-colored eyes had turned so cold.

Mae Belle saw none of it. "Perhaps you'll come to my

musical evening next week, Grayson. Mrs. Lucton has promised to play the Vienna Piano Concerto for our entertainment. She is a most accomplished musician."

He smiled, faintly. "I'll have to decline. One of my guiding principles is to avoid amateur musical performances at all costs."

Cassandra was appalled by his manners. She expected her hostess to chide him for his rudeness, but Mae Belle's attention was already elsewhere. There was an angry silence after she departed. Grayson was sorry he'd succumbed to the unexplained urge to anger Cassandra; it was stupid of him to antagonize her since, if his plan succeeded, he'd be seeing a lot of her in the near future.

For her part, Cassandra was sorry that her upbringing kept her from tossing the insult back in his face. There were equally effective ways of cutting him. She let her gaze drift away. "If you will excuse me," she said, "I believe I see a friend across the room."

Damn her! Grayson made a stiff bow and tried not to watch as she moved away. Haughty as a duchess. Not that he blamed her. He'd acted like a fool.

They avoided each other for the rest of the evening. Cassandra attached herself to a group near one end of the reception room where Mrs. Merrivale and several ladies were listening to Major Malone hold forth on the fortunes to be made in silver mining. Carried away by his own eloquence and forgetting his audience, he suddenly switched to the bloody Apache uprisings in the territories. His gruff voice, honed on countless parade grounds, carried.

"But why are the Apaches attacking innocent people?" Bernice Godwin exclaimed. "Can't the government do something?"

"But they already have, madam." Cassandra recognized Grayson Howard's deep voice. She looked up to find him almost behind her chair.

His eyes blazed with anger. "The government has stolen their land, and under the Indian Appropriation Act it has nullified all the treaties and made the Indians wards of the United States. Furthermore, they've starved them, sold them whiskey and tainted pork, and murdered their women and children. And your California legislature had just paid out hundreds of thousands of dollars in 'bounty' money to supply private armies to rid the state of its native inhabitants."

He made a bow to the lady. "I think that shows that the government is hard at work on the 'Indian Problem.'"

"Well, yes." Mrs. Merrivale uttered faintly. "I—I'm glad to know that Washington is not asleep on the issue."

Grayson turned away, and only Cassandra saw the mask of bitterness that his face had become. Her first instinct had been correct. Something wild and fierce had entered the room with him.

She rose and pushed through the throng until she reached the terrace doors. She glimpsed his reflection in the glass panes. He was watching her again. With a shiver she opened the door and went outside. Cassandra didn't know what had come over her.

It was ridiculous to flee just because Grayson Howard had dashed cold fact over the warm glow of the evening. But it was more than that. For a fleeting instant she'd seen something in his dark gaze that had shocked her—a hidden rage, an agony of soul that transcended mere pain and anger.

It was something that she knew and recognized.

Something that she had learned to live with, day by day. And Grayson Howard, who was so much more vivid, more alive than she could ever be, felt it even more keenly. Her pain was dull and blunt. A fading echo of emotions that had been shut away too long, in the secret corners of her soul. But in him, it had sharpened into a deadly weapon.

She pitied anyone foolish enough to cross such a man.

Cassandra descended the terrace and followed a wide path. Her slippers made no sound over the flagged stones. An ornamental fountain splashed nearby. Starshine and moonglow turned the jetting sprays into cascades of diamonds and lace. The air was still but there was a restlessness about the night, pulling a great swell of longing through her soul like a rising tide until she ached with it. Perhaps it was only nostalgia for happier, simpler times. In their girlhood, on warm, still nights like this, she and Margaret had often slipped away into the gardens of their childhood home. In the darkness, the crumbling ramparts and towers of Castle Fayne had taken on a sheen of magic. Transformed by moonlight, the worn stone towers had seemed perfect and whole. Camelot.

Cassandra wished that she could turn back time, just for a moment, to see her dearly loved sister once more, and bask in the peace she had known then. She leaned down to touch a late-blooming rose, still clinging valiantly to its thorny stem. Its pale color had been bleached to lavender by the moonlight. Her fingers brushed against the velvety bloom. The flower fell apart in absolute silence, showering her slippers with its delicate, curling petals.

Cassandra stared at the empty calyx and bare stem through a sheen of tears. *Oh, Margaret!*

"Cassandra!"

A shadow coalesced from beside an old tree and she squeaked in alarm. Then she realized that it was only Tyler. For a second she had expected to see Grayson Howard. The man had certainly had a detrimental effect upon her nerves.

Tyler strolled over to her side. The tip of his cigar glowed dull orange through its ashy coat. In the light of the paper lanterns his face held a fixed intensity. He flicked the ash into the fountain. "You've met Grayson Howard. What do you think of him?"

"I haven't given him much thought." Even as she spoke the words Cassandra recognized them for a lie. She had definite views on Grayson Howard. He was a dangerous man, and she wanted to have nothing to do with him. Now, or ever.

Tyler took a puff of the cigar and blew it out slowly. "It doesn't matter. You'll have the chance to get to know him soon enough. I've invited him to dinner tomorrow night. In fact, I've invited him to give up his hotel suite and be our guest for the remainder of his stay in town."

Cassandra was dumbfounded. "What on earth inspired you to extend such an invitation?"

Tyler shot her an unreadable glance from the corner of his eyes. "We have six empty guest rooms. They might as well be put to use. I want him treated like a king while he's with us. You'll do me proud, of course. I have no worries there. But see that Kitty is up to snuff, and rigged out in her finest. And none of those girlish dimity dresses, by God!"

"Kitty?" A cold chill filled Cassandra's heart. "What has she to do with this?"

He dropped the cigar stub and ground it beneath his heel. "I've been thinking over what you said about the age difference between Clayton Everett and Kitty. There was a good deal of wisdom in it." He turned to face her fully. "So much so that I've changed my mind."

Cassandra listened in growing alarm as he continued. "Grayson Howard is a wealthy man. He'd make an ideal partner for me on the Colorado mining venture. We might even get Simon Fiddler to agree to come in with us. And if Kitty plays her cards right, she'll end the little season as Grayson Howard's wife."

She stared at her husband in horror. It was like a waking nightmare. And this "brilliant" idea of Tyler's was all her own doing, for putting the idea of an eligible, younger suitor in his mind.

Tyler saw that he'd shocked her. "Think about it. I'm sure you'll agree it would be the best solution." In more ways than one, he thought, now that Clayton Everett had discovered the discrepancies in the warehouse books. He'd smoothed it over tonight but there might be trouble ahead. But once word got out that his niece was engaged to Grayson Howard, his other creditors would back off. Goddammit, he *had* to pull it off!

He went back inside, leaving Cassandra in complete turmoil. The fear and rising anger made her begin to feel alive again. It surprised her to realize how numb, how dead she had been. But naive, innocent Kitty married to a bitter, mocking man like Grayson Howard? No, she must do everything in her power to prevent it. This proposed alliance must never take place.

Tyler saw nothing wrong with marriages of convenience. Matings of bloodlines, of power and wealth. It was the way of their world. But, oh! She had wanted so much more for her adored niece. A loving partnership, a sharing of interests, even a meeting of souls.

Cassandra looked down at her wedding band. Perhaps she was as naive as Kitty. Perhaps such things were only the stuff of girlish dreams and romantic novels.

Her own wedding night had been a disaster. She knew it was her fault more than Tyler's. She was cold by nature. He had told her so a dozen times and she could not refute it. Her bridegroom's advances had not succeeded in arousing any emotion in her other than fright. He had left their marriage bed in anger and she had cried herself to sleep.

They had never overcome that unfortunate beginning. He had spent the following night with his mistress. Within a week it was all over town that Tyler preferred Elaine DuVale to his new young bride. The humiliation had devastated Cassandra. The scalding lecture on a wife's duties, given by her own mother, had made it even more difficult for her to hold up her head. But she had been so young, only fifteen—frightened and inexperienced—and as inert as a block of wood.

If it had been so terrible for her, what would it be like for a tender girl like Kitty to be given to a passionate man like Grayson Howard? For passionate he was. It was clearly marked in every line of his dark face, and the shifting depths of his eyes.

It didn't bear thinking of.

Cassandra went back to the house slowly, crushing the fallen rose petals beneath her feet. Her head throbbed. She wanted to go home. And she didn't want Grayson Howard to be a guest beneath her own roof. His very presence would be intolerable. The mere thought of it made her stomach ache and set her heart pounding erratically.

Earlier she had pitied anyone who made an enemy of him. Now, she could think of nothing worse than being Grayson Howard's wife.

3

Ling Cheung took a carriage back to the out-skirts of town where the Orloff Circus was set up. A distant skirl of calliope music—if something that assaulted his ears so horribly could be called that—was almost drowned out by the barker's voice outside the main tent.

"*Step* right *up!* Step *right* up, *la-a-a-dies* and *gen-nel-mun!* The *show* is *about* to *begin!* See Prince *Or*-loff tame the *migh-ty* beasts of the *jun-gle*. See *Prin-cess Zen-ora*, the Cir-*cas*-sian *slave girl*, ride bare back on the *Wild Hor-ses* of the *Sun! Chills, tha*-rills, and *danger* await you under the *big top!* Yes-sir-ee, *step* right up!"

Ling Cheung realized his timing was poor. A girl in a spangled circus costume ducked around the side of a tent, laughing. A muscular young groom glared after her. He wondered if they were lovers.

"Miss?" He hurried toward her with one of Grayson's posters in his outstretched hand as a steady stream of eager customers pushed past the little barker and through the opening of the main tent.

She refused the flyer. "What do you want? I'm in a hurry."

"I'll be on my way in a minute, miss." He held up the flyer so she could see Annette Mason's picture. "Have you seen any young miss of this description passing through since yesterday."

"Sure did." She tossed her hair. "About twenty or thirty of 'em."

Ling Cheung had too many years of politeness to show his annoyance. "Thank you for your trouble."

He could hear her laughing all the way to her gaily painted caravan. His ears burned with chagrin. He scanned the grounds and spied a man grooming horses and decided to try him next.

The calliope burst into greater volume and the air throbbed with it. The tumblers and clowns went spilling into the tent to the sound of laughter and applause. Boris Vetter, better known to circus-goers as Prince Orloff, was counting the house through a peephole. He turned around as his star performer joined him.

"Looks like a good crowd, Bedelia. And there'll be more by tomorrow when word gets around."

The young woman beside him nodded. "My new act is drawing them in like crazy. You'd better give me another raise, Boris. I'm worth it."

The circus owner eyed her with more than passing interest. "You be a little nicer to me, sweetheart, and I'll show you just how nice I can be in return."

She laughed in his face. "When pigs fly. I've heard about you, Boris. Just keep your dirty hands off of me or I'll pack up and leave you flat."

His face darkened. She was new and one of his biggest draws, but Boris was getting tired of her tormenting him. Teasing and flaunting herself, but never coming through with the goods. He'd made a mistake in letting Bedelia think that she was better than the rest. Before long he was going to have to teach her what her proper place was in this circus: in the ring and in his bed.

He swung away from the tent and stopped short. A man in a dark suit and bowler was just outside the door of his caravan. "Goddamn bill collectors!" Hadn't he given the feed merchant half of his money yesterday? Boris flexed his brawny arms and advanced menacingly.

"Hey, you! What're you doing snooping around here? Git!"

Ling Cheung spun around. A beefy man with strawberry hair and a ringmaster's suit was coming at him, accompanied by a veiled girl in harem costume adorned with glass jewels. He held up the flyer.

Bedelia stared. "Jesus, Boris! It's a Chinaman. In a suit!"

"Damned chink!" Boris waved his meaty fists. "Off with you, or I'll have the roustabouts kick your yellow butt down the hill and all the way back to Chinatown."

Anger burned inside Ling Cheung's breast but he held it in check. His people had been civilized for thousands of years, while this brute's ancestors had still been wearing skins and living in caves. He gritted his teeth and stood steadfast. He had a job to do. "I am looking for the man who calls himself Prince Orloff."

The ringmaster bent the coil of whip back and forth in his hands. "I'm Orloff. And I don't want your kind around here, mister. No slant-eyes allowed."

It took great effort for Ling Cheung to control himself. It demeaned him to even have to speak with such an uncouth person. There was only one universal language among such barbarians. "A five-hundred-dollar reward is offered. Perhaps you have seen this girl in your travels?"

Boris nudged the bareback rider. He was too proud to admit that he could only read with great difficulty. "Take it, Bedelia. I don't want any of that yellow stuff to come off on my hands."

She gave her boss a look of intense dislike and snatched the broadside from Ling Cheung. With the veil drawn across her face and her eyes heavily outlined with kohl and paint, he couldn't tell what she might really look like—but there was crafty intelligence in her blue eyes. And hunger. If she'd seen Annette, Ling Cheung thought, she'd remember. For five hundred dollars.

Bedelia scanned the lines and examined the demure face that might have belonged to a hundred others. *Annette Mason.* Too bad. She could put five hundred simoleons to good use. Damn good use.

Boris was getting to be a problem.

She gave Ling Cheung a quick scrutiny. "How'd she come up missing?"

"There was a misunderstanding. The young miss left home eight years ago and has not been seen since by her loving family."

Bedelia's gaze flicked over the reproduced photo again. Well dressed, well fed, and cared for. And the family was wealthy, too. You could tell by the expensive boots the girl and her mother—that must be her mother —wore. That, and the fact that they had hired this fellow to look for her, and that they had five hundred dollars to give in reward money. What a stupid little fool. All that and she ran away. Bedelia couldn't think of anything that would have sent her running from them. Some people didn't know where their bread was buttered.

She tried to hand the broadside back. "No," Ling Cheung said. "Keep it. Show it around to the troupe. If anyone remembers her, I can be reached by a note to this post office address at the bottom."

The talk of five hundred dollars impressed Boris so much that he forgot to be threatening. Ling Cheung tipped his hat to Bedelia and walked away. Boris stared after him. "Now, how do you suppose that fellow had enough money to hire a hack?"

Bedelia shrugged. "If the girl's people can post a five-hundred-dollar reward they can afford a Chinaman in a suit."

She folded the flyer carefully and tucked it into her bodice; but when Boris went off she tore it to shreds and threw them away in the nearest box of trash. Her memory was uncanny. And she'd memorized the man's post office address as well. If she saw Annette Mason she'd recognize her, all right.

And she'd be damned if she'd share that reward with Boris, or anyone else.

The calliope changed its tune, light ripples of sound charging down the scales into booming thunder. Bedelia hurried between the tents, ignoring the looks and whistles of the carny men. It was time for her to finish her transformation from Bedelia Brown to Princess Zenora, the Circassian slave.

Ling Cheung got into the carriage. The last of the flyers would be distributed by noon. Now he had nothing to do but sit back and wonder what Grayson was up to, getting himself invited to dinner at the house of his sworn enemy.

He settled back against the leather seat and thought

of his boyhood in China, of his time lugging water for the coolie gangs who'd built the Central Pacific tracks east from Sacramento, and of his arrival at the Thunder Ranch, where his mother was still cook. Life had been hard. But it had been so much simpler then.

Cassandra paused and looked for signs of Grayson Howard's arrival from the arched window on the second-story landing. From this vantage point she had an expansive view all the way down the hill. There wasn't a single carriage in sight. He was long overdue, and that pleased her greatly.

Mr. Howard would earn no points by arriving late and failing to send his excuses. Tyler was a stickler in some areas. He considered unpunctuality to be one of the unwritten cardinal sins. He'd planned to take Mr. Howard up into the hills to look at some property before dinner, and was growing increasingly irritated. Cassandra smiled. All to the good. Perhaps she could do something to fan the flames. Gathering her skirts, she hurried lightly down the stairs.

As she reached the entrance hall the great door opened inward and Kitty came flying in, cheeks rosy and eyes sparkling with excitement. One day very soon, Cassandra thought, she will become a great beauty. The assurance of it was there in the girl's lovely bone structure and wide hazel eyes. It struck her as odd that so few of Kitty's contemporaries could see it yet. Indeed, Kitty herself could not.

Her niece was wearing her new bronze habit with black frogging, and her veiled hat and whip dangled from one hand. The color of the habit brought out the bluer shades in Kitty's eyes. Her resemblance to Margaret was stronger at that moment than anytime in the past; but when she saw her aunt she stopped dead in her tracks and the bright glow faded. She darted a glance over her shoulder and lowered her voice. "Is—is our guest here yet?"

"No. He's late—and your uncle is ill-pleased."

Hope and color lit up Kitty's face once more. "Perhaps he's changed his mind."

Her niece's words gave Cassandra an idea. If there was no way of dissuading Tyler, then it must be the sardonic Mr. Howard who backed off from a proposed match with Kitty. She smiled with growing confidence. "Run along and dress for dinner, darling. I think your new green gown would be suitable for tonight, since it's to be just a quiet evening at home."

Kitty raised her eyebrows. "The French muslin? I thought you meant to have it returned. Uncle Tyler dislikes the color. He said it made me look insipid."

Their eyes met in a conspiratorial way; but in a household of this size, there were always servants nearby to overhear. "Nonsense," Cassandra replied. "I think it is the perfect outfit for our dinner party. And you must admit that my taste in fashion is more to be trusted than your uncle's."

The shadow lifted from Kitty's eyes. She understood the game, and was pleased to be treated in such an adult manner. "How can I ignore the advice of the most elegant woman in San Francisco. I shall gladly wear the green muslin."

Kitty went up the stairs quickly, relieved not to have been questioned over her own tardiness. She and Helena Pettigrew had spent the afternoon with Helena's cousins visiting from Massachusetts. There had been talk of a picnic in the botanical gardens or a visit to the circus that had just come to town—Kitty was dying to see Princess Zenora ride bareback upon the Wild Horses of the Sun, and the wire walking act of the Flying Sabatinis. Neither promised treat had materialized.

Instead, Edward and Jerome Mercier had bored her with bragging stories of their prowess at sports and their sparkling acquaintance on the East Coast. Kitty had little interest in sculling and hurdling, and none at all in the golden Mercier cousins. Despite their patrician faces, they were rather ordinary young men. Kitty knew they felt the same regarding her. She'd overheard one of Jerome's pointed comments to that effect. "A little brown mouse," he'd called her, "with no conversation and not the slightest inkling of what constitutes feminine charm."

His remarks had cut her to the bone. The outing had been completely spoiled for Kitty, and she hadn't exchanged more than two more words with either of the Merciers on the ride home. Helena had been furious with her. Later, upon returning to the house, Kitty had lingered near the stables in hopes of seeing Jake.

He'd been nowhere to be found and of course she couldn't ask after him. Then, insult to injury, Tomms had sent her packing as if she were still a gawking, horse-mad girl of nine or ten. The entire afternoon had been miserable.

But as she was leaving the stableyard she'd spied a small twist of paper that he'd tucked into ivy growing along the stone archway. That was where Jake had promised to leave a note for her. Unfortunately, Tomms had been there, so she hadn't been able to retrieve it. Yet. But she might be able to slip out before dinner, or perhaps send Jenny to fetch it. Jenny thought it was all very romantic.

Cassandra watched her niece vanish up the staircase in a flurry of youthful energy and bronze twill. Blue and rose and white were Kitty's best colors. The French muslin dress was to have been made of blue on blue. Instead, Madame Lucine's new assistant had sent over the proper pattern, but done up in a dull shade of green that only an olive-skinned brunette could wear successfully. A shade that drabbed Kitty's soft brown hair, sallowed her complexion, and changed the predominant color of her hazel eyes from blue to a muddied moss. A hint of a smile played about Cassandra's mouth: a most fortunate mistake.

She followed the branching corridor that led past the music room and the library to Tyler's study. As Cassandra approached the open double doors of the music room, a blonde girl in the blue-sprigged dress of an upstairs maid shot out of the room, giggling and coyly looking back over her shoulder. She almost collided with her mistress.

With a little squeak the girl pulled up short. Her starched maid's cap was knocked sideways and a lock of dark hair had come loose from her bun. An inspection of the music room, Cassandra surmised, would probably reveal an abashed and frightened footman. She eyed the girl's telltale uniform and a pointed silence ensued. They both knew an upstairs maid had no business in this part of the house.

"G-good afternoon, madam." The serving girl bobbed awkwardly in a poor attempt at a curtsy and tried to regain her composure. She stood, alternately flushed and pale, biting her lower lip between broad teeth and twisting the frill of her starched apron with nervous fingers as she waited for the ax to fall.

It took Cassandra a moment to place her. "You are Rosaleen, Moira Purcell's niece, I think?"

"Yes, m-m-ma'am."

Moira had been Stoneleigh's head parlor maid until severe rheumatism had forced her early retirement. "I am glad to hear her condition is improving. When you visit her next you must ask Cook to prepare a special basket to take to her."

"Y-yes, m-ma'am."

"I shall follow your progress with great interest." Cassandra gave a slight smile of dismissal. "You may return to your duties."

Reproof nested in reprieve. Profound relief spread over the maid's face. "Yes, ma'am! Thank you, ma'am!" With a marionette's jerky curtsy, the girl whisked away, grateful it had been Madam and not the master who had discovered her folly. And determined not to let a handsome devil lure her away from her new duties again. Why, that rascal, Jake Adams, could have gotten them sacked, with no references! Mr. Lucton, from all Rosaleen had heard, would as soon give you the sack as look at you. Rosaleen hurried away.

Cassandra found Tyler's study empty, and went to confer with her housekeeper. When she went back a short time later he was at his desk, the red leather account books stacked neatly to one side. He was preparing the envelopes with the servants' quarterly salaries. Juno dozed contentedly at his feet. Cassandra had always marveled at the strange relationship between them. Tyler never seemed to notice the dog, except as an encumbrance, but the creature worshiped the ground he walked upon. Tyler was more than Juno's owner: he was her god.

Cassandra entered the study as her husband sealed

another envelope. "Why, I thought that surely our guest would be with you. Has Mr. Howard had a sudden change of plans?"

Tyler rose impatiently. "If so, he hasn't bothered to let me know of it."

She pressed her advantage. "Perhaps he has mistaken the day."

The frown deepened to a scowl as he looked out upon the empty drive. "Damn it, he should have been here two hours ago!"

Better and better. Cassandra hid her triumph. "Shall I have Morton tell Cook to set dinner back an hour?"

"There's still time. And wear those rubies tonight."

She was aghast. "I'd feel like an utter fool. And I'd look like one, as well."

He turned back and strode over to her. "Listen to me, goddammit! I am master of this house, and you'll do as I damn well say you will!"

He'd never spoken to her so roughly before. As she stood rooted with indignation, Tyler clamped his hands around her shoulders. His eyes narrowed. "I've made up my mind, and none of your frosty looks will change it. The girl needs a husband, and a wealthy one to keep her in the high style to which she has long grown accustomed. And a young, red-blooded one, at that."

She steeled herself. "Really? I've heard rumors that blood in Mr. Howard's veins is that of a Cheyenne Indian. Is it true?"

A strange expression crossed Tyler's features. "So that's it. I don't know which loose-lipped gossip informed you of the rumors regarding his background, but I'll tell you here and now—he may be the son of a redskinned chief—damn it, he might be one himself and live in a tipi for all I know! But get this through your head. His bank accounts weigh more heavily with me than his bloodlines."

"And what do you expect Kitty to do?" Fear made her angry. She would not let this travesty of a marriage, this merger, take place. She appealed to his innate snobbery.

"My niece has the blood of earls and great ladies in her veins. She is made for a gentler life, and could never adapt to life on the plains. Or do you expect her to live in a hide tipi, with a-a *papoose* on her back?"

Tyler's face grew ruddier. His fingers dug into her flesh so hard she winced and tried to pull away. He held her all the more firmly. "Listen to me! When we married, Cassandra, I gave you free rein over household matters, to hire whom you would and spend whatever you thought necessary. But your authority does, and always will, end there. This is business, damn it! *My* business."

He shook her once, hard. One of the pins fell from her hair and it tumbled down over her shoulder. Tyler was so enraged that he didn't notice. He shook her again. "I don't give a good goddamn for Grayson Howard's pedigree. And I won't have you fouling things up with your hoity-toity airs and graces."

Cassandra's arms felt bruised to the bone from his cruel hold. In the many years of the marriage Tyler had never once laid hands on her before. She was frightened and enraged. For just a moment primal fury blazed out from her eyes, savage and raw.

Tyler was startled. He'd never seen her show such spirit before. It was almost like seeing his wife turn into another woman—or a marble statue come to life. He let her jerk herself away, but his jaw settled into the rigid, stubborn lines Cassandra knew so well.

"Control yourself!" He threatened, "Or you'll suffer worse from me. I've been patient with you, Cassandra, but no longer. And remember that *I* am Kitty's legal guardian. And her sole support. I control her destiny, and I will cut her off without a penny if she goes against my wishes."

"You would never do so!"

"Would I not? Try me, and she'll suffer the consequences. As for you, you've been lax in your chaperonage. Tomms tells me that one of the grooms has been making up to her."

That infuriated Cassandra even more. "I think you may trust Kitty to know where to draw the line. If Tomms can't discipline the groom, then he should be dismissed at once."

"I've just taken care of the matter. You may tell your precious niece that there will be no more rides accompanied by that jack-o'-worts, Jake Adams. Tomms found a note the young scoundrel left for Kitty. Adams was dismissed and escorted off the property at once." With one of Tyler's boots applied to his behind and a hard clout to his ear.

Cassandra's hands clenched and unclenched as her brief rage cooled and hardened into implacable determination. She eyed her husband stonily.

"We do not see eye to eye on this matter, Tyler. And we never will. But I give you fair warning. I will do everything in my power to save Kitty from making the kind of marriage that"—Cassandra caught herself in time—"that her mother did. She will not—she *must* not —marry a man like Grayson Howard."

She left without a backward glance, seemingly cool and in control of her emotions. Inwardly she was bursting with rebellion. She heard the library door slam behind her. Tyler was in a towering rage now and she regretted that. It would be Kitty who suffered for it.

She rubbed her bruised arms, distraught over Tyler's behavior and herself for defying him so openly. It was futile to try to fight his whims face-to-face. He would only overwhelm Kitty with his anger, demolish her with his loud, booming voice and vulgar condemnations. He would browbeat her into accepting a proposal of marriage from a man who was half barbarian and totally intimidating.

Carriage wheels crunched up the long gravel drive and Cassandra saw a flash of glossy black picked out in red through the sidelights and peered out. Her unwanted houseguest had just arrived. She didn't want to have to speak with Grayson Howard now. In a swirl of silk she went past the panel of clear leaded glass and swept across the floor toward the stairs—only to find that she had been mistaken.

The carriage was not arriving, it was heading for the stables after dropping off its passenger. Grayson Howard stood at the open drawing-room door. From the odd light in his eyes, she was sure he'd arrived in time to get an earful.

A restless tension filled the air. For the first time in her life, habits of good-breeding deserted Cassandra. She stared at him wordlessly while crimson flooded her cheeks. The study door had been open. How much had he overheard? She realized that her hair had come loose and lifted her arms to twist it hurriedly into place with the ivory pins.

The gesture was feminine and natural. It charmed Grayson against his will. Cassandra looked younger and less aloof with her curls tumbling loose from her chignon. He wanted to go to her and take out the remaining pins and slide his fingers through her hair. It was so rich and shining he knew it would feel like satin.

Then he saw the shadows of the bruises already forming on her arms. He wondered what had caused them . . . or who.

Cassandra blushed. Why was he staring at her? She felt like a butterfly, skewered by a pin. He lifted his hat and bowed slightly, smiling his dark, ironic smile.

"Good afternoon, Mrs. Lucton. It is good of you to invite me to stay with you for the rest of my visit."

His sardonic tone was not lost upon her. She gave him the faintest of polite smiles. "Any guest of my husband is welcome at Stoneleigh, Mr. Howard." The words felt smooth and cold in her mouth, like stones from an icy river. "I sincerely hope you will enjoy your visit with him."

Grayson smiled. "A shot to the heart, but as you see, I am scarcely wounded. And I'm afraid that the press of business renders me unable to accept the invitation to stay at Stoneleigh."

Morton came gliding out of the side hall to take his hat and cane, mortified that he had not been there when the guest arrived. "Mr. Lucton is awaiting you in his study, sir."

"Thank you." Grayson gave Cassandra a swift, ironic glance, then allowed the butler to lead him away.

She remained frozen on the bottom step until the library door closed behind Grayson. With his advent a restless tension filled the air. She gathered her skirts and fled up the staircase, as if a ravenous wolf had been loosed in the house.

*   *   *

Kitty dressed for dinner with her mind in utter chaos. Her hopes had been dashed by Grayson Howard's arrival. She had seen him from the windows. He was not as handsome as Jake, and was also quite *old*. Perhaps as much as thirty.

Jenny entered. "It wasn't there, miss. Not where you said it was nor anywhere else along the wall."

Kitty's stomach sank. "Do you think Tomms found it?"

"That old wart? No, he'd have taken it straight to the master, and he would have sent for you straight away."

"Perhaps the wind blew it out into the field."

There was no time now for disappointment. Kitty examined her reflection in the oval mirror on her dressing table, twisting and turning to see the effect. The green dress made her look faded and dull. For the first time she was glad that she hadn't inherited her mother's fabled beauty. Men would not fight duels over her, or write odes to her grace. Uncle Tyler had once said that men had been despondent to learn that her mother was already a married woman when she first came to London and took the town by storm.

Kitty dusted on another coating of rice powder for good measure, noting with satisfaction that it hid the bloom of her complexion and washed out her features. "How do I look, Jenny? Is that a freckle on my nose or only a reflection?"

Her maid licked a finger and daubed at a speckle on the mirror. Jenny was a blunt Irish girl and not at all in awe of her young charge. Hadn't she known Miss most of her life? "Really, miss, you should have a proper looking glass like Mrs. Lucton has in her room, now that you're courting and all."

"I'm not courting, Jenny. You mustn't go about saying such things." Kitty moved away. "And I like this room just the way it is." Although she could take her choice of far more elegant and costly furnishings, she still clung to her white-painted wardrobe and bed. She knew every pink and yellow rosebud painted along the decorative borders, and every place where the green enamel of the leaves was chipped away.

A china doll with eyes that opened and closed and a gown of blond lace was still propped against a velvet bolster in one chair. It was past the time to set such things aside, yet Kitty hadn't the heart to relegate Monique to a dark cupboard. Uncle Tyler had had the doll sent from France only two years ago.

Time was moving much too fast for her. Soon, if Uncle Tyler had his way, she would have to leave all this behind. He had told her this morning exactly why he had invited Grayson Howard to visit, and exactly what behavior he expected from her. Panic welled up in her chest until she felt robbed of breath. Kitty closed her eyes and waited until the sensation passed.

Jenny picked up her mistress's discarded garments from a pile on the floor. "Oh, miss, look what you've done! You've gone and put a big rent in your riding dress."

Kitty hadn't even noticed the large three-corner tear. "It must have caught on something. I don't even remember doing it."

Jenny sniffed again. "You never do, begging your pardon, miss."

Kitty grinned. Not for her, the fancy lady's maid with airs and graces and a nose in the air, whom Uncle Tyler would have bestowed upon her, if not for Cassandra's backing. Kitty felt much more at ease with dear Jenny. With those she knew well she could be her own unassuming self. It was only with strangers or new acquaintances that she felt stupid and her tongue turned to lead. And of course with Uncle Tyler. She held him in considerable affection that was well tinged with awe. He was so sure, so powerful, that she felt small in consequence. Usually he was a benign, if distant, deity dwelling under the same roof and showering her with gifts. But the few times when she'd incurred his wrath were imprinted deeply on her memory. She tried not to think of them.

She let Jenny adjust her wide sash and clasp a necklet and earrings of seed pearls around her throat, amazed that the bounding pulse didn't show. There was a soft rap on the door and then Cassandra, in a gown of watered silk in a deep rose color, entered. "You look perfect, my dear."

"Thank you." Kitty lowered her head. Cassandra could see the neat center part in her shining brown hair, the childish vulnerability of her white swan neck. She dropped a light kiss on Kitty's nape.

"You have no need to be nervous, darling. Remember what I promised. You will not be forced into anything you do not want. I won't fail you."

No, Kitty thought with a qualm, but I might fail you.

They went down the gothic staircase together and entered the long drawing room arm in arm, unaware of the charming picture they made. Tyler was showing Cassandra's collection of blue and white porcelain to Grayson. Built-in cabinets flanked the fireplace, filled with bowls and plates and temple jars from China. He turned.

"Ah, there you are, my dears. Mr. Howard, you have already met my wife, of course."

Grayson bowed over Cassandra's hand and was surprised again at how delicate it was. And how cold, even through her evening glove. The rubies flashed at her white throat. She was overdressed for the occasion, he thought, trying to intimidate him with grandeur. It only angered him.

Cassandra saw the flash in the depths of his eyes and flushed. She knew exactly what he was thinking. That disconcerted her. She pulled her hand from his strong grasp.

Tyler beamed proudly. "This is my wife's niece, Miss Hamilton. Kitty, make your curtsy to Mr. Howard."

Kitty tried not to look directly at her uncle's guest, but found herself staring. How brown he was, and how fierce his eyes! She stumbled as she took a seat in a gilded chair, flushing with embarrassment. She shot her aunt a frightened look.

Tyler saw it and was furious. Aware of his disapproving scowl, Kitty sat in a cloud of misery, praying for the sound of the gong and Morton's announcement of dinner. She found Grayson Howard even more alarming at close quarters. His wit, she thought, bordered on sarcasm, but perhaps that was just because she was so nervous and ill at ease.

He must have just said something to her, because he was looking her way expectantly. Everyone was looking at her. Juno snuffled at her master's feet, then rose and somehow knocked a china ornament off a shelf with a wag of her tail. It bounced on the thick carpet and smashed to pieces against a brass floor urn, which rang like the call of Judgment Day. Kitty sprang to her feet with unflattering eagerness. "Was that the gong?"

It was the first time she'd shown any animation since his arrival and Grayson smiled sardonically. Evidently she preferred her dinner to his conversation. He was almost beginning to regret the necessity that had brought him here. He felt the medallion burning beneath his shirt, and hardened his resolve.

The dinner itself went more smoothly. They ate formally in the gold dining room beneath twin chandeliers of faceted lead crystal, a footman behind each chair. All through dinner Kitty never once gave her opinion or uttered an unsolicited comment on any subject unless prodded. Then she flushed and stammered so that it was almost as painful for her listeners as it was for her.

Cassandra, seeing that Grayson had not taken to Kitty immediately, was heartened. She exerted herself to keep the conversation afloat without involving her niece too often. Cassandra caught Grayson looking at her with speculation in his eyes, and more than a touch of amusement.

He was indeed amused. So, the white queen didn't approve of him for her little princess. No one, he reflected wryly, had thought to ask for his approval. By the time the women rose after dinner, leaving the men to cigars and port, he'd already made up his mind. Nothing on God's green earth would make him offer for Kitty Lucton. The girl bid fare to bloom prettily, in a fluffy, candy-box sort of way. Other than that she seemed to be a blank slate.

He was amazed now that he'd even contemplated the idea. Jaime was right. He must have been mad.

If he meant to torment Lucton he'd have to think of something else. There were other ways to skin a skunk.

After port the men joined the two ladies in the drawing room. Cassandra had her embroidery frame set up and was threading her needle with crimson silk. Kitty was rummaging through the cabinet where the family albums of travel drawings were stored, hoping against hope that her presence would be forgotten. Grayson felt sorry for her.

Kitty Lucton seemed like a little brown sparrow who had wandered, unwillingly, into an aviary of more exotic birds. And she was ready to fly away at the first opportunity. Every time she thought that her uncle wasn't looking, her glance slid over to the face of the mantel clock. Her whole manner was nervous and high-strung. He couldn't tell if she disliked or feared him, or if this edgy nervousness was the girl's natural state. And Kitty Lucton, although of marriageable age, was definitely a girl. Not the kind of female a man would want to have snowed in with him for the long Colorado winters.

Nor was the girl's aunt. He narrowed his eyes and examined Cassandra, while pretending to be listening to another of Tyler's overripe anecdotes. She was not a girl, but an elegant china doll of a woman, ruffled and jeweled and perfumed. Utterly sure of herself and her superiority to the common run of mankind. And, he was sure, she disliked him as heartily. Especially since their encounter earlier. Every time they exchanged words or their eyes met, animosity grew, crackling through the air like the uneasy aura of an approaching storm.

While Tyler's story wound toward its end, his wife sat behind her standing embroidery frame, plying her golden needle with great skill. The white queen in her ivory tower. She stopped to snip the thread with golden scissors. The jeweled band around her throat caught the light. It was a constant reminder of her wealth and privileged status.

Grayson turned his scrutiny on his host. A less outwardly polished man would be called a banty rooster. Tyler Lucton was more of a grackle, handsome and colorful and boldly aggressive. He punctuated his current story with sharp, birdlike nods of his head, as he came to the punch line. "And then the duchess of Devonshire said to the maid: 'Never mind, my dear girl. If you have seen *one* duke in the bathtub, you have seen them all!' "

Grayson smiled, although he'd been listening with only half an ear. Tyler rose abruptly. "I'll help Kitty find that album."

Grayson was left alone with his hostess. As she took up a piece of brilliant green floss to rethread her needle, he tried to place Cassandra in his imaginary zoo. Tried and failed. But he knew that she mistrusted him.

Her instincts, he thought, were remarkable.

Meanwhile, Tyler had joined Kitty at the cabinet. He'd noted the indifference in Grayson's eyes when they alighted on his niece. Things were going badly. If the girl didn't mend her ways tonight it would be too late. Future invitations would be sloughed off with trumped-up excuses. Tyler made a show of rummaging through the compartments of the heavily carved cabinet while Kitty struggled to subdue her anxiety.

She glanced at him from the corner of her eye and her cup of woe brimmed over. Uncle Tyler was in a rare taking. She felt all of five years old with skinned knees and a rent in her stockings. She had been anticipating this moment—and dreading it—from the time he had entered the room.

Tyler cleared his throat. "I know that your aunt has already spoken to you about the import of Mr. Howard's visit," he began, glowering impatiently at the top of her bowed head.

"Yes, Uncle T-Tyler."

"I didn't expect to be required to speak to you also."

"No, Uncle T-Tyler." She stared at her green kid slippers, wishing herself a hundred miles away. Lectures by Uncle Tyler were always uncomfortable, but fortunately rare. That he was taking the time out for one now, with Mr. Howard in the same room, only served to highlight his displeasure.

Tyler's breath came out in an impatient gust. Kitty was being obstinate and ungrateful. The girl grew more like Cassandra every day! Impossible to read her thoughts even if she looked straight at him, and how could he begin to judge what she was thinking if the chit kept her head down the whole time?

"Kitty. Look at me." He waited till she complied, then lowered his head to hers, as if conferring on some point. "I have purposely cultivated Grayson Howard's acquaintance and invited him here as a suitable candidate for marriage."

She gave him the look that was all frightened eyes and trembling mouth. It infuriated him. "Perhaps your aunt did not explain things fully. I will be frank. You have no portion of your own." A heavy flush spread over his cheeks. "You are, in effect, a pauper."

Kitty's stomach knotted. "Yes, Uncle Tyler."

"I don't like to mention it, of course. Still, I must impress upon you how important his visit is. He wishes to become better acquainted with you before making a formal offer—that's only natural. But I'll tell you to your head that the whole of San Francisco knows why he is here.

"If this engagement doesn't come about, if Grayson Howard returns to his ranch without offering for you, you'll be a laughingstock. And when you make your official bow to society, you will have the pleasure of knowing that people are talking behind your back, saying that you could not bring him up to scratch."

Kitty's head drooped lower. For a moment Tyler's heart was wrung. Cassandra was right. She was very young after all, and not much accustomed to society. Despite the uncomfortable feeling, he went on. Unless the *Lady* sailed into San Francisco Bay by the end of the week, he was going to need this alliance with Grayson Howard. He hardened his heart against her obvious distress.

"You have none of the fetching ways cultivated by other girls your age, and though you are quite pretty, there are many greater beauties making their come-outs this season. You will be a candle to their suns. You will find yourself sitting along the wall with the matrons and spinsters who will eye you with curiosity, trying to fathom what it was about you that turned Grayson Howard away. Is that what you want, Kitty?"

She raised her face at that. It was white as a paper narcissus above the frail stem of her throat. "N-no. Oh, no!" She tried to go on but her clumsy tongue adhered to the roof of her mouth.

"Good. Then that's settled. You will make yourself agreeable to him. You will cease jumping like a frightened mouse when he takes your arm or flinching when he speaks directly to you. And you will stop looking at him as if he were an ogre."

"Y-yes, Un-cle Tyler."

"Good." Reaching one of the higher shelves inside the cabinet, Tyler extracted a large book bound in red morocco. "Here. Take this album of engravings over to him."

She did as he directed, pressing the album tightly to her chest. No matter what Uncle Tyler said, she couldn't . . . she *couldn't!*

Cassandra was alarmed by her niece's sudden pallor. "Kitty, what is it? Are you ill?"

"I . . . I have the headache . . . and I think . . . I'm going to be . . ." White-faced, Kitty suddenly bolted from the room.

Cassandra went after her, leaving her husband and guest alone together. Grayson departed shortly afterward, thanking Tyler for his invitation to stay at Stoneleigh. "The hotel will be more convenient for my business, but I do appreciate your kind offer."

Tyler was angry and disappointed. He recovered quickly, "Perhaps you'll dine again with us tomorrow?"

"I'd prefer you all to be my guests for dinner at my hotel tomorrow—unless you have other plans?" Grayson said.

The tension drained from Tyler. He didn't care what plans Cassandra might have made: they were dining at the Dillon tomorrow. "We'd be delighted."

Grayson shook his hand and resigned himself to another dull evening. He didn't know what had prompted him to extend his invitation. As he drove back to the city he smiled wryly. Jaime had cautioned him that revenge was dangerous. He hadn't warned that it could be damned boring, as well.

Grayson returned to his hotel room in a strange state. The buildings and the press of people closed in upon him until he longed for the freedom of the Cheyenne lands. He had always imagined he would stay on them, living the life his father had before him. His thoughts turned back to the time when his mother had brought him to the Cheyenne, to honor a blood vow made to his dying father. He had been seven years old.

Buffalo Heart was ancient, the oldest and wisest of the band. He lifted his head and sent Grayson a stern look. "You say, son of Small Eagle, that you have come to know your Tsistsistas heritage. And what if I say that your destiny is to live among us many years? What then?"

Grayson's answer came strong and clear. "I will stay."

"Ah." The wise man stared into the fire. "And what if I tell you that one day your destiny will take you far away from the Tsistsistas, to live among the white-eyed ones again?"

Pain lanced through Grayson's heart but he held his head high. "If you say I must, then I will go."

Silence stretched out, humming with tension. Buffalo Heart stared into the whispering flames while Grayson waited, holding his breath. At last the old man leaned forward.

"And what if I say to you, Gray Wolf Born of Thunder, that when you go away from us, it will be forever?"

Grayson swallowed, hard. "Then I will still stay away . . . forever."

And so he had. Grayson rubbed his eyes. He had turned his back upon the Cheyenne willingly. It had been the first and greatest sacrifice that he had made in his quest for vengeance. There was not a day that he didn't feel an exile. But it had been necessary to adopt his white heritage once more. To learn the white man's games and beat him at them.

Grayson stripped off his clothes and got into bed. The hour was late but sleep eluded him for a long while.

When he did finally fall into dreams, they were deep and disturbed.

A huge black bird soared overhead, talons dripping blood. He swung his rifle up and shot it. Feathers exploded in midair. The scavenger's smooth flight changed to an awkward, desperate tumbling. When it struck the ground Grayson felt the vibration of the thud through his feet.

He ran toward it, eager to examine his kill. But instead of the raptor, he found only a dying swan. Its elegant neck was twisted awry and the feathers of its soft white breast were matted with gouts of blood.

Blood as red as rubies.

The dream changed. He was back at Bitter Creek, searching through the burned tents and bloodied bodies. Searching for his uncle, Smoke Along the Ground. Searching for his wife and infant son. He knocked aside a pile of charred blankets with his boot and found Cassandra Lucton staring up at him with bloody, vacant eyes.

He woke up screaming.

Three A.M. The dream surrounded him, merging with reality until the heavy draperies looked like tipi walls stretching toward a midnight sky. The dark shapes of the furnishings looked like coffins, or bodies stacked up like bales of hides and furs. The fine hairs stood up on his arms and the back of his neck. Grayson rose and lit the lamp. The draperies were just heavy curtains at the windows, the sofas and chairs just furniture. But the horror remained.

He got up and poured himself a drink from the bottle of whiskey he kept only for guests. His hands shook and the pungent liquid spilled over them. He stared at the whiskey, breathing in the peaty fumes. He hadn't touched anything but wine in years. He could control the wine. Anything stronger controlled him.

Grayson struggled with himself briefly, then lifted the glass and downed it at a gulp. It scalded his throat like acid, and ate away at the edges of his pain. It softened and blurred the horror. He poured another.

That was the last thing he remembered.

In the morning he woke up to brash sunshine and a room in shambles. His body was stretched crosswise atop the sheets and his head throbbed violently. He forced himself to a sitting position. The whiskey bottle lay empty beside the bed and two chairs were overturned by the door. The leg of one was broken.

A shattered mirror and long splinter of broken glass caught the light and threw it back mercilessly. It stabbed at his eyes, but he couldn't draw the draperies: he'd torn them from the rods.

And he didn't remember any of it.

Grayson muttered a savage oath. It was a wonder that they hadn't broken down the door and hauled him off to the nearest jail. He suspected that Jaime had spread a few dollars around to ensure against it. Perhaps Jaime had calmed him down and gotten him back to bed. He didn't remember that either. It didn't matter.

He touched the medallion that was both talisman and shackle. This was all that mattered. This and the vow he had made. He closed his eyes and was once more upon the banks of Bitter Creek, wandering among the mutilated dead.

His hands clenched convulsively. *I will remember!*

4

"*Bedelia! Get a* move on!"

It was almost time for the show to start and the circus troupe was gearing up for it. Bedelia knew she should be changing for her first act, but she took more than a casual interest in the fellow Boris was talking to. He was well setup, tanned, and handsome with curling dark hair and the devil in his hazel-blue eyes. Just the sort that attracted her. Like to like, as the saying went. And he seemed to know his way around horses, too. Boris needed a little convincing.

"Why did they let you go, eh?"

Jake flushed. "There was a young lady of the house took a shine to me. So you see, they gave me my marching orders out of fear it would lead to something else."

"And did it?" That from Bedelia. She jumped off the hitch where she'd been sitting and sauntered over to them.

The newcomer's face darkened. "That it did not!"

"And would it have?" she teased.

Jake gave her a bold wink and turned back to Boris. "Well, will you take me on or not?"

"All right. You're hired." Boris poked a finger at him. "But if I find out you're wanted for thieving or murder, you'll be on your way in an instant."

"Fair enough."

Jake went off to see to the horses for Bedelia's act, aware that both she and Boris were watching him. They noticed that he worked hard and had an instinctive understanding with the animals. Except for the fact that he kept glancing down the road with a frown between his eyes—which might indicate he'd lied and the police were after him—Boris couldn't find a thing to complain about.

It wasn't the police Jake was watching for, but Miss Kitty Hamilton. He knew she'd gone out to picnic and that the route home would lead her past the circus. He wondered if Jenny had really given his note to Kitty. He hadn't tried to deliver it himself. He was still bruised from the beating her uncle had given him before throwing him off the property. Damn Tyler Lucton's black heart to hell! Well, he hadn't heard the last of Jake Adams, no matter what he thought!

Jake slipped the glass-jeweled bridle on the horses for Bedelia's first act, still watching the road.

Kitty's outing with Helena and her two cousins was not a success. Helena was irritated and Jerome and Edward no longer hid their boredom with her. She felt like a leper.

Helena whispered in her ear, and gave her arm a

pinch for emphasis. "*Really, Kitty! You could at least try.*"

But she couldn't. Kitty didn't like either of the cousins. Their supercilious attitude infuriated her. Edward's direct questions and comments, made in a sincere attempt to draw her out, had only flustered her. It had taken Jerome's superior airs and condescending ways to intimidate her into tongue-tied silence.

The Merciers' fine carriage made light work of the bumpy road, and while Helena amused her cousins with idle chatter Kitty sat quietly, pleating and unpleating the skirt of her rose linen dress. Jake had never made her feel silly or commonplace. Jerome and Edward were the ones who were stupid and silly, their heads filled with nothing but racing and who had been to whom's party, and what a lot of tedious young men and women had said to them.

Let them think her ill-mannered or worse. Kitty didn't care at the moment. Her eyes were on the road ahead. Indeed, all her concentration was focused there, and she was the first to hear the distant wail of the calliope. Her insides lurched. Clasping her gloved fingers together tightly, she pretended she hadn't noticed it, but her heart hammered against her ribs.

It was a good five minutes—five inordinately long minutes—before Helena paused for breath and heard the music. "Oh, what is that?"

The carriage crested a low hill. A line of painted wagons, as colorful as gypsy caravans, ringed the flat meadow. Tents with bright banners filled the center of it and a stream of carriages and riders came toward it from town. Helena clapped her hands together in delight. "The circus! Oh, do let's stop!"

The two young men were equally enthusiastic. Only

Kitty sat mute. Helena put a dainty hand upon her friend's arm. "Now, don't be a wet blanket, Kitty, and offer up a dozen reasons as to why we shouldn't stop. I'm sure your aunt won't care if we're a little late returning, and she knows that we'll be perfectly safe with Edward and Jerome."

"I've no objection," Kitty answered diffidently, but her pale cheeks flushed with warm color. This was what she'd been waiting for all morning. Praying for, to be more exact. Helena's cousins were delighted. A circus might yet salvage a wasted day with a girl who, no matter how charming, was still their cousin, and her colorless little friend. Edward obediently turned the carriage off the road to a track leading to the circus grounds and in a few minutes they had joined the gathering throng.

The shirt-sleeved barker, straw hat tipped back over his rusty hair, was hustling the crowd into the main tent.

Edward procured their tickets while Jerome gawked at the freaks. "I say, do you think that bearded lady is truly a woman, or a man in disguise?" Edward laughed. "I don't believe I care enough to find out, coz. I'll leave that up to you."

Helena quelled their boisterous spirits with an indignant look and they all went off to see elephants staked behind one of the tents. A wiry boy was setting down buckets of water for the huge beasts. The smallest of the three dipped his trunk in the bucket and let loose with a playful spray from its flexible trunk. The boy was doused from head to toe. Outraged, he picked up a long prod and struck at the elephant, cursing the air blue.

"Here, that's no way to talk in front of ladies," Jerome began, advancing on the urchin. The elephant took umbrage and squirted Jerome in the face with a well-directed stream. Helena shrieked, the urchin laughed, and several onlookers joined in. Only Kitty seemed oblivious.

She stood apart from the rest, staring past the string of dappled circus horses, bedecked in gold-colored leather harnesses and tassels and braids, with nodding gold plumes strapped to their foreheads. From nearby a man's voice called: "Bedelia? Get a move on. They're lined up and ready to go."

Kitty's heart gave a lurch. That was Jake's voice. He was here, just as he'd told Jenny he would be. Now, if she could only get her courage up to slip away and meet him and . . .

Edward took her by the arm, none too gently. His cuff was sprinkled with dark water spots. "Come, let's go inside before we all get a soaking. I've managed to obtain front row seats."

It was warm inside the tent and the jostling crowd was loud with excitement. They had no more taken their seats than the circus master stepped into the ring, welcoming them all with a flourish of his corded whip. He cracked it twice, with the sound of a rifle shot, and the grand parade began, accompanied by the wild skirls of the calliope. Strong men, freaks, capering acrobats, and strutting tightrope walkers marched through the curtains and around the sawdust ring, followed by camels and bridled zebras, colorful clowns, and prancing dogs in ruffled collars.

Then the music changed and the horses entered with a flourish, all flashing hooves and bobbing plumes. The air was rich with the scents of sawdust and horses and sweat. Kitty felt a thrill of excitement. She hadn't seen a circus since she was a child; but it was seeing Jake that had set her heart pounding. Love, she thought, was a frighteningly wonderful thing.

Jerome felt a different sort of thrill and forgot his soaking when a team of plunging horses entered. A lovely equestrienne straddled their backs. She was dressed in a form-fitting spangled outfit with a revealing bodice and a short, flaring skirt. Pink tights and matching boots encased her shapely legs. With a quick glance over one shoulder, she somersaulted backward, landing easily on her feet.

Edward was equally enthralled. "By Jove, isn't she something!"

The horses went around the ring three times, sufficient for their rider to spot the "swells" in the crowd. Bedelia had been with Prince Orloff's circus for only three months, but she was a seasoned performer. And an excellent pickpocket. Leaping to the back of the off leader, she struck a pose. It was second nature to adjust her balance fractionally with every movement of the horses, while holding the reins effortlessly. As the team thundered around a second time, her brilliant smile lingered on a certain spot in the front row.

Yes, those two green fellows in the front row would be easy marks. A couple of young dandies with more money than sense. Bedelia was well acquainted with their type. And these two at least had a look of good humor about them, without that touch of debauchery she'd learned—the hard way—to avoid.

Holding the reins with her left foot, she arched backward until her hands touched the horse's rump. It wasn't happenstance that she'd managed to do it where Edward and Jerome could get the full effect. Bedelia had a sharp brain and soft body, and she used both to full advantage. With a twisting somersault, she vaulted up and flipped over to the near leader. A roar of applause and wild cheers accompanied her triumphal exit from the tent.

The new horse handler came up to catch the lead bridle and Bedelia gave him a wink as she slid off. "What do you think, Jake?"

He grinned in admiration. "I think you're a hell of a woman, if that's what you're wanting to hear. Are you so talented in bed?"

She sent him a saucy look. "If you stick around long enough you might find out for yourself."

Without waiting for his reaction she ran to her wagon and stripped off the top and stiff skirts of her costume, leaving only a dancer's leotard. She threw on a tight sleeveless jacket that didn't quite meet in front and was held together by three strategically placed golden chains. A pair of sheer pantaloons, a belt heavy with disks of jingling coins, and a sheer veil that went over her head and wrapped securely around her throat completed the transformation. Princess Zenora was ready for her next act.

Bedelia glanced in the freckled mirror. Thinking of the swells in the front row, she loosened the chains that held her bodice together by several links. The curves of her breasts were more noticeable, but they weren't in danger of flopping out of the bolero when she did the back flip this time. That had gotten them run out of Sacramento, and "Prince Orloff" had been really pissed.

He didn't have the guts to fire her, though. He didn't dare. With two aged tigers and a moth-eaten bear for the animal act, her three routines on horseback were the heart of the circus. Boris worked both Bedelia and his horses hard, but without them he wouldn't have much to draw the crowds.

The aerial acts were crowd-pleasers, but they worked

with a net; and since Mario's broken arm had healed crooked, he missed the bar almost half the time. No, it was the young men who had the money to spend, and what drew them in was the idea of watching a half-naked woman ride horseback around the ring. And she could always collect a little bonus money from them. It was a hard world, and a girl had to look out for herself.

Weaving seductive plans, she ran out to join the horses in high good humor. At the best she'd get a good dinner and a bauble or two out of those fellows, maybe some good times: at the worst, a little rough play, and before they knew it their fine gold pocket watches and the contents of their wallets became hers. But that was only for the last night of the circus, before they packed up and left town.

Someday, Bedelia dreamed, she'd hit a real bonanza. Maybe reap enough to leave the bogus prince and his mangy troupe before things got too out of hand.

Boris was *really* becoming a problem.

The Princess Zenora act was always a crowd-pleaser. Bedelia rode out of the tent after her act filled with a heated elation that was almost sexual. Controlling the plunging horses, aware of herself and her body at every instant, aware of the men in the crowd gaping at her costume and trying to catch a flash of her bare breasts, always excited her. And the look on the faces of those two marks she'd picked out earlier! They'd be eating from the palm of her hand.

She jumped down, leaving the horses to Jake, and started toward her caravan to change for the "Innocence in Peril" routine, which was her last except for the finale. Halfway to the wagon, she rounded the bales of

hay and was accosted by Boris. He was dressed in jodh-
purs with a fancy shirt, and a jacket dripping with fray-
ing gold braid. He brandished his looped-up whip in her
face.

"Goddammit, Bedelia, what do you think you're doing? Didn't I tell you to keep that jacket laced tighter?
Or are you trying to bankrupt me while you entice the
men? Slut!"

Without warning he slid the handle behind the chain
links holding her bodice together and yanked it open.
Pulling her toward him, he thrust his hand inside and
fondled her breasts. "Is that what you want them to see,
hey?"

Bedelia went white with rage. "Damn you, Boris!"
Her hand lashed out to slap his face and her knee came
up between his legs.

Orloff was faster. He caught her wrist in his free
hand, at the same time clamping his legs over her knee
before she did any damage. Slowly, to prove his superior
strength, he immobilized her and pressed her close. The
stiff wires of his gold braid scraped her bare flesh.
"Maybe," he said between his teeth, "you need to learn
who's boss here."

He half dragged, half carried her away and toward
his private wagon. She was too winded to yell for help
and she knew that no one could hear her over the calliope's ear-shattering music. In any case, she couldn't believe that he meant to follow through with his threat.
Boris had insinuated a few things lately, but he'd never
approached her outright. Then she saw the odd light in
his eyes and understood.

He was one of those. The kind who needed anger or
fear or pain to spur him on. Memories assaulted her and
she choked on the bitter taste of bile.

She went purposefully limp in his arms. Boris was startled at first. "Oh, no!" he said. "None of your tricks!"

He picked her up bodily and knocked her head against the side of the wagon. Light and darkness exploded in her head. Bedelia's brain was numbed and her reactions were slow. She grasped at his lapels to keep from falling.

"That's better," Boris said. "And don't be thinking they'll miss you for the grand finale. I already told them you were out of it."

She was sick with fear and loathing. She still didn't know if he meant to beat her or rape her, but one thought burned bright in her frenzied mind: She'd roast in hell before she let him do either. Goddamned filthy swine!

Bedelia watched for her chance. As he lifted his arms to strip off his jacket, she leapt forward, butting her head into his midsection with all her strength. He fell backward and his boot heel caught in a coil of rope. His head cracked against something and Boris grunted in pain. As she dashed past his hand jerked out to catch her ankle and she crashed down beside him. Rolling away, she scrambled to her feet, expecting him to follow. But Boris lay unmoving, his tanned skin changing rapidly to a horrible gray.

Bedelia knelt beside him cautiously, but it was no trick. Boris was dead to the world. Relief came first, followed by fury. That miserable rat had ruined everything. She'd meant to stay with the Orloff Circus at least through summer. They were scheduled to head for Denver then. But when Boris came to, there'd be hell to pay. It looked like she'd have to make it to Denver under her own steam.

She went back to the wagon she shared with Biddy, the bearded lady, and Flo, the snake charmer. It smelled of greasepaint and jasmine perfume and the disgusting brown cigarillos that Biddy chain-smoked every evening. As she closed the door something slithered across the table into a space behind the cupboard. Bedelia glanced at the cages below the bunks. One of the cages was empty. Goddammit, Flo's baby python was loose again. Sneaking, slithering thing. Well, at least it kept the wagon free of mice and rats, she thought.

With a sharp glance to make sure it wasn't coming out again, Bedelia yanked her battered valise from beneath the narrow bunk and began jamming things into it. Her own possessions were few and she augmented them with Flo's purple silk robe—a gift from a recent admirer—and some glass beads that belonged to Biddy. She'd never liked either of them very much, anyway.

It was mutual. Homely women had a way of standing together against one who was young and pretty. Bedelia had known that from her first day at school. Experience had reinforced it. Not that pretty had gotten her anything but grief so far.

Quickly stripping off her costume, she folded the outfit and tights and arranged them neatly in the valise, then donned a plain brown dress whose folds hid the fact that it was a divided skirt, and a pair of serviceable but scuffed boots. She grinned at her image in the spotted mirror on the wall. She looked like a country schoolteacher in this, all right. Her own mother wouldn't recognize her. The smile faded abruptly. Her mother had left her on the doorstep of the foundling hospital when she was six years old. Some mothering instincts.

As Bedelia was closing the lid she heard loud voices coming toward the wagon from the direction of the animal cages. Good God Awmighty, Boris was coming after her already! She'd been sure that he'd be out for an hour or more, the way that block had smacked into his head.

She pulled back the flour-bag curtain and glanced out the window nervously. Biddy was running across the uneven ground on her short, stumpy legs with one of the strong men behind her.

"Oh, my Gawd! He's dead," Biddy cried out in her deep, masculine voice. "Boris is dead!"

The strong man—Bedelia saw it was Andy—caught up with Biddy and clapped his hand over her mouth, simultaneously lifting the bearded woman off her feet. Con, Andy's brother, came hurrying up to them. "Shit! Biddy's right. He's broke his bloody neck, but we don't want the police to find out and send us packing."

With Biddy still kicking and thrashing, they carried her back the way she'd come. Bedelia was stunned. Boris was really dead. Jesus. She blotted her damp forehead on the cotton curtain, suddenly aware that she was sweating and her hands were trembling. She plumped down on Flo's bunk and put her head between her knees until the nausea and dizziness passed.

Andy and his brother were partners in the circus. They'd know enough to keep things quiet until after the show. But it was only a matter of time till one of the roustabouts reported seeing her arguing with him. What was she going to do now?

After several moments she felt her panic easing. Boris was dead and there wasn't much she could do about it. She'd never killed anyone before. God, he'd looked awful. She hadn't really meant to hit the bastard so hard. But given the chance to live the moment over, she'd have done the same. No man—*no man*—would ever touch her like that. Not again.

Andy would try to hush things up before the police got wind of it. Circus people were always at the mercy of the local law officers, who would use any excuse to get rid of them. Chances were that Boris's body would be hidden until nightfall, then taken out and left in a ravine. Meanwhile, they'd be asking questions. She had to get away, fast!

Her best bet was to disappear while the show was still in progress. And before anyone came looking for her. Bedelia opened Flo's box of greasepaint and found what she wanted. Dipping a finger in the jar of silver, she rubbed a small amount between her palms and streaked it over her hair at the temples and forehead. A few dabs of brown greasepaint beneath her eyes and in long grooves from nostril to chin, and her face had aged as well. She grinned at her reflection. Her younger years, spent with Colonel Faxon's acting troupe, came in handy at times. Very handy.

She took out a wide-brimmed straw hat that bent in at the sides to hide her face. Bedelia tore the blue ribbon from around the crown and stuffed it into her pocket, then jammed the bonnet down over her hair. Taking a shapeless shawl from a peg, she wrapped it about her upper torso. Her shoulders sagged and her back curved to fit her adopted role, and she slipped out of the caravan. No one would recognize her.

The music told her that the tumblers were already in the ring and the elephants were just entering. No one paid any attention to the small hunched woman making her way through the crowd, occasionally stumbling and apologizing in a soft, trembly voice. Not Edward and Jerome, who had ogled the pretty bareback rider so shamelessly. And a half hour later, when Edward missed his wallet and monogrammed stickpin and Helena found her reticule slit and its contents missing, neither would remember the nondescript woman with graying hair, in a faded brown dress and shawl.

Jake was the only one Bedelia had to worry about now. She knew his type. They were always on the lookout for the main chance. They saw too much and knew too much. Jake had told her earlier that they were two of a kind. Bedelia hadn't liked that at all. It had cut too near the bone.

She ducked behind one of the elephants and scanned the area for signs of Jake. He was supposed to be grooming the gelding for the Roman chariot in the grand finale; instead he was lounging against the feed wagon, practicing his charms on a young girl in a rose linen dress and fashionable bonnet. It seemed to be working just dandy. The girl's face was turned up to his, glowing with patent adoration. Silly little fool.

Bedelia stepped carefully around until the wagon was between them, and made her way toward the gray mare that she had been training to ride for the Wild West routine. The horse snuffled softly as Bedelia murmured in low tones and stroked the velvety muzzle. The mare was skittish and precious minutes were lost soothing her before she allowed Bedelia to put the bridle on. She was just about to throw the practice saddle over the horse's back when Jake's hand clamped down on her shoulder.

"And where might you be off to, my high-tempered beauty?"

The saddle fell heavily, bruising her foot. Bedelia rounded on him. "God damn you, Jake Adams, you've broken my toes!"

"Feeling nervy, aren't you now. You wouldn't be trying to make off with one of Boris's horses would you?"

Bedelia glared at him. Jake was the kind of fellow

who made trouble just for the sake of it. The truth—or a portion of it—was her best chance. "Boris is dead. Fell and hit his head on one of the tackle blocks. And I'm not about to cool my heels until the police come and start poking around. I'll take the horse for the money I'm owed."

A dark gleam sparked Jake's hazel eyes and his teeth flashed white. He already knew of Boris's demise. Now he knew something else, as well. "Not a lover of the police, eh? You wouldn't be running from them on another matter, would you?"

Her own smile was hard and bright. "Not me, love. It wasn't me dipped my hand into the strongbox yesterday."

Jake's face froze. "I don't know what you're talking about. You couldn't of seen anything."

Bedelia felt a keen edge of danger, but made a saucy face at him. "Happens I did. But if I'm gone when anyone comes asking questions, why, there's nothing I could say about anything either . . . is there?"

With a low curse Jake lifted the saddle for her and threw it on the mare, cinching the girth. Bedelia wrapped her valise in a brown-striped saddle blanket and tied it on behind while he adjusted the stirrups. Then he stood back, arms akimbo. "All set. Now, be on the way with you, you brass-plated vixen. I've got better fish to fry."

She let Jake give her a leg up into the saddle. "Yes, I saw that little wren in peacock's feathers you were trying to charm with your brogue and that good-looking phiz of yours. I never marked you for a fancy man, Jake. Or are you hoping her daddy will buy you off?"

"Ah, that black devil. May he rot in hell!"

Jake's features twisted into a black scowl. Suddenly

he didn't look handsome at all. "Just keep your mouth shut—and I'll do the same."

She looked down at him through narrowed eyes. "I saw you ogling that girl. She's not your kind. You'd best keep to your regular games. You're not half as smart as you think you are."

"You think you're the one with the brains and all, don't you." He was flushed with anger. "I might be deep in love with the girl, for all you know."

Bedelia's mouth twisted with scorn. "There's no love inside you except for yourself, Jack-O." She nudged the horse with her knees and it started forward.

Jake scowled after her. "I'm that glad to be seeing the back of you. You'll come to no good end!"

Bedelia glanced back over her shoulder. "You'd better hope you're wrong. Didn't you say we were two of a kind?" With a bold grin and a jaunty wave, she guided the mare through the knots of circus-goers.

Jake turned away, cursing, and searched the throng until he spied Kitty in her rose dress and fancy bonnet. There was fresh color in her cheeks and a sparkle of excitement in her eyes. From this distance she looked like one of those Dresden dolls he'd seen in a shop window, all dainty and ruffled. Every inch the pampered darling of a wealthy family.

He picked up the hayfork and moved back toward the horse enclosure, frowning. Bedelia just didn't understand.

Cassandra sat alone in the yellow sitting room, ignoring the lures of a perfect late-summer afternoon while she checked her lists. There were a hundred last-minute details to go over for the ball. The drone of bees came on the still, warm air.

A faint clicking noise sounded from the open door to the corridor, growing louder. Next came the scuff of boots across the floor, point and counterpoint. The sounds always came together when her husband was at home: Tyler and his faithful spaniel, Juno, returning from the stables. Cassandra smiled to herself. Juno would follow her master over a bed of glowing coals without whimpering. A moment later the two appeared in the doorway.

"Where is Kitty?"

"Resting. She just got back from a drive with Helena and her cousins. It's good to see her enjoying herself with other young people."

Tyler frowned. Young people. He knew very well what Cassandra was saying, but refused to rise to the bait. He prowled the floral carpet that covered the center section of the polished parquet floor and Juno snuffled along.

Cassandra went back to her lists. She knew all of Tyler's moods, this one particularly well. He made another circuit of the carpet until his pacing brought him to the fireplace. Above the mantel hung an oil portrait of his wife and her late sister. Margaret had already been five years older than Cassandra. The painting had been done at Castle Fayne one sunny June when they were twenty and fifteen respectively. Now that summer was captured forever on canvas. Margaret had already been married to Hamilton then.

It was a romantic portrait: two sisters, dressed alike in ruffled white gowns sashed with blue satin, straw hats with matching ribbons trailing from their fingers. Closer examination, as in real life, had shown that the likeness was really a trick of coloring and posture. While Cassandra's nose was delicately patrician, her sister's had been shorter and slightly retroussé. The artist had caught the sensual fullness of Margaret's mouth and something of her casual arrogance, softened by a delicate jaw. The same sure hand had captured Cassandra's quiet grace, at odds with her firm mouth and the subtle stubbornness of her chin.

They had been a striking pair, and if their dowries had matched even half their beauty, Tyler knew that their mother wouldn't have entertained his proposal for a minute; but a drowning man would clutch at any rope thrown to him. He knew that for a fact.

His glance fell to the portrait of Kitty hanging on the adjacent wall. A pity that she hadn't inherited the Fayne beauty. But with his help, she'd do well enough. If this arrangement with Grayson Howard worked out as Tyler planned, Kitty would be set for life. And everything else would be settled, too.

He frowned at his wife. "Shouldn't you be dressing for dinner?"

"Yes, I'm going up now." Cassandra set her lists aside and rose. "Don't worry, there is plenty of time."

But there wasn't, Tyler thought. Time was the one thing he lacked. He went out through the garden door with Juno padding at his heels.

At eight o'clock Cassandra was ready for their dinner engagement with Grayson. The gas lamps hissed softly inside their etched glass globes as Povey twitched one last fold of Cassandra's gown into place. The simple lines of the gold silk enhanced the beauty of the Fayne

Rubies, which she was wearing by Tyler's edict, without seeming overly ostentatious.

She waved away the leaf-shaped diamond earrings that Povey had brought out from the drawer of her dressing table. "Not those, if you please. I'd like the gold snood instead."

"Yes, my lady." The master wouldn't like it and that was all Povey needed to spur her on. She hadn't taken to him in almost fifteen years and wasn't about to start now.

She caught Cassandra's long hair at the nape, gave it a few deft twists, and captured the glowing auburn mass in the golden snood. After checking the effect, Povey had to admit that her mistress had chosen wisely.

Once her toilette was complete Cassandra went to Kitty's room to offer subtle encouragement and discreet advice. A first venture into a very adult environment could be difficult for any young girl: for someone as shy as her niece, it would be an ordeal.

She rapped softly on the door and entered. In the half-light she saw Kitty's ivory fan laid out on the dressing table along with her thin gold bracelets, and her pink gown with the embroidered forget-me-nots was waiting to be donned. Cassandra was startled. Kitty should have been dressed and ready long ago.

She hurried through the connecting door. The lamps were unlit but a shaded candle gave off a soft glow at the bedside. Kitty was curled up on her side, just beyond the circle of light. At first Cassandra thought that Kitty was sleeping, but as she drew close she saw that the girl's eyes were red-rimmed, unnaturally bright, and ringed with shadows. Cassandra's surprise changed to alarm.

"Darling, what's wrong?"

In answer Kitty made a small sound, half moan, half sob.

"Oh, my poor sweet, you're ill!" Cassandra bent to touch the pale forehead with her lips. No fever, thank God.

Kitty closed her eyes and turned her head away. "Not ill. Just . . . just my monthlies. But the cramps have never been so bad. And . . . and I've got the most dreadful headache. And Uncle Tyler will be so *dreadfully* angry with me."

Cassandra sighed. He would indeed, but there was nothing he could do about it. She leaned down and kissed Kitty's cheek. "Obviously you can't accompany us tonight. Don't worry, I'll take care of it. But where is Jenny?"

"It's her half day off. She's gone to Dr. Vertrees's lecture on mesmerism with Cook's nephew. They're walking out together."

"Really, Kitty, you shouldn't be gossiping with the servants." Cassandra smoothed the hair back from her niece's brow. "I'll bring you a headache powder and have Povey make up a hot water bottle to put on your stomach. She can tend to you until I return. We won't make it a late evening."

Kitty grasped her aunt's hand. "Don't let me ruin your plans. And I'd just as soon not have a lecture from Uncle Tyler tonight, so stay as late as you like. I'd—I'd really prefer to be left alone to sleep. You know how Povey is, always hovering about and fluffing pillows and asking if one is feeling better."

"Very well, darling. I'll have her peek in before she retires, but I'll tell her not to wait up. You'll feel better by morning."

Cassandra wafted out in a rustle of silk and a subtle

cloud of French perfume. Kitty waited until the door closed behind her, then rolled over and buried her face against the soft down pillow. The tears fell hot and fast but she muffled her sobs as best she could and cried herself out. She was horrible, despicable. The worst beast in nature, for lying to her aunt—but she had no other choice. Uncle Tyler had made that quite clear. It was his fault for trying to force her into marriage with a man she could never love. Grayson Howard frightened her.

Kitty wiped her eyes with the edge of the pillow slip. Aunt Cassandra had embroidered it for her, and that almost started another fall of tears. They prickled behind her eyelids but she fought them back. Someone was coming.

Povey entered with a vial of medicine on a tray and a towel-swathed hot water bottle under her arm. "Poor sweeting," she murmured soothingly. "It's a terrible curse a woman has to bear, but it often eases after the first child is born. Now drink this down quickly, and you'll fall into a sound sleep. When you awaken you'll be good as new."

Kitty took the vial. Her feigned headache had become quite real. Her temples throbbed and her eyes felt like pits of burning sand. She pretended to take a sip. But as soon as Povey turned to draw the draperies, she dumped the contents into the water pitcher on her night table.

"Is there anything else you require, miss?"

"If you would just put out the light before you leave, Povey. My eyes ache so."

"Of course, sweeting. Rest well now. I'll inform the other servants that you're not to be disturbed."

Kitty waited until she heard Povey descend the stairs, then slipped quietly down the corridor and into Cassandra's room. Within minutes she was back in bed, her heart beating erratically.

When Povey returned to her mistress's chambers to straighten up she saw that the diamond earrings she'd intended to put away were not atop the dressing table. Lady Cassandra must have put them away herself, earlier. She shook out the folds of a blue-green dressing gown and hung it up properly, then swept away a light dusting of face powder and set the silver hairbrush and comb neatly to one side.

The door opened and one of the upstairs maids entered to turn down the bed and see that all was ready for her mistress's return. Povey greeted her. "Madame said not to wait up, Nellie, and Miss Hamilton is not to be disturbed. I'll be going down to visit with Mrs. Llewellyn in her chambers."

"Yes, mum." Rosaleen started to drop a curtsy to this very superior lady's maid but caught herself in time. Mrs. Llewellyn had been trying to break her of the habit. As she smoothed the coverlet and plumped up the pillows, Rosaleen thought of Povey having tea with the stately housekeeper in her private apartment, and only hoped that one day she might aspire to such heights.

Kitty waited at her door until she heard their footsteps move away. She glanced at the clock. Only one more hour to go.

She didn't know how she could endure the wait.

The Golden Room at the Dillon Hotel was the finest dining in San Francisco, and the most expensive as well. Grayson surveyed it from the doorway. Amid the tinkle of crystal, the gleam of cutlery, the elegant china, a man could get the very best viands and wash them down with pale golden champagnes. For a price. The Prince of Wales and Oscar Wilde had been guests.

Jaime came from the bar to join him and shook his head wonderingly. "I never thought little Jaime McFee would be dining at such a fine place. I could buy a little farm in Ireland for the price of a good dinner here."

Grayson laughed. "Sad, but very true. Zacharias Monroe came to town with a sack of gold, and spent it all here at the Dillon in three days—on whores and on champagne dinners for his chums. And he swears to this day that it was worth every penny."

Despite its prices, the Golden Room drew diners like a magnet draws iron. Ranchers and gold miners, gamblers and grifters, and traveling sopranos and actors mingled with scions of European nobility. The women were resplendent in silks and satins and taffetas, their bared shoulders rising from low-cut gowns, their throats and ears and fingers adorned with dazzling diamonds. Here a duchess might rub shoulders with the queen of the demimondaine, and a man might sup with his wife one night, and his mistress the next.

They strolled to Grayson's reserved table, stopping now and then to answer a greeting from an acquaintance. The women followed his progress, not just because he was handsome and wealthy, but because of the air of suppressed danger that he carried with him. The men watched warily. No matter how urbane their manners, they were a tough breed; yet there was something about Grayson Howard that made them feel, singly and collectively, like fattened sheep with a sleek wolf in their midst.

Jaime followed in his wake, basking in the reflected glow. His position as Grayson's mining agent, helped along by his Irish blarney, had certainly aided his success with the ladies. He caught the eye of a pretty blonde in red satin, who was obviously bored with her elderly companion's company. Yes, the evening was starting off well.

They took their seats and Grayson found himself under intense scrutiny from a stunning brunette at the next table. Her blue gown and sapphire and diamond jewelry were impeccable and there was nothing in her appearance to disclose that she moved, not on the upper levels of society, but in the shadow world of the demimonde. But it was there in her eyes. He knew her by reputation: Arabella Collingsford. She was a young widow and the mistress of Simon Fiddler, the British financier who had settled in San Francisco some ten years earlier.

She noticed his regard and shifted her carriage, presenting her dimpled shoulders and full white bosom to best advantage. She smiled at Grayson over the rim of her champagne glass, and she lifted it infinitesimally with an elegant, gloved hand. He sent her an answering smile and a small bow. Then Cassandra Lucton entered the room and he was suddenly blind to everything else.

He had to admit that she stood out among the over-ruffled and overribboned beauties at the surrounding tables, their coiffures adorned with diamonds and pearls and dyed plumes. Her gold silk gown was cut low to show off her fabulous shoulders and the womanly curves beneath the shimmering fabric. Grayson felt a tightening in his loins.

Other men noticed Cassandra as she made her way toward his table, preceded by the obsequious maître d'. Tyler, in evening dress, followed, a dark shadow to her radiant sun. Grayson narrowed his eyes. Lucton was enjoying the sensation his wife made, gloating in the knowledge that other men wanted her and envied him.

Grayson rose and took Cassandra's hand in his, bowing low over it, then shook hands with Tyler. It was going to be a very long night.

Kitty counted out the passing minutes in a fever of anticipation. At last it was time. She gathered her things and was almost at the door when she heard a small sound from her dressing room. How could she have forgotten that Povey was going to check on her again! She scooted back, shoving her two bandboxes beneath the bed, then climbed in and pulled the covers up to her chin to hide her clothing.

The door opened inward a few inches. Kitty made her breathing slow and softly audible. Povey's voice was a mere whisper. "Ah, the dear little thing is asleep."

The door closed and Kitty almost dissolved in tears again. She was betraying everyone who had loved and cared for her. If only Uncle Tyler hadn't forced this cruel decision upon her! But didn't the Bible say that a man and woman should leave their parents and cleave to one another? Really, this was the same. She wiped a traitorous tear that leaked from the corner of one eye. Wasn't it?

The next ten minutes were an agony. She daren't slip out yet until she was sure that Povey was in her own room—but what if Jake didn't wait for her? He'd told her how risky it would be if anyone noticed him. She couldn't bear it if anything happened to Jake.

Steeling herself, Kitty threw off the covers once more, then put the cushions from the window seat beneath the comforter, just in case. A last, tear-blurred look around the room, and she was gone.

She slipped down the stairs without being seen. Morton would be dozing over one of the hot toddies he drank nightly for his rheumatism. Then it was easy to cut through the Chinese breakfast room and out into the rose garden. It was very dark. Kitty had never been out this late at night, alone. The symphony of crickets seemed surprisingly loud. There wasn't even a moon to light the way, but the stars bloomed across the sky like a garden of diamonds, illuminating a fairy world, all silver and black.

Avoiding the stables, she cut through the ornamental maze and across the night-dewed lawn, keeping to the deeper shadows. She jumped and squeaked with alarm when a rabbit ran across her path, startling her. Another bounded past, equally surprised to find a human interloper.

Kitty had always found the night mysterious, romantic, serene—from the safety of her window. The reality was quite different. A shiver ran through her. There were strange rustlings here and there, the darting movements of hunter and the hunted. Of dark things ready to pounce and rend and feed. She hurried on.

The ground soon changed, turning to open meadowland. Kitty had spent happy hours here, chasing blue and orange butterflies and picking bouquets of wildflowers. It seemed unfamiliar by night. Ahead, silhouetted by the starlit sky, a long stand of trees whispered to one another in the light breeze. Beyond them was a service road leading back to the barns and storage buildings, and the small valley that sheltered the home farm and a few head of grazing cattle. It was there that Jake was waiting for her.

Jake and their new life together.

Kitty was breathless from agitation and effort but she hurried on, catching her cloak on the brambles and stumbling over protruding roots. She slid the cords of the bandboxes over her wrists to free her hands and parted the tall grass. A bird screeched at her feet, flapping suddenly upward from its hidden ground nest, to lure her away. Kitty had to stop to still the wild beating of her heart. She was trembling with reaction.

As she pulled in a deep, shuddering breath a tall shadow peeled away from one of the tree trunks. Her heart seemed to fly up in her throat, blocking off her air. The shape came forward and she recognized Jake. She had made it! She was safe.

"Oh, Jake!" Her eyes gleamed with emotion more brilliant than the reflected starshine. "Oh, Jake!"

Kitty ran toward him, hands outstretched, with the bandboxes banging against her knees. He caught her in his arms and crushed her against him. All worries and concerns fled as she felt his mouth come down on hers.

His kiss was hard, almost brutal. Not at all like the tender kiss he'd given her at the circus when no one was looking. Kitty tried not to be afraid. This was the moment she had waited and prayed for: the start of a new and perfect life.

In the meadow a hapless field mouse peeked timidly out of its burrow, then scurried between the tall stalks of grass. Intent on its own goal, it didn't see the owl swoop silently down until the predator's shadow fell over it.

And then it was too late.

5

Cassandra toyed with her chocolate trifle. The dinner with Grayson Howard was not going well— at least from her point of view. Although he had refrained completely, she had drunk just a little too much champagne herself. It hadn't helped one whit. She was just as aware of him as ever. Of his strength, his masculinity—and his disapproval.

She wished Mr. McFee could have stayed through dessert and was sorry that he'd had to leave early— unlike Grayson, she hadn't seen him depart with the pretty blonde in red.

Tyler leaned close while their host was engaged with the wine steward. "See that man at the corner table with the white goatee and old-fashioned coat? That's Judge Julius Milvern, down from Sacramento. The one across from him is Seamus Rooney. He'll be elected to the senate, mark my words."

He had also spied Sylvanus George, who reported on society doings for the *Chronicle,* avidly scribbling a description of the Fayne Rubies on his shirtcuffs. They'd be in the next edition. Tyler all but rubbed his hands in glee.

Cassandra knew that Grayson had overheard, and blushed. She turned her head slightly and became aware of a man staring at her. He lifted his glass and toasted her with an exquisite smile. Only his eyes mocked, and only for her to see.

Tyler, witnessing from an angle, was pleased. He leaned close to Cassandra's ear. "A rare compliment, my dear, from such a noted connoisseur of beauty."

She leaned closer. "Who is that gentleman with Arabella Collingsford?"

"Simon Fiddler. He'll be at our ball, as well."

Cassandra was surprised. She had never met the famous financier, but she had heard of him. He was the younger son of an English peer, who had come to the untamed American West and shrewdly parlayed his portion into a fortune in supply trains, cattle, and real estate. Now he wielded immense power, and had recently enlarged his operations to San Francisco. According to rumor, Mr. Fiddler visited the boudoirs of grand and titled ladies with more frequency than did their husbands.

He looked like neither a hardheaded man of business nor a philanderer. He looked, she thought, like a romantic poet, with his softly waving blond hair worn long, and his beautifully shaped white hands ornamented with a single emerald. His mouth was firm and masculine, yet softly bowed, and thick lashes beneath arching brows. Despite his personal beauty she felt faintly repelled by him.

Tyler hooked his thumbs in his waistcoat and beamed. "He'll come over to our table, I'm sure."

Cassandra was certain that Mr. Fiddler had seen her husband, but that he chose to ignore him. She looked down at her gloved hands, toying with the stem of her champagne glass. She was embarrassed for her husband, and strangely protective. Impulsively she rested her fingers on Tyler's sleeve. The touch surprised him, while it amused the man who had caused it to happen.

Grayson had watched the silent exchange, while appearing not to. His eyes lingered on Cassandra. Somehow, he'd picked up the impression that the Luctons' marriage was not one of intimate sharing. Perhaps he'd judged wrongly. Still waters ran deep. He was fleetingly envious, not of what they had but of what he himself had lost. Then he remembered why he had lost it, and his brief compunction vanished.

He tried to keep the memory at bay, but the restaurant hazed and vanished before his eyes. He was suddenly far away from the Dillon Hotel, surrounded by an awful stillness, riding once more through the bloody carnage at Bitter Creek.

A waiter clattered a tray. The sound yanked Grayson back to the present with a jolt. The contrast filled him with a sick and icy rage. There were no bodies here, sprawled lifeless on sandy soil, hacked and defiled. The bodies here were alive and well fed, dressed in silks and satins and fine linen. The only reminders of the bloody memories were the dark rubies that ringed Cassandra Lucton's slim white throat. He looked away.

Cassandra had been watching him and saw the sudden change in Grayson's expression. Set and stern, with an underlying pallor and the skin pulled tight over his sculpted bones, until he looked almost inhuman. She shivered and reached for her wineglass. Their eyes met, silvery gray and sea-green. Cassandra was unable to look away. Then the waiter came between them as he lifted Tyler's dessert plate and the spell was broken. She looked into the golden bubbles rising in her glass, too disturbed to chance it again. In that brief moment she had been more aware of him than she had ever been of any man. And more aware of herself as a woman.

It was odd. She knew that Grayson didn't like her. The waves of antagonism were palpable. She felt suddenly cold and sipped her champagne. It warmed her slowly but the chill remained, centering about her heart. She felt, even more strongly, that she must do everything in her power to prevent a marriage between Grayson and Kitty. He would destroy her. Cassandra's fingers tightened on the stem of the glass. There was a tiny snap as the thin crystal stem fractured between her gloved fingers. The cut-crystal bowl fell away and shattered against the rim of her plate. The wine ran out between the glittering splinters and soaked into the linen tablecloth. It was Grayson who first noticed the blood. "You've cut yourself, Mrs. Lucton. It should be attended to at once."

Cassandra was amazed to see the bright crimson staining the palm of her glove. She didn't feel anything. Pulling the glove off gingerly, she discovered a small gash in the fleshy part of her hand. "A scratch," she said quickly. "Nothing to cause concern."

Grayson had already taken out his linen handkerchief. He took her hand in his, surprised to feel the fine tremors as it rested in his grasp. He looked at her and once again their eyes met and held. He looked back at the cut and swiftly bound his handkerchief around it.

His ministrations were strong, sure, and surprisingly

gentle; but his touch was agony for Cassandra. She couldn't think or speak. It was as if they were alone, sharing a moment of intimacy. She was afraid of betraying herself by look or gesture, and sat still as a stone. "Thank you," she said in a cool voice that covered her inward agitation far too well.

A shadow fell across their table and they looked up in unison. Simon Fiddler stood beside them, smiling. He was a connoisseur of beautiful women. He let his gaze pause a moment too long on Cassandra, and was gratified by the flush that tinted her skin. He imagined her naked, that wonderful thick hair tumbling down in flaming tendrils against her ivory skin. His smile widened. Tyler Lucton had indicated that he was eager for an alliance with the Fiddler Import Company. Simon suspected that he was desperate for it—but was he desperate enough to allow his wife to be seduced?

Because, Simon decided, that would be the unspoken condition. A delicious prospect.

The men rose and bowed over the introductions. Fiddler took Cassandra's hand. "I am charmed, madame. I shall look forward to your ball eagerly, in hopes that you might spare me a waltz . . . or two?"

Cassandra sensed danger. She gave him a bright social smile. "Then you must come in time to sign my dance card, Mr. Fiddler."

Her response pleased him. He always enjoyed a challenge.

Tyler introduced Grayson as a cattleman and avid cardplayer, and Simon responded by inviting Grayson to attend a gaming house with him after dinner.

Grayson thanked him, but declined. "I've a previous engagement."

Simon was not to be rebuffed. A graceful bow and

negligent wave of the hand. "Breakfast then, if you're free. At my new hotel. And I'm giving a little dinner party tomorrow evening to show my new Oriental collection. A bachelor affair." He gave them the particulars.

Tyler was caught between gratification at being asked and fear that Grayson would decline. An invitation to Simon Fiddler's dinner parties was a sign to one and all that a man had arrived.

Grayson's eyes were opaque as agate. "I've heard of your lavish hospitality, Mr. Fiddler. I'd be pleased to attend as your guest."

Tyler was delighted. "Mr. Howard is interested in expanding his investments. Perhaps you can give him some advice on succeeding in San Francisco."

"But of course." Simon smiled coolly. "No need to wait until tomorrow. My best advice, Mr. Howard, would be to follow Mr. Lucton's example. Make your fortune in trade, and then wed a beautiful aristocrat."

Cassandra was stunned by the insult. Her glance flickered across to check Grayson's reaction. His face was smooth and blank, with no expression at all. Tyler's hadn't changed. Again she felt that surge of protection. Was he too eager and blind to see that Simon was ridiculing him? Or was he just so in awe of the man's position and power that he would let such rudeness pass?

Simon took her hand and raised it to his lips, but instead of brushing the air above it, he pressed them against the back of her hand. Even through her glove, his breath was hot on her skin. An unpleasant sensation prickled along her spine. Looking into those angelically blue eyes, Cassandra saw through them to an infinite black void. If Satan walked the earth, she thought suddenly, he would not come with horns and hooves and a forked tail. He would come as Simon Fiddler, full of grace and charm.

While she struggled to maintain her poise, his fingertips traced suggestive circles in her palm. A tremor of revulsion rippled through Cassandra. Simon smiled and released her hand. He was delighted with her response. Arabella was wanton by nature, a willing whore. This woman would be different. He would use her buried passions to enslave her against her will.

Another smile, a murmured good-bye and he was gone. Cassandra simmered with rage.

Grayson watched her face as she struggled for control. Her anger barely showed. He only knew it was there because he was learning to read her eyes. Initially he'd thought her cold and aloof. Then he'd seen her with Kitty and learned differently. Something was very wrong in the Lucton household. His keen senses picked up anger, confusion, and fear. He wondered why.

There was one thing Grayson could tell for certain: Beneath Cassandra's calm there was boiling emotion. If it wasn't released, one day it was going to blow sky-high and scald everyone in range.

Suddenly the manager hastened over. With a series of jerky bows and a hushed whisper, he handed Cassandra a sealed note. It was marked "Urgent." She recognized Povey's spiky handwriting at once. "Excuse me," she said, agitatedly breaking the seal.

As she scanned the lines her face went as pale as the snowy damask tablecloth. She was rigid and shaking like a willow in a high wind. For a moment Grayson thought she was about to pass out. She swayed and he caught her about the shoulders to steady her.

"It's Kitty," she gasped hoarsely. "She's . . . she's ill. Forgive us. We must leave at once!"

Grayson had already signaled for their hats and canes and for Cassandra's cloak. Tyler jumped up and pushed back his chair. "Have they sent for Dr. Jamieson?"

"No."

"Then we'll stop and notify him ourselves. It's on the way."

Her eyes were wide with distress, greener than the sea. She fumbled for the cloak's button with shaking fingers. "No. Povey says it isn't necessary."

"Damn it, what does the woman know? She's just a servant."

"I would trust Povey with my life," she said flatly. *And with Kitty's.*

They left the restaurant hurriedly and Grayson walked with them to their waiting carriage. The night was warm and a fat yellow moon grinned down from the cloudless sky. "I hope your niece is not seriously ill."

Tyler grunted. "Just a minor indisposition. You know how women get about such things."

As the carriage wheels grated on the cobbles, Cassandra leaned back, closed her eyes, and prayed.

Grayson waited until their carriage was out of sight, but instead of calling for his own, he vanished between the buildings and made his way on foot to another section of town. A closed carriage waited at the end of a street of narrow houses crowded shoulder to shoulder. He climbed in and settled back, going over the evening's events in his mind. Tyler Lucton was exactly the kind of man he'd imagined him to be. Shrewd, ruthless, amoral.

A profitable end would justify any means. But Cassandra? He still couldn't put her in a cubbyhole.

He'd been wrong about her before. Initially he'd thought she opposed him as a suitor for Kitty because of his Cheyenne blood. He'd faced prejudice before. It was only after spending time with them that he realized she was protecting her niece from Tyler's ambitions as fiercely as a lioness protecting her cub. Her instincts were valid. He'd be the very devil of a husband for a girl like Kitty.

But then, he'd be a bad husband for any woman.

He had nothing left to give. The caring part of him had died long ago. He thought of the years of planning and effort it had taken to prepare his vengeance. For once it gave him no comfort. And it didn't banish the image of Cassandra Lucton that haunted him. What was she afraid of? Her husband? Himself? And why?

The carriage stopped and he got out, losing himself like a shadow among the seemingly deserted streets of Chinatown. Grayson knew he was not alone and that his passage was observed. He'd had the same feeling out on the prairie and among the folded mountains of Colorado and New Mexico Territory and it had never been wrong; but discerning whether the watcher was friend, foe, or neutral observer was beyond his powers.

He found the joss shop and slipped in the unlocked door. It was eerie inside with nothing but a hint of brass and the ghostly shapes of the porcelain statues. The bead curtains stirred with dull clickings and he froze in place, but it was only the movement of the door that had caused it. The rooms beyond were cramped, their blackness impenetrable. He found the handle and opened the door. The room smelled of cooking oil and shrimp and kerosene. He looked into the gloom. "Light the lamp. This place is like a cave."

A scratch, the sharp odor of sulfur, and a match flared, illuminating Ling Cheung's smooth dark head. The wick caught and the burning kerosene lamp sent the shadows leaping back. They were in a kitchen of sorts, with open shelves for storage and two narrow cupboards. The remains of a mostly uneaten meal sat congealing on the table.

Ling Cheung sat before it. He had changed his western clothes for a robe of dark embroidered silk and the lamplight cast deep shadows in the hollows of his face. Grayson pulled out a chair and sat opposite his friend. The other man withdrew an envelope from inside his wide sleeve and placed it on the scrubbed wooden table.

"It is all here. Everything that you asked for and more."

He spread out the sheaf of papers and Grayson flicked through them. More than he'd dared to dream. More than enough to topple Tyler Lucton's far-flung empire and ruin him completely. He waited for the triumph he'd expected. He was surprised to feel nothing but a cold, emptiness. Ten years was a long time to wait.

"I am forever in your debt, Ling Cheung. If ever you need me, you have only to ask."

His companion fixed him with a somber look. "I had not expected to ever call you on your promise, old friend, but now I find that I must do so."

"Name it. It's yours."

"It is a matter of great discretion. I have spoken with my grandfather and he agrees that you are the man to help us." Ling Cheung folded his hands. "Several young women have disappeared of late."

Grayson heard the pain in his friend's voice. He pitied

any girl alone in San Francisco—for all its surface sheen, it was a rough place. And a Chinese village maid far from home and not knowing the country, the language, or the customs would be in a far worse position.

"Young women disappear every day in San Francisco. A seamstress from Philadelphia vanished on her way home from a dry goods store, and I just heard that a scullery maid disappeared from Market Street yesterday."

"Yes. A lone female here and there. But you see, in this case there were ten of them."

Grayson leaned forward as Ling Cheung went on. "Madame Wu, the woman who runs the joss shop, is a respected matchmaker, and has arranged many successful marriages. When a match is agreed upon she is paid a fee, and when the girl arrives she receives the rest of what is owed to her. To insure that this is done, Madame Wu has also taken on the task of collecting their passage money in advance from the men, and arranging for the brides to be brought here from China.

"Until this past month all has gone smoothly." Ling Cheung met Grayson's eyes. "Ten young women of good family—the most beautiful from the villages surrounding my home—set out from China aboard the *Java Prince*. The crossing was smooth and the ship docked three days early in San Francisco. Madame Wu did not expect them so soon, but a message was sent to her at the joss shop. Being unable to go herself, Madame Wu sent her most trusted servant with a wagon to fetch the young women. When he arrived there was no sign of them at the wharf."

"Are you sure that they were really aboard the *Java Prince*?"

"Yes. The servant made inquiries of the harbor master and some of the dockworkers. The young women had indeed been aboard. They had disembarked earlier and gone off with a white man and a woman who claimed they had been sent by Madame Wu." He spread his hands helplessly. "They were never seen again."

Grayson frowned. "And now the men who paid for the brides are angry."

"Yes. They say that Madame Wu has tricked them out of their money and sold the brides to the houses of joy instead. If she does not produce the brides—or the money—she will suffer the consequences."

"If they've disappeared into one of the brothels in Chinatown, you're in a better position than I to learn of their whereabouts. My face makes me a stranger there."

"That is true." Ling Cheung lowered his eyes. "But there is not a whisper abroad. The brides are nowhere to be found."

Grayson's eyes narrowed. There was more to this than what it appeared to be on the surface. He wondered just what dainty items Simon Fiddler had in his "Oriental collection." He kept the thought to himself. "I could easily pay off this debt of Madame Wu's, if that is what you wish. But I don't think that's what you're asking of me."

"No. I am asking you to help me find the girls." Ling Cheung's face set in lines of misery. "They came here in good faith to marry honorable men. One of them is my affianced wife."

Grayson swore. It was a bad situation. The missing girls were—or had been—virgins. Virtuous women were highly regarded. Fallen women would not be considered marriageable to men of Ling Cheung's class.

Grayson was careful to preserve his friend's dignity. "These prospective bridegrooms. What do they want, the girls or their money returned?"

Ling Cheung sighed heavily. "That depends. If the girls are soiled the men will of course demand their money back from Madame Wu."

A heavy weight settled over Grayson. He was going to have to do some investigating. And he had a pretty good idea of where to look. What to do with the women afterward was another matter. "We'll work out something to see them safely settled one way or another. I'll start things rolling tonight. I have an idea—no, I don't want to say anything just yet. But if all goes well you'll hear from me within the next day or two. Perhaps sooner."

Grayson left the joss shop by another route and eventually made his way back to the livery stables where his own carriage awaited him.

Half an hour later he was back in his suite at the hotel, conferring with Jaime McFee. There was no evidence of Grayson's rampage in the rooms. The mirrors and smashed china had been replaced and new draperies hung at the windows. They were undrawn, and beyond the panes a fog was drifting up from the bay, muffling the moonlit world in layers of gauze. Grayson closed them. He'd had his fill of San Francisco. Not that it wasn't beautiful in its own way, but he was weary of fog and rain and busy streets filled with traffic.

His soul hungered for wide, empty horizons bounded on one side by the thrust of mountain peaks. For clean, fresh air without the stink of burning coal and gas lamps. He longed for a sharp wind whipping jumbled clouds across a piercing blue sky. There would be snow in those clouds, enough to bury the plains in an ermine blanket that blotted out the scars the white men had made upon it, and to hide the stains that still darkened the ground at Bitter Creek.

But there was work to be done here yet, and McFee was waiting. Grayson sprawled in the chair opposite his right-hand man. "Any more responses to the broadsides we sent out on Bronco's sister?"

"Just the one girl I told you about earlier. She was supposed to meet you tonight, but never showed."

Grayson's face hardened. "Another liar, no doubt. That makes five. You probably frightened her when you said there would be an investigation and imprisonment for impostors."

Jaime took one of Grayson's cigars from the humidor and cut the end. "Did you really expect to hear anything?"

"After all this time, Annette could be anywhere."

"She could be dead."

"I agree. Bronco is sure she's alive. I'm not nearly as hopeful. I've hired a fellow to do some digging through the records, in case a burial was registered. Every female between the ages of thirteen and twenty. And there are others making inquiries."

"You've been very busy in the last few weeks," Jaime said, striking a match.

"Yes, and I'll be busier tomorrow. I'm meeting with Simon Fiddler tomorrow morning, joining his dinner party in the evening and . . ." Grayson pulled a small square of paper from his pocket and opened it flat. An address and time were written in a delicate hand. "It seems I have an assignation at noon with his chief mistress." Not that he meant to keep it.

"Arabella Collingsford? You have been busy. But

watch your back, amigo. Mr. Fiddler has more eyes than a potato and more ears than a cornfield."

Grayson laughed. "Still the farmer at heart? Don't worry, I can take care of myself."

He rolled up the paper and held it over the wick of the lamp until it charred and burst into flame. Then he placed it on an empty plate and watched it burn.

He was silent for a few minutes. Then he made a swift decision. "You've got my power of attorney, Jaime. I want papers drawn up, placing my interests in the Morning Star Mine as collateral for Tyler Lucton's loans at the California Investment Bank."

Jaime was stunned. "What the hell . . . ? You can't be serious?"

"I have never been more so."

"Jesus Christ, you're mad as a hatter!" Jamie was almost sputtering he was so upset. "If he goes under, you'll lose everything!"

Grayson's eyes were suddenly dark as slate. "It's mine to lose. By the way, I'll require some unusual materials tonight, but I'm sure you can come up with them."

He ticked off the items on his list. They made no sense to his companion, and McFee eyed him with concern. "Damn it, I don't like this one bit. I wish you'd tell me what you're up to."

A cynical smile touched Grayson's mouth. "Why, no good, of course!"

His companion frowned and shook the ash from his cigar. "Laugh if you like, amigo. But if you keep this up, someone will shoot you and put an end to your misery."

Grayson looked away into the shadows of the room. "One can always hope."

* * *

By the time the Lucton carriage rolled up the long drive, Cassandra was in a state of high nervous tension. Dear God, what could be wrong to put Povey in such a panic?

She transferred some of her anger to Grayson. If he hadn't invited them to be his guests at the Dillon, she would have been home with Kitty. She opened the door without waiting for the groom and jumped down before Tyler could stop her.

Morton, still dressed in the long apron he used when polishing the silver, had already opened the door. His face showed only mild concern, quenching her alarm. Perhaps Tyler was right and Povey had overreacted to a minor indisposition. She did worry over Kitty so.

She went quickly up the staircase and found her maid hovering on the second landing.

When she spied her mistress her homely face crumpled like an old sock. "Oh, my lady! Thank God you are here at last. Miss Catherine has been asking for you."

The cold hand of fear squeezed Cassandra's heart. "Is she much worse?"

Povey, for once unconscious of the deference she felt due her mistress, didn't take the time to answer. She turned and went up the stairs quickly. Cassandra lifted her silk skirts and ran up behind her in a blind panic.

Tyler watched her dash up the staircase. He had no place interfering in problems peculiar to women's bodies. Really, Cassandra was making too much of it. If they cosseted Kitty's every little ache, she would grow up to be an invalid, like his great-aunt Agnes.

After letting Morton take his hat, cloak, and cane, he retired to a glass of brandy in his study, where the butler had thoughtfully had the fire lit. Lifting the crystal snifter, he watched the liquid within seem to turn to flame. He took a sip and rolled it around on his tongue. Things were starting to look up. First Grayson Howard, and now this flattering attention from Simon Fiddler. Tyler took another swallow and let the quiet seep into his soul.

He was glad to have a private moment to himself. With Kitty under the weather tonight and all the ongoing fuss for the coming ball, this was likely to be his last peaceful moment.

Povey opened the door to Kitty's room and Cassandra went in. Her maid locked it behind them. Kitty's favorite music box lay smashed on the floor beside a broken scent bottle. Her driving cloak was crumpled on the floor beside her new bonnet. The bed was empty, the covers thrown back, and an empty wooden jewelry box lay upturned on the sheets. Cassandra's heart thudded against her rib cage.

"Where is Kitty? What has happened?"

"In here, my lady." Povey began to weep as she led Cassandra toward the adjoining dressing room. "I thought she was sleeping! I didn't want to wake her . . . and when I got up to use the water closet I—I h-heard the sound of breaking glass . . ."

The gas lamps were lit in the dressing room, casting their orange glow on an eerie scene. The carpet was splotched with powder and shards of crystal. Every item on the vanity was knocked over and the oval mirror above it showed a spider's web of splintered glass. The whimper of a small animal stabbed Cassandra to the heart and she turned toward it, sick with fear. Kitty lay curled up on the floor in one corner of the little room, her back to the wall. She was swathed in a thick comforter with only the top of her head peeking out, rocking and mewling with hopeless, wrenching sobs.

Cassandra flew across the room and knelt beside her. Kitty's hair was disheveled and matted with burrs and bits of leaf mold. One of her eyes was bruised and swollen almost shut and her lower lip was split and puffed. There was a red abrasion at her temple, and when Cassandra pulled the blanket away she screamed.

Cassandra knelt beside her. "Dear God in Heaven, what has happened here!" But somehow she already knew.

Kitty shrank back, but not before Cassandra saw the scratches that raked across the girl's exposed shoulder and breast. A rush of murderous rage shook Cassandra with its power and primitive force. She'd never suspected herself of harboring such savage emotion; but if the man who'd done this were in still in the room, she would have tried to rip him to pieces with her bare hands.

But righteous wrath wouldn't help Kitty. She gathered her niece into her arms. "Oh, my darling. Hush. Hush, now, my sweet darling."

Cassandra tried to think of what to do next, but her own thoughts were as shattered as the mirror. She had sworn on Margaret's deathbed to guard and guide her infant daughter—and she had failed terribly.

She smoothed Kitty's hair, feeling the thick burrs scrape her palm. How could an intruder have gotten in unheard? She looked up at Povey. "Have the police been notified?"

"No, my lady—"

"Then they must be sent for at once!"

"But, my lady, surely . . . it would ruin Miss Catherine!"

Cassandra's head was swimming and she was grateful for Povey's logic. There was more than Kitty's reputation at stake. If the assault became common knowledge, her fragile spirits would be hopelessly crushed. If they weren't already. She shook off her grief. "You are right, of course, Povey. We will have to alert everyone that there's been an intruder in the house. Tyler will organize a search—"

"No! I mean, no, my lady—you see—it's not like you think."

Povey didn't know how to go on. Her angular face grew stark. "Miss Catherine . . ." Her voice trailed off but she recovered herself. "Miss Catherine wasn't in the house at the time. She was out beyond the kitchen gardens—in the grove."

Cassandra's head jerked up. "That's preposterous. What would she possibly be doing out there in the middle of the night?"

Povey swallowed. There was no way to sugarcoat the bitter truth. Kitty hiccuped on a sob and answered, driving the sword deeper into Cassandra's heart. "I w-went there to m-meet him. To m-meet Jake . . ."

A shudder ran through her body and her face was a mask of misery. She dissolved in tears once more, beating her fists against her knees. "Oh, Aunt Cassandra! He said he loved me," she sobbed. *"H-he said h-he l-loved me!"*

6

Bedelia was not happy. Her escort had promised her a night of wining and dining. Champagne and chateaubriand. Instead she had gotten ale and stringy beef in a dingy waterfront saloon that catered to a rough and scruffy crowd. The piano player was lousy, too. Why, she could play better with her eyes closed.

There was one compensation: Her companion, a young sprig named Willy Guest, was already three parts drunk. Any plans he might have had for hiring one of the upstairs rooms for the night, would do him no good. Another mug and he'd be under the table with the soiled sawdust and moldering scraps of food. Willy leaned close to her ear, blasting her with alcoholic fumes.

"Wanna 'nother glash of beer, B'delia m'love?"

"Naw." She watched the dark-eyed fellow at the next table pour out a glass of pale yellow wine. "Get me a bottle of that horse piss he's drinking. You promised me a good time, remember?"

She didn't really want the wine. She wanted to attract the other man's attention. His hair was as brown as his eyes and he wore a gold and onyx ring on his index finger. He was a good-looking fellow and free with his money. When he'd bought drinks for two of the saloon girls, she'd seen the bundle of green he'd flashed in his bulging wallet. Now *there* was a fellow who knew how to treat a lady! And he was at his table all alone for the moment.

Bedelia felt the same thrill she experienced just before riding into the circus tent to begin her act. Like the barker used to cry out, there were thrills, chills, and maybe a little danger involved. Especially if she could manage to lift his wallet.

If she timed it right, she could leave Willy to snore it off and try her luck with the well-heeled gent. He looked up and caught her eye. Bedelia sent him a smile that could have melted candles. He raised his glass to her in a salute, nodded, and drank the contents. Yes, she decided, poor Willie Guest would sleep alone tonight. His eyes were getting glassier by the minute and he was sprawled back in his chair. She wondered if she dared purloin his wallet yet. One way or the other, there was bound to be enough money to get her to Denver in style. If not, she would have to fall back on her alternate scheme—although that one seemed like a long shot.

She waited until the man at the next table was talking to the slattern taking orders. Her hand snaked into Willy's pocket and her nimble fingers did the rest. As she removed the bills and counted them beneath the table her eyes narrowed. The bastard had sixty-five dollars on him, and he'd been feeding her hog swill! Cheap son of a bitch. Well, let this be a lesson to him about treating a girl right. Bedelia tucked his bankroll in her bodice, while pretending to adjust her gown, and waited for Willy to pass out.

Unknown to her, the man at the next table had seen it all. It paid to sit facing the corner mirrors behind the bar. She wasn't exactly what he'd been paid to find, but she was a real looker. And she'd been around long enough to learn a few tricks. Besides, he was horny as hell. Joe Scudder grinned and wiped the beer foam from his mustache. He needed sixteen girls to fill Mr. Fiddler's order, and he'd only found fifteen so far.

His smile widened to include Bedelia. A *prime* looker. And it wasn't as if he was doing anything against Mr. Fiddler. After all, he was more or less a merchant, and a merchant always made sure his wares were good before putting them on the table. He watched Willie Guest slide down in his chair, then rose and approached the wide-eyed little lady. Little tart, was more like it, he thought. It was all he could do to keep from licking his lips. He'd have a good time and kill two birds with the same stone.

Yessir, he'd have his cake, and eat it, too.

Bedelia returned his smile archly. She'd never met a man she couldn't interest. Not unless he had both feet in the grave. She shifted her skirts to expose a good deal of shapely ankle. Give him a little something to think about.

It didn't take long. The minute Willie sank into an alcoholic stupor he was at her side. "The name's Joe Scudder," he said with a bow. "I run a lumber camp outside Sacramento. Ordinarily I wouldn't intrude on a lady such as yourself. But with your escort out of commission . . . well . . . this isn't the kind of place a pretty lady like you should be frequenting, you know."

She favored him with a flirtatious look from beneath her thick lashes. At the same time she calculated the cost of his suit and pearl stickpin to the penny. And that gold ring on his right hand was the real McCoy, all right. "You wouldn't know of someplace where I'd be more at home now, would you?"

"Would you feel safe with me at the Golden Room of the Dillon Hotel? I'm very well known there."

The Dillon Hotel! That was the clincher. Joe Scudder was evidently a man of substance. Bedelia decided not to steal his wallet and run. This could be the start of a cozy little arrangement. She rose and put her hand on his arm. "I'd be delighted, Mr. Scudder."

As they went out to his waiting carriage she envisioned a wonderful evening ahead. Their late supper at the Dillon was everything she'd imagined, right down to the last glass of champagne.

An hour after finishing it she was bound and gagged, lying on the floor of Joe Scudder's carriage in a drugged stupor.

It was late when Cassandra returned to her boudoir, exhausted. Povey moved about in her dressing room, putting the ruby necklace away in its special box. Kitty had been bathed, dosed with laudanum, and put to bed. Between herself and Povey they concocted a believable story for the rest of the household, but Tyler had to be told everything. She dreaded it.

Cassandra shivered thinking of what his response might be. It had been wicked of Kitty to deceive them, and had been terribly foolish to believe Jake's blandishments—but she had already paid dearly for it.

She waited at the door connecting her boudoir with

Tyler's dressing room, her forehead pressed against the cool wood, until she heard him enter. There was no use putting it off any longer. She summoned her courage and attempted to slide back the lock that had closed the door between their suites for so long. She wondered if he'd ever realized that it had been locked. Cassandra couldn't remember the last time he had come to her bed. It had been years since he'd thought of her as anything but the mistress of his house and a hostess to his guests.

She had to hit the lock with the heel of her hand to loosen it. Tyler looked up in surprise as she stopped dead on the threshold. Reed, his valet, was with him. She should have expected that. Cassandra swallowed. "Tyler, may I speak to you privately?"

One look at her pale, set face and he dismissed Reed. Tyler followed her into her own bed chamber and frowned when she shut the door. He'd heard that there was illness down along the waterfront, but thus far it hadn't affected the upper-class homes high in the hills. "Good God, Kitty hasn't caught something infectious, has she?"

"I only wish it were so simple. Perhaps you had better sit down."

Puzzled, he nevertheless sat on the end of the blue brocade sofa and waited. He'd never seen her look so distraught before.

"Kitty has been . . . has had . . ." She took in a ragged breath. "She went out to meet Jake Adams tonight, while we were at dinner." Cassandra began to paint a picture of a young girl, mistaking a first crush for abiding love, slipping out by moonlight at the behest of her beloved.

Tyler interrupted fiercely, rising to his feet. "Is that

what this is all about, by God! She ought to be thrashed!"

"Wait, please. There is more." Her plans to couch the tragedy in softer words vanished in her anxiety. "Kitty . . . he—he raped her."

She had expected an explosion of rage from Tyler. Instead there was utter, disbelieving silence. The beating of her own heart grew to fill the vacuum, until it thundered in her ears. Her husband seemed to be in shock.

"Tyler . . . ?" His reaction to the terrible news was far worse than she had anticipated.

"By God, I'll—" His voice broke off abruptly. His face, normally ruddy, took on a deeper, unhealthy hue. She had seen him angry before, but never like this.

"As for that blackguard who attacked her, I'll—I'll—unh!" He choked on his wrath, gasping for breath and crumpling before Cassandra's eyes. Tyler reached for support and collapsed against the curving back of the sofa. He seemed unable to catch his breath and his skin darkened to a hideous slate color.

Crying out for Povey, Cassandra ran to his side. Her husband's lips were purple and his breath whistled as he struggled for air. With every wheeze his eyes seemed to sink deeper into his skull. The episode lasted scarcely half a minute, leaving him gray and suddenly old, and Cassandra half paralyzed with terror.

Povey entered and Cassandra sent her for the decanter of brandy that Tyler kept in his dressing room. She forced some between his lips and gradually his color came back. "I—I'm all right," he managed at last. His voice was thick. "My father used to have these spells when he was angry. It will pass."

While she knelt beside him his breathing became normal. Despite their entreaties, Tyler refused to rest, pushing himself up shakily despite their protests. "I must see Kitty now."

Cassandra went with her husband to her niece's room. She was afraid that seeing Kitty might cause him to suffer another fit of apoplexy. Tyler, now that he was prepared, showed that he was made of sterner stuff. He stood grimly looking down at Kitty's still form and his hands curled into fists at his side. Her hair had been brushed free of the burrs and bits of leaf and woven into a single plait. Except for the marks on her face, she looked like a sleeping child, innocent and untouched.

He turned away and his voice was hard as iron. "No one is to be admitted to this room excepting the three of us. Not even Jenny. Think of some excuse to keep her away and we may yet pull out of this coil."

Cassandra was dizzy with relief. "Yes. We'll say that Kitty has been feeling out of sorts for several days and that the episode has led into an epic migraine. Jenny is too full of vigor and would only disturb Kitty's rest, which is why only Povey is to wait upon her."

Tyler's jaw relaxed. "That will do nicely. In the meantime, the important thing is for you to be yourself." He eyed Cassandra sharply. "No sighs, frowns, or tears."

Before she had time to respond, Povey came rushing in behind them in a twitter. "My lady!" she whispered hoarsely. "Your diamond earrings are missing, my lady, and the aquamarine necklace as well. I've checked everywhere!"

Tyler cursed beneath his breath. "No doubt taken by that young villain. It's a wonder he didn't murder Kitty as well." He smashed a fist into his palm. "By God! I'll see him hanged for this."

Povey hovered, wringing her hands. "And all the silver plate brought out of the vault in order to polish it for the ball. Shall I have Morton put it away?"

A flash of the old vigor lit Tyler's eyes. "No. There's no need. We will need it polished and ready."

Cassandra was stunned. "Are you mad? We can't attempt to pull it off. The ball must be canceled!"

His face darkened again. "By God, that it won't! Do you want to start tongues wagging? We'll hold the ball and you'll do your part in making it a huge success. You'll wear your new gown and the Fayne Rubies. You'll flatter the women and charm all the men. And we will make the ball the social success of the season!"

He turned on his heel and walked away.

Despite his late hours, Grayson was up early the next morning. He had an appointment to meet Simon Fiddler. They were served a private breakfast in the restaurant of his yet unopened hotel. The tour of the building that followed was impressive, but Grayson was disappointed. He hadn't found what he'd expected. If Simon Fiddler was involved in the disappearance of the Chinese girls Ling Cheung was seeking, he'd hidden them elsewhere.

Simon was already installed in his private suite, which occupied the entire top floor. The tour ended there, in the magnificent salon. The bronze velvet draperies and the sheer curtains had been fully opened and Grayson realized that even this panorama had been planned as part of the room's adornment.

"My little hideaway," Simon murmured.

Grayson had the sensation of sitting in the midst of a stage set. Everything about this private dining room was meant to awe. From the painted ceiling to the precise angle of each bibelot on the mantlepiece, it bespoke wealth, an appreciation of beauty, and power. The ornate mirrors reflected sofas, various cabinets and vitrines filled with treasures, and two chairs flanking a table inlaid with ivory, onyx, and emerald-green malachite. It had originally been commissioned by a king of France, Simon explained, then rescued from destruction and sold after the Terror to a Venetian doge, and later confiscated from the king of Naples by the Emperor Napoleon, for his own use.

They sat on either side of the table. Simon leaned back in his chair and smiled his beautiful smile. "An omelet and grand tour:—I'm sure you expected a more entertaining time when you accepted my invitation."

"It's freely said in certain circles, Mr. Fiddler, that an hour or an evening spent in your company always ends with the unexpected."

Simons' eyebrows rose. "Am I really so predictable? How tiresome. I must rethink my habits."

The easy drawl didn't fool Grayson. Simon's eyes were extraordinarily blue. Something was afoot. Grayson waited.

Simon watched him, biding his own time as well. Two minutes passed, three, then four. He'd underestimated his guest. Whatever the quality of his bloodlines —and there were interesting stories making the rounds regarding Mr. Grayson Howard—he might prove a worthy opponent. Worthy, but ultimately defeatable. The unspoken war of silence had gone on too long, and he broke it suddenly, caressing his sapphire stickpin with a long, graceful finger.

"I've heard on good authority, Mr. Howard, that you're thinking of dissolving your interests in the Thunder Mine. I might be interested in acquiring it."

"Your informants are out of touch. I've decided against selling it." Grayson drummed his fingers on the tabletop. "Although I'm mystified as to how you've learned of it. There are only two men with whom I've discussed the possibility. Two very discreet and loyal men."

Simon smiled. "But you see, Mr. Howard, that I am also in the business of acquiring information."

Grayson appeared to digest this. "I suppose it was Jaime McFee," he said slowly. "I'm disappointed in him."

The smile on Simon's face widened. "Ah, yes. Mr. McFee. A good man, and devoted to your interests. But every man, so they say, has his price. Wealth, power, recognition. The acquisition of knowledge. The pleasures—or sins, if you will—of the flesh." He leaned forward. "What is yours, Mr. Howard?"

"Hasn't your information told you that?" Grayson settled back in his chair. "I like fast horses and fast women. I enjoy challenge. And, as you've no doubt heard, I'm a gambler. High-stake card games are my particular vice."

"Then let us propose a challenge. Your gold mine against . . . what?"

Everyone knew that Simon Fiddler was one of the richest men in America. His interests ranged from shipping to cattle ranching to the importing of rare objets d'art. There was a spark of light in Grayson's eyes. "You tempt me. But perhaps my stakes are too high to suit you."

"Name them."

"I'll put up the Thunder Mine—if you'll stake something of equal value. Your new hotel perhaps. Or the latest additions to your, ah, 'Oriental collection,' as I believe you called it?"

"Ah." Simon was startled and barely hid it. He lifted his crystal glass and watched the way the facets sent out rainbows of light. "I don't like your stakes, Mr. Howard."

Grayson gave his host a measuring look. "I imagine that a simple wager of mere gold would bore you."

"Infinitely."

"Then I'll be on my way. Thank you for a most interesting morning."

Simon rang for the butler. "Mr. Howard is leaving, Timmons."

He nodded pleasantly to his guest. "One day we'll agree on the stakes. I'll look forward to our match."

He escorted Grayson from the parlor, a marked sign of personal favor. "As I said yesterday, you will be meeting my good friends tonight. Friends it would behoove you to cultivate if you wish to do business in San Francisco, Mr. Howard. Men of wealth and power in the community, some with international ties. Afterward there will be, ah, a bit of entertainment that I am sure would interest you, as well."

Grayson's face was a smooth mask and totally unreadable. "I'm looking forward to it."

"Nine o'clock, then. At warehouse sixty-one on the wharf."

Grayson's eyebrows rose a fraction. "An interesting setting for a dinner party."

Simon merely smiled quizzically. "Until this evening, Mr. Howard."

But the moment the heavy door of the private apartment was closed, all of Simon's languor vanished. A dark-eyed, dark-haired man stepped out of the adjacent parlor. He was a well-dressed, fellow with a gold and onyx ring upon his index finger. "That the one?"

"Yes. See that he's followed, Mr. Scudder. Look into his background. Investigate his finances. Find out his hopes and dreams. What drives him. And try and discover exactly what he knows about me." Simon frowned. "I need to know everything there is to know about Mr. Grayson Howard."

The man went to the window and signaled to another fellow waiting in the street below. "He won't spit, that you won't know about it, Mr. Fiddler."

"Excellent." Simon sprawled back in his chair. "Now," he said, in one of his quick changes of mood, "what have you brought for my especial entertainment tonight? Or should I say whom?"

Joe Scudder smiled. "A rare one, Mr. Fiddler. A very rare one, if I do say so myself."

Cassandra awakened, thinking she'd just experienced a terrible nightmare. Then she realized she was in the wing chair in Kitty's room, with her feet propped on a footstool and a blanket thrown over her. For a moment she was disoriented. Then memory came flooding back on an evil tide. A wave of nausea washed over her. It was all true.

She rose, feeling groggy and ill. A few hours of troubled sleep had done nothing to refresh her. Tyler had vanished behind his locked door all night, but she had been awake until well after sunrise while Povey dozed in the narrow truckle bed. Cassandra's brain seemed filled with cotton wool.

Kitty was sleeping quietly, her breathing more regular

since the last dose of laudanum. Povey heard her stir. "She's resting quietly, poor lamb."

If Cassandra's heart had not already been broken by Kitty's rape, it would have been by the sight of Povey, grown old and hunched overnight. "I must meet with Mrs. Llewellyn," she said with regret. "I shall hurry back and have Jenny or Rosaleen carry up a tray."

"No need, madame. I couldn't eat a single bite."

"Some tea, then." Cassandra stooped to press a kiss on Kitty's brow. Helpless pity and tenderness swept through her, followed by impotent rage. Kitty was curled on her side, one hand cradled beneath her cheek. The bruises were dark stains against her pallor. It wrung Cassandra's heart. She had tried to shield her niece with love. It hadn't been enough. She swallowed her tears. This was no time to succumb to hysterics. If she meant to see Kitty through this she must be strong. And, if there was any justice in this world, then Jake Adams would suffer for his sins.

She sighed and went through to her own chambers to dress. Her mirror showed a pale woman with haunted eyes. That would never do. She bathed her face in cold water and brushed her hair, arranging it in a loose knot at her nape. A touch of rouge to her cheeks and lips masked her wan appearance.

There were a hundred details to check for the ball, and her heart was too heavy to deal with them. She had no choice in the matter. Before leaving for the city earlier, Tyler had impressed upon her again that it was essential they follow their normal routine. Cassandra was prepared to fill her role in this tragic charade.

Despite her frayed nerves and lack of sleep she had few doubts that she could carry it off successfully. She had been raised to be a lady in every sense of the word.

To bury her own feelings beneath a calm and gracious exterior, to hide her deepest emotions from society's cruel scrutiny. It had become second nature for her to show a brave face to the world when her life was in utter turmoil. God knew she'd had plenty of experience at doing so, beginning in childhood.

She straightened her shoulders and went downstairs. She swept down the gothic staircase, her hem whispering as it brushed the steps. Voices were raised and she was surprised to find the household at sixes and sevens. Mrs. Llewellyn was in the hall, arguing with Morton. When she saw her mistress she bustled toward her, trembling with outrage. "Oh, my lady, I don't know what we've come to. I never thought to see the police called in to Stoneleigh, that I didn't. It's a wonder we weren't all murdered in our beds!"

Cassandra's fingers gripped the railing. "Whatever do you mean?"

"Why, didn't the master tell you? A robber was loose in the house last night."

Morton gave her a quelling look. "It is true, madam. A window in the dining room was forced. I am deeply disturbed to report that several pieces of the Georgian silver plate are missing. And," he added mournfully, "also the Charles II silver punch bowl which I had placed there, after polishing it last night."

"I told you that you should have locked it up in the butler's pantry," the housekeeper said darkly. "If more heed had been given to my words . . ." Mrs. Llewellyn broke off before the butler's icy glare.

Cassandra felt a dull headache starting. "Has Mr. Lucton been informed of this?"

"Yes, madam," Morton intoned. "The moment Mr.

Lucton came down for breakfast this morning I apprised him of the fact."

"Thank you. You have done all that you should."

"But," Mrs. Llewellyn said indignantly, getting to the heart of her concern, "what are we to use for the champagne punch for the ball?"

"Send one of the footmen to Pennynton's tomorrow and have him procure a crystal bowl. The best they have."

"Very good, madame."

Cassandra realized that, while the ball might be a test of her endurance, the preparations for it were proving to be her salvation. There was something comforting in organizing such unimportant details, when she'd lost control over the rest of her life.

Mrs. Llewellyn was eager to go over the list of preparations for the ball and they all went to check on the progress in the ballroom. The great chandelier had been lowered near the floor, and the footmen were polishing the crystal drops and swags. Morton stood by, to see that no damage was done to it. Its cost would have paid the wages of the entire forty-member staff at Stoneleigh for several years.

Cassandra walked through to the conservatory where an army of men on ladders and scaffolds had cleaned the hundreds of panes. Two others were hanging swags of tasseled silk from the ceiling. When the decorating was finished, the conservatory would look like a sheik's tent from the Arabian Nights, set against a dark, starry sky. Unfortunately, one of the silken swaths was obscuring the door to the garden, and she had to make them change it. She wished that her other worries were so minor.

The last stop was the green drawing room, which

would be set up for cards. Dozens of new decks, still in their wrappers, were stacked atop a sideboard, and the extra gilt chairs she'd rented for the event were lined along the wall, awaiting placement. Outwardly, at least, preparations for the ball were shaping up well. Cassandra didn't know how she was going to go through with it.

The hours passed quickly and she was astonished to hear the clock chime. She wanted to check on Kitty and took a shortcut through the yellow sitting room, through the formal dining room, and out into the entrance hall. Cassandra stopped in astonishment. The hall was submerged in a sea of roses.

Baskets, bowls, and china vases of golden roses were on every surface, including the floor, and more being brought in from outside. The air was already heavy with their spice. She gazed at them, completely bewildered. In the first place, the flowers she'd ordered weren't to come until the following afternoon; and in the second, these weren't at all what she had ordered.

Cassandra forged her way through the massed blooms. Morton stood by the entrance, harassed beyond endurance. "Deliveries for the ball are to be taken to the tradesmen's entrance," he announced for the third or fourth time, to no avail. Another enormous basket of roses came through the door with a grinning delivery man behind it. Morton was forcibly backed up against the console table.

She stepped in quickly and addressed the man who appeared to be in charge. "What is the meaning of this? I did not order roses, I ordered mixed bouquets with ivy, and you're a day too early with the delivery. You must take them all back, at once!"

At her astringent tones the activity came to a halt.

The fellow handed her an envelope of heavy white paper inscribed to her. Puzzled, she broke the seal and found a bold, unfamiliar scrawl: "No rose on earth can match your beauty—or even dare aspire to it."

There was no signature, only a carelessly scrawled "S." Cassandra shivered in the warm afternoon light. Simon Fiddler. Sybarite and seducer of women. He was stalking her with poetic phrases and a fortune in flowers, but he was still stalking her. And, a voice in her head warned, very sure of success.

An image of Kitty, seduced by Jake's lies and honeyed words, flashed into her mind. Jake and Simon Fiddler were two of a kind. The card fell from her hand, as if she'd touched something vile. She turned to Morton. "Send them back. Every last one of them."

"Send them back?" The butler was surprised out of his decorum. "But, madam . . ."

The head delivery man grinned. "Can't take 'em back, ma'am. Orders."

Her anger got the better of her. "Then deliver them to St. Anne's Foundling Home and Orphanage." The children would enjoy them.

She didn't see Grayson in the doorway. He had ridden up a moment earlier, a clouded amber cane over his arm. He hadn't expected to find such chaos in Cassandra Lucton's orderly domain. At first glance the foyer seemed buried by masses of roses, all gold as coins. She stood in their midst like Danae surrounded by the golden shower. But instead of Zeus in all his splendor, there was only a confusion of men in florist's livery, and one very bewildered butler.

Grayson stepped inside. "You heard the lady. Get those flowers out of here."

The delivery men jumped at the voice of masculine

authority and began retrieving the floral offerings. Cassandra moved backward to avoid one of them and bumped into Grayson, off balance. He caught her by the shoulders, saving her a nasty tumble. "It appears that I'm in the way," he said smoothly.

Cassandra's control had slipped as well as her feet, taking her good manners with it. "Very much so!"

She jerked away from his touch. It had burned through her silk morning gown to her flesh beneath, as if he'd touched her naked skin. As if he'd caressed it. She was flushed with internal heat and the confusion that only Grayson Howard seemed to cause. Dear God, how could a man she scarcely knew make her feel like this?

Grayson lifted his eyebrows. So, the rose had thorns, did she? "I can see you have your hands full. I only called to inquire after Miss Hamilton. I hope she's fully recovered from her indisposition."

"Recovered?"

For one near-fatal moment Cassandra forgot the hurried explanation she'd given at the Dillon last night. She controlled the flutter of panic in her stomach and forced a smile that was more of a rictus. "Oh! Yes, thank you, she's much improved. Kitty is subject to migraine. I'm sure she'll be herself in time for the ball."

"I'm glad to hear that. I'll hope to dance with her."

With a smile and a bow he walked out into the sunshine, crushing the golden petals beneath his heels. Once outside Grayson's smile vanished. By the time he'd retrieved his horse from the stable boy he was in a rare temper. In the way, was he? Arrogant bitch.

But that wasn't fair. Directness had always been a virtue in his book. What angered him had nothing to do with her curt response. It was the way his heart had sped up at the sight of her and the swift rise of desire that came with it. He'd wanted to take her there and then, amid the crush of golden roses. And she wasn't unaware of it. She couldn't be. Not after the way she'd jumped when he touched her and the way the heat had flushed her cheeks.

He dismissed it as mere lust. He didn't know Cassandra Lucton. And he didn't know how to love anymore. Not since Bitter Creek.

He reached the end of the long drive and gave his horse its head. The roan sensed his master's roiled emotions and set off at a spanking pace. Grayson was glad to leave Stoneleigh behind him.

He didn't need any distractions from the dangerous evening ahead.

By late afternoon Grayson was down along the wharf, listening for gossip. The Hanged Man Saloon was a shabby affair with a sooty tin ceiling reclaimed from an abandoned house, battered tables and chairs, and a long bar on one wall. The oak was black with grime and age and the mirror behind it spotted from the salt air. At the moment the place was filled with smoke, the odors of onions, and the sweat of unwashed bodies and lively curses.

Grayson stood at the bar, one boot upon the tarnished rail. No matter how late or early the hour, the saloon was always busy. The regulars, leery of passing strangers, had gotten used to his presence. He'd been stopping in at about the same time every day for several weeks. The bartender was surly but the whiskey was strong and the rumor mill the best along the waterfront.

"A drop of that blue ruin." Grayson put his coins down on the bar. He always ordered gin. That and rum and hearty ale were the most common drinks in such places—and it didn't stain when he poured it up his sleeve. He took the glass and pretended to knock it back in a smooth gesture, then ordered a second.

Three men sat at the table behind him, rolling their cigarettes and nursing their drinks with an unusual caution that spoke of threadbare wallets. Grayson seemed to pay no attention to his surroundings, staring morosely into his gin or at the dim reflections in the speckled mirror behind the bar. In reality he was keenly interested in the conversations around him.

A sour-looking man, well into his cups, was grousing to his cronies at one of the tables. " 'You know I can't give you no raise with the *Lady Cassandra* still out,' 'e said. 'You'll take 'alf wages and bedamned to ye,' 'e said, az if 'e were a bloody king."

"Ah, it's at the bottom of the sea, don't you know," one of his companions joined in. "And poor old Barney Svenson with it."

"Shut up, Miller. Let the man talk." He leaned forward. "Well, what happened next?"

"Well, then," the first man continued, "we had words, ye might say. 'A man can't feed iz family on that,' I said to iz face, I did. And 'e tol' me if I thought that, then I could jes' light out and never show my face agin. So I'm out on my ear after five years." He thunked his empty gin glass down for emphasis. "Black-hearted bastard!"

"That he is. Seven years I've worked for Lucton Shipping, long before he showed up here with his fancy wife and built his fancy mansion in the hills. Seven years, working my way up to head man, and never a kind word nor a bonus from him."

"And then you got the boot."

"Right up my arse, I did. Insubordination, he said. He's the brains, he said. And all I asked was why couldn't we put the overload in building number sixty-two, since it was half-empty. Ten seconds later I was out on my ear. And I'm not the only one to have the same experience, boys, I can tell you."

Grayson listened as the complaints degenerated into general grumbling about working conditions and the greed of all bosses. He joined in the conversation, as he occasionally did, cursing a mythical boss in Galveston. Eventually he worked the talk around to Simon Fiddler. "Is he as bad as all the rest?"

"Dunno. He must treat 'em right, mate, 'cause they're loyal to 'im and they've got plenty of coins to jingle. No, you don't hear no complaints from Fiddler's men. Keeps to themselves, they does. But I wouldn't work for him for all the tea in China. Not if 'alf of what I 'ear is true."

After buying another bottle to grease the man's tongue, Grayson listened carefully without appearing to pay much heed to the conversation. The bits and pieces fell into place and he sauntered off to look around the wharf. By the time he slipped back into the Dillon Hotel through the tradesmen's entrance, he'd learned everything he needed to know.

Jaime McFee was waiting for him, drinking his whiskey with his boots up on the ottoman. He stared when he saw Grayson in grimy workman's clothing. "What are you up to, now?"

"Were your ears burning earlier? I maligned your name to Simon Fiddler a few hours ago. I'm sure you'll hear from him soon."

"I thought you were up at Stoneleigh, courting your bride-to-be." He eyed Grayson's clothes. "Although, if you dress like a dockworker I doubt you'll make any headway."

The smile left Grayson's face. "Don't ring the wedding bells yet." He peeled off the jacket and dropped it in a chair. "Any news?"

"A message came an hour ago from Ling Cheung. Some young woman showed up yesterday claiming to be Annette Mason. She's supposed to return this afternoon. He said he'd try to hang on to her until you got there."

Grayson looked at the clock and swore. There was no sense taking time to change. "Someone tried to follow me from Fiddler's hotel. I lost him in Chinatown. Stay a little distance behind me, and if he shows up again, find out who he is and what he wants."

"And who's behind it."

"You're quick on the uptake, Jaime."

"That's why you pay me so well."

Grayson handed Jaime an envelope. "Don't forget that appointment at the California Investment Bank today. They'll need those papers putting up the Morning Star mine as collateral against Lucton's new loan."

Jaime shook his head. "One day you're trying to get Lucton by the balls and twist them by letting him overextend his credit, and the next you're bailing him out. Either there is more to this than you're telling me, or you've lost your mind."

Grayson stared out the window to the Lucton mansion high above the city's sprawl. "Perhaps I have."

The whiskey decanter was near to hand. Jaime lifted it and poured himself another drink. A stiff one. "I hope you won't live to regret this."

The corners of Grayson's mouth lifted in an ironic smile as he turned away. He already rued meddling in

Tyler Lucton's affairs, and in ways that Jaime couldn't begin to imagine.

The woman in the joss shop greeted Grayson with a smile. He went up the stairs to Ling Cheung's private office two at a time. By the time he was halfway to Chinatown the man trailing him had disappeared—no doubt into some convenient alleyway, where Jaime would meet and persuade the man to supply the information he wanted.

He threw the door open and was disappointed to find it empty. Damn it, where were they?

He paced the floor restlessly for several minutes before Ling Cheung returned, alone. Grayson stopped. "Where's the girl?"

"She was supposed to have met me an hour ago. The hotel where she said she was putting up had no record of Annette Mason."

Grayson shoved his hands into his pockets. "What did you think of her?"

"There was something very familiar about her. She has some resemblance to Annette, as she might be now. But, as you know, a young child's face is a blank slate. Life can write many stories upon it."

"Did she remember anything? Did you try to trap her?"

"The woman claims she suffered an illness that affected her memory, but that seeing your broadside helped her to remember. She had a slip of paper—part of an envelope—with Annette's name written upon it—and a set of rosary beads that matched the ones in the picture."

"She could have gotten those easily enough." He hit

the table with his fist. "Damn it, I'd like to see her and get this settled. I'd know in an instant if she's lying or the genuine article.

"By the way, I've a lead on that matter of yours. I'm off tonight to a dinner party given by Simon Fiddler. You might be interested to learn that it's being held at his warehouse on the wharf."

A gleam came into Ling Cheung's dark eyes at the tone in Grayson's voice. "You know something, then?"

"Like you, I have contacts in interesting places. Is everything set on your end here?"

"Everything is in place—if the missing women are found."

"Good. This is the plan . . ."

Twenty minutes later Grayson was on the way back to his hotel, deep in thought. This business of Bronco's was complicating things; but if the girl claiming to be Annette turned out to be genuine, it was worth it. He had been afraid to give credence to Bronco's assertions that Annette was alive and well somewhere. It was either a miracle or a hoax. Grayson leaned toward the latter.

He'd lost faith in miracles a long, long time ago.

Cassandra tiptoed into Kitty's room. With the curtains and draperies closed, the room was dim as twilight. Povey had eschewed the comfort of the wing chair by the window for a hard wooden one at the bedside, in hopes it would keep her alert; but as Cassandra entered softly her head was nodding lower and lower toward her thin bosom. The click of the door shutting brought her awake with a jerk. Kitty slept on.

"Dear Povey, you really must rest. Go lie upon your bed. I'll sit with Kitty awhile."

"Perhaps I should, or I'll be no good to either of you, madame. A quarter hour or so, and I'll be quite myself again."

Cassandra agreed, smiling inwardly. The preparations for tomorrow's ball were well in hand. She had no intention of waking Povey up until dinnertime at the very earliest. Settling herself in the wing chair, she listened to the slow, steady rhythm of Kitty's breathing. It was more natural now than during the night, when she'd been heavily drugged with laudanum. Time would heal the physical bruises. Cassandra feared that nothing would heal the deep wounds that Kitty's spirit had suffered. The memory of her frenzied weeping was terrible. The reality of the rape was worse.

Cassandra was too restless to sit still for long. She crossed to the bedside. How young and vulnerable Kitty looked. In the delicate bones of the girl's face, she could trace the child she had been and the woman that she would one day become. As she leaned forward, she felt Kitty's breath flutter across her skin, light as the brush of a butterfly's wing. *Oh, Kitty!*

She knelt down beside the bed, washed over by a great wave of love and hopeless regrets. Something sharp scratched her ankle through the silk of her stockings. Cassandra rubbed her leg and bent down to see what had caused it. Kitty's reticule was beneath the bed, lying there in the darkness. She pulled it out, not realizing at first that it was upside down.

As she lifted it, a mass of cool metal and glittering stones spilled out upon the floral carpet. Cassandra stared in astonishment at the missing aquamarine and diamond necklace and the diamond ear clips that Margaret had left to her. "What on earth?"

Although her exclamation was low, it was loud enough to startle Kitty from her doze. Her shadowed lids flew up and she raised herself on her elbows. Then she saw the jewels spilling from her aunt's hand.

Kitty's face crumpled inward and she burst into tears. "H-how you must hate me . . . to repay your kindness with t-treachery after all you and Uncle Tyler have done for me. I never intended to take anything that wasn't mine. But w-when I saw them j-just lying on your dressing table . . ." She couldn't go on.

Her words were muffled by tears, but their message was chillingly clear. Cassandra felt as though she'd been kicked in the stomach. The gold and faceted stones grew leaden in her palm. Her whole arm seemed to ache from the weight of them. "Kitty, *you took the jewelry?* But I . . . we thought that Jake had stolen them!"

Kitty struggled to sit up, her face swollen and tear-streaked. "I went into your d-dressing room to get the silk shawl I'd left there, and saw your j-jewel case and the earrings. I only took them in case J-Jake and I r-ran out of money. And you had said that one day you would g-give them to me. On my wedding d-day . . ."

The gems slid from Cassandra's numb fingers to the satin coverlet. She stumbled up and her shoulder hit the bedside table. An empty teacup fell, shattering against an inlaid table. Echoing in Cassandra's ears like the shattering of her own heart.

7

Cassandra didn't know how she had gotten through the day. Literally. The preparations for the ball seemed to be well in hand, and she found a completed checklist in her own hand on the rosewood secretary, but she had no recollection of writing it. In the same manner she found herself dressed for dinner in a gown of emerald silk, without quite knowing how she'd managed it. She must get a grip on herself, she thought. For Kitty's sake.

Those three words had become her litany.

The clocked chimed sweetly, startling her. Tyler would be in the drawing room, waiting for her to join him. First she must stop in to check on Kitty and Povey. Her niece seemed to be dozing, but it occurred to Cassandra that she might be pretending to sleep, to avoid more painful, but inevitable, discussions.

Povey had placed a vellum screen between the lamp

and the bed. The room looked warm and cozy and, to her surprise, Cassandra realized her maid was smiling. Povey rose and came to her. "Miss Catherine has gotten her monthlies," she whispered. "No worry on that score."

Cassandra closed her eyes in silent prayer. "Thank God!" The one fear she'd been unable to face had been that of a pregnancy from the rape. She smiled, but her hands trembled with relief. "I'll come up immediately after dinner."

Tyler was not in the drawing room. She found him in his study. His skin was sallow and there were new lines around his eyes. The leather volume that contained the household inventory lay open on the blotter beside the whiskey decanter and a heavy-bottomed glass. He was dressed for an evening on the town. Cassandra was rigid with indignation.

"I did not think that you would be going out this evening, under the circumstances!"

Tyler cleared his throat. "This is something unavoidable. I have an urgent meeting and I am also expected at Simon Fiddler's dinner party, you'll recall. It will look bad if I don't show. I may take a room in town and go straight to the warehouse in the morning."

She squared her jaw. "I need you here, Tyler."

"That can't be helped. And there is nothing I can do for Kitty now." He gestured toward the inventory book. "Morton or Mrs. Llewellyn will have told you about the break-in and the missing silver."

"Yes."

Tyler's face was strained. "There has been an interesting occurrence. It seems that the body of a young man was found behind a tavern on the waterfront. The owner told the police he believes it to be that of Jake

Adams, who labored on the docks before coming to work at Stoneleigh. He'd been shot to death."

A rush of emotion filled Cassandra: surprise, horror, relief—and a deep-welling, primitive satisfaction that shocked her with its rawness. Jake Adams, answering to a higher court, had paid for his crimes. Kitty would never be the same again—but at least she would suffer no further harm from that quarter. "I am glad that he's dead."

"Yes, by God! The police found my monogrammed silver card case and my favorite gold cufflinks in his pocket. They recognized the Fortuna wagon wheel symbol on them and notified me."

Cassandra shuddered. "Then . . . why, it must have been Jake who stole the silverplate."

"And your jewelry, as well. The police would like me to see if I can identify the body, since the tavern fellow wasn't sure." His eyes locked with hers.

"It wasn't the groom who stole my jewelry," she said slowly, lowering her voice. "It was Kitty who took them. I'd promised them to her and she meant to . . ."

Tyler was frozen for a second. Then jumped up and grabbed her arm. "Shut your mouth!" he whispered fiercely. "The door is open. Do you want the servants to hear?"

"But . . ."

"I've already sent a report listing them as being stolen. The filthy bastard is dead. It won't hurt his reputation, but it would destroy Kitty's! You must get hold of yourself, Cassandra. At once!"

She saw that he was within an inch of losing control. And, of course, he was right. "I understand. You may count on me to carry off my part."

"There is no part to play. You must merely tell the

truth." Both his hands now clamped her shoulders. "And the truth is that Kitty is completely out of this. Listen to me, Cassandra. She had been feeling poorly all yesterday afternoon, and retired early to bed with a debilitating headache. She was dosed with laudanum and remained in her room all night, with Povey in attendance." His fingers dug into her flesh. *"Nothing happened."*

"Very well." Cassandra kept her voice steady. "Nothing happened."

"No, goddammit!" He bruised her arms. "It must be more than mere words! You must believe what you are saying—or no one else will. You discovered some of your jewelry missing from its case, and this morning Mrs. Llewellyn reported that some of the best silver plate was missing. I notified the police and told them that a groom, recently fired for insubordination, was seen near the house. Later I was notified that a body, presumably his, had been found in the bay."

Cassandra tried to control her trembling. She agreed with her husband. There must be no suspicion that anything was amiss. They must focus attention on the missing silver. Jake was dead. It couldn't matter to him if the jewelry was added to his lists of sins. Cassandra closed her eyes. When she opened them her voice was clear and direct, and as impersonal as an automaton.

"We dined at the Dillon with Grayson Howard last evening. Kitty stayed behind because she had a sick headache." Her voice broke and she paused a moment to contain herself. "Povey gave her one of Dr. Matcham's patent powders, but it became much worse and we were sent for. Povey never left Kitty's side from the time we left until we returned home."

Tyler let out a long, gusty sigh. "Excellent. You'll

do." He released her. "If I have to spend the night in the city, I'll take a room at the Dillon."

She clutched his coat sleeve. "I wish you would stay here with us."

"Don't worry, my dear. Do exactly what I say, and we'll see Kitty out of this coil, with no harm done." He rang for his carriage.

Cassandra followed him out into the hall. *No harm done?* Perhaps Kitty's reputation might escape unscathed, and that was no small thing, but there was far more than that at stake. The physical damage was bad enough, but it was the emotional damage that Cassandra feared even more.

Kitty might never recover from the betrayal of shattered trust and the terrible alchemy of the rape had turned her glowing first love into fear and hate and horror.

She turned away at the sound of carriage wheels. Tyler had warned her that she must pull herself together and go on as she normally would. There were many things to attend to and Cassandra suddenly was determined that the ball would be the success of the season, no matter how difficult it would be to carry on the charade. She would laugh and dance as if she hadn't a care in the world.

For Kitty's sake.

Eli Hawkins reached for his worn jacket. It was chilly here along the waterfront, and he was set for night watchman duty. The day had been beautiful, but as the sun vanished behind the hills, a thick fog rose from the bay, drifting in eerie wisps along the docks. It muffled sound and distorted vision with its fluid shifting, rendering the commonplace and familiar, alien and strange.

A form materialized out of the shadows in front of the warehouse, startling Eli. It seemed to him that one second there had been only a slight thickening in the hazy air, the next that it had coalesced into a dark man in evening dress, leaning idly against the warehouse wall. The watchman scratched his head and considered whether it was any of his business to investigate. No use in questioning the swells about their reckless doings. Plenty of them about the waterfront of a night, looking for trouble. Finding it, more times than not. And able to buy their way out of it, as well.

No, Eli decided, the man's presence was nothing to him. He shrugged and went about his duty. But when he spied a fellow in laborer's clothes behind the warehouse a few minutes later he was quick to act. He smacked a wicked piece of heavy pipe against a piling. It made a sound like a gunshot. "Off with you, now! You've no business back here."

The laborer glanced back over his shoulder and gave a double-noted whistle, then took off, running, into the disguising fog. Eli smiled in quiet triumph. No dirty, two-bit thief would be breaking into Mr. Fiddler's new warehouse. Not when Eli Hawkins had the watch. He wondered if he'd scared off that swell in evening dress, too. But when he made his rounds the man was still there, melting into the growing shadows as if he were part of the fog.

Grayson hadn't moved an inch, although he'd heard the boom of the pipe, the whistle, and the shouts. He'd been expecting them. As the watchman departed he lounged against the side of the building, carelessly puffing on a cigarillo. Droplets of mist formed in the thickening air and clung to his dark hair. He dropped his cigar, ground it out beneath his heel, and watched as the scenery was silently blotted out. Soon all that could be seen of the ships at anchor was a ghostly forest of spars, furled shrouds, and tapering masts, floating like a mirage against the rapidly darkening sky. Simon Fiddler had picked a strange place to entertain his friends.

The warehouse was on the end of a row of buildings, with an empty one immediately beside it. Lights glimmered through the veils of fog and Grayson's mouth turned up in a sardonic smile. Some of the richest and most influential men in town were, like himself, responding to Fiddler's invitation. From the number of hacks and private carriages wending their way toward the warehouse, the casually worded request to join their host for an evening's amusement was tantamount to a command performance.

One by one the vehicles disgorged their passengers, and Grayson was not surprised to see prominent bankers, landowners, shipping magnates, and descendants of the old Californios. Eighteen men in all. In his weeks in San Francisco he had never seen such concentrated wealth and power in one place—and never in lowlier surroundings. The men milled about, entangled in ribbons of shifting fog. Grayson kept to the shadows.

Tyler Lucton was absent, which surprised Grayson. Perhaps Kitty Hamilton had suffered a relapse. Or perhaps, on such a damp and chilly evening, Cassandra Lucton's charms held more allure than dinner with Simon Fiddler. If that was the case Grayson couldn't blame him.

As the puzzled invitees made out friends and acquaintances, their comments and speculations rose. Simon Fiddler's residence was one of the finest in the city, and the new hotel that he'd designed and bankrolled was almost ready to open; it seemed strange to most of the invitees that he would instead invite his distinguished guests to a warehouse along the waterfront.

"What the devil is the meaning of this?" Judge Milvern asked. He was affronted at being invited on this fool's errand, and then left outside in the fog. He pulled at his white goatee. "I've a mind to get back into my carriage on the instant."

"It's one of Simon's jokes, Judge," a prominent landowner replied. "Our host prides himself on his unusual dinner parties. I'm sure he has something unique in store for us."

Judge Milvern wasn't mollified. "All I've got to say is that Fiddler has a very peculiar sense of humor. I don't like it."

"Stick around. He had harem dancers at a party in Paris, so I've heard tell. I've always wanted to see a real harem girl."

"Goddammit," Seamus Rooney said irritably, "how long is he going to keep us waiting out here?" His big jaw thrust out as it had years before when he'd been in the ring. Seamus Rooney was not used to kicking his heels at others' pleasure. He broke off his complaint at a sound from within.

A gong had been struck somewhere in the depths of the warehouse. Its echoes rang through the creeping fog, deep and hollow. On cue the massive doors were pulled open. The blue smoke of incense mingled with the tendrils of fog and Simon Fiddler appeared in the midst, like a djinn. Over his evening clothes he wore a Chinese gown of embroidered silk, and his eyes shone with wicked amusement. "Welcome, all my friends," he said softly. "Welcome to the Forbidden City."

Grayson's instincts warned him to be on the alert. As he followed Simon inside the huge doors, his heartbeat was strong and true, like the rhythm of a war chant, and his blood began to sing. The others were right behind, more curious that surprised.

Initially the entrance to the warehouse was black as the maw of a cavern. Someone tripped and stifled an oath in the gloom. When they entered strings of paper lanterns were lit, splashing color and illuminating an exotic scene. Banners of silk hung from the rafters and thick rugs, woven in elaborate patterns, covered the floor. From an unseen source at the far end of the building, music came, sweet and seductive. A wizened man in a mandarin's robe appeared and led them through a maze of banners and screens of bamboo or lacquer inlaid with mother-of-pearl and semiprecious stones.

They followed the music slowly toward the back of the building, winding through paths formed by the panels. In angles and corners there were ornate tables, chests, and breakfronts of teak and ebony. Lengths of opulent fabric were draped artfully, displaying priceless porcelains and statuary, temple jars, bowls, and bottles carved from amethyst and opal and every color of jade, and boxes of aromatic wood banded with gold and jewels.

A beefy magistrate ran his eyes lovingly over a T'ang horse and Judge Milvern oohed aloud at a life-size hare carved from mutton-fat jade. Seamus Rooney ignored the beautiful objects. They were not the treasures he sought most avidly.

Grayson looked overhead, where the rafters were lost in gloom. More rugs were rolled and stacked on pallets above, next to dump boxes filled with sand in case of fire. With a fortune worthy of a king in his main warehouse, Simon Fiddler was taking no chances.

As they moved through, Simon appeared before them once more. The gong sounded again and dinner was announced. The doors to the next section rolled back to reveal a long table with twenty-one intricately carved chairs. Silver and gold glimmered among the crystal glasses, mirroring the fire of myriad candles. On a small dais in one corner, a string quartet played chamber music. Otherwise the room was bare.

Puzzled, the guests took their assigned places and partook of an excellent meal; but they had come to expect far more than good food and drink from Simon Fiddler. Where, their slanted looks said to one another, is the surprise? Where is the joke in this elaborate plan?

By the time the tablecloth was removed and the port was passed around, they had silently agreed that this time the joke was on them. Simon was known for the unexpected, and this certainly filled the bill. A sense of disappointment stirred through the group. And as the unspoken thought spread, Simon pushed back his chair. He had tired of watching their faces, reading their glances. Slowly he surveyed the table. A pack of fools. With, he amended, one or two exceptions. He rose and the conversation ceased.

"I won't offer you cards or gaming tonight, my friends. Instead I have other entertainment in mind. If you'll come with me . . ."

Intrigued and mystified, they followed as he led them forward in the darkness, holding a branch of candles aloft. Suddenly he stopped. Other tapers were lit by servants and behind him shimmered cloth of gold, as wide and as high as the eye could see. The air was thick with a sickly sweet fragrance. Simon set the candelabra down and addressed the assemblage:

"Five years ago I came to this city a mere stranger. Now, due not only to my own efforts, but to your friendship and support, I've made a place for myself here, both socially and in your circles of commerce as well."

He made a sweeping bow to his guests. "Tonight, I am celebrating the completion of construction on my new hotel. And to commemorate the occasion, I've a parting gift for each of you. A token of my great esteem. You may each choose any treasure from this place for your own. Anything at all, from the smallest snuff jar to the largest inlaid cabinet. Or . . ."

The gong sounded and the cloth of gold parted like the curtains of an opera house. "Or," Simon continued, "you may choose from one of these lovely works of art."

The whisperings and comments ceased abruptly. Lamps of pierced brass cast golden pools of light inside a mammoth barred cage. There were banks of colorful cushions and long, low couches along the sides, like those in the opium houses. And on each one lay a young woman, seemingly asleep. The missing brides that Madame Wu had brought to San Francisco—and, Grayson surmised, the seamstress and scullery maid who'd vanished within the past few days. The women were gowned in loosely wrapped silk robes, which left little to their observers' imaginations. One woman struggled up weakly, only to fall back again.

Grayson saw the despair in her eyes and swore viciously beneath his breath. Drugged, and still terrified. Egon Pierce glanced back over his shoulder but the attention of the other men was fixed upon the captives.

Simon strolled to one woman and tugged at her robe. It fell away, exposing a slim ivory body, newly ripened into womanhood. There was a stirring from the group, although no one spoke. Someone whimpered.

Their host turned back to the men. "Some of you will, no doubt, make your selections here. Others— Phelps and Appleby, I'm sure—would prefer to choose from among the furnishings and bibelots."

"You say that you are giving these women to us? Just what," Judge Milvern said shortly, "do you expect us to do with them?"

Simon smiled silkily. "Anything you wish, gentlemen. *Anything* you wish. There are rooms upstairs for those of you who are rather more modest; but for the rest of us . . ."

He signaled and two men in his livery went from couch to couch, unlocking the shackles that restrained the girls. Grayson couldn't decide if they were too drugged or too frightened to react. He stepped into the shadows and yanked hard on a length of rope depending from the ceiling. Somewhere outside a bell rang, but its sound was lost in the laughter and cries inside the warehouse.

Seamus Rooney began peeling off his coat. Jerold Giddings moved forward, his face darkening with primitive lust. He passed the first two couches and stopped by the third. "This one. I'll take this one."

He bent over the girl and tried to tear her robe free, then uttered a cry of outraged pain when she bit his hand. He slapped her so hard her head hit the bars of the cage and she was knocked unconscious. Giddings didn't stop. His clothes were half off and he threw himself upon her. The smell of burning oil drifted through and moments later the air was filled with thick, roiling smoke, as black as tar. Simultaneously the doors closed to seal off their portion of the warehouse where the girls had been kept prisoners.

A servant in Simon's livery came through from the back. "Fire! The whole front of the warehouse is on fire! Get out or you'll go up with it!"

Simon shouted something, but his voice was drowned out by shouts of panic. The smoke grew thicker and he vanished into it. Some coughed. Others cursed. From all sides, voices picked up the warning cry: "Fire! *Fire!*"

The drugged girls were no longer of primary interest as the men pushed their way through toward the back of the building. "This way," a loud voice called. Laborers with dampened cloths over their noses came through the back and led the terrified men out to safety. Grayson joined Ling Cheung and his men who were disguised as coolie dockworkers. They moved through the maze of aisles they had made with crates earlier, leading or carrying the captives toward the front doors where the wagon was waiting. They'd have the girls far and away before anyone noticed they were missing.

Closed wagons awaited, the cloaked drivers and dark horses looking ghostly in the thickening fog. "Out. Hurry! We'll meet at the appointed place."

Grayson lit a torch and threw it deep inside the warehouse, into a pile of carpets. They'd make a lot of smoke but they wouldn't burn well, and once the dump boxes were opened they'd quench the flames. Ling Cheung set a small pile of oil-soaked rags aflame outside the door. There had to be a real fire to cover the escape of the women, or Simon Fiddler would turn the town upside down. If he knew, if he even guessed, Ling Cheung and Madame Wu would not live long.

While shouts of "fire" still carried on the air, Ling

Cheung ran for the carriages. One of the girls was lying on her side and light from the lanterns pooled on her features. Ling Cheung rubbed his eyes. Unbelievable. He knew now why Annette Mason hadn't returned to meet with Grayson—she'd been abducted by Simon Fiddler's henchmen, possibly as she was on her way to the joss shop. Ling Cheung offered up a prayer of thanksgiving. Truly the ways of Heaven were strange.

The wagons pulled away with their drugged cargo. The hooves of the team were well muffled, and their faint clop and the creak of the wagons wheels were soon lost in the fog. Grayson went back inside the warehouse where the fire burned brightly, creating a quantity of choking black smoke. Bales of exotic silks ignited with whooshing noises, and exploding glass tinkled against the beams. The fire was spreading.

He unwound one of the lines that kept the dump boxes upright and let it free. The box swung down, empty. Grayson tried the next, with the same result. There was a distinct smell of kerosene. The side of a wooden crate marked "Jade Carvings" fell away. Inside there was nothing but straw and stones. The heat ignited the straw and Grayson pushed his way past it toward the back door.

As he was dodging past the cage he saw a new area of flame shoot up near the wall. Something was wrong. The odor of kerosene was stronger. He heard a man scream. Jerold Giddings stumbled through the smoke. He was drunk and had lost his bearings. "Help! Help me!" he cried, clawing at the golden hangings. "Oh, God! We're going to die!"

"Not that way. Follow me!" Grayson tried to herd Giddings toward the back of the warehouse, but the man was beyond reasoning. He tried to dodge past

Grayson, thinking safety lay in the opposite direction. Grayson tackled him and they went sprawling across the floor. A broken violin lay smashed up against a chair. Suddenly Giddings jerked away, knocking one of the brass lamps against the gold curtain. Flames shot out, then ran up the curtain in greedy streaks, like fiery caterpillars eating their way up a crumbling yellow leaf. They turned the gold to brown, then to a dusty, bitter black. The satin curtain shimmered and swayed from the breeze of its own burning. Flakes of light broke from it, showering down on everything.

A roar went up, as if of shouting voices, but it was only the fire from the front, leaping the gap as new air reached it. Giddings fought like a wild thing. Grayson had no choice. He pulled back his fist, delivering a solid blow to the other man's jaw. He went limp and Grayson beat out the flames with his hands.

The coat was saved but the warehouse was fast becoming an inferno. Crashes, booms, and dull thuds echoed from all directions. Voices carried in the heated air. "It's the fire brigade."

"Hurry! There's folks inside!"

"Man the hoses!"

The bright flames were obliterated by the thick smoke and Grayson couldn't see a foot past his face. The atmosphere in the warehouse was thick and black as carbon. Something fell, grazing Grayson's temple. He staggered up, pulling Giddings after him. "Over here!"

He heard Judge Milvern shout. A section of roof fell, trapping Grayson on the other side. Dodging around, he searched for a path to safety. The smoke was clogging his lungs, sucking the breath from him. Coughing wracked his body and his eyes watered fiercely. Then he saw it—a pale gray rectangle near the floor that marked the doorway. He pushed around a barrel and was half-way there when something came whistling down out of the dark. He tried to throw himself out of the way.

Too late. Fire exploded in his head as he pitched forward. Then there was nothing but darkness and utter silence.

The sun rose too early for Cassandra the next morning. She'd lain awake, remembering the morning of her birthday, and her image caught in the golden cage of light. She had longed for change, and it had come. Disastrously.

Her comfortable world had been shaken up and turned on end, like a glass water globe filled with swirling bits of tinsel. She sat up and hugged her knees beneath the satin coverlet. Would her world . . . *could* her world and Kitty's ever be righted again?

Cassandra got up and opened the draperies. Outside the sun was bright, the gardens in bloom, the colors sharp and vivid. Everything was very much alive. Inside this house there were only shadows. False images of a falser life, where nothing and no one were as they seemed. Inside herself there seemed to be nothing at all.

She couldn't feel, she couldn't think. But she should be thinking, and hard, for something kept nagging around the edges of her mind. Nebulous ideas that she refused to let take form, for they were dark and frightening. There was no time to face them. Tonight her house would be thronged with the cream of San Francisco society.

After dressing she went to check on Kitty. Povey was asleep on the truckle bed. Kitty had her eyes closed, pretending to be asleep, too, but Cassandra knew she was awake. If I'd watched her more carefully this would never have happened, Cassandra thought. But oh! Didn't she know that I would never have forced her into a distasteful marriage? Didn't she realize how much I love her? Oh, Kitty. I would give my life to have spared you this.

Cassandra pressed a kiss on Kitty's cheek. "I love you, darling," she murmured.

There was so much more that she wanted to say, but it seemed that Kitty wasn't ready to hear it. She went out and closed the door softly.

Kitty snuffled away the tears she'd been trying so hard to hide. Cassandra still loved her, despite everything. Somehow that made it all the harder to bear. She was choking in guilt.

Her own silly notions of love and her willfulness had caused pain and misery to those she most loved. Povey had always been Povey—a doting and unchanging presence. But during the long morning hours, while her aunt's maid dozed in the chair, Kitty had looked at her. Really looked at her. When had Povey grown so old and thin and frail? Had it happened so gradually that she hadn't noticed—or had it occurred all at once when she'd stumbled in from the woods, bruised and bleeding, and collapsed in Povey's arms.

And Uncle Tyler—when he'd looked in on her yesterday he hadn't uttered a single word. His face had said it all.

Worst of all was seeing what she'd done to Cassandra. Her aunt had always seemed serene and poised like a beautiful fairy-tale princess. Now her green eyes were haunted and dark with emotion. Kitty kept her lids together tightly, but a single tear squeezed out. Everything had changed because of her. She'd ruined her own life, and theirs as well.

She turned her cheek against the pillow and wept, quietly and hopelessly.

After breakfast Cassandra was accosted by Mrs. Llewellyn. The housekeeper was in a terrible dither. "Oh, madam! Richards went down to Pennynton's yesterday to get a new punch bowl and brought it back all wrapped and boxed. I've just unpacked it, and I don't know what to do."

"Did they send the wrong item?"

"Oh, no! A beautiful thing it would be—if not for the crack running right through the middle. Richards swears he never dropped it. I sent him right back to Pennynton's." The housekeeper's face crumpled with woe. "But there's not another one to be had anywhere."

Cassandra had more things to worry about than cracked punch bowls. If necessary she could borrow one, but she remembered that there was one she had never used since coming to San Francisco. It was old-fashioned in style but would certainly do.

"I believe I have another which would be suitable. I'll look it up in the household inventory book."

Her words worked like magic, and the housekeeper beamed. "Another punch bowl! And to think that Morton never mentioned it!" Reassured, and armed with more ammunition in the ongoing battle for supremacy between Morton and herself, Mrs. Llewellyn marched off to beard him in the butler's pantry.

Ordinarily Tyler removed items from the vault but Cassandra knew how to get into it. That seemed the most likely place to keep the punch bowl, which was more valuable as an antique than for the gold and silver from which it was made.

After conferring with a harried caterer's assistant, Cassandra headed for Tyler's study to get the inventory list. Something was still wrong, nagging at the edges of her mind like the ringing of discordant bells. She was so lost in thought she went right past the door and had to double back.

As she entered the study, closing the door behind her, Cassandra realized what it was. The house was filled with smaller items of silver and gold, which would have been far easier for Jake to carry off and sell. Why had he taken such heavy, bulky items as the punch bowl and the Georgian plate? It was very strange, to be sure.

She unlocked the side drawer of the polished mahogany desk where Tyler kept his father's hair-trigger dueling pistols. The inventory book was kept in its own leather-bound volume beneath them, along with a metal box that held papers and some ready cash. The pistols were kept unloaded but she hated to touch even so much as their case. Dilbert Lucton had killed seven men with them.

Shifting them aside, she rummaged for the inventory book without success. Then she remembered that Tyler had had it out earlier. Perhaps he'd left it in the hidden safe when he'd gotten the silver place settings out for Morton. She locked the study door before going to the bookcase and twisting one of the carved bosses on the molding. The next section slid forward and away, revealing a large steel vault built into the wall.

It was higher than her head and when she opened it the steel-lined interior ran back for twelve feet. It was almost as wide. Cassandra had always hated entering it. It reminded her of the Fayne mausoleum in St. Stephen's churchyard. She half expected to see coffins stacked along the walls.

The shelves were crowded although the silver chest and the gold serving platters had already been removed. On the left she spotted the velvet case that held the Fayne Rubies and a large strongbox. Her eyes were unused to the darkness as she went deeper into the vault, and she didn't make out the solid gold candelabra and the twelve matching plates swathed in dark gray cloth. Instead she caught the glint and glimmer of silver where none should be. Those same jangling bells she'd heard earlier sounded a warning in her head.

Cassandra turned slowly toward the silvery gleam. Someone had moved the gold pieces. Crowded in beside them were five pieces of incomparable Georgian silver plate—and the priceless Charles II punch bowl.

She reached her hand out and touched them to convince herself they were real. In the chill air of the vault the sterling felt cold but no colder than the icy blood congealing in her veins.

Cassandra turned and fled the strongroom, slamming the door shut as if to seal off the demons of knowledge that assailed her. The bookcase slid into place with a groan and a whisper. Dazed, she stumbled across the room to the desk and eased herself into the chair. She was trembling violently.

Jake had had nothing to do with this: the only person who could have put the "missing" silver into the vault was Tyler. He must have slipped downstairs sometime during the night, taken the silver from the locked cupboard in the butler's pantry with his own set of keys, and hidden it in the vault. Then he had led them all to think that Jake had stolen the silver.

Her husband had acted out an elaborate lie. But why?

Because, a still small voice said, the truth of what Jake had done could not be told without destroying Kitty. A pair of diamond earrings could be misplaced and mistakenly thought stolen; but the large sterling pieces were another matter. Therefore, if Jake could not be branded the rapist that he was, he could at least be branded as a thief.

Again that question came unbidden: Why?

She unlocked the side drawer again and slid it open. The leather of the pistol case was dark as spilled blood. She willed her hands not to shake and carefully opened the case. The pistols were nested neatly inside. Cassandra had grown up around guns and knew more about them than Tyler imagined.

She lifted one gingerly, checking to make sure that it was unloaded, and sniffed the barrel. It hadn't been fired since the last time her husband had cleaned it. Hope suffused her. Cassandra took up the second one and repeated her actions. An acrid odor stung her nostrils. There was no doubt that it had been fired recently.

Very recently.

Cassandra put them back exactly as she'd found them and relocked the drawer. She felt physically ill. The room tipped and reeled. She bent down and leaned her face against the leather pad, so sick she thought she might vomit.

She didn't know how long she stayed like that. It was the chiming of the case clock in the hall that roused her from her stupor. Twelve o'clock. Time to spell Povey for a few hours. Cassandra rose and checked herself in the small mirror that hung beside the door. Every hair was in place. She looked exactly the same as she had when she'd entered the room. How could that be, when what she'd found in Tyler's drawer had changed her so completely?

She went out and up to Kitty's room like a sleepwalker. She would take care of Kitty now and think later. It was the only way she could survive the dreadful hours until Tyler returned home.

Povey came toward her, speaking in a papery whisper. "Jenny just brought up a tray. She said that Jake Adams is dead. Found washed up along the wharf yesterday morning, and half eaten by the fishes. Slipped and bumped his head, so they say."

She folded her hands primly. "'Tis like in the Old Testament: Young Jake was evil through and through. He sinned and he was destroyed by the hand of God."

Cassandra looked away. She couldn't meet Povey's eyes.

The hand that had destroyed Jake did not belong to God, she was quite certain, but to Tyler Lucton.

8

Ling Cheung sat in the joss shop staring at the plum blossom painting on silk that hung in Madame Wu's shop. His eyes were bleary from a sleepless night and the smoke of the warehouse fires. Suddenly Madame Wu came out of the back room. He rose and hurried toward her. He was afraid to speak.

The old lady smiled. "The maids from your village will all recover from the smoke and soot with a little medicine and a good deal of soap and water. They are otherwise untouched."

He understood her meaning. The girls of his village had suffered a terrible fright but they were unharmed and still virgins. It was far more than he had hoped for. Madame Wu would deliver the promised brides, the young maids would find suitable homes with their contracted husbands—especially the one who was to be his own wife. Ling Cheung would make up to her for the horror she had faced in coming to this new land.

"The gods are merciful," he said humbly. Now if he would only hear from Grayson, he could rest. He was increasingly worried. He had followed directions in bringing the maids to Madame Wu, even though he had not wanted to leave until he knew his friend was safe. They were to meet here afterward but Grayson had never shown up. Ling Cheung rubbed his eyes with his forearm. Surely Grayson would have sent word by now. Something was very wrong.

"And the other one?" he asked, remembering the Caucasian girl he'd rescued with them.

"She has not awakened from the medicine given to her. I do not think she has sustained any injury. What are we to do with her when she awakens?"

"Keep her here for now, if you please." He drank his tea down. "I shall see if I can find my friend. Meanwhile, if he should arrive, tell him I shall return within the hour."

Ling Cheung started out for the Dillon Hotel but was saved a trip when he came across Jaime McFee outside an imposing bank building, escorted by a distinguished-looking man who was beaming jovially. "It is a pleasure to do business with you, Mr. McFee."

Jaime joined Ling Cheung, shaking his head in wonder. "Ten years ago fellows like that wouldn't have even let me inside their banks. Now they fall all over and call me Mr. McFee!"

He grew agitated when he learned that Grayson had failed to keep his meeting with Ling Cheung. "He never came back to the hotel last night, but then Grayson told me he might be away for a few days. I don't like this one bit! I'll check his usual haunts."

"I will go down to the warehouse area."

"Christ! You don't think—"

"I am afraid to think," Ling Cheung replied softly. A short time later he was on the waterfront with a gang of laborers. The destruction was unbelievable. The fire had spread farther than he'd guessed. Nothing was left except burnt timbers and blackened metal scaffolds, twisted by the enormous heat. Twelve buildings were reduced to warm ashes and the air reeked of smoke.

He found the remains of Simon Fiddler's warehouse. In some places the debris was seven feet high, composed of ruined goods and portions of fallen walls and roofs. He recognized Tyler Lucton sitting in his fine carriage, staring out at the devastation. Ling Cheung picked his way through to what had been the back of the building. An oak desk leaned drunkenly among the rubble, half of it burned away before the flames were extinguished. The breeze played with the pages of a book that looked like a rectangular, black cinder. The paper peeled away in wisps of ash. He was surprised to see undamaged pages of text beneath it.

He called to his crew. "You will start here and work back and sideways toward that gap. Most carefully, if you please."

They began lifting aside the sections of collapsed wall. Glass tinkled beneath their booted feet. By midday they had combed through a quarter of it without finding anything more valuable than a melted brass inkstand and small tarnished black lumps that had once been silver forks and spoons. It was very strange.

A shout went up from one of the crew, an Irish fellow who had joined them on a lark. But the men had only found some intact bottles of spirits underneath a pile of sodden carpets. Then O'Malley called out to him. Ling

Cheung hurried through the slippery mass of water-soaked ash. "Jaysus, Mary, and Joseph," the Irishman said, "will you take a gander at that!"

Ling Cheung knelt down. A soot-covered hand protruded from beneath a fallen cabinet. He peered into the space where the piece of furniture had wedged itself against the wall. Grayson was lying on his side amid the debris. "Over here!" Ling Cheung cried.

The rest came running. They had to be careful in lifting the cabinet away so it wouldn't fall on Grayson. It was a slow, nerve-wracking task but it was finally accomplished. They pulled him from the wreckage. He didn't move and his face was pale as death.

"Mother of God!" O'Malley said. Then he crossed himself slowly and whispered the prayer for the dead.

Preparations for the Luctons' ball were in full swing at Stoneleigh, despite Tyler's continued absence. He'd sent her a note that he would be detained until evening. Povey was shocked by her mistress's appearance. There were taut lines of strain and darkening circles beneath Cassandra's eyes. Suddenly she felt like a young nursemaid again, scolding the six-year-old girl that Cassandra had been when first Povey had gone into service at the Castle.

"You must rest, madam. A glance from you would break a mirror."

Cassandra laughed shortly. "Yes, I know. I look like something cast up by the sea." Povey straightened up from placing a cloth wrung out in lavender water over Kitty's forehead. Dear Povey. The one blessed constant in a world that was rapidly disintegrating.

Kitty gave her a wan smile. "Yes, do. I'm quite all

right." Cassandra reluctantly retired to her chamber. She didn't want to be alone, yet she must be ready for the ordeal to come. It would be difficult to hold her head high and carry out her hostess duties in the usual manner. To look beautiful, dance gracefully, and carry on light conversation until the small hours of the night. To do it all while Kitty lay upstairs, her dreams and innocence shattered.

To smile at Tyler and play the hostess to his gracious host, wondering—knowing in her heart of hearts—that he'd killed Jake.

She didn't think she could bear to have Tyler touch her ever again. Yet, wasn't that hypocritical? She'd wanted to kill with her bare hands the man who'd raped her niece. And she was still glad that Jake was dead and Kitty was safe from him forevermore.

Dear God, take me back to yesterday. Let me start all over again, she thought. But nothing changed. Cassandra pulled the curtains and stretched out on her daybed. Her body was tense as a coiled spring. The strain was taking its toll. For the first time she began to doubt her ability to pull it off. Hiding it from acquaintances might be easy enough, but could she escape the shrewd eyes of Mae Belle Lorenz? Or worse, of Grayson Howard?

Perhaps a glass of Tyler's brandy might help. The decanter wasn't in his dressing room but she found it on the marquetry table beside his armchair. Dust motes danced in the late afternoon sun but the fire was unlit and she found the room chilly. Cassandra felt as if she'd never be warm again.

She splashed enough into the glass to fill it halfway. The brandy glowed inside the glass like old gold, and went down like silk. She took another swallow and felt the fire of it chase away the numbing cold. She'd finished it before she realized it, and poured another. Within a short time of drinking it down her cares seemed to be gradually slipping away. She returned to her room and fell into a light and dreamless sleep.

In the late afternoon Cassandra had another meeting with the frenzied caterer in the yellow sitting room. Juno looked up eagerly from her place on the hearth rug. Her eyes and ears were failing but her nose was still acute. When she realized that neither of the intruders was her beloved master, she settled her muzzle on her outstretched paws and went back to sleep.

The caterer had just departed when Morton entered and coughed discreetly. "These just arrived, madam. Delivered by hand."

She thanked the butler and waited until he withdrew before breaking the seal on the first note. The narrow upright lettering belonged to Bernice Godwin. Mr. and Mrs. Leslie Godwin regretted that a sudden indisposition had made it impossible for them to accept Mr. and Mrs. Tyler Lucton's invitation to their ball.

Cassandra set it aside. It was inevitable that a few people, out of the three hundred invited, would be unable to attend. The second was from Mrs. Perry, who also pleaded indisposition. In the next half hour more notes arrived. Mrs. Merrivale and her sister, Miss Howington, deeply regretted that they would be unable to attend due to illness in the family. Colonel Richmond had been suddenly called away on duty, and Mr. John Trowbridge had been unexpectedly summoned to the bedside of his ailing uncle.

As she finished the last missive, Morton appeared with another. General Morgan Dutton, that fearless veteran of the Battle of Glorieta Pass, had been felled by a painful attack of gout. Butterflies danced in Cassandra's stomach. She had never had so many guests cancel their acceptances before.

The last note was from Alfred Lorenz, written in his narrow, sloping hand. He sent regrets on behalf of his wife and himself. Mrs. Lorenz had been stricken with a severe case of quinsy following their reception. On doctor's orders, he was taking his wife to their estate in southern California where she could recuperate in the warmer and more salubrious air. There was nothing more. No polite wishes that the ball would be imminently successful. No mention of calling upon the Luctons when Alfred and Mae Belle eventually returned to the city.

Cassandra stared at the bold signature. Mae Belle always boasted that she had never been ill a day in her life. Had Alfred written this note with his wife's collusion, or against her protests?

Dear God, had word of Kitty's shame spread already despite their precautions? It was an axiom that no family secret was ever kept long from that household's servants. Although Stoneleigh's location kept it more isolated than the mansions of Nob and Russian Hills, news could conceivably travel back and forth with a speed that defied logic. Already today there had been a number of delivery men and the caterers and extra help had been hired on to assist the household staff. There must be twenty serving people brought in for the occasion; yet Cassandra couldn't think of any way rumors might have leaked.

The only people who knew of Kitty's tragic plight were Tyler, Povey, and herself. And Jake Adams, of course. But he was dead. Another idea struck her. Could someone have discovered that Jake had been shot—and that Tyler had done it? *Murder*. The word echoed in her head. Her husband was a murderer.

No, a cynical little voice said, the Godwins, the Mrs. Merrivales, and the Alfred Lorenzes of the world would not condemn Tyler for it. Not because Jake deserved to die for his foul deed, but because he was a member of the common class. Bribes were paid and such things were hushed up. It was a conspiracy of wealth and power compounded by silence. By arrogance so sublime it made its own laws and broke them at will.

Cassandra tried to shake off her alarming fantasies. Her imagination was running away with her. It was absurd to be upset by a handful of written regrets. Coincidences did happen. Rising briskly, she continued her tour of the house as if her only cares were those of a well-bred hostess.

The silver and brass shone to perfection, the windows sparkled, and every sconce was filled with new beeswax tapers. The hothouse flowers, from the great sprays of golden lilies, blue delphinium, and emerald ivy in the foyer, to the cascades of pink and yellow tea roses massed with ferns, white delphinium, and purple salvia in the ballroom, might have come from the gardens of Paradise.

The Venetian chandelier sent darts of light across the polished floor and the gilt chairs and divans, upholstered in pink silk, were arranged exactly so around the sides of the long room. Reflected back from the long gilded mirrors between each pair of windows, it was all breathtaking. Stoneleigh had never looked more beautiful.

The musicians had just arrived and one of the footmen was leading them to the dais at the far end of the ballroom. There was nothing for Cassandra to do except look in on Kitty and ready herself for the ball. Along with her magnificent gown and the Fayne Rubies, she would don her bright social armor. Safe behind its polished facade, she would smile at Tyler and his guests, as if Jake Adams had not been murdered, as if Kitty were not lying wan and listless in her darkened room.

She went up to dress as the florist's men added the final touches. When she came down an hour later the ballroom was perfect, every detail just as it should be. The banks of flowers perfumed the air with a light, spicy scent. The light of the beeswax candles shone on the polished dance floor, unmarred by the slightest scuff. The immense chandelier with its sparkling prisms reflected in the mirrors into infinity.

The musicians glanced at her and away. Their conductor steeled his courage and approached her for instructions. "Perhaps I mistook the hour, Mrs. Lucton. When would you like us to begin?"

The case clock in the hall struck the quarter hour. Cassandra kept her head high. "You have not mistaken the time, Mr. Vincinelli. You may start the music now, if you please. Something gay and lilting."

He made her his deepest bow, and went back to the dais. The waltz began and Cassandra took up her post at the head of the staircase, to Strauss's "Tales from the Vienna Woods." Tables of refreshments were set up in the white salon with wine punch and chilled champagne, iced cakes and other delicacies. The kitchens were as full as they could hold of lobster and shrimp, sirloin of beef and succulent ham for the late supper that would never be served. Dozens of servants stood at the ready, to wait on guests who would never arrive.

Cassandra was still standing there, back as straight as

an arrow, when the clock tolled the passing of the hour, as if, at any moment, colorful throngs of people would ascend it with smiles and warm greetings.

Morton stood below in the entrance hall, three footmen at attention beside him. The youngest was starting to fidget. The butler quelled him with a single superior glance. Cassandra didn't know how much longer she could keep up her pose. Tyler had wanted this ball to create a sensation. His wish had been granted. They would be, but certainly not in a way that either of them had anticipated. Wild thoughts of returning to England or of emigrating to New Zealand or Australia flew through Cassandra's head. They must go somewhere, anywhere, where Kitty could start afresh and build a life untainted by the past.

She waited alone at the foot of the staircase, head high and cheeks pale, until it was definite that not a single guest would come. Cassandra dismissed the servants, thanking them quietly. Then she turned in a rustle of silk and ascended the stairs, like a condemned woman mounting the scaffold.

A wild storm reached Stoneleigh that evening and although the downpour stopped near midnight, the wind raged unchecked. It clawed at the treetops, snapping branches and battering the windowpanes until they rattled in their frames. Cassandra, in a rose silk peignoir, sat stiffly upon the carved chaise in her room listening not to the storm but to the thoughts echoing down the lonely corridors of her mind. She felt like a discarded shell. Sea-tossed. Empty.

Her orderly existence had shattered like a glass ball and she could make no sense of the scattered shards.

Kitty was drifting in poppy dreams and Tyler had neither returned from town nor sent a message. Pulling a shawl around her shoulders, Cassandra rose and crossed to her dressing room to check on her niece. A single candle burned upon a side table, shaded by a portable screen. She tiptoed in. "How is she?"

Povey looked up from her vigil. She had aged ten years since morning. "She was fretful a while back and I gave her another dose."

Cassandra's face was a white flower in the dimness. "Shall I send for the doctor?"

"No need for that, madam. She's young and strong. Best to let nature do the healing." And keep tongues from wagging.

"I'll sit with her awhile. You must rest sometime, Povey."

"I can't, my lady, nor do I want to." She shifted her bony frame in the hard chair she had chosen to keep herself awake. The wind howled and whistled angrily. A gust rattled the windowpanes. "The Wild Huntsman is out tonight," she said, almost to herself.

Cassandra shivered, remembering Povey's old North Country tales of the ghostly Huntsman and his fiery-eyed hounds, whose appearance presaged death and disaster. But this was California, she reminded herself, where the Yorkshire ghosts and goblins held no sway.

She found herself too restless to sit quietly now, and left the dressing room so her fidgeting would not disturb Kitty. Shortly after two the squall blew itself out with the abruptness of a quenched flame. Suddenly she was able to distinguish a faint sound in the distance. Cassandra hurried to the window and peered out.

Darkness pressed in at the window with velvet hands. Then the cloud bank shifted and the vista was filled with cold gray light from the crescent moon trapped by the limbs of an ancient oak. Lights flickered, vanished, and reappeared along the sweeping drive, but Cassandra could not tell if they were will-o'-the-wisps or the lanterns of Tyler's coach. Or, remembering Povey's comment, the glowing eyes of the Wild Huntsman's fearsome pack.

She dismissed the chilling fantasy and went out into the hallway, then down the stairs to the second landing, where she could see and not be seen. It was airless and humid there, and the great house creaked around her like an old man's bones. Her hands and feet felt cold and clumsy, mere lumps of ice.

Down in the hall the candles burned low in their sockets and Morton dozed on the brocade cushions of a black oak settle. He had been instructed to retire for the night and could have left one of the footmen in his place, but a strong sense of duty kept him at his post. In his Bible it was not fitting that the master of the house should end his homeward journey without a suitable welcome. Especially on such a night.

Cassandra heard the jingle of harness and the clatter of hooves in the cobbled courtyard. Morton stirred, yawned, and went to open the door, donning his usual unflappable facade as he flung the heavy door open wide. Tyler strode in, the capes of his driving coat spattering water upon the marble floor. Cassandra let out the breath she hadn't known she was holding.

A shadow moved from beneath the oak settle and Juno came snuffling out. Ears brushing the floor, the old dog made unsteadily for her master, uttering soft yips of joy. He hardly noticed her and greeted Morton, his manner more curt than usual. Relinquishing his coat and hat to the butler Tyler headed not for the stairway but toward the side corridor leading to his study.

After a moment Cassandra followed him. Except for a tall stand of candles at the far end, the corridor was in shadow and there was no sign of her husband. Cassandra stopped at the open study door. It was dark, the two windows at the far end luminous rectangles in the gloom. She started to retreat, thinking he had gone into another room, when she heard his chair scrape back from the desk and the sound of a drawer opening. A match rasped against the scratch.

"Tyler?"

A point of light wavered, then spread into a yellow glow as he lit the desk lamp. It cast sharp shadows on his face, obscuring his eyes as he faced her from his chair behind the highly polished desk. "Up so late, my dear?"

"I've been waiting for you. Tyler—"

"Your concern touches me. Now that I am here, you may seek your pillow with a quiet conscience."

The sarcasm in his voice frightened her so that she forgot her carefully rehearsed words. Cassandra stepped closer, then halted abruptly. A long-barreled dueling pistol lay in the open drawer, nested in its open leather box like a snake in its den. It gleamed menacingly in the soft light. She was suddenly afraid. "What do you mean to do?"

Shifting aside the box, Tyler removed a sheaf of papers from beneath it. "I have business to finish tonight. Go to bed, Cassandra."

Relief bubbled up inside her. She could have laughed if not for what had happened to Kitty earlier. Tyler began sorting through the papers, ignoring her presence. She couldn't bring up Jake Adams and chose a less explosive topic. "I had expected you would offer me an explanation for your absence tonight. Are you aware of what happened? Every one of our guests sent their regrets. Even old Mr. Glenforth, who never misses a chance to dine out."

She leaned forward. "What has happened, Tyler? Why have we suddenly become lepers?"

"An apt expression, my dear." He sighed, a short impatient sound. "I am sorry for your embarrassment. But you are young and will soon get over it."

Cassandra felt she was walking on quicksand. The familiar ground was rocking beneath her feet while the man with whom she had lived intimately looked at her with the cold detachment of a stranger. She wanted to shake him. "For God's sake, Tyler, tell me!"

The dark head lifted, and while he gazed at her with opaque eyes, his voice was brutal. "It seems you have made a bad bargain after all, Cassandra. My investments have not prospered and the risks I took to save them were in vain. I am ruined."

"Ruined?"

"Destroyed, paupered, penniless! The Lucton Luck has turned against me. The *Lady Cassandra* lies at the bottom of the sea. Three other ships of my fleet are overdue and likely lost in the Pacific storms, as well. The banks have called my loans in. All my assets must be sold to satisfy my obligations."

"But . . . my jewels. We can sell them. Surely the Fayne Rubies are worth a fortune!"

"Your jewels are paste. All but the rings on your fingers. I had them copied and sold the stones to pay my debts." His voice was low now, almost disinterested. "Even if they were genuine, it would still be useless to sell them. Attempting to stem the floodtide of my losses would prove as futile as trying to drain the ocean with a sieve."

Cassandra couldn't believe him. This was some terrible jest. "You cannot be serious. Surely you shall come about again. We have connections, and with your business acumen—"

"The faithful wife." He cut her off ruthlessly. "Ready to throw her lot in with the penniless failure. How well bred of you. But you rub salt in my wounds, Cassandra. I did not expect you to react as you have. And I have not deserved such loyalty."

Juno stirred at his feet and whined softly. Tyler sat back, arms resting along the arms of the chair, like a marble statue of Judgment in repose. "Well, I absolve you of your loyalties and your vows.

"I have never been faithful to you, Cassandra. Perhaps you've guessed that. Whore and servant and great lady—I've had them all. Some of them under this very roof."

He paused with cruel deliberation. "One of them, your own late sister."

She was in shock, unable to move, scarcely able to take in his swift and deadly attack, the meaning of his words. "M-Margaret?"

"Ah, that stuns you out of your ice queen role. Yes, Margaret was my mistress, from before she married Hamilton to the day she died. I admired Hamilton. He was a most complacent husband. I must admit to feeling remorse when he was stricken with the fever in India while on business for me, although it did make things easier. It was unfortunate that when he came back he was a changed man."

"I don't believe you. Why are you saying such terrible lies?"

"For the first time in our marriage I am telling you the truth. You have such a civilized, bloodless nature, my dear. Margaret was filled with passion. Fire to your ice. It was Margaret I wanted to marry in the first place. Of course, you were only a schoolgirl then, and I had not made my fortune yet. Your father did not think me a good enough catch for a potential earl's daughter, and married her off to a wealthier suitor. He never expected to break his neck taking that fence, did he?"

"Why did you offer for me?"

He gave a curious little shrug. "It was Margaret who suggested it."

Cassandra clapped her hands to her ears. "Why are you saying this? I don't believe a word of it."

"Don't you? Then what will you say to this? Before Hamilton arrived at our townhouse, Margaret dashed off a note and asked you to send a footman with it to a house in Cadigan Square. I owned that house, and I was the man waiting for her. I'd convinced her to come away with me. I'd booked passage for us on the *Pride of Scotland*. But Hamilton was suspicious. He got to her before I did, and shot her to death before turning the gun on himself. And you know the rest."

Cassandra was frozen in place, unable to move or speak. How could she have been so blind, so foolish? Beautiful, charming Margaret, the older sister she had so adored, the mother of her beloved Kitty, had betrayed her with Tyler. She felt shriveled and dead inside.

Tyler watched the transformation with perverse satisfaction. "And now that I've told you this, I will tell you everything. Kitty—"

"No!" Cassandra flung her hands out to ward off any further soul-shattering revelations. "No more."

"Kitty," he went on implacably, "is more than just your niece. She is also my daughter."

He turned his chair at right angles to the massive desk.

Cassandra stared at him in shock. She could find nothing to say. Everything she had most valued, he had stripped from her: the warm memories of charming, bright-eyed Margaret, even her special relationship with Kitty. Lies and lies and more lies.

Whirling about she stumbled from the room, fleeing Tyler's harsh laughter and the bitter taste of the fruit of knowledge.

The sound of her footsteps echoed and died away and the house settled down to its usual nighttime stillness. Shortly after the case clock in the great hall struck three, one of the under parlor maids sleeping in the attic above the west wing was wakened by a sound. She lay listening a few moments, but heard nothing more over the gusting wind. The night was dark and a foretaste of autumn chilled the rain-soaked earth outside her gable window. A poacher in the woods, she thought, too groggy to realize no one would be out in such a windstorm, and fell back asleep.

Povey, dozing on the truckle bed set up in Kitty's dressing room, started at the noise. Thunder, she thought, and drifted back into her semislumber. Kitty, deep in a laudanum haze, heard nothing at all. Only Cassandra, lying curled atop the covers of her silk-hung bed, understood what it was.

A sharp pain passed through her temples, reverberating through her skull. A moment later a second shot followed the first. Long after the echo died she was still holding her breath.

Then she was running, running for the door and down the long stairway, running toward Tyler's study, and already knowing what she would find.

9

"Let the light of Thy mercy shine upon him, O Lord, and bring Thy humble servant, Tyler Emory Lucton, into the bosom of Heaven, and to Thy everlasting life . . ."

Cassandra listened without hearing, and the vicar's mumbled prayers became a turgid drone, like the hum of distant bees. Her heavy black veil blurred a landscape already half-obscured by inclement weather. An ill wind had come blowing out of the north. It had rained for three days and was drizzling still, as Tyler Lucton, the man she had been married to, but had never known, was laid to rest in the churchyard.

A fitful wind tore at her veil. She scarcely felt the cold raindrops against her face. All her senses were numb. She tried to concentrate on the ceremony but time and again her mind drifted away. The trodden grass and sodden leaves, the rows of slanting headstones, glistened coldly. The flowers of the funeral wreaths were so drenched they looked as if they had been dipped in glass. Cassandra stared over the heavy coffin at the line of trees beyond, until they were blurred by mist or the sheen of her own tears.

She pulled her veil closer and was alarmed to note that her hands were shaking. The loneliness of her position was terrible. In addition to herself, the clergyman, and his acolyte, the only others present were the upper servants and employees—Povey, Morton, and Mrs. Llewellyn. Picard, the estate steward. Josiah Craig, who represented the Lucton Lines' legal concerns, and bespectacled little Mr. McCauliffe, who was their personal solicitor.

Cassandra tried not to feel bitter. She had expected the comfort of friends. It seemed she had none.

She gazed at the smattering of mourners. Where were all of Tyler's cronies, the dazzling crowds who'd dined at their table and shared their opera box? And where were their wives and sisters and daughters, who had so eagerly sought the company of the Lucton family? They had fled at the first hint of scandal, vanishing from view like fog over the bay.

Cassandra tried to be charitable but could not. Their absence was a sign of their fears springing from Tyler's precipitous fall from grace, as if bankruptcy and suicide were contagious. Cowards, she thought, angrily wiping away a tear. Cowards and fools!

But not all her anger was for them. A great portion was for Tyler, who had left his wife and his own, unacknowledged daughter to deal with the aftermath. Leaving them to face the consequences of his actions, while he himself had escaped.

"Ashes to ashes, dust to dust . . ." The vicar sprinkled a few clods of earth over the heavy coffin, then wiped his hands, eager to be done with this affair. He had been reluctant to bury a suspected suicide in hallowed ground, and only Cassandra Lucton's oath that the death was accidental had overcome his deep-seated scruples.

She wondered what he would do if he knew there was another body in that solid wooden box. That Juno's cold form lay at her master's feet now, just as she had in life. The corners of Cassandra's mouth quivered in a tremulous smile, then turned down once more. Tyler had shown more concern for his dog than for her or for Kitty.

A cold wind snatched at her veil. She had never felt so alone and frightened, so small and insignificant before. But she must be brave, because the worst was still to come.

She focused on the vicar's head, fringed with tarnished silver hair, like old Christmas tinsel. It seemed wrong that so ancient a man had outlived her vigorous husband. An accident while cleaning a gun. Did anyone really believe that? She had always thought Tyler indestructible, a man with sufficient rashness to brazen out any challenge that life could offer. Yet pride had been the strongest aspect of his personality. Unable to face the prospect of his ruin, he had chosen his own way out.

Was there something she could have done—should have done that might have prevented this? Guilt mingled with her shock and confusion. It had hurt deeply to hear him say that she was cold. Icy. And all the while she was bursting with a life and passion that had found no outlet. If only. If only . . . The words beat like a drum inside her ears, and then she realized it was the wet clods falling with the dull thud of finality.

". . . through the mercy of God, rest in peace. Amen." It was over and the few mourners stirred uneasily, like a stand of dark trees shivering in the wind. Cassandra sighed. Now the task of picking up the pieces would begin. Perhaps, when all the debts and obligations were discharged, she might take Kitty away for a few months. Sunshine, a change of scene. A chance to forget or pretend to forget the nightmare of the past few days. It would do them both good. She would discuss the matter with Mr. McCauliffe after the official reading of the will.

Things could not be as bad as Tyler had said, but if necessary she would even sell off some land. A simple life would suit her, and Kitty could recover her spirits more easily away from the rigors of high society.

That thought sustained her through the cold collation that followed, and she was still turning it over in her mind when it came time for the reading of Tyler's will. Out of deference to the situation the reading of the will was held in the yellow salon rather than Tyler's study. A cheery fire in the grate helped dispel the gloom of the day. Morton had pulled the draperies shut to block out the sodden gray landscape, and set out decanters of imported sherry and fine old brandy. The solicitor had been detained at the churchyard, and Cassandra waited patiently.

She approached Kitty's portrait over the mantelpiece. Cassandra had bewildered the servants by having it changed with the one of herself and Margaret that had hung there before. She couldn't bear to look at her sister's likeness. The pain of it went too deep.

Kitty smiled down from the painting. The three years since it had been finished stretched out like strands of thin copper wire. At one end a happy child, eager and untouched by life—and at the other a frightened young woman, scarred forever by betrayal. Cassandra turned away and contemplated the leaping glow of the fire.

She and Kitty would go away somewhere. One of the islands, warm and sunny, with never a trace of cloud. Or they might return to England and find a small cottage in the countryside. A pleasant little hideaway beside a meandering stream, where she could tend to a garden rich with stocks and wallflowers and a knot garden of herbs. Her imagination embroidered the details.

Cassandra pictured herself with a garden shears in one hand, a basket of larkspur and early roses over her arm. The whisper of a light breeze through the trees and the sleepy hum of bees would come in counterpoint to the snick of the metal shears. One could lose oneself in a garden. From time to time she would look up and wave at Kitty, who would sit in the sunny bay window with a book on her lap, or on a comfortable wooden bench, in the shade of a sprawling tree.

Yes, she promised herself, there must definitely be a garden. And a serene, retired life, where no hint of gossip would destroy their peace. There would be a comfortable room for dear Povey, who was much too old and set in her ways to start anew. The three of them would sit before the fire together on wintry evenings and walk along the lanes in fine weather.

She took comfort in her plans. Now and then she would entertain the neighborhood squire and his wife, give small dinner parties for the local gentry, or go up to London for a whirl of the shops; but for the most part they would lead a cozy existence, content with hearth and garden and each other's company. Away from scandal and wagging tongues, and people who turned a friendly face one minute and a rigid back the next. Away from the whispers.

But the sound that disturbed her was not whispering. McCauliffe entered, wheezing his dry lawyer's wheeze and shattering her rose-colored fantasy. He bowed deeply, despite his age. "A sad day, my dear Cassandra. A very sad day."

For years he had harbored a secret admiration of her, shining like a beacon in the cramped corners of his heart. It pained him to see her reduced to the present state. He escorted her to one of the sofas, thinking that even in stark mourning with her hair severely dressed, she was lovely indeed. In other circumstances a beautiful and aristocratic young widow might have made another advantageous marriage, once the scandal died down. Ah, me!

He shook his head and signaled Morton to bring his mistress a glass of brandy. The poor woman looked as if she needed it. The butler brought her one on a silver tray. Cassandra stared at it blankly, then cupped the snifter in her hands, concentrating on the play of light along the crystal facets. Anything to avoid thinking. Remembering. She still had nightmares about it.

Povey came in with Kitty, saw her young charge safely ensconced on the sofa beside her aunt, then retired. Kitty sat with her hands folded in her lap. For all the attention she paid to her surroundings she might have been on the other side of the world. It grieved Cassandra to see her niece so wan and dispirited. She had been able to keep Kitty from attending the funeral only by letting her think that her presence, in such a weakened condition, would be an extra burden of worry to herself. Cassandra rose and went to her. "Dearest, you should be resting."

Her niece lifted her chin in a brave little mannerism that any of Cassandra's acquaintances would have recognized. "I'm quite all right. Please . . . let me be with you."

Mr. McCauliffe, watching them together, was struck by the resemblance. Two beauties in distress, he thought, and clucked his tongue. His days as knight in armor were long over; only his heart remained stout and true.

Taking a seat beside Kitty, Cassandra composed her features. With so many dire rumors of Tyler's financial affairs flying about, she dreaded this moment. "We are ready, Mr. McCauliffe."

A discreet nod from the solicitor and Morton went out, closing the double doors behind him. McCauliffe pushed his spectacles up on his bony nose and gathered a sheaf of papers.

"I have before me, Mrs. Lucton, the last will and testament of your late husband, Tyler Emory Lucton. The appropriate papers have been filed and the formalities tended to. To spare you the dry legal terminology, I will put this in lay terms."

He paused and cleared his throat. "There are the usual small bequests to Morton, Mrs. Llewellyn, Miss Povey, and several of the upper servants. Everything else —the bulk of the estate—is left to you, madame, with the provision that you will discharge the debts and obligations of your late husband's estate. And that is it, in a nutshell."

Cassandra looked at him sharply. She had expected funds and trusts and other ways of tying things up. This seemed too easy. "Surely there is more that you must tell me. I know that there are many obligations outstanding. . . ."

The solicitor rubbed his age-spotted hand over his forehead. "Forgive me. I should have explained, perhaps, that I have already gone over the estate books with the steward, and through most of the business papers as well. I am afraid that in trying to spare you, I have put things rather badly."

He groped for words and seemed to find none appropriate to the situation. With every passing second Cassandra's dread increased.

"It is very bad then. Well, I'm sure something can be salvaged." She glanced at Kitty, who seemed utterly rapt in tracing the pattern of flowers on her skirt with a fingertip. "Perhaps you can tell me, in general terms, Mr. McCauliffe, what might be left after the debts are settled."

McCauliffe tugged at his collar and looked exceedingly unhappy. "Unfortunately, Mrs. Lucton, after the debts are discharged there is very little at all. I doubt that the bequests to the upper servants can be satisfied. But there might be enough, I daresay, to provide a small —a very small—income for you for life. It would involve considerable retrenchment on your part."

Cassandra took Kitty's hand in hers. "I do not anticipate doing much entertaining in future, so my expenditures will be much smaller, and I can let a good deal of the under household staff and the gardeners go. With good references, of course. Kitty and I shall be quite happy living a retired life."

A long silence filled the room. McCauliffe took a healthy swallow of his own brandy. "I am afraid, Mrs. Lucton, that, er, it is painfully clear to me now that you do not understand the extent of your husband's losses."

Suddenly Mr. McCauliffe felt his age, and more. He wished this day were over. "Your late husband recently mortgaged Stoneleigh and the surrounding land. I've spoken with the creditors, who have been most understanding. You will be able to stay on until the end of the month, but then you must remove to other lodgings."

There was a loud humming in Cassandra's ears, drowning out the lawyer's grim tones. She caught only snatches of what he was saying: ". . . retain the pieces of furniture you brought with you upon your marriage . . . personal effects . . . your own clothing and such . . . your late grandmother's settlement . . . New Zealand and Australia, which unfortunately was not a successful venture . . ."

Fighting for control, Cassandra was unaware of how hard she was holding on to Kitty's hand. Her head cleared slowly and the humming faded. Mr. McCauliffe was droning on, his eyes avoiding hers. ". . . and everything else must go on the auction block."

"Everything!" Cassandra closed her eyes a moment. So many emotions swirled through her it was impossible to sort them out. Foremost were fear for her future and Kitty's, and a savage, guilty anger; but she couldn't tell if the latter was for Tyler, for setting up this fall from grace and abandoning them to the consequences, or with herself, for being such a blind, naive fool.

She marshaled her courage. "Tell me exactly how things stand. Do not try to spare me."

"You should have enough to rent modest apartments in an unfashionable part of town. Without the need for servants you might be able to eke out a respectable allowance from the minor stocks that were put in your name as part of your marriage settlement. The rest must be sold."

Kitty lifted her head and spoke for the first time since she'd entered. "Even Cassandra's piano?"

JOIN THE
TIMELESS ROMANCE READER SERVICE AND GET FOUR OF TODAY'S MOST EXCITING HISTORICAL ROMANCES FREE, WITHOUT OBLIGATION!

Imagine getting today's very best historical romances sent directly to your home – at a total savings of at least $2.00 a month. Now you can be among the first to be swept away by the latest from Candace Camp, Constance O'Banyon, Patricia Hagan, Parris Afton Bonds or Susan Wiggs. You get all that – and that's just the beginning.

PREVIEW AT HOME WITHOUT OBLIGATION AND SAVE.

Each month, you'll receive four new romances to preview without obligation for 10 days. You'll pay the low subscriber price of just $4.00 per title – a total savings of at least $2.00 a month!

Postage and handling is absolutely free and there is no minimum number of books you must buy. You may cancel your subscription at any time with no obligation.

GET YOUR FOUR FREE BOOKS TODAY ($20.49 VALUE)

FILL IN THE ORDER FORM BELOW NOW!

YES! *I want to join the Timeless Romance Reader Service. Please send me my 4 FREE HarperMonogram historical romances. Then each month send me 4 new historical romances to preview without obligation for 10 days. I'll pay the low subscription price of $4.00 for every book I choose to keep — a total savings of at least $2.00 each month — and home delivery is free! I understand that I may return any title within 10 days without obligation and I may cancel this subscription at any time without obligation. There is no minimum number of books to purchase.*

NAME_____

ADDRESS _____

CITY_____STATE____ZIP_____

TELEPHONE_____

SIGNATURE _____

GET
4
FREE
BOOKS
(A $20.49
VALUE)

TIMELESS ROMANCE
READER SERVICE

120 Brighton Road
P.O. Box 5069
Clifton, NJ 07015-5069

McCauliffe blinked. He'd almost forgotten she was there at all. "Yes, I am afraid so." Kitty fell back into her glazed abstraction.

Cassandra grasped at her one hope. "You spoke of stocks, and of foreign holdings earlier."

"Yes. Nothing elaborate. Or productive for that matter." He glanced at one of the papers. "A few shares in a paper mill that has sunk into insolvency. A played-out opal mine in Australia, and a two-hundred-acre parcel in Nevada. I believe that your late husband won the deed to the acreage from Simon Fiddler recently, in a game of faro. I have not had time to receive full reports on the holding, but it may be possible to sell it back to him. If you wish, I will set matters in train immediately."

"No! I—" Cassandra stopped herself. She couldn't afford to be choosy over where she sold her properties. "Thank you, Mr. McCauliffe. I would like to see the reports when you acquire them. I am too weary to make such a decision just now."

"Very well." He gathered his papers. "In the meantime, if you have any immediate need for funds, Mrs. Lucton, you may apply to me for an advance."

After the solicitor had departed the day passed slowly. Kitty went upstairs again. "To read," she said, but Cassandra knew she would find her niece sitting with an unread book open in her lap, or staring emptily at nothing. The happy child was gone forever, replaced by a grave young woman who spent as much time lost in her thoughts as she did in the world around her. It broke Cassandra's heart.

She was terribly worried. If Kitty was so withdrawn here at Stoneleigh, what would happen to her when they were reduced to living in lodgings, with neither dignity nor privacy? What would happen to Kitty, who should be experiencing the happiest days of her young life now? With the scandal of Tyler's ruin and whispered suicide, and with no dowry, there would be no hope of arranging an advantageous marriage. Cassandra saw the future stretching out before them, an unknown and lonely road with misery at the far end. She hadn't shared Tyler's revelations with Kitty. Let the poor child be spared that, at least.

She was so lost in thought she took a wrong turning at a branching corridor. This wing was rarely used. It had been one of her husband's elaborate fancies and she rarely entered it, but it provided a shortcut to her suite of rooms. Tyler had purchased the entire Tudor wing of Fayne Castle from her senile old grandfather, complete with tapestries and furnishings.

The paneling, the great stone fireplace and chimney breast, and the oriel windows had been numbered, dismantled, and carried 'round the Horn in the bellies of the Lucton Line's merchant ships, to be reassembled at Stoneleigh. Tyler had expected her to be pleased and Cassandra had tried to hide her dismay. Castle Fayne had been legally looted of its history for no better reason than her grandfather's debts and Tyler's wish to show off to his peers.

The corridor jogged abruptly left, then opened into two small reception rooms. Cassandra passed through one and into a wide corridor. Above her a series of faces stared moodily out from time-darkened portraits. She didn't know who the people in the portraits were. Tyler had purchased them at auction from various estates and their histories had vanished along with their owners' fortunes.

She expected to find a staircase at the far end of the

gallery but the double doors opened to a long, dark gallery. She stopped and looked around to get her bearings. The room was musty and filled with shadows. A fleeting panic caught at her.

She turned and hurried in the opposite direction. Yes, there was the door that led back to the gold salon in the main section of the house. Cassandra opened it but found no glittering chamber, only a gloomy hall that ended in a crooked flight of well-worn stairs. Retracing her steps, she turned another corner—and came up against a blank brick wall. She didn't recall ever having seen it before.

For a terrible moment Cassandra didn't know where she was. Everything seemed to alter and shift, like a dream. She'd lost all sense of direction. She was in a stranger's house, wearing a stranger's clothes. Living a stranger's life.

Turning again, she fled down the corridor and stumbled on the corridor that led past Tyler's study. She ran to the entry hall and up the stairs to the safety of her boudoir, as if pursued by demons.

A warm golden glow penetrated through Grayson's closed eyelids. He heard sounds of rain and smelled the intermittent odor of smoke. He thought that he was back in his lodge among the *Tsistsistas*. Back along the shores of the river, in a favorite campsite called Where the Willows Are. Gunshots shattered the remnants of his restless dreams. He opened his eyes, expecting to see She Laughs and Two Bears playing on a buffalo-hide blanket nearby.

It was a shock to find himself on his bed in the Dillon Hotel, and to realize the scent of smoke came with his every exhalation. His bare chest was scraped in a dozen places and he was wearing a pair of pajama bottoms he'd never seen before. What the hell!

He could hear the sound of steady rain and realized that the gunfire was only thunder beyond the drawn draperies. Jaime was sitting in the armchair, reading one of Ned Buntline's dime novels by the light of the cranberry lamp. The whiskey decanter and a glass were beside him along with a discarded newspaper.

Grayson shut his eyes again. He had no idea of how he'd gotten back to the hotel and into his bed. His last recollection was waiting in the fog down along the wharf, and the bobbing lamps of approaching carriages.

His head ached with trying to remember it all. He'd arranged for a screen of smoke to create a diversion so the captive girls could be rescued. Something had gone very wrong.

He glanced down. His right arm was bandaged and the top of his hand was crusted and blistered. His left was a mass of scratches and bruises. He tried to speak but his throat felt rusty. A first attempt brought a faint croak. Jaime turned a page. Grayson realized he hadn't been heard. He took a deep breath and steeled himself to try again.

"Jaime." It was only a raspy sound, like the quiet scraping of a wooden chair shifted backward.

Grayson tried to sit up and fell back against the pillows, muscles weak and aching with disuse. Jaime sprang up and hurried to his side. "Don't try to talk yet. Here."

He took a small brown bottle and poured a thick, greenish liquid into a glass, then splashed a dash of whiskey in as well. "Drink this down. Doctor's orders."

Grayson frowned and waved it away. His friend

wouldn't back down. "Drink it, amigo. Because otherwise I have orders to kneel on your chest and pour it down your gullet."

He meant it. There was nothing for Grayson to do but take the glass and swallow. It wasn't as vile as it looked, but close enough. It burned like rotgut and ate a hole in his stomach. A wave of nausea swept over him, bringing a cold sweat to his upper lip. He forced the rest down and kept it down.

Jaime laughed softly. "Worse than buffalo piss, eh? Well, it'll do you more good. You ate a hell of a lot of smoke. The next time you set out to rescue a passel of women, I hope you let me in on it!"

Grayson struggled up, this time more successfully. Although his entire body was stiff, the joints eased a bit with movement. He felt a hundred years old. "What happened?" His voice was stronger, but very hoarse. It hurt like the devil to speak.

"The ceiling came down on you. A beam grazed your thick skull and knocked you out. Ling Cheung got a crew and dug you out the next day. Giddings wasn't so lucky. They could have buried what was left of him in a cigar box."

Giddings. Flames flared in his memory, orange and yellow-white . . . shouts and high-pitched screams . . . men in evening dress stampeding like steers in a lightning storm. Thick, choking smoke and the blazing inferno that had been Simon Fiddler's warehouse. A man named Giddings, running the wrong way . . .

The echoes of screams danced through Grayson's throbbing head. "And the women?"

"The Chinaman says he got them away without any trouble. They're probably squirreled away over one of the gambling houses in Chinatown, playing fan-tan and

eating whatever their version of bonbons is called."
Jaime frowned. "How the hell did you get mixed up in
it? And why didn't you take me into your confidence?"

"Ling Cheung wanted it kept quiet, for obvious reasons. And he had men available. I didn't think it would
turn into a conflagration."

"Don't worry. No one knows that you were involved."

No, Grayson thought, but I wonder how long it will
take Simon Fiddler to suspect. And how long it would
take for him to retaliate. The next few days should
prove quite interesting.

He shifted and caught sight of his face in the tilted
shaving mirror on the bureau. His face was gaunt and
hollowed and his eyes were sunken into his head. He'd
been out of touch for more than a few hours. "How
long have I been laid up?"

"Fiddler's dinner was five days ago."

That was a shock. "Four days flat on my back and
the world still managed to turn without me. Well,
there's a blow to any man's self-esteem."

"We found you among the rubble of the warehouse
the next day. You came around shortly after and didn't
seem that much worse for wear, except for the burns
and a bump on your head. You collapsed in the carriage
on the way here. An inflammation of the lung, from
breathing all that smoke."

Grayson pushed himself up to a sitting position. The
room wobbled, then steadied as he exerted his will-
power. His body, toughened by long days in the saddle,
responded to his steely discipline; his memory did not.
"It's still a damned blank. What else have I missed?"

"One hell of a lot." Jaime held up a hand and began
ticking things off on his fingers: "A million-dollar ware-

house fire on the wharf, which cost Simon Fiddler and several other importers a pretty penny. A certain red-haired dancer at the Empire Saloon, who sends her regards. A good horse race yesterday—Queen's Pleasure won at twenty to one, like I predicted."

He paused and eyed Grayson somberly. "And Tyler Lucton's suicide."

"What?"

"Lucton was deeply in debt, as you know. He borrowed from Peter to pay Paul to pay the next fellow in line, all the way from here to New York to London. And when his vouchers were suddenly called in all at once, he couldn't meet his obligations." Jaime met Grayson's glance squarely. "He blew his brains out with a dueling pistol in the middle of the night. His wife found him."

Grayson cursed. "The man was a fool! He should have been able to fend off the worst of his creditors another month or more, since I put up the Morning Star Mine as collateral. His debts must have been worse than even I knew."

Jaime looked puzzled. "You did what you set out to do, didn't you? Lucton had emptied all the best stuff from his main warehouse and hidden it in a smaller building near Fiddler's. Meant to torch his main building and claim the insurance money. The wind was so strong the fire at Fiddler's warehouse roared out of control—and destroyed Lucton's secret cache as well. It was the final straw."

Grayson's mouth filled with the taste of ashes. He'd come to California with one end in mind: to destroy Tyler Lucton. But at the time, "Lucky Lucton" had been only a faceless name. That had been enough. Now it all seemed so long ago.

Rain pattered against the windows. Jaime threw back

the draperies, revealing a dark mass of clouds scudding against a misty gray sky. The temperature outside was dropping rapidly. He listened to the rain, picking up its hidden rhythms. He was glad to be snug inside four walls and not meeting up with it in Colorado, out on the rangeland. "Hear that wind? It's going to get mean."

Grayson stared at the drops of water hitting the glass panes and racing down in twisting rivulets. "What of Lucton's family?"

"Mrs. Lucton is holding up. The girl is still confined to bed by her mysterious indisposition but supposedly recovering."

"Look into their financial affairs. Before leaving town, I'd like to know how things stand with them."

"No need. It's common knowledge. They won't starve, but life won't be easy for them. Now they'll learn how the rest of the world lives."

Grayson sent him a sharp look but before he could reply there was a rap at the door. Jaime opened it. Simon Fiddler entered, rain dripping from his cloak. Beads of moisture on his hair caught the glow of the lamplight, giving him a false halo. His smile was equally counterfeit.

"Ah, Mr. Howard. I'm delighted to see you've come round. You gave your friends quite a little scare."

Grayson motioned for him to take a seat. "Perhaps you underestimated the thickness of my skull."

"Who would dare to utter such irreverence? You're the city's latest hero, you know. It's not every day that a wealthy landowner risks his person for the life of one so far beneath him." He set his hat down on a chair beside the door. "I refer to the late Jerold Giddings, of course."

His smooth words carried a jagged edge but his eyes held a curious reflection. Grayson recognized malevolence, tinged with something suspiciously like amusement. Fiddler was the kind of man who enjoyed the fire and fury of the battle, even if he was bested. The kind who would be back to fight again, on grounds of his own choosing.

Simon flung himself down in the armchair with casual elegance. As he pulled off his thin gloves, the gold and emerald ring was stark against the whiteness of his hand. "Are you too weary to speak of business matters? No? Good. First, I must tell you that you did me a good turn by refusing to sell your interest in the Thunder Mine. I've had my men prospecting on the other side of the mountain, just south of the little town of Aureus. We've struck the mother lode: a vein of silver so massive and so pure that it can be mined with a spoon, as they say. I've named it the Pegasus."

Jaime glanced at their visitor but Grayson kept his own face impassive. "My congratulations on your good fortune."

He knew the mountainside above Aureus well, and the rock was all wrong for silver. Simon's mine was as mythical as the flying horse he'd named it for. Grayson wondered what the charade was all about. The warehouse fire must have cost him dearly. He had a vague image of empty crates and one filled with stones and straw. Was it real or an effect of the blow to his head? He wondered if Fiddler could be trying to fend off his own creditors with stories of a silver strike.

Simon toyed with the ring on his left hand. "Thank you. Things are going very well for me. But I didn't come here to brag of my good fortunes. I am seeking a partner in an interesting venture, and have a proposition for you.

"I'm sure you've heard of poor Lucton's death. Although his flagship sank off the coast of Java, Tyler Lucton had three others still at sea. The moment they come into port, they'll be confiscated by his creditors. The goods will be auctioned off for a pittance. Their cargo," he said smoothly, "is rumored to be rich."

Grayson leaned forward. "Why are you telling me this?"

"My dear fellow, I feel I owe you something, since you almost came to an untimely end under my roof, so to speak. I hope you'll form a partnership with me. I will speak frankly. If the ships were to be met off the coast and, ah, shall we say, *diverted* to another harbor?—the wealth in their holds would bring a much higher price."

"Piracy on the high seas?"

"Nothing so daring. I'm sure that the fair Cassandra would agree to sign the rights over to us. She and her niece are paupers, you know, or as near to it as they can come."

Grayson leaned back against the pillows. "And the profits to be given to the widow and her niece, of course."

Simon smiled at his sardonic tone. "I am a businessman, Mr. Howard, not a charitable institution. And even if I were, the profits would not pay a tenth part of Lucton's bad debts."

He steepled his hands and watched Grayson intently. A hungry cat, waiting to see what kind of mouse he might lure from its nest.

Grayson's hands fisted against the linen comforter but his voice sounded calm. "I'm a rancher, Mr. Fiddler. I have no interest in intercepting ships at sea."

"A pity. And I thought you were a gambler." Simon rose with the same languid grace. "I regret infinitely that urgent business calls me away from California. We'll meet again, Mr. Howard, I'm sure. Perhaps in Aureus."

He shrugged back into his cloak and took his hat from the chair. Jaime had already opened the door. On the threshold Simon paused and looked back. "I'd heard you have been courting Lucton's niece. Kitty, isn't it? How fortunate that you didn't offer for her. A pretty child, but nothing like the delectable Cassandra."

He sighed in rueful exaggeration. "Do you know, I once sent the widow Lucton a fortune in roses—and she gave them away to the poor?"

Grayson smiled. "A woman of spirit."

"Yes," Simon agreed. "Really, one shudders to think of what might happen to the lovely Cassandra and her niece now, cast out upon an uncaring world. Most of the servants have fled and there will be bailiffs in the house by week's end."

He went out, closing the door behind him. The room seemed suddenly brighter. Grayson thought that Fiddler carried a dark cloud with him that tainted everything it touched. And if he had read the silky threat in the man's voice correctly, Fiddler's plans for the remains of Tyler Lucton's empire extended to his widow as well.

He threw back the covers, willing his strength to return. There was something he must do . . . yes, he must ride out to Stoneleigh and . . .

Fatigue and the dose of medicine caught him in midthought. He sank back against the pillows, fighting the sleep that closed in on him like a dark cloud.

Later someone held a glass of warm liquid to his lips and he drank it gratefully. "Just a little more," a soft voice said. His eyes flew open. Jaime and a young woman stood beside his bed.

Jaime grinned. "Another surprise for you, but this

time a more enjoyable one." He turned to the woman. "Come closer, he won't bite."

Grayson's first thought was that she wasn't the type of woman Jaime usually admired. She had a trim, athletic build, in contrast to the more opulent beauties he usually favored; but it was her face that struck him even more. Instead of indolent good humor and frank sensuality, this one had mobile features and shrewd, intelligent eyes.

She came forward and dropped a light and graceful curtsy. "I'm very pleased to meet you again." A dimple played at the corner of her mouth. "And I must say that I like this place a lot better than where we last met." She paused. "You don't know who I am? I'd hoped that you might recognize me."

Jaime saw Grayson's puzzlement. "They say that Heaven repays its debts, old friend. Well, the hand of Fate brought this young lady to us, in repayment for your good deed. She is one of the women you rescued from Simon Fiddler."

But that didn't explain what she was doing in his suite. "I'm edified, Miss . . . ?"

Her laughter was merry as a bell. "How formal you are. You really should know me."

Bedelia stepped closer into the circle of lamplight by the bed. Her face was scrubbed clean of the heavy cosmetics she'd worn in her circus act. "After all, you've paid to advertise in the newspapers and you've had my name and picture spread all over San Francisco. Why, I even met with your agent before I was unlucky enough to be abducted from the streets by Simon Fiddler's henchmen."

Grayson was speechless with amazement.

Bedelia looked from one to the other, and laughed

low in her throat. She had leapt without looking, and landed in a pot of cream. She put her hand on his. "I'm Annette Mason, Bronco's little sister. And I intend to go back to the Thunder Ranch with you."

Cassandra and Kitty took their evening meal in the breakfast parlor. The long dining room was already swathed in holland covers and would have been too gloomy for just the two of them. Suddenly Kitty jumped up with a shriek, knocking her chair over. Cassandra followed her pointing finger. Two young men in dirty clothes lurked among the roses, their faces pressed against the windows. They laughed at her reaction but scampered away when Cassandra advanced toward them and pulled the draperies shut.

She put her arm around her trembling niece. "They're just curiosity seekers, darling. I'll speak to Tomms about having them chased off the property. Meanwhile we'll spend the evening upstairs, where we can be undisturbed."

"It's just that they surprised me so." Kitty swallowed. "I'm sorry. I will be strong for you. I promise." Kitty smiled tremulously and went up to her room.

Even the haven of the yellow sitting room did not go undisturbed. Cassandra looked out at the lawn where gawkers were congregating. She stepped out to the open glass doors. "This is a house of mourning. Please leave us in peace."

Hoots and catcalls followed her inside, and someone threw a piece of apple at the window. Cassandra was becoming frightened. The estate agent had warned that looters were not uncommon in situations such as hers, but she'd hoped that the isolated position of Stoneleigh would spare them that.

She rang quickly for Morton. "We must get Tomms and the grooms to help patrol the grounds. Jenkins and the gardeners must help, also."

The old butler wrung his hands. "They've gone off, my lady. All but Tomms and Johnny MacCrae. Shall I give them rifles and ammunition from the gun room?"

"Yes. They can frighten off intruders. Can you handle a gun, Morton?"

"No, my lady."

"Then we must stay awake through the night. The sales agent's men will be here in the morning and we will be safe then."

Cassandra had no experience with a rifle, but she did know how to load and fire a pistol. Being raised in the country, she had grown up among dogs and horses, hunters and guns. It was something everyone learned.

But the only pistols were the two locked in Tyler's study. Much as she dreaded going there, she would have to do it.

Night had fallen quickly and the lamps were not lit below. It was like descending into a pool of still black water by the light of a single candle. The carved apostles of the gothic staircase were silent as she descended, but their hollowed eyes winked and shifted in her wake.

The pool of darkness melted away before her taper's small flame, but only for a few feet around her. The ceiling of the great entrance hall was lost in flickering shadows and the white marble that floored the chamber seemed as cold and forbidding as an ice floe. The auction was scheduled for the end of the week but Cassandra had been able to sell some of the furnishings privately, through an agent whom Mr. McCauliffe had recommended. Already Stoneleigh seemed like a stranger's place, foreign and forbidding. The Venetian chandelier in the ballroom had been swathed in holland cloth and the Jacobean court cupboards and the knob-kneed chairs were gone from the foyer. Odd, how she missed them: she had disliked them excessively.

She passed the empty place on the wall where the Turner had hung, painted sea and sky ablaze with incandescent light. Tyler hadn't liked the painting, but had purchased it on her advice. Ironically, the proceeds from its sale had gone to pay off his most pressing debts.

Her collection of Oriental porcelain in the drawing room was another boon. The agent had complimented Cassandra on her exquisite taste and said that the blue-and-white vases and matching temple jar should fetch a very good price. These, along with her personal jewelry, were the basis of a nest egg that would pay their food and modest lodging until—until what? No answer came to comfort her.

Her footsteps echoed hollowly as she wandered through the empty house. Rain hammered at the windows. She quickened her step. The house servants had already deserted, one by one. Mrs. Llewellyn had been the first. She had packed up and left after Tyler's funeral, without a word to anyone. Only Povey and Morton and Jenny were left, along with Cook and one of the scullery maids who had a cleft lip and no place else to go yet. By week's end even they would be gone, Morton to his brother in England, Jenny to Simon Fiddler's new hotel as chambermaid, along with Cook and the scullery maid. All of them with fine recommendations, but without the pensions they deserved.

Povey had no family and was too old to seek another position. She had begged to stay on without wages. It would be difficult to house and feed three mouths, but Cassandra could not have done otherwise. A deep affection bound them. They would take up lodging in two rooms on the top floor of a shabby rooming house, next to a greengrocer's shop. It didn't seem possible.

The door to Tyler's study loomed ahead in the light of the taper. Cassandra didn't think that she could enter the study again. Then she heard laughter and pounding at the front door. She must protect Kitty and the others dependent upon her. Her hands were cold and stiff as she unlocked the door and entered.

Her first action was to light the lamp. Coming into the tomblike silence in the dark would have been unendurable. The air smelled dead and close. She hurried to the desk, trying to not see the stains on the carpet and the wallpaper behind the desk. Trying not to remember the hideous, shattered thing that had been Tyler, lying there in the glistening pool of blood.

Like Margaret.

Tyler had left them bankrupt and ruined, but Margaret's betrayal had wounded her more deeply than had Tyler's. What would their lives, their marriages, have been like under better circumstances? If Tyler hadn't been in love with her sister, would he have given his love to her? And Margaret—if she had been able to marry her childhood sweetheart, with whom she'd been violently in love, would she have lived out her days happily, or would she still have been shot by her jealous husband and left to die in a pool of her own blood?

Cassandra fumbled at the drawer. The more she hurried the more difficult it was to fit the key in the lock. Her ears seemed preternaturally tuned to pick up the echoes of his two fatal shots—once for Juno, once to end his own life. Against her will her eyes were drawn to the dark blotches that marred the floor and wall and smattered the draperies. So much blood. The drawer came open and she took out the box with the dueling pistols and ammunition. Only one shot in each. Enough, perhaps, to scare off any bold intruders.

She took the box up with her to her bedchamber before removing the pistols. They had hair-triggers. Cassandra sat in her armchair, fully dressed, with a blanket across her knees and set one of the loaded pistols within easy hand's reach. Her eyes were heavy from weeping and lack of sleep but Cassandra didn't dare doze off. Povey took up her vigil in Kitty's room, with a fringed paisley shawl around her shoulders and a stout walking stick across her bony knees. With the connecting doors open, the two of them would guard the upper floor, with Morton and the two gardeners below.

At midnight she heard a shot and shouting, which frightened away the would-be intruder. When dawn came without further incident she sighed and closed her eyes.

She dreamed of walking the battlements of Fayne Castle with her sister. The day was fair and sunny and a hawk rode the currents of air, king of the sky. "Look, Margaret!"

Her sister turned and Cassandra screamed. The figure beside her was covered in blood and it was not Margaret, but Kitty. Cassandra screamed again and the picture broke apart into sharp segments, like shattered glass.

She woke with her heart beating wildly and realized that the breaking glass was not part of her dream, but coming from the drawing room below. Whispering to Povey to stand guard, she grabbed up the loaded pistols and made her way silently to the head of the stairs.

10

Cassandra heard a moan of pain from the hall below. "Morton?" The only answer was the sound of muffled laughter followed by the shattering of more glass. *Dear God, what now?*

Hurrying down to the entrance hall, she held the pistols gingerly before her. The sidelights were broken and the outer door flung wide open. Dirt and bits of grass and sticks had been tracked over the marble floor. In the alcove the statue of Victory glistened with the stream of brown tobacco juice that had been directed at it. The sharp smell of urine filled the air.

A wicked laugh startled her. It came from the drawing room. Cassandra ran to the doorway and then froze on the threshold. Two ruffians had broken into the left-hand china cabinet and were pawing through its contents. The swarthy man had the head of a small china shepherdess poking from the pocket of his grimy leather vest, and a Sevres bowl lay in pieces at his feet.

Cassandra recognized him as one of the under-gardeners who'd left earlier in the week. While she'd given in to fatigue and slept in her armchair, he'd gained entrance with his crony and ransacked the lower floors. As she stood paralyzed with shock, the other fellow grabbed one of her prized blue and white vases and dashed it down on the marble hearth. It shattered with a hollow pop and a tinkle of tiny shards. Cassandra was sick. She and Kitty could have lived comfortably for six months on what it would have brought at auction.

"Oh, no!" She ran toward them, forgetting the pistols in her hand. "Stop at once!"

"What're you doing with those popguns, princess." The man grinned. "Here, give them to me. You're like to hurt yourself if you're not careful." He came at her and she raised the pistol. *"Stop, or I'll shoot!"*

The second man started working his way toward her from the other side. Cassandra backed up until she felt the hard edge of a cabinet behind her back. The pistol wavered in her hand. The two were closing in on her.

"You ever have a lady, Bert?" one asked the other, grinning. "I've always wanted to see if they're any different beneath their fine, silken gowns from the girls at Maisie Packer's place.

"There's two of 'em here. The other one must be upstairs. Real pretty young thing."

Cassandra leveled the pistol at the nearest one and cocked the hammer. He stopped. "She won't shoot," his friend said. "That old-fashioned toy's not even loaded."

Then she heard a moan. From the corner of her eye she saw Morton trying to rise from behind the sofa. The hilt of a thick knife protruded from his back. He fell over the front of the sofa, rolled to the floor, and went completely still. She knew he was dead.

The first man lunged at Cassandra. She pulled the trigger without conscious plan. Although her aim was off, the pistols had been made by a master and still had the power to destroy. The looter was less than a foot away when she fired. He was blown back by the force and crashed against the sofa, slithering down the satin brocade in a smear of bright blood. Cassandra stared at what had been his face.

Her stomach turned and she retched violently. It was all the second assailant needed. He caught her around the waist and grappled for the gun. It went spinning away behind them, discharging when it hit the wall. The bullet missed Cassandra by inches, but shattered the Chinese vase before thudding into the attacker's knee. He went down with a terrible howl, grasping his injured limb. Blood pumped out at an alarming rate.

She grabbed up a poker from the fireplace and stood over him, afraid he would get up again. Four other men, hearing the ruckus, came running in from the hall. Their hands were filled with antique snuff boxes from Tyler's study and one held the gilded birdcage from the conservatory. "Bloody bitch! Look what she's done to Bert and Eddie."

The man with the birdcage backed away. "I don't want no part of this. I'm clearing out." He wheeled and ran, throwing the cage away. The others eyed each other, then came after Cassandra, their lips pulled back from their teeth like feral beasts.

One picked up a beautiful temple jar and heaved it at her. It missed, but the flying fragments grazed her cheek and drew blood from her thumb. She cried out, not from pain but from the wanton destruction. From fear at what might happen next, and from the knowledge that she had killed a man. She held the poker before her with both hands, ready to smash it down if they came too close. It was slick with her blood.

"Cassandra?"

Oh, God! Kitty's voice came from the stairway. "Don't come down. Lock yourself in with Povey!"

Kitty didn't obey. She ran inside the room and stopped dead. Cassandra was wild with fear. "Run! Hide!"

The urge to protect and defend swelled inside her, exploding into a primal rage. The man called Bert vaulted over the small sofa and landed on the body of the man Cassandra had shot. When he got to his feet there was a knife in his hand. One of the others cursed and fled through the garden window.

Cassandra hurled herself at the marauders. Wielding the implement like a sword, she attacked with the ferocity of an ancient warrior queen. The two men were thrown off guard. As the younger man jumped back she caught him with a glancing blow to the tip of his elbow. He howled in pain and retreated, cursing.

The quick rush of victory made her concentration waver. She whirled and brandished the poker menacingly. Before she could press her advantage Cassandra realized, too late, that the second man had used the distraction to run up behind her. He struck her wrist with the side of his hand and her own went numb up to her shoulder. The poker flew in a wide, downward arc, shattering a rose bowl to smithereens and landing beneath a console.

Her breath came in great, heaving gasps and her throat was too tight to scream. Kitty picked up a jar of *famile rose* porcelain and heaved it at the man's head, but she was shaking so badly it missed. The other man caught her and shook her like a terrier with a rat.

Time slowed down with Cassandra caught in the center of its web. The long gold pin that held her chignon in place came out. Her hair spilled down, hanging in lustrous waves to her waist. She was aware of the younger man, nursing his injured arm in the corner, of Kitty's danger and her own helplessness. The hands on her throat began to squeeze and she gasped for air . . .

Suddenly another body hurled itself into the room and Cassandra looked up, dazedly. Grayson Howard lunged toward the looters. He had already chased three off the property, and had a gash over his right eyebrow for his efforts. The younger, injured man gave a warning shout and escaped through the window. Grayson tackled the second and brought him crashing to the ground. It was soon an unequal match. The thief was thickset and brawny but his adversary, despite four days in bed, was far younger and quicker. And he was sober.

The two men barrel-rolled across the floral carpet and crashed into the pedestal table. It tottered and fell, sending the brass bowl spinning against the fireplace screen and scattering in colorful, fragrant heaps the potpourri that Cassandra and Kitty had made. Attar of roses and lavender mingled with the odors of fear and sweat.

A fluted crystal candlestick was the next to go. It exploded in glittering shards. Grunts of exertion, the curses of the thief, and the thud of fist on bone filled the room.

Grayson took his adversary by the shoulders and banged the man's head against the floor. The robber was putting up less and less of a fight. Already the man's eyes were swollen half-shut and his face was a bloody pulp from Grayson's battering knuckles. With a low moan he went suddenly limp. A string of red spittle drooled from his puffy mouth and there was a dark smear of blood across the white marble of the hearth. And still Grayson struck out at him in a fury.

Cassandra was appalled. "Stop it! Stop it at once. You're killing him!"

But Grayson couldn't stop. Cassandra ran to him and tried to stay his punishing hands. Grayson rocked back on his heels, pushing the hair from his eyes with the back of his bandaged hand. The dressing was half off, revealing the singed and blistered skin beneath.

"Why didn't you stop?" Cassandra sobbed.

Grayson looked up at her in surprise. Hadn't she heard what they'd been saying? Apparently not. Or if she had, it had been too horrible to acknowledge. All of her horror was focused on him, instead of the intruders. His gorge rose at the thought of what would have happened to her, had he not heard the commotion in time.

Cassandra had never seen such raw savagery. It confirmed every dark fear she had hidden in the back of her mind about Grayson Howard. "Is he . . . is he dead?"

"Not yet."

She glared at him as if he were a murderous savage who had dared to wander into her drawing room. "But you meant to kill him!"

Grayson was sore and aching all over, and mad as hell. He wanted to throttle her. He rose, wiping the blood that was dripping into his eye with the back of his torn sleeve. "You're damned right, I did! And what did you intend to do with that poker you were waving around, Mrs. Lucton? *Knight* the son of a bitch?"

She stammered something and went pale. Her glance went to the man lying half under the sofa with a bullet through his head. Grayson crossed over to him. "What the devil! Who did this?"

Cassandra shook like an aspen leaf in a windstorm. The smell of gunpowder was nauseating. All the defiance drained from her. The world tilted before her eyes, and spun around and around like water going down a drain. Grayson swooped down as her knees buckled and caught her in his arms. Cassandra found herself deposited on a settee, roughly.

He knelt beside Morton. The steel blade had caught the old butler in a vital spot. Grayson rose, shaking his head. "I'm sorry."

She covered her face with her hands. Morton would never sail for England. He had died trying to defend them. It was too much to bear. Grayson went to her and put his arm around her. She wept silently against his shoulder, then sat up and wiped away her tears. Povey came down, took in the scene in a glance, and led Kitty back upstairs.

Cassandra tried to rise but Grayson kept her pinned to the settee by the force of his arm. "We can't stay here," she said numbly. "We'll leave today . . ."

Grayson's arm tightened about her shoulders. "A wise decision. I've made arrangements to house you at my hotel."

"Thank you, but I have leased a—a place in town."

"Cancel it." His eyes were hard. "Unless you prefer that rat trap next to the greengrocer's. Yes," he said when she flinched. "I know all about that."

"Really!" The bright red of mortification flooded her face but her tone was stiff and regal. "It was kind of you to come to our aid—indeed, I'm most grateful for your assistance. But—but you must let me be the judge of what is best."

"Don't be a little fool! Or do you think it's in your best interest to share lodging with a syphilitic poet and a woman who entertains strange men in her room?"

Cassandra rose, trembling from head to toe with indignation. He seemed bent on humiliating her. Grayson blocked her intended retreat. There was a smear of dried blood across his right cheekbone. She shrank inwardly before the intensity of his gaze but held her ground. "*Where* I may go and *whatever* I may do, it is none of your business."

"Damn it, I'm making it my business. Before the week is out, I intend to make you my wife!"

Cassandra's heart skipped a beat. "You are completely mad!"

"Perhaps. My friends think so."

Cassandra tilted her chin. "You mock me, Mr. Howard. My husband was buried only a few days ago. I think you should go now."

"I'm not leaving your side until I see you and the rest of your household safely established at the Dillon Hotel. Or do you plan to shoot a few more looters?"

She gasped and tried to slap his face. He caught her wrist and held it. "Forgive me! That was uncalled for." He brushed a strand of hair back from her face with his bandaged hand. "I think you are a very brave woman."

There was no doubt in her mind that he was a raving lunatic. With a sob, she tried to push her way past him. Grayson blocked the doorway. "New debts have come to light. Bailiffs will be here to dispossess you. Unless you wish to be thrown out on the street in your shift, I'd advise you to listen to what I have to say."

It infuriated him to see the fear in her eyes. He gentled his voice but aimed for her soft spot. "I'm fully informed of your financial affairs. Without a miracle you and your niece will be out in the gutter. I know how much you love her. What hope of happiness will she have then?"

Cassandra bristled. "If you are so concerned with Kitty's happiness, why don't you offer for *her*?"

"Kitty is a mere girl." A spark of heat smoldered in the depths of his eyes. "I am a man. And a man wants a woman."

He pulled her closer. Cassandra felt giddy. He was warm and full of life and incredibly strong. "I cannot help thinking that this is some sort of insane jest," she blurted.

His eyes held hers. "I have never been more in earnest."

Cassandra was unable to tear her gaze from his. She was convinced, against her will, that he meant it. "You are a wealthy man, Mr. Howard. You could look as high as you please for a wife. Out of all the women you might choose from, why choose me?"

He couldn't admit the truth to her. He was having a difficult enough time explaining it to himself. "My home is an isolated ranch. There are few amenities and no luxuries. Except for my cook, the nearest home to mine is ten miles away. It's not a situation that would tempt most women. But I can give you a roof over your head and a secure future. Neither creditors nor gossip will hound you. And when the time comes, I'll see that Kitty has her pick of suitable young men. God knows there are a hundred fellows to every eligible girl in Colorado, and fortunes made every day."

A shudder ran through Cassandra's body. Her thoughts were jumbled. This man, this lean and dangerous stranger, was offering her a way out of her terrible predicament. She understood him now. He chose her because no one else would be so foolhardy as to accept his offer. His reasons were cold and impersonal, but he held out the only hope within reach. Despite her fears, the temptation was overwhelming. She turned her face away.

"You are forgetting that I am in mourning. My husband is barely cold in the grave—and you are proposing marriage!"

"You needn't hide behind convention. I know exactly what kind of life your husband led you." And that they hadn't been intimate in a long time. "I will not speak ill of the dead. Nor," he said savagely, "will I let you play out a tragedy for me, when I know that your marriage was a goddamned farce!"

She blanched, and Grayson could have bit his tongue in chagrin. Devil take it, he'd done it again. He lowered his voice. "Don't be afraid of my rough tongue. I've spent too many years in the company of men. The fact of the matter is that I need a wife. The nights are long and the winters cold—and a man gets lonely . . ."

Cassandra looked up at the change in his tone. His eyes were still intent, yet there was a softening in their depths that unnerved her. Grayson released her wrist, but held his hand out to her. "Come, we can do better than this, Cassandra."

It was the first time he'd ever said her given name. The syllables seemed to vibrate in the air between them. Cassandra didn't know which way to turn. Grayson Howard was the last man she'd have expected to come to her rescue—and he was offering her his name and protection and escape from the past, adventure and risk and the opportunity to really live again. Perhaps even to love.

She knew then what answer she wanted to give. But

there were things he hadn't considered. It was painful for her to drag her private shame into the harsh light of day, but in fairness he must know the truth about her and her great failure. She must give him his out.

"There is one thing that you have not taken into consideration. You are in your prime, Mr. Howard." She clenched her fingers so tightly together that they almost went numb. "A man—a man wants heirs. Sons to carry on his name." God knew that Tyler had. Her voice dropped to a hoarse whisper. "And I am barren."

The result wasn't at all what she'd expected. Grayson exploded in anger. "Goddammit! Is there nothing you won't say in order to turn me away? Will you next claim disease or madness in the bloodlines? Or perhaps it's more personal? Perhaps you've also contracted the pox?"

"What?" She went whiter than the shards of porcelain at her feet. "How dare you!"

While she sputtered in rage he grabbed her by the shoulders. Her face, so pale before, was suffused with high color. Grayson loomed over her, his own features hard with anger. "Enough of these excuses! Don't waste my time playing fool's games." His mouth twisted bitterly. "If you can't stomach me as a husband, Cassandra, at least have the courage to say it to my face!"

The room went suddenly still. A door opened and closed somewhere. Cassandra found herself unable to think, much less move or speak. He caught her hands between his. Fire to her ice. Warming her, heating her. And as her blood quickened, his wrath cooled. He might have been carved from granite. "Well, Cassandra? What is your answer?"

The spell that held her shattered abruptly. Once more

she struggled to be free. "Let me go. You're bruising me."

As she yanked her arm away he released her suddenly. She staggered back against the table and steadied herself. Grayson made no effort to assist her. His eyes were cold and remote. He gave her a chill parody of a smile.

"You needn't fear, madam. I won't touch you again. You've made your wishes abundantly clear."

He spun around on his heel and went toward the door without another word. Cassandra watched him with her heart pounding as if it would burst. Grayson was a proud man. Once he left he would never return. And she and Kitty would be alone, friendless, and unprotected in a very hostile world. So alone. And when he'd had his arm around her earlier she had felt so safe.

She stretched out her hand. "Wait. Don't go, please!"

Grayson turned reluctantly, as if sensing a ruse; but the look on Cassandra's face was genuine. The hauteur had vanished and she looked frightened. Haunted. The angles and planes were suddenly stark and the circles beneath her eyes looked like bruises. The sudden gauntness only emphasized the fragile beauty of her bone structure, the eloquence of her eyes. He waited, not moving.

Cassandra came to him slowly, haltingly. "If . . . if you still wish it, Mr. Howard, I will accept your proposal to be your wife."

"Why?" The single word was torn from him involuntarily. He had to ask—and damned himself for doing so.

The question startled Cassandra into an unfortunate truth. "I—I have no other choice."

His face closed and shuttered instantly. "My compliments on your refreshing honesty. When would you like this happy event to take place?"

His sarcasm numbed her. Cassandra would have given anything to be able to take back those blurted words. Any attempt to explain would only make things worse. She squared her shoulders. "I will leave the details of the arrangements up to you."

A slow smile played over his mouth. He hesitated only a few seconds. "Pack whatever you need for the two of you and your servants. I'm taking you to my hotel. You needn't worry about the house. I'll post guards."

"To your hotel?" Her sense of propriety was outraged. "Really, you presume too much!"

His voice cut across her objections. "Do you want to spend another night under this roof, waiting for intruders to find their way up to your bedchambers? I think not. And if it's your reputation that you're worried about, it's a bit late for that. Whatever is left of it will be shredded to pieces when the word gets out that you've married me so suddenly."

It was true. Cassandra knotted her fingers together to keep them from shaking. "Very well. When will we . . ." She couldn't say it. "When will the ceremony take place."

"Judge Bruckner is in my debt. I'll try to persuade him to perform the marriage this afternoon."

So soon! Sinking fast in the sea of sudden change, Cassandra grasped at straws to keep afloat. "A civil ceremony! I would prefer to wait and be married by a priest."

His eyes flashed with sudden amusement. He'd like to see the priest that would marry them without banns, two days after her husband's burial. Not to mention the looter she'd shot. Discretion seemed the wiser course.

"With all due respect to your religious principles, I believe our best course is to have the legal affairs seen to first. If you like, I'll arrange for the rest after we're settled."

"Very well. I'd like—" Cassandra saw movement behind Grayson and broke off. Povey, hearing the noise and their raised voices, had come back in search of her mistress, and heard all that she needed to know. She curtsied among the wreckage of the drawing room. "Shall I begin packing, my lady?"

Cassandra was so dazed that she could only nod. Povey bustled off, leaving them alone together once more.

Grayson lifted Cassandra's hand to his mouth and kissed her fingertips. "I'll check the grounds. Be ready to leave at noon."

Her fingers tingled from his touch, and her emotions were a turbulent mixture of unacknowledged longing and of unremitting dread. When he left her she ran upstairs. As she braced herself to make the announcement, Cassandra still could not believe that she had agreed to marry Grayson Howard.

Povey had already begun laying her gowns out upon the bed. She must put her whole life, until this moment, completely behind her. It had been nothing but an elaborate—and ultimately humiliating—lie.

Grayson spent the next two hours with his bankers, assessing the damage from his loans to Tyler Lucton. The afternoon was brilliant with sun when he finally helped Cassandra, Kitty, and Povey alight at Judge Bruckner's law office. The elegant building had survived two fires that had leveled half of San Francisco, and had been covered in white paint to hide the flame-scorched brick. A fluttery woman of indeterminate years ushered them into Judge Bruckner's inner sanctum. "His Honor will be here shortly," she said. "Please make yourselves comfortable."

The homely office was a far cry from the gothic stone arches and stained-glass chapel of St. Anselm the Younger, where Cassandra had been wed to Tyler. There were no massed flowers and lighted candles, no swirling notes from a big pipe organ to announce the nuptials, no dignitaries or family friends present to wish her well.

One wall was filled with cases of books in brown leather bindings, another with unflattering political cartoons cut from the newspapers, depicting: Judge Calvin Bruckner, The Only Man For Working Men. The room smelled of cigars and whiskey and garlic salami. Someone had missed the spittoon recently. Povey sat stiffly on the worn leather sofa with Kitty, and Cassandra felt suddenly stifled. Things had moved too quickly.

An hour ago she had still been garbed in widow's weeds. In deference to the occasion and Grayson's express wishes, she had changed into a plain dress of dark mulberry silk, neither too somber nor too festive. She was suddenly terrified of the step she was taking. She hardly knew Grayson. He had courage. He was direct to a fault. And he was, no doubt, one of the handsomest men that she had ever seen. His professed style of life was simple, yet she sensed that he was a very complicated man. She had seen him gentle and fierce, savage and suave. But he was still, in truth, a stranger.

Dear Lord, was she making the same mistake a second time?

She went to the window, hoping for a peaceful view

of the bay; it overlooked the peaks of the neighboring building and the trough between two where a dead pigeon was wedged. Cassandra whirled around and almost bumped into Grayson.

Grayson caught her and kept her from falling. A wave of pity swept over him. "It's not too late," he said for her ears only. "Tell me now if you've changed your mind."

A second ago she had been ready to bolt, but he radiated such sureness and confidence that some of it rubbed off on Cassandra. She got a grip on herself. "I gave you my word, Mr. Howard."

"Then you'll have to stop addressing me so formally." His smile softened his words. He was relieved she hadn't taken him up on it. He'd no more wanted a wife than he'd wanted to catch typhoid—but that was before he'd met Cassandra.

She didn't have time to reply. Jaime arrived with Bedelia on his arm and Judge Bruckner came in through a side door simultaneously. A quick round of introductions followed. The judge didn't meet Cassandra's expectations. She had envisioned a dignified man in black robes, projecting the weight of his worldly responsibilities; instead she found a round little pumpkin of a man with a smile to match. He had shrewd brown eyes, a fringe of ginger hair, a backwoods accent, and a set of bad dentures that made it difficult for her to understand two words out of every five. The situation seemed so farcical she didn't know whether to burst into laughter or tears.

Bedelia eyed Cassandra with interest. The bride was not at all what she would have expected a masculine fellow like Grayson to choose. Too hoity-toity and proper by half. If I'd met him first, he'd never have given her a second glance, she thought and cursed her luck. Ah, well. She'll never hold him.

Cassandra extended her hand to the newcomer. "I am very pleased to meet you, Miss Mason." She was surprised by the strength in Bedelia's grip. Although Bedelia smiled and seemed pleasant enough, Cassandra noticed the thin, dissatisfied line of her mouth in repose, at odds with her ingenuous air and guileless blue eyes.

Bedelia was cordial enough to Kitty but didn't even favor Povey with a nod. She knew a servant when she saw one. No use wasting her wiles on such a vinegar-faced old prune.

Cassandra took the slight to heart and developed an immediate dislike of Grayson's protégée. And when Bedelia gazed at Grayson there was a look in her eyes, deep and incalculable, that set Cassandra's teeth on edge. It was not the kind of look a woman about to be married wanted a young and pretty woman to give to her intended groom.

Kitty was too miserable to pay much attention to Bedelia. She didn't understand why Grayson had proposed to her aunt, nor why Cassandra had consented. She would have been perfectly happy living above a greengrocer's shop; but moving away from San Francisco to Silver Creek was even better, for they would be far away from everything familiar, with no reminders of the cruel past.

Judge Bruckner took up his position before his desk, a small leather book in his pudgy hands. "Shall we begin?" At least that was what Cassandra thought he meant. "Shully buhgin?" was actually what she had heard. The words sounded so distorted to her ears that he might have been speaking Urdu.

"Wers thuh brahd?"

She looked for Grayson to interpret. He left Jaime, went to her side, and took her hand, leading her forward. Bruckner beamed.

Povey and Jaime stepped forward together, as incongruous to Cassandra as everything else about this unorthodox ceremony. The judge launched into his preamble and once again she felt as if she were listening to a foreign language that, on rare occasions, bore a vague resemblance to the English tongue. It added a more bizarre note to the proceedings.

He cleared his throat and opened the book. "Durly beelovit . . ." Cassandra felt more and more that she was in the throes of a vividly peculiar dream. But then Grayson took her hand in his and slid a thin gold band on her ring finger. Suddenly every face was turned to look at her. She hadn't been listening and had missed her cue. "I—I will."

The sound of her own voice startled her. As the judge read out the words she found herself repeating the rhythms of the familiar ceremony in her mind. It seemed unreal . . . *for as long as we both shall live* . . . There was a terrible finality about that phrase. Her fingers trembled. Grayson's hand tightened on hers momentarily and she closed her eyes.

Judge Bruckner cleared his throat. "Wull, thas that." He grinned amiably. "You kin kiss yer wafe."

There was an awkward pause. Her fingers were like ice against Grayson's warm hands. He smiled reassuringly before leaning down to plant a chaste kiss on her cheek. She'd thought he was aiming for her mouth, and turned her face a fraction at the last minute. Grayson read her mind. He was suddenly furious.

He put his arms around Cassandra and pulled her tightly against his chest. She was too thin and delicate beneath the rustling silk. Grayson felt the soft swell of her breasts and the rapid flutter of her heart. His own blood picked up the echo and it thundered in his ears. By God, this would be a real kiss! His mouth came down upon hers squarely, hot and hard. Possessive and possessed. He wanted her so suddenly, so fiercely that he could have cleared the room and taken her then and there.

Against all conscious will, Cassandra felt herself melting into the heat of his firm body. His strength surrounded her, buoying her up even as her legs turned to wax. She felt as if she were falling, sinking into the power and dominance of his passion, until she feared that she would lose herself in it forever.

She pulled back, breaking the contact and the sensual web that had bound them. She didn't dare meet his eyes. To let him know how shaken she was would be to give him a weapon to wield over her. Grayson watched her face closing like a flower to him. For a few fleeting moments he had been sure that he had found a core of warmth deep within her, burning to be free. Now he feared that he'd only imagined it, conjuring it up from his own violent need.

When he looked up nothing had changed. His back had shielded their kiss from curious eyes.

All but Bedelia, who had watched them avidly. *Yes, she's cold, all right. She'll never keep him. She doesn't know what a man like that wants. But I do.* Bedelia hugged herself with smug satisfaction.

And I'll be waiting in the wings . . .

The sun set over the water in wreaths of glory. Sea and sky were liquid gold, then molten rose, then regal purple shading into dusk. Cassandra watched it through the open doors to the balcony of the hotel suite until the last spark of light was quenched. She dreaded the night. The others had gone to their rooms, leaving her alone with her new husband for the very first time.

It was strange to be separated from Kitty and Povey, and to know that her new life had begun. She couldn't remember ever being so terrified. Not even on her wedding night with Tyler. She had been ignorant then, not only of the duties of a wife, but of life. She had still believed in wishing upon stars.

Grayson stood next to the fireplace, remembering the first time he'd seen her face in the photographs. The irony amused him. He'd come to California seeking vengeance and instead had taken her for his wife. What was she thinking? What did she expect of him?

What did she want?

He waited to take his cue from her. The wind ruffled her hair and he ached to touch her, to fill his hands with her. The night was cooling rapidly. She must be cold in her summery dress. He began to think she'd stay framed in the doorway until Judgment Day, rather than come to him. Jesus, he wanted her!

He acknowledged now that he had wanted her from the first moment he'd seen her portrait. That night at the Lorenzes' Nob Hill mansion, when he'd seen Cassandra arriving, he had known that they were fated for each other. Known and fought against it from the start. He'd told himself from before their first actual encounter that she was everything he most despised, when all the while he'd realized, deep and instinctively, that she was the sum of his desires.

He went to the door. "Cassandra . . ."

She didn't meet his eyes but moved into the room

slowly, without speaking. Grayson went to her until only a few inches separated them. He lifted his hand and touched her hair. It was like skeins of dark silk against his callused fingers. She made him think of sheets and French perfume and the most intimate of acts between a man and a woman. Grayson tipped her face up to him. What he saw surprised him. She was afraid. He didn't want her to be. Not of him. Not ever. He touched the back of his hand to her cheek for reassurance. His skin caught fire from the contact. It burned a track along his arm and went through him, straight to his loins.

He took her hand and brought it to his lips, then touched them to the sensitive inside of her wrist. It bound them together in a sensual spell. Nothing existed but the two of them, alone in the cool dimness. Grayson leaned forward. His mouth brushed her temple, her cheekbone, the tender hollow at the angle of her jaw. He sensed the heat rising within her and put his hands on her shoulders, drawing her close. Her breasts were soft and their nipples were hard through the fabric.

Cassandra wanted him to kiss her. She wanted him to hold and caress her; yet at the same time she was so afraid. She didn't want to fail again, to see Grayson turn from her and walk away, perhaps forever.

He misunderstood what he read in her eyes. She'd been through hell in the past few days, and this hasty marriage hadn't helped her state of mind. He'd acted like a fool riding out to Stoneleigh like a maniac. Offering marriage to a woman he scarcely knew. But he would do it all over again, if need be. She was a fever in his blood. Desire blossomed and grew. He cradled her fragile face between his strong hands. "I want you, Cassandra. Will you lie with me?"

It wasn't what he'd meant to say.

She couldn't answer but Grayson saw the sudden flare of longing that lit her eyes. He swept her up into his arms and carried her into the adjoining bedroom, placing her on the bed where the sheets had been turned back. He leaned over her and touched his mouth to hers softly, then with mounting hunger. Caution vanished. He'd planned to take his time, let them become more acquainted. Grayson realized that he'd been lying to himself. He couldn't be near her without making love to her. He wanted to possess her, to make her ache for him the way he did for her. Jesus, he wanted her!

Cassandra was terrified. Not of Grayson, but herself. She hadn't expected this so soon. She would disappoint him as she had Tyler. He would turn from her with disgust because she was cold, incapable of satisfying a man. Even now, while his lips brushed her throat and her blood sang with longing, she felt her limbs growing heavy. Turning to wood.

He was unbuttoning her bodice. He slipped his hand inside and cupped her breast. Heat and fear warred with one another. Fear won. "Wait." She tried to push his hands away. She wasn't ready. "Please," she whispered.

Grayson's inner struggle was severe but short. He cursed his rashness. He'd acted like a damned barbarian. Curse it, she'd only been widowed a few days. That gold ring he'd put on her finger didn't make any difference to her heart. After all, she had been married to Tyler Lucton for half her life. He rolled away.

"Go to sleep," he said wearily. "You've had a long day." He rose and left the bedroom, closing the door behind him.

Cassandra stared at the closed door. Their wedding day and she was already alone. What had she done? She heard him pacing the parlor floor and tiptoed to the door. He was talking to someone—a woman. Then she heard the door to the corridor close and she knew that the parlor was empty. She climbed into the bed, her teeth chattering with reaction. History had repeated itself: two marriages, and two disastrous wedding nights.

Fear and pride had held her back. Yet when Grayson had touched her she'd been torn between that fear and a deep and passionate longing. To be held, to be loved, was such a human need. Her heart cried out for it. Her body burned for the warmth of his upon it, her breasts ached with the yearning.

False pride was a lonely bedmate. Cassandra wanted this strange marriage to succeed. She had come to it as a grown woman, not an inexperienced young girl. Her eyes had been wide open when she accepted Grayson's proposal and when they'd exchanged their vows. She didn't expect romantic love, but she did hope for the sharing of joys and sorrows and physical intimacy. For passion and affection.

When Grayson came back she would go to him. But the minutes turned to an hour, the hour to two, and still he didn't return. A dreadful fear grew in her mind. Perhaps, like Tyler, Grayson didn't really want her, only what she represented.

She couldn't bear it. Her nerves were shattered, her spirit bruised. Cassandra buried her face in the pillow and wept herself to sleep.

11

Four days later Cassandra stood on the bare railway platform at Promontory, Utah, with the Central Pacific engine s-s-s-ing out small puffs of steam behind her. Povey and Bedelia had already gone back inside. There was nothing much to see. The platform was surrounded by bleak alkaline flats. A purple-brown jumble of barren mountain rose up on the horizon, breaking the monotony of the sterile landscape.

The wind whipped at her yellow taffeta skirts and tugged at her bonnet. Grayson had insisted—rightly so, under the circumstances of their marriage—that she discard her widow's weeds. She felt overdressed and out of place in her neat traveling suit with the lace froth of her shirtwaist foaming over the collar. Even the ropes of jet beads and matching earrings, which were her only tokens of mourning, looked frivolous in such a drab, forbidding place.

She strolled up and down the platform to stretch her legs, thinking of poor, faithful Morton, buried in the churchyard instead of sailing home to England. This was a hard country, even its cities untamed and perilous. She was not the same woman who had come to America ten years earlier.

She was not even the same woman she had been ten days ago. She had been ostracized, widowed, impoverished. In less than a day's time she had shot a man and married a man she didn't really know. The wish she'd made on her birthday came back to haunt her. She'd asked for change, and had gotten it with a vengeance.

Grayson joined her, squinting into the strong sun. "A year ago Leland Stanford stood here and swung at the golden spike to unite the Central Pacific and Union Pacific railroads. He missed."

Cassandra had heard the story before from Stanford himself. It had been an amusing drawing-room anecdote back in San Francisco; but here, in the wilderness of the alkali flats, the joining of the railroads and the drama of their construction was a vivid and daring undertaking. Gangs of Chinese laborers had built the Central Pacific east from Sacramento, through great pine forests and rushing rivers of the Sierra Nevada Mountains and down to the inhospitable shores of the Great Salt Lake. Gangs of Irish navvies had built the Union Pacific to the west to join them in a monumental feat of human will. It had taken vision, courage, and power—and cost many lives—before that symbolic golden spike united the raw and sprawling nation from east to west.

She was awed at their accomplishment, and grateful to Grayson for finding a safe, neutral subject. He'd been avoiding her as much as possible. The strain between them grew worse with every passing day. In public he was polite and considerate. In private they were two strangers, sharing the same room. She noted the frown between his eyes. "You don't approve of this taming of the wilderness, do you?"

Grayson was startled. Was he becoming that easy to read? "I'm a cattleman. Without the railways I couldn't get goods to the ranch so easily, nor my cattle to the eastern markets. And it's certainly a fast and comfortable way to travel."

His surprise was as transparent as his attempt to cover up the fact that she'd seen through him. She smiled. "Tell me what it is that you dislike so much about the railroads."

He gazed out over the flats and when he spoke the timbre of his voice was rich and low. " *'Great beasts will come, with hooves of iron and fire in their bellies, belching foul smoke. White men will come and the buffalo will go, as Sweet Medicine foretold us. We will be banished from out hunting grounds and the rivers will run dry. There will be great sorrow in* Tsistsistas *camps, and weeping in the lodges. This, I have seen.'* "

She understood that he'd been quoting from his Cheyenne heritage. The side he kept hidden from her, locked away behind a door that was closed to trespassers. Even his wife. "How tragic," she said softly. "Whose words are those?"

But Grayson didn't hear her. He was turned inward, listening to voices of the past. Long ago, when he'd first gone to live among the *Tsistsistas,* old Buffalo Heart had warned that one day he would leave and return to the white man's world. The old seer had been wrong in only one way: Grayson lived in the white world now but he was not of it. He never would be; yet he was bleeding inside, torn between the two halves of his soul.

Cassandra sighed. Grayson had gone wherever it was that he went when his face took on that bleak, forbidding look. She left him to his inner devils and walked to the end of the platform again. A rawboned young man in dungarees and a plaid shirt pulled up in a canvas-covered wagon. He clambered down and stretched, then spied Cassandra and sauntered over.

"A hard place, ain't it? Think of them emmirant settlers trying to cross this godforsaken land by wagon train. Must've been right gruesome."

Cassandra tried but her imagination failed her. Her knowledge of the area's history was scant. "A grim trial, no doubt. Did many of them survive?"

He grinned, placing her accent correctly. "'Course they did. Les'n they gave in to thirst and drank the alkali water. Us Yankees are a tough breed."

"Indeed, you must be!"

She learned a lot about the young man in the next few minutes, much to her dismay. His name was Tex Sample and his own parents had traveled the Oregon Trail in a covered wagon much like his own, walking beside their oxen most of the way. Mr. Sample was on his way to Johnsonville, just south of Salt Lake City, and intended to make his fortune there.

"Cats," he said confidentially. "I got a whole load of 'em. Cats is better than gold."

"I beg your pardon?"

He reached inside his coat and pulled out a sable kitten, which had been sleeping in his vest pocket. "They get rid of the rats," he informed her, looking over his shoulder for eavesdroppers. "And the saloon girls love 'em."

His face pinked with earnestness. "There's a little yellow-haired filly at the Red Garter in Johnsonville.

Thought I'd give her one. Soften her up, so's I can pop the question. Cats is better than flowers, too. It's a lonely life out here."

The sable kitten yawned, exposing a tiny pink tongue, and opened its eyes to look right at Cassandra. They were bluer than the cloudless Utah sky. It was love at first sight. Cassandra reached and stroked the long, silky coat. She could feel the vibration of its purr through her gloved fingers. The kitten closed its eyes in bliss. "What a dear little creature."

"Why, he likes you!" Tex Sample exclaimed. "Gosh, I sure wanted to give this little feller to that blondheaded girl in Johnsonville. But I can see you've taken to one another. If your heart's set on him, I suppose I could give her one of the others instead."

Cassandra looked up into the young man's guileless gray eyes. She couldn't believe that he was capable of conniving her—was he? "Are you truly going to Johnsonville to sell your cats, Mr. Sample, or are you planning to make a fortune from gullible train passengers?"

He had the grace to blush. "I *am* going to Johnsonville, ma'am. Next week. And I *was* thinking of taking a load of cats along. A teamster carted a wagonful to Deadwood a few years back and did right well for himself. And I did think as how a nice lady like you might be bored on the long train run—and how playing with a gamboling kitten could help to pass the long, weary hours."

Sample glanced at her from the corner of his eye to see how Cassandra was taking his stories. They seemed to be working. "Found this little feller hanging 'round the milk shed this morning. Cute, ain't he? I'd sure hate to hafta put him in a bucket."

"Mr. Sample!" Cassandra began indignantly.

Grayson had been watching the scene unfold. Her sharp exclamation brought him to Cassandra's side in a few long strides. "Leave my wife alone, you young scalawag, or you'll be picking your teeth up out of the dirt! Go on, and take that flea-ridden animal with you."

Sample stepped back quickly but gave it one more try. "Now, how could a fine gentleman like you be so unkind to such a pretty lady? She's set her sweet heart on this little whisker. Wouldn't you like to purchase this fine little kitten for your lovely wife, sir?"

"No, by God."

A forlorn expression flitted across Cassandra's face. It was gone in an instant but Grayson had seen it. He made a wry face, took a silver dollar from his pocket, and flipped it to Sample. The young man caught it in one hand and pressed the sable kitten on Cassandra with the other. "Much obliged!"

He was off like a shot, grinning all the way back to his wagon. Cassandra cuddled the warm, furry bundle, careful of its delicate bones and needle-sharp claws. The kitten winked at her, blue eyes meeting blue-green. She smiled in delight, then looked up to thank her husband. Grayson wasn't there to receive them. He had moved away to speak to the engineer. Perhaps he didn't want her gratitude.

She got back on the train to show off her cuddly acquisition. Kitty would be enchanted.

They were traveling in luxury. Grayson had arranged the use of two private cars from a vice president of the railway. The floors of both cars were covered with thick Oriental carpets and wainscoted in rosewood. The second was divided into a fabulous parlor and a smaller but elegant dining suite. The walls of the dining section were hung with blue silk and swags of the same material framed the windows. The rosewood table had matching high-backed chairs and could seat twelve comfortably. The men spent their evenings smoking cigars and playing cards there after dinner, while the women talked or read or worked on puzzles in the parlor.

The car ahead of it was divided into a small parlor, guest quarters, and a luxurious bedroom at the end for the honeymoon couple. No one knew that once the door to the bedroom was closed for the night, they rarely spoke. Or that Cassandra slept in the bed alone, while Grayson wrapped up in a blanket on the floor. "We'll go slow," he had told her, "until you're settled on the ranch. There's plenty of time."

She fervently hoped so. The alternative would be intolerable. From what she could glean from her husband and Jaime McFee, the Thunder Ranch was in an isolated valley. There were few social contacts, and they would all live in each other's pockets, especially in the long winter months.

She found Kitty sitting in an armchair by the window, staring blankly out the window. The parlor was like a long formal drawing room, with beveled mirrors, pier cabinets, and scrolled wallpaper to match the gold draperies. The chairs, sofas, and ottomans were upholstered in rose damask with a faint gold thread woven through, and there were glass-fronted cases of books and objets d'art.

When Kitty saw the little ball of fur her face lit up. "A kitten! Oh, what a sweet little face he has. Poor thing, he is hardly weaned. We must get him a saucer of milk."

Cassandra hadn't seen such animation in Kitty's face since that terrible night. She was glad she'd met Tex Sample, engaging scoundrel that he was. If he'd only known it, she would have given him gold, just to see the smile of delight on her niece's face.

By the time the train left Promontory even Grayson was playing with Cassandra's new pet, baiting it with a dangling piece of twine, and laughing at the kitten's antics. He smiled at Kitty. "You'll have to give the little rascal a name," he teased. "We can't have two 'kittys' under the same roof."

"Then I shall give him the name you used. I will call him Rascal." She looked away, suddenly embarrassed, but Cassandra could tell she felt increasingly comfortable with Grayson. Thank God.

Later, its pink belly full of milk, the kitten curled up happily in the wooden crate Grayson had procured for it. He had even lined half the bottom with a piece of flannel. Cassandra was pleased. She smiled her thanks as they bent over the carton and Grayson's breath caught in his throat. She had some unexplained magic that could turn him inside out with a look or a touch. He didn't want anyone to have such power over him. Long ago he had learned that pain came hand in hand with love, and desolation in the wake of hope. It wasn't worth the risk.

He rose abruptly and went into the small parlor, leaving Cassandra to wonder. She was sound asleep when he retired for the night. Sometime after midnight Rascal awakened and complained loudly of loneliness, until Kitty took him into her berth. Their bond was sealed. By the following day he had won everyone's hearts and made himself quite at home in the swaying parlor car.

The journey to Grayson's ranch at Silver Creek, even in the luxury of two private railroad cars, proved long and tiring. The confinement was not as difficult for Cassandra to bear, as was the loss of her music. How she would love to be able to lock herself away with a piano and weave all her tangled emotions into a tapestry of thundering sound! But there was no outlet for her confused emotions, except her troubled dreams.

Grayson found a message from Bronco waiting for him at the next stop. He and Jaime discussed it as they leaned on the rail of the back platform, smoking their inevitable cigarillos. "Two offers for the Thunder Mine within two weeks," Grayson told him. "Interesting, isn't it?"

"Are you thinking of taking any of them up?" Jaime shook a column of ash into the wind. "You lost a bundle when Tyler Lucton blew his brains out. I warned you."

"The money wasn't the important thing to me . . ." Grayson broke off. He blew out a cloud of smoke. "At least I didn't lose the Morning Star Mine. I'd intended to meet him at the bank the next day and sign the papers."

Jaime dropped the cigar stub and ground it out quickly. The wind was picking up and they didn't want any more fires. Grayson handed him another. "I'd give my eye teeth," he said, "to know what's behind these sudden offers. I may have to take a little trip to Aureus to find out what Simon Fiddler and his fellows are up to on the other side."

"Maybe there *is* a Pegasus mine," Jaime said with a shrug.

"And maybe the moon is made of green cheese. According to Bronco there's silver coming out of the mountain—just where is the question."

"Bronco probably knows by now." Jaime puffed out a cloud of smoke. "Seems he's got more than his ear to the ground."

"Well, I hope he hasn't heard that we've got an extra passenger on board. I'd hate to ruin the big surprise."

"You're really looking forward to Bronco's reunion with his sister."

"Yes, it should be something to see."

Grayson was thoughtful, watching the tracks converge and dwindle into the distance. The fresh air and wind cleared the cobwebs from a man's head. Annette talked constantly of seeing her brother again. Jaime had produced a picture of Bronco with his mother and sister and she kept it close beside her, sending fond looks at it from time to time. She'd even written their names on the back in pencil: "Annette and Bronco Mason, with our dear mother."

He ground the butt of his cigarillo in the sand bucket kept there to stifle minor fires en route. He couldn't wait to witness that first meeting. "While the ladies are getting settled in tomorrow night, call the ranch hands together in front of the porch. And don't tell them why. I want this to be a complete surprise."

"But . . ." Jaime hesitated. "Bronco and Annette have been parted for years. They might want a few moments alone, first."

"Nonsense! The more the merrier." He smiled and went inside.

The journey seemed to go on forever. Nothing brought the changes in her condition home to Cassandra as much as the alien landscapes that they'd passed through. They'd switched to the Union Pacific tracks from Promontory to Cheyenne, then gone south on the Kansas Pacific offshoot to Denver and changed to the Silver Spur Line. Flatlands had given way to dull brown hills pocked with dusty green scrub. Long purple ridges and green piney slopes were scarred with reaches of bald rock and capped by icy peaks so tall that they choked out the clear blue sky.

The novelty of train travel had worn off after the second day. They were all inured to the clack of the wheels and the rumble of the cars. Povey, who was a magnificent needlewoman, passed the time with her embroidery and cut-work. Cassandra and Kitty talked or read or played at draughts and anagrams. Bedelia had no interest in their pastimes. The company of women bored her.

An after-dinner sherry was not her idea of a high time. She knew Jaime had a case of gin but hadn't dared ask for a drink, or to get up a hand of euchre. It was damn hard to have to watch her tongue constantly, too. When she'd answered the flyer and claimed to be Annette Mason, she hadn't had all the facts. She hadn't expected to be a frigging pioneer, stuck out in the middle of the frigging wilderness. By the time she figured out what was what, they were smack in the middle of it. She invented a case of travel sickness and retired to her tiny bedroom to daydream of better days ahead.

Grayson joined Cassandra and Kitty in the parlor the day before their scheduled arrival. "Where's Annette?"

"Sleeping." Cassandra jerked her embroidery thread too tightly. She hoped Annette would sleep until dinner. In fact, she wished she'd sleep right through it. Grayson and Jaime might find her lively and attractive, but Cassandra felt a growing dislike for the person she knew as Miss Annette Mason. She was rude to Povey, condescending to Kitty, and flirtatious with the men. There was something consciously artful and calculating in her wide blue eyes. And it grew when she fixed them upon Grayson. And he seemed to enjoy it thoroughly. Men were blind: they never noticed the things a woman did. Not where a pretty young female was concerned.

Cassandra stabbed her needle into the cloth and right into her finger beneath. She winced and pulled it out, quickly pressing her handkerchief against the wound. Oh, how she wished she could turn her turbulent emotions into thundering music, release her anxieties in the swift rush of sound! Forgetting for a few minutes the travail of the past weeks and her apprehension for the future.

While Cassandra fretted, Bedelia was lying stretched out on her comfortable berth with the curtains closed. She wasn't really napping. She was bored to death by the monotonous scenery and hours of female company. Jesus, this sedate life was killing her! She had to figure out her best course of action. She was torn between jumping ship at Denver and setting her cap at Grayson. From what she'd gleaned from Jaime, life on the Thunder Ranch was not her cup of tea. If she went along with them, there were two courses open to her. One was to convince this Bronco person that she was his long-lost sister, take him for what she could get, and light out to Denver. In a booming town there'd be work there for an enterprising woman. The other was to stay on at the ranch and insinuate herself with its owner. And that was tempting.

Grayson Howard was rich and he was handsome. She smiled in the dimness. There was something about him that bypassed a woman's brain and went straight to her deepest feminine instincts, and clubbed them over the head. Not that he was rough or uncouth. More like untamed. Yes, and dangerous, too. Bedelia liked that in a man.

It hadn't taken her long to realize that there was

something odd about the newlyweds. It never occurred to her that the marriage hadn't been consummated. Not with a man as virile as Grayson. She only knew that there was trouble there—a distance that shouldn't be, between two people who jumped straight from a funeral to a wedding. Maybe he found his bride a little too milk-and-water for his tastes. He was a red-blooded man with a man's needs. And, Bedelia thought, she could show him what he was missing. It might be worth her while to stick around the Thunder Ranch for a while and see which way the wind blew . . .

In the morning she joined everyone for breakfast and was annoyed to learn that they'd changed tracks outside Denver during the night. They'd been shuttled to the Silver Spur Line while she slept and Denver was miles behind them. She was stuck for now.

During luncheon the brakes suddenly screeched and squealed so loudly that conversation was impossible. The engine clanged and chuffed to a halt and the china in the glass-covered breakfront rattled. Steam boiled up in billowing clouds that obscured the view through the windows, then quickly dissipated. Kitty was anxious. Tales of desperadoes ran through her head. "Is something wrong?"

Cassandra set down her cup and went to the window. Several blank-faced sheds clung to the side of the brown hill, their red paint scarred and faded. A long chute on an elevated trestle ran from the largest one down to the railroad tracks. "I think we're stopping for water and fuel. There are some rude sort of outbuildings up ahead by the side of the tracks."

Grayson entered. "Rude sort of outbuildings? That's no way to speak of the closest thing we have to a town hereabouts. Welcome to Silver Creek, ladies."

It was a subdued group of women who assembled on the plank platform a short time later, surrounded by crates and trunks and dressing cases. Silver Creek was even more unprepossessing than it had appeared from the train window. There was no station. No town. Nothing but the worn red buildings, the sere hills, and the hard, bright sky. Across the tracks the land rolled featureless to the horizon. There, the hazy blue of the distant mountains blended into the heavens, with only cloudlike streaks of snow to mark the boundary between them.

There was not a house, a horse, or even a stray dog in sight for as far as the eye could see. It was as if they had been dropped off at the ends of the earth. Even the few plants that clung to the rocky soil seemed dead or dying. After the racket of the train, the very stillness was unnerving. It was broken only by the activity on the platform and the low, constant moan of the wind.

Cassandra was aghast. Dear God, what had she done! Kitty stared about them silently and Povey's dour face settled in sterner lines. Bedelia plopped herself down on a flat-topped trunk and sulked. Shit! She should have got off in Denver. This place was deader than a graveyard at midnight!

The private cars were switched onto a siding and the train, reduced to an engine, a coal tender, and a lone passenger coach, started up in a clang of bells and a hiss of pressurized steam. They watched forlornly as it vanished up the track and around the side of a hill.

Kitty picked Rascal up from the traveling basket she'd fixed for him, and rubbed her cheek against his softness for comfort. She had never imagined a place like this in her entire life. She had wanted to escape from the press of people, but this was as alien to her as the moon.

When the baggage and goods were safely stowed, teams were hitched and Grayson brought out the newer and smaller of the two carriages. It was elegant and built for speed, as were the two fine horses harnessed in tandem. He held the restive bays easily and Jaime handed Cassandra up into it. The carriage had only one seat, but there was room for Kitty. Cassandra looked around for her niece, but Jaime was already assisting her into the second vehicle.

Grayson started off. "The others will follow." He saw her hesitation. "Don't worry, you can trust your niece to Jaime."

She sent a sidelong look at her new husband. His profile was beautiful, in a stark, masculine way. His bronzed skin and honed features suited the vast, jagged landscape. He belonged to it, in a way that she never could. Her blue taffeta traveling dress and yellow gloves seemed frivolous against the barren hills and the distant gray-blue peaks. Her kid boots would not last a mile.

Grayson seemed to follow her thoughts. "If the weather holds we'll go into Aureus next week. You'll like it, I think."

Grayson snapped the reins. The team responded with vigor. "The bays are eager for a good workout," he said, cracking the whip high over their backs.

With the faster rig they soon outdistanced the others. The horses flew down the road, stretching their powerful legs in gracefully matched strides. Cassandra held her hat with one gloved hand. She admired Grayson's skill with the reins while at the same time deploring his increasing speed. They thundered over a rude wooden bridge—little more than a few long boards—that spanned a dry arroyo.

"You'll overturn us!" she gasped as they took the crest of the road.

"Nonsense." He let the horses have their heads and they raced along with the wind streaming through their manes. The faster they went the more nervous she became, grabbing the sissy bar for dear life; but Grayson exulted in their wild dash. His eyes shone like silver and his face looked young and eager. It was as if a part of him long held in check were suddenly set free. The answer came to her. He was going home to the land he loved.

While she was headed into exile.

But she mustn't think that way. "How far is it to the ranch?"

That evoked a laugh. "You've been on it since you got off the train. The Silver Creek operation is one of my holdings. As for the house itself, we've a good long way to go."

"I know as little about your ranch as I do about you."

He didn't answer. She settled back against the seat, overwhelmed by the immensity of it. In some places sudden small rises were capped with greenery. Others were huge wedges of tilted stone, bare except for small patches of emerald moss and splotches of tan lichen. Eventually they entered a wide valley, thick with a variety of grasses and dotted with cattle. A river wound through it, small and swift. The water was incredibly clear and there were trees clustered along its banks. Grayson turned to her, frowning. "Do you ride?"

"Of course. Before I . . . before I left England, I used to spend all day in the saddle on my grandfather's estate." She had almost said "before I married Tyler." That seemed a little inappropriate under the circumstances.

"Good. I'll take you around and show you the property. It will tell you more about me than anything I can say."

"I should like that."

He fell silent after that. A turn past a grove led them into a second valley, backed by green hills. Behind their rounded humps rose the spikes of jagged peaks, their wrinkled seams white with last winter's snow. Their way seemed straight ahead, but as they swung past the grove of trees the ground fell away rapidly. The drop was sheer and at least a thousand feet.

It made Cassandra dizzy to look down, but she spied a small town on the far side of the low valley. In the clear air she could make out houses and a street of shops, a church complete with steeple and two large buildings. The first was painted a bright scarlet with white trim, the second white with dark shutters and an ornamental balcony running around all three floors.

"That's Aureus," Grayson told her. "You'll fit right in. It was founded by English expatriates—mostly land speculators, retired colonials, and make-believe cowboys, with a fair number of remittance men and black sheep."

"I don't know why you imagine I should fit in with such a group!"

He grinned. "No offense. There are some blue bloods, like yourself. They drink gin tonics and tea from china cups, toast the queen's health, and hunt coyotes instead of fox."

Cassandra knew that some of the largest cattle operations on the plains were owned by European investors, particularly the British. Sir Harry Bascomb and his syndicate of American partners owned a quarter-million acres on the other side of the mountains from Aureus. Bascomb and Tyler had been partners in a highly profitable venture several years back. Most owners were absentee landholders; others had taken up western life with enthusiasm, sending home studio photographs of themselves in chaps and spurs and cowboy hats to shock their relatives.

"The nearest woman to us is Beth Leslie," Grayson told her. "She's the widow of an Englishman, Philip Leslie. They met in Charleston and came out here after they married to manage his cousin's spread."

"I shall look forward to meeting her soon."

Grayson kept his eyes fixed on the dusty road. "The Lazy L is about ten miles as the crow flies. Twenty if you take the trail."

The consequences of her marriage settled over Cassandra like a leaden cloak. Grayson had warned her that his life was a lonely one. She wished now that she'd taken his words at face value.

His team covered the miles quickly. Soon they arrived at a fence of peeled logs, pierced by a high wooden gate. The crossboard above was burned with a double lightning emblem: The Thunder Ranch.

Beyond the grove of hardwoods, several long outbuildings came into view—barns, stables, a smithy shop, and corrals, miniaturized with distance. Grayson slowed the team, prolonging the elation of his homecoming. It had never looked more beautiful to him. He turned to Cassandra. "Well? What do you think?"

What did he expect her to say about outbuildings? She wasn't a farmer. "The view is lovely," she ventured. "The stables are quite large and . . . and the barns are very well kept." Someone had even planted a lilac bush and flowers outside the door.

He reined in sharply. "That's not the barn."

She looked again, shading her eyes against the afternoon glare, and stared at the building in dismay. Not only flowers, but gingham curtains at the windows peeking through the leafy lilac. Her heart seemed to plummet to her toes. Dear God, was that . . . that *cowshed*, their residence? It could have fit comfortably into the drawing room at Stoneleigh. She glanced at Grayson. He was angrier than she'd ever seen him.

He was furious. At Cassandra for denigrating his home, at himself for not preparing her for it. Because he had built it himself, he loved every inch of it. He hadn't realized until this moment how it must seem to her.

"It's small from your standpoint," he admitted, "but you'll get used to it. And it's damn snug in the winter when the wind howls down out of the north with a load of snow. We had fourteen feet of it last February."

She shivered. "A goodly accumulation! Are the winters always so severe?"

"That," he replied crisply, "was from one storm."

At first Cassandra was struck mute with dismay. Then she became angry. He was either trying to frighten her, or this was an example of American exaggeration. Fourteen feet of snow at one time, indeed!

The light faded abruptly as the sun lowered behind the rocky tip of a mountain, purpling the valley with false twilight. Long shadows stretched across the ground, stealing toward the cluster of buildings. By the time they reached them the sky shaded from lavender to indigo and the crest of the mountain was limned in gold.

Stars bloomed overhead, larger and closer than Cassandra had ever imagined. The air seemed tinted a luminous, pastel lavender. "Are you hungry?" Grayson asked. "Ping will have a good meal waiting for us."

Cassandra was tired and answered without thinking: "It's late. I would prefer to have a tray sent up to my room."

Colorado Territory was as foreign to her nature as San Francisco was to his, Grayson realized. She'd never stick it out. When the train made its next monthly stop at Silver Creek she would probably be on it, this time traveling west. And that made him angrier.

"*You* don't have a room. *We* have a room. Together. And we don't run to maidservants here. Ping has enough to do cooking for the ranch hands. You'll take your meals family style with the rest of us, or go without. And you'll do your share of the work and the cleaning up!"

Cassandra gave him a cool look. "I see that I was under a misapprehension. I thought it was a wife that you wanted, not another serving woman."

He narrowed his eyes. "That was my original intention when we married. Let me remind you, however, that it was you who changed the rules."

"That is unjust!" She felt her face redden. "I haven't barred you from my bed."

"Nor have you enticed me to it."

Her flush deepened to a crimson. "I wasn't aware that it was necessary between husband and wife."

His eyes glittered dangerously in the starlight. "Your point, madam, is well taken."

His words sent a chill up the back of her arms. There was no time to answer.

A rangy tow-haired boy came out of the barn with a sheepdog at his heels. He saw them and ran up to take the horses, goggling at Cassandra. No wonder they'd had word to have the carriages brought down to Silver

Creek. She looked like one of the fine ladies in the mail order patterns his mother used to have. Or maybe a princess.

"Welcome back, Gray! I've been watching for you." He waved to the side. "They finished the addition while you were gone. Got enough lumber cut to add on more, but Bronco didn't know what you wanted for sure."

Grayson helped Cassandra get down from the carriage. "That's good. The entire second floor will be ours. It's not luxurious, by any means, but you won't be as cramped as you might imagine."

Top floor? Cassandra leaned forward in the direction the boy had indicated, and saw the house for the first time. Grayson hadn't realized that the trees had screened it from Cassandra's view. It was nestled against the hill to the right. The building she'd mistaken for it must be the bunkhouse then, she realized with relief.

The house was solid and serviceable, standing four-square against the elements. A low porch supported by square pillars ran along the front. Long shutters framed the tall windows and the central door, stark against the horizontal split logs that formed the walls, and the white chinking between them. The steeply pitched roof hid a smaller second floor. Two broad chimneys and an enormous woodpile by either end of the house gave evidence of long, hard winters.

A lamp burned in the front window, casting a warm, apricot glow through the panes. The house looked cozy and welcoming. Cassandra gazed beyond it, where the tall evergreens on the rim of the hill were still tipped with gold by the last long rays of sunlight. The scene was perfect and oddly familiar, like something from a half-remembered dream.

Grayson saw her smile. He was ashamed of the way

he'd tried to bait her, and felt the constraint of the past few days dissolve as they went up the path to the front door. He was tired of words—polite ones, sharp ones, angry ones. She was his wife, and it was time that he did something about it.

There were times when a man and woman could communicate on a level so deep and intimate there was no need to speak. Grayson wanted that with Cassandra. He wanted to sweep her into his arms and carry her upstairs to his bed and make love to her. To fall asleep afterward with her naked in his arms.

He was so tired of being alone.

But already the sounds of an approaching vehicle echoed from the rim of the valley. Grayson muttered an oath beneath his breath. Jaime and the rest were about to descend upon the Thunder Ranch. There was business to catch up on and people to settle in first.

He had to content himself with swooping Cassandra up in his arms and carrying her onto the porch. He laughed at her gasp of surprise. "Let's start out right. I'll carry you across the threshold for luck."

She put her arms around his neck for balance, feeling silly and rather shy. How strong he was. She liked the way he smelled and the rough texture of his coat against her cheek. *I shall be happy here.* The idea came into her mind fully formed and certain.

Grayson reached for the door handle, thinking how light and warm she felt against his chest. The scent of her hair was intoxicating. He was tempted to fulfill his marital obligations and damn the rest of his responsibilities to hell. His long fingers groped for the handle and brushed against the metal fittings. Before he could turn it the door opened wide. The odor of roast beef and apple pie wafted out.

"Welcome home, Gray! When I heard the train whistle I drove over to see that everything was ready for your return."

The voice was low, and distinctly feminine. A small woman, with a classic cameo face, dark blond hair, and eyes as brown as pansies stood just inside, her heart-shaped face aglow. When she saw Cassandra in Grayson's arms the light was abruptly quenched.

He was as amazed as she. The woman moved back from the door with awkward, jerky movements and he stepped inside. "Beth! I didn't expect to find you here."

"Yes." Her glance went to the woman in Grayson's arms. "That's quite obvious."

He set Cassandra down. She flushed and smoothed her rumpled skirts. Grayson went directly to the introductions. "Cassandra, this is Mrs. Leslie, whom I mentioned earlier. Beth, this is my wife . . ."

The other woman was even more startled. She struggled but seemed to recover her composure. "How do you do," she said briskly—and burst into tears.

Grayson took Beth's hand. "What is it? Has something happened?"

She sniffed and dabbed at her eyes. "It . . . it is just . . . so joyful an occasion. To have you home at last . . . and with a new wife . . . I never expected . . ." She conquered her tears. "You are so deserving of happiness, Gray. I wish you both good fortune."

Grayson bent down and kissed her cheek. "You've been a good friend to me, Beth, and it was kind of you to plan such a nice reception. I'm glad that Cassandra has another woman—and a compatriot, as well—to hail her arrival. And once you know Cassandra, I'm sure you'll welcome her as much for her own sake, as for mine."

Neither woman seemed to share his sentiments. They eyed each other like two cats with a fish bone. An awkward pause ensued. Cassandra felt a sharp twinge of emotion and mistook it for pity: she knew without a doubt that Beth Leslie was in love with Grayson, that she had expected someday to marry him herself. It was equally plain that he was unconscious of it. She realized it was up to her to bridge the widening gap. Smiling, she held out her hand.

"Grayson has spoken of you to me, Mrs. Leslie. I am most sincerely pleased to meet you and know that we shall become great friends."

"Thank you. You are very kind." Beth gave her a brittle smile. I can see why Grayson was smitten with you, it said quite clearly, but as to the matter of friendship, I will hold my opinion in reserve.

The other carriage pulled up and in the general excitement there was no time for more. Kitty was more concerned with getting the kitten into the house and procuring some milk for him. Povey climbed down with an assist from Jaime, and stood looking at the house. Cassandra couldn't read her expression at all, but then Povey had had many years of hiding her thoughts.

Bedelia was the last to descend. It wasn't exactly what she'd expected, but after riding for hours she was ready to fall asleep in any convenient corner. God, she wanted a drink!

Grayson ushered them all inside. Beth Leslie, taken aback by the arrival of three more women, met them with fortitude. As he made introductions, Cassandra had her first chance to look about. The small parlor served as dining room and study. The rosewood sofa and armchair were covered in deep garnet velvet. The rest of the room was plain, solid, and masculine, from the scrubbed pine floor to the smoking stand, and the enormous rack of antlers over the mantelpiece.

The glassed-in bookcases at one end were filled with account books and the heavy trestle table before them held a double inkstand, a small globe, and two framed photographs. One was a quiet family portrait, showing a lovely woman with a small boy—who was obviously Grayson—and a tall man in buckskins, who might have been Spanish or Indian. The other was less formal, and had captured an outdoor scene. Two Indian braves, dressed in buckskins, flanked a smiling young Indian woman mounted on a pinto pony. Suddenly Cassandra looked closer. One of the men was Grayson. She was reminded for the hundredth time of how little she knew about her husband.

Beth offered to make tea. She spoke as if she were the hostess and the newcomers were visitors, merely passing through. Cassandra's hackles rose. "I'd prefer to go to my room and freshen up first."

Grayson sensed trouble and took charge. "Povey can have Jaime's room, next to the kitchen. He won't mind bunking with the men for a few nights. Kitty and Annette will have to share the spare bedroom until the addition is furnished."

Bedelia spoke up quickly. She didn't want her options limited. "I'm a terrible sleeper," she lied. "Toss and turn and talk in my sleep. I wouldn't want to keep Kitty awake. There must be a storeroom or such where I could set up my bed."

Beth stepped into the role of hostess again. "There is that old staples pantry next to the kitchen. It's snug with a window facing the hill, but isolated from everyone else."

She led them through to the kitchen, with its great

stone hearth, and threw open a door. Bedelia peered in. The pine floor was clean and the walls had been white-washed and the single window covered in red gingham. It faced the hill and suited her just dandy. She could come and go as she pleased.

Maybe not for long, though. Once she built up a stake she could light out for Aureus or Denver, where a hard-working girl could set herself up just fine. Of course, she'd have to save up some money for a stake, first. That wouldn't be too hard to do. There were a lot of lonely cowboys on a place this size.

"What a dear little room!" she said brightly. "All empty and clean."

Beth's color rose. She had thought that the storage pantry would make a nice little sewing room someday; but that was before Grayson had come home with an unexpected bride, and changed everything.

"I'll pass on the tea. If there's an old mattress or a pile of blankets I'll just curl right up in the corner. The only thing I want to do right now is shuck off these dusty clothes and fall into bed."

Kitty looked at Bedelia in astonishment. "But don't you want to see your brother?"

"My brother? Oh! Yes, of course. But it's so late—"

"Yes, and the men get up before dawn," Grayson added. "I think you ladies should have some refreshments and make an early night of it. You've been traveling all day. I'll see that your things are unloaded."

Beth led them into the dining room, where a roast stood ready to carve, surrounded by browned potatoes, fresh bread, cookies, jellies, and jams. A plate of cookies and a brown sugar cake were on the sideboard near a brown earthen teapot covered with a cozy. Two plates and two place settings. How intimate, Cassandra thought. Mrs. Leslie had been a busy little bee! The others were glad to have hot tea and refreshments, but she found that her appetite had vanished.

As Grayson went outside he heard the sound of the women's footsteps and their mingled voices. It seemed very strange. No woman had ever lived beneath this roof before—and now there were four of them. It was going to take some getting used to.

Cassandra was having similar thoughts. She went upstairs, staking out her claim. She found a wide landing, with a long window facing the front yard, and three doors. Two stood open. To the right was a bedroom with a high truckle bed, covered with a colorful patchwork quilt stitched with red, yellow, and blue calico. The windows were hung with red fabric and tied back with yellow bows. The wood-framed mirror over the dresser threw back a pale image of her own face. No comb or brush marred its surface. The room had none of the small personal articles that would have declared ownership.

She opened the middle door, feeling like Bluebeard's wife, and found only a narrow storage space beneath the eaves. A small window looked out to the hills. She wondered, with a pang, if it had once been intended for a nursery. How little she knew about her new husband. Nothing of his past. Nothing of his future hopes and dreams.

The larger bedroom was on the left. A small flowered valise was just outside in the hall. Mrs. Leslie's? The furniture was made from dark wood in clean, masculine lines, and polished to a fare-thee-well. The chinking between the honey-toned wood of the flat-sided logs was white as icing. Heavy blue draperies framed the double windows. Although dusk was closing in rapidly, she caught a glimpse of distant, twilit peaks. A fire blazed cheerily in the fireplace, and the sleigh bed facing it was piled high with feather comforters, and spread with an exquisite blue and white patchwork quilt.

She went inside. A brass bathing tub and tall wooden shaving stand were visible through the half-open doorway. The room smelled of cedar and pine and expensive leather. Grayson's room. Had Beth Leslie expected to spend the night here? Cassandra looked around but there wasn't so much as a hairbrush or a hatpin to be found.

She was turning into a jealous cat. And for what? Because this was the only life she had. Because she intended to make the best of it, for all concerned. She would be a good wife and she would be happy here. Whether she was wanted or not.

But for all her fine resolution, the words rang hollow. There were other, deeper reasons that she was unable to acknowledge. She went to the window, shielded the glass pane with her hand, and looked out. She could not have gotten farther from her previous life unless she sailed to Africa and pitched a tent among the Bedouins. The river gleamed like pewter and the stark shadow of the mountains edged a star-strewn sky. Cassandra closed the curtains. She hadn't realized how tired she was. The bed looked soft and inviting. Until she remembered that she wouldn't be sleeping in it alone. Ignoring its invitation, she sat in the rocker before the fire, and watched the dancing flames.

A moment later—or so it seemed—she opened her eyes. The house was silent, sleeping. The door to the landing was closed and the flames in the fireplace had mellowed to glowing orange embers, beneath a coat of thick white ash. Someone had thrown a crocheted carriage blanket over her lap. Cassandra realized that she had been asleep for some time.

And that she was no longer alone.

12

Grayson leaned against the mantelpiece, watching her. There was weariness in the chiseled lines of his face, but his eyes were intent. He'd removed his boots and coat. His shirt was half-unbuttoned, the sleeves rolled up, and his hair carelessly tousled, as if he'd raked through it with his fingers. The hour was obviously advanced. Cassandra felt very foolish.

"How long have I been asleep?" *How long have you been watching me?* But she didn't say that aloud.

"It's half-past midnight. The others are in bed, fast asleep."

"I didn't mean to keep you from your bed."

The glow from the hearth reflected warmly in his silvery eyes. "I had no intention of getting into it alone."

The moment of truth. A shiver raced up her spine. Grayson crossed the floor soundlessly toward her. The urge to run almost overwhelmed her—but whether to the door or his arms was unclear.

Grayson recognized her feelings. Hadn't he gone through them himself? From their first meeting this moment had been inevitable. They had gotten off to a bad start in his hotel suite on their wedding day. He wanted to begin anew here, away from the shadows of the past.

"This is our first night together under this roof. Let us begin our life here in the right way, Cassandra. As man and wife."

He held out his hands to her. Slowly, tentatively, she placed her hands in his grasp. His fingers closed around them. Cassandra only had an instant to feel the callused strength of Grayson's hands, the leap of current that bridged the small gap between them. Then he pulled her to her feet. The carriage blanket fell to the floor and she was in his arms.

She hadn't begun to realize how much power was contained in his sinewy frame. His chest was wide and hard, his arms like iron bands around her. She found herself caught between them, overwhelmed by the fierce possessiveness of his embrace. Her emotions were chaotic, a blend of exhilaration, fear, and things she couldn't even name.

His breath stirred her hair, warm and clean with his male scent, and she could feel the swelling in his loins and the pounding of his heart. She clung to him out of sudden physical weakness and the shattering knowledge of her need. She wanted him to make love to her. Grayson sensed the change in her.

"I want you, Cassandra, in my arms, and in my bed!" He tipped her face back so his mouth was only a whisper away from hers. "Will you come to me?"

"Yes."

Her voice was so soft he could scarcely hear her. Words were unnecessary. Her rose and lavender perfume filled the air. Her perfume was so much a part of her he would have singled her out of a crowd by it. It stirred his senses, intoxicated him with desire.

Grayson pulled the pins from Cassandra's mass of midnight hair. It fell in shining ripples almost to her knees. He brushed her cheek with the back of his hand and felt her tremble in response. He'd known there was passion beneath her cool surface, but as she came awake, alive in his arms, he realized that he hadn't even begun to guess at the depth of it. Nor of his own desire.

From the moment of their first meeting there had been a potent sexual attraction between them. They had both denied it. Now it was an unstoppable force. The dam was breached and it washed over them in a deluge, sweeping away all restraint.

"Cassandra . . ." He buried his face against her hair, weaving his hands through its silky length. The softness of her body molded to the unyielding lines of his. His lips traced fire along her temple and down her cheek and the rhythm of her heart accelerated. When his mouth covered hers, hot and urgent, she surrendered to it. Her fear melted away and her blood sang with fierce, wild joy.

Grayson unbuttoned the taffeta jacket and slid it away from Cassandra. His fingers fumbled with the buttons. The loops were too tiny for his big hands to manage. He'd been patient too long. He grasped the edges and yanked them apart. Buttons skittered across the floor, a hail of small glass beads to mark the rising storm of their emotions. He pushed the fabric aside slowly and pressed a kiss against her bare shoulder.

She sighed as his mouth skimmed lower, across the

upper swell of her breasts. His lips touched the pulse point at the base of her throat, setting her skin afire with sensation. She shivered against him. Grayson found her mouth again and kissed her, long and deep. Her aching loneliness was swept away by sheer physical longing; the hunger for something deeper, truer, surged up in an implacable tide.

She clung to him while he rained kisses upon her upturned face. Time had no meaning. She clung to him, dizzy with delight as his hand cupped her breast. Cassandra didn't remember moving but suddenly they were stretched out across the bed. She was on her back, stripped to the waist. Grayson was there beside her, his lips skimming over her collarbone, pausing at the base of her throat and moving lower. The firelight glazed his body, highlighting the sculpted muscles of his bare back and burnishing his dark hair.

His palms cradled her right breast and his warm breath brought the nipple tinglingly erect. His cheek was rough against her, his lips hot and seeking. He whispered her name softly, then took the tip into his mouth. A shock of pain, of pure animal pleasure shot through her. Her back arched against him as she groaned aloud. Her fingers tangled in his dark hair, pressing him closer, nourishing him with the shudders of delight that shook her slender body.

His hands rustled against her remaining garments. Skirt and petticoats and the rest went the way of the shirtwaist, dropping with a sigh to the thick rag rug. She had nothing left but her sheer stockings and satin garters, and the ropes of tiny jet beads that wound around her throat and over one breast. Their tiny edges were sharp against her flesh. She reached up to remove the necklace, but Grayson stayed her hand. "No. Leave them."

He sat back. How beautiful she looked in the firelight. Her limbs were smooth and shapely and the contrast of her white skin and the ropes of shiny black beads inflamed him more. He wanted to take her then. Wanted her so badly that he closed his eyes a moment. Not yet. Not yet.

He taught her the play of passion, lifting one of the strings of beads and letting them dribble back against her breast like drops of water. Catching his hand in a loop, pulling hers into it until they were bound together, wrist to wrist. Rubbing the jet lightly over her skin so that it became an exquisite torture. Pressing the beads against her nipples until she felt their bite. Her mouth formed a perfect O. He took it with a searing kiss, promising so much more.

The sensations he evoked in her were beyond Cassandra's experience. Almost beyond her comprehension. She arched toward him, offering her breasts, aching for more. Feeling his lips, his tongue, his teeth, upon her breast, as soft as the feathering of her own hair across her skin, as sharp, as teasing, as the nip of his teeth. As relentless as the wind.

She went where he led her as the play grew wilder. Never before had she been touched like this. Never before had she known such fullness of arousal. When he looked at her, his eyes intense and heavy with craving, she felt bold and wanton, seducer and seducee. Her body grew hot and moist and eager; yet when he touched her intimately she was suddenly shy.

"Cassandra . . ." He sighed her name against her breasts, her navel, the gentle mound of her abdomen. The tip of his tongue trailed over her flesh in tantalizing movements and she groaned and tried to turn away. Grayson pressed her thighs apart with his hand and felt the slight resistance; yet he knew she was ready for him. He whispered her name once more, but her eyes were closed and she refused to look at him. He was going too far and fast for her.

Grayson reined in his need and stretched back down beside her, bringing her trembling body against the length of his. Smoothing the contours of her back, cupping the firmness of her buttocks, her satin thighs. Slowly, he wedged his knee between her legs, caressing and murmuring soothing words. Her scent filled the room like incense.

He turned her on her back and covered her with his warmth, and wondered how much longer he could hold off. His need for her was greater than his wisdom. He put his hand gently between her legs and this time she didn't protest. Cupping his hand against her feminine softness, he let her get used to his touch.

He wanted to know her innermost secrets and to bring her with him to the brink. Sweet Cassandra. Honey in the comb. The shock of his touch had her twisting away. His touch heated her blood but she was so unsure. His touch became more intimate, invading gently. Seeking to give pleasure and to teach her to accept it.

Dark pleasure stirred her blood, smothering the dull spark of shame at her arousal. She had never dreamed of being touched like this. Her body shuddered and she cried out his name.

His fingers moved, drove into her with pounding rhythm until she could no longer discern ecstasy from torment. Her breasts ached from his suckling and her swollen nipples ached. And yet she wanted more. He pulled his hand back and she tried to keep him from stopping. Cassandra was lost to frantic desire, aching for release. He pushed her gently back against the pillows.

He entered her with unintended roughness and her body arched up to meet him. He filled her with heat and rising passion. She sheathed his need in her own urgency. They surrendered to mutual need and their sweat-slicked bodies came together with a violence that was the inevitable result of their long denial. He plunged deeply and she cried out his name and arched to meet him, thrust for thrust.

Afterward they drifted into satiated sleep, each knowing they had pleasured the other. She awakened in the middle of the night from a dreamless slumber to the light feathering of his fingertips over her breasts. He saw that she was awake, and pressed a kiss against her mouth. He leaned over and caressed her breasts, taking her hands to cover them.

"Touch them," he murmured. "Don't be afraid. Feel what I feel."

The globes of her breasts weighted her hands. Her nipples contracted into tight buds beneath her palms. Grayson kissed her fingers, then spread them apart to hold the tips erect. His breath danced over them, and she felt a deep pulling in her loins. She wanted him to make love to her again.

Grayson sensed her willingness. He wanted her more than ever. His voice was low and husky with arousal. "I am on fire with need. I cannot satisfy my hunger for you, nor quench my thirst."

His mouth claimed hers again with fierce possession. His hands moved down to touch her throat, her breasts, the rounded curve of her abdomen. His mouth followed, hot and seeking. She was silk, she was perfumed satin and musky womanhood. Grayson lost himself in the touch and taste of her, in the heat of her body and the answering fire in his. He had wanted her, but until this moment he hadn't realized the great price he would have to pay for having her: he was caught up in the spell of her enchantment, beyond any hope of escape. If he could not fight it, he would work the same magic on Cassandra. Ensnared, he touched and teased and tasted, carrying her away with him on the wings of abandon.

This time he took her along with him into a place she'd never gone before. Cassandra felt the earth fall away, felt herself falling down and down. She clung to him in fear and longing. He cried out with her as her body shuddered in ecstasy, held her safe in his embrace. They sailed the dark night wind together, soaring higher and farther than either had ever imagined, up past the burning stars.

A chickadee's song awakened Cassandra. She yawned and opened her eyes. It was past sunup and Grayson was already gone. Her clothes were scattered all over the room and the shirtwaist lay in a ruined heap by the fireplace. Smiling, she touched the empty pillow where his head had lain, breathed in the scent of his body from the sheets.

The fire was low and the room was growing cold. She didn't even know how to build up the fire, but she would learn. In the night hours she had learned things about Grayson that she had never expected, and more about herself. She had learned to be a woman. Giving and wanting and taking. Reveling in the difference between male and female, the joy of forsaking restraint to embark on marvelous adventures of the senses. Feeling for the first time the unleashed power of the sexual act.

She had never imagined the sheer pleasure of it. And she'd been unable to keep her body from responding eagerly to his every stimulus. The things he'd done . . . The things that she'd let him do . . .

Her face grew hot with the memory of their wild lovemaking. His bold caresses, by hands and lips and tongue, had aroused a wantonness she'd never known she had. Yet she could never let another man touch her the way Grayson had. Tyler had certainly never done so. Unless . . . with Margaret . . .

She dashed the images from her mind. This was a new life, a new beginning. She must set the hurts and failures of the past behind. Her fingertips brushed across her breasts and her womb felt heavy with longing. She wanted Grayson to come back and make love to her again. A slow smile touched the corners of Cassandra's mouth. She knew now that her nature wasn't cold—far from it! This strange and wonderful new life was supposed to have begun when she'd exchanged vows with Grayson back in San Francisco. In actuality it had begun in this room, amid the tangled sheets, with only the firelight for witness.

She didn't know how she could look at Grayson without blushing. She counted the hours until nightfall. So long until they were alone together in this big, comfortable bed.

She heard voices below. Cassandra was shocked to think that she hadn't given a thought to Kitty, Povey, and Bedelia until this very instant. She sighed and pushed the covers back. There was fresh hot water in the stoneware pitcher. A thoughtful gesture from her new husband, and a promising start to the day. He hadn't spoken tender words. He hadn't whispered words of love. It was too soon for that. But he had said that he wanted her, and then he had proved it. Over and over again.

For now—perhaps for always—it would be enough.

Grayson met up with Jaime as he came up from the stable. In the early light the sky was pink and gold and the mountains took on a reddish hue. The sun revealed new shadows beneath Grayson's eyes and picked out his cheekbones in high relief. Jaime took note of it. "Dreaming again?" he asked quietly.

"No. I slept like a stone." The realization surprised Grayson. He hadn't had a single nightmare about the massacre since he'd awakened in the Dillon Hotel after the warehouse fire. Even then, that last dream had been filled with contented memories, viewed as if from a distance.

He bounded up the porch steps. Jaime had already assembled the men there. They sent up a throaty cheer that startled the robins from the branches, and set one of the hounds baying. When the noise abated, Grayson announced the results of a very successful trip. ". . . and with the cattle going to Kansas City for such a good price, there will be bonuses for all."

That was the arranged signal. A second cheer drowned out the opening of the door and Bedelia stepped out beside him, as he'd instructed her to do. She was wearing a dress of sprigged dimity with her hair worn long and loose, and tied up with a wide white ribbon. The same hairdo, in fact, that Annette Mason had worn in the broadsides he'd distributed. How clever of her.

The men fell silent, doffed their hats, and gaped at Bedelia. A woman, in this bastion of men, was as unexpected as snow in August. Especially a young and pretty one. A sigh rose through the ranks of the men like wind through the meadow. Hal Mundy was always the boldest. "Jasus, Mr. Howard, did ye take a wife, then?"

"That I did. And a new niece by marriage, as well as a most superior ladies' maid."

The men looked at one another, burning curiosity mingling with apprehension. A woman could create a lot of unpleasant changes on a ranch. Especially one who had her own fancy ladies' maid. Clean shirts and hair trimmed regular. Prayer meetings at all hours, and no spittoons around the table. A collective shudder ran through them. It had happened on the Cooney spread: it sure as shit could happen here.

Grayson suppressed a grin and placed his arms akimbo. "Mrs. Howard will have the running of the house. What she says in and around it goes. But don't get your hopes up for any major changes: I'm still in charge of the Thunder Ranch."

The hands threw up their hats and cheered so loudly that three female faces appeared at the house windows. Their reactions to the men below differed. Cassandra, looking down from the upstairs landing, was pleased to know that Grayson had the respect and liking of his men. They seemed a cheerful and noisy lot.

The door to Kitty's room stood open and the beds were empty. Cassandra started down the stairs, afraid that their loudness might have frightened Kitty. Povey looked out from the parlor. Their arrival, after the luxury of the train, had been a shock to her system. Her eyes filled with sudden tears, blinked back with staunch ferocity: she hadn't expected her poor lambs to end up like this!

Kitty turned away from her window and picked up Rascal. She was glad that she didn't have to go outside alone, as Annette had done. She didn't like having people stare at her. Noise and loud voices didn't frighten her: except for the end, everything that Jake had done to her, he had done in utter silence. The kitten's needle-sharp nails drew blood from her arm. Kitty didn't even notice.

Outside, Grayson continued his speech.

While everyone's attention was fixed upon him, a tall man with short blond hair and bright blue eyes came out of the cattle barn. He stopped short, took a good, hard look at Bedelia, and started running toward the porch. "Annie! Gawd Amighty, Annie, is that you!"

Bedelia stepped down from the porch hesitantly. "Bronco?"

"Annie!" He held out his arms and she began to run to him. Then she caught a flash of Grayson's face from the corner of her eye. Her ability to read an audience had been honed to an art. Something was wrong. She came to a halt.

The man raced forward and swung her up in his arms and whirled her around. "By Gawd, you have the look of Maw about you! Don't you know me, little sis? Don't you remember old Bronco?"

Bedelia almost sagged with relief. She hadn't jumped in at the wrong cue. It was all right. "How could I forget you, Bronco? Why, you haven't changed a bit! Except for that mustache! Every night since I've been gone, I've knelt and said my prayers, just like you taught me. And the one thing I've prayed for hardest is that someday I'd see my wonderful brother again."

He set her down abruptly. "Then you gotta wait some, sweetheart, 'cause Bronco's gone to Aureus and he won't be back till Tuesday!"

He grinned and slapped his knee in high good humor. Bedelia itched to slap his face. Suddenly she realized that Grayson was immediately behind her. "I—I don't understand," she said to the big fellow, trying to cover her tracks. "Aren't you my brother?"

"Hell, no! I'm Ole Jansson, but I been called Swede since I was a tadpole. Guess it's 'cause I was raised in the Lake Superior copper mining towns, surrounded by five hundred Finns."

"But . . . but . . ." Bedelia tried to think fast. "You look so much like Bronco! It was a natural mistake."

Grayson took her by the arm and marched her back to the porch while Jaime dismissed the men. His face was dark with anger as he pinned her shoulders back against the log wall. "I'll have the truth now, you lying little hussy! You're no more Annette Mason than I'm the man in the moon."

Bedelia knew when the gig was up. In her early days on the boards, before she'd connected with the circus, she'd learned that a bit of sauce might work where tears would not. She rubbed her arms where his fingers had left red marks and laughed. "What gave me away?"

Grayson's fury was tempered by reluctant admiration. "You're a cool one, aren't you?"

She took a deep breath, thrusting her breasts forward, and licked her lips. "There's some would say the opposite."

He shook her again. "Is that what you are? A common whore?"

Jesus, he was strong. Bedelia felt the heat radiating

from his body. Ooh, but she'd like to try him out! Her little room was directly below the newlyweds' chamber, and she'd lain awake half the night listening to them. Give her a chance and she'd give him the ride of his life. She felt a dampness between her legs at the thought of it. If he was looking for a whore, she could play that role, too, and willingly. But instinct told her to back off.

"That's cruel of you to say. I'm just a poor farm girl who went to the big city. Got me a job as chambermaid in one of those big, fancy houses on Rincon Hill. I was working real hard, planning to send money back to my ma."

She coaxed a single tear to fall as she combined a little bit of fact with a lot of sheer imagination. "But Ma died, and then the master of the house started getting ideas about me. Got me alone in one of the spare bedrooms when I was turning down the beds one evening. Before I could stop him, he tore my clothes off, pushed me down on that bed, and got on top of me. He would've had me, too—lecherous old bugger!—but I hit him on the head and ran outside in my knickers. I was running around, hysterical. That's when I got caught by the baboon who drugged me and stuck me in that cage with the other girls."

Grayson shook her. A lock of her hair came loose, curving seductively against her throat. His eyes were hard. "That's a very nice story. Did you make it up just now, or had you planned it all along, in case I saw through your masquerade?"

"That's the honest truth." She leaned forward until her breasts brushed his shirtfront. "Why don't you spank me, if you think I'm lying." The thought of it made her hot.

Her attempt to use her wiles on him was so blatant

that Grayson almost laughed in spite of himself. "I've a better use for you somewhere. Maybe mucking out the stables."

That startled her. Did he know somehow about the circus . . . about Boris? No, Bedelia decided, or he'd have never let her on the train with his precious bride and her precious niece. But just in case he'd heard and was testing her . . . She looked up at Grayson through her lashes. "You can do anything you want with me . . . but that. I'm terrified of horses. I'll scream if one even comes near me!"

"Then how do you propose to earn your keep—or your fare back, if you choose to leave."

Again, that small flick of her tongue against the corner of her mouth. "I'm sure we could think of something . . ."

Yes, Grayson thought, she knows all about enticing a man. If he hadn't found Cassandra, if she hadn't filled his bed and his life, he might have taken this eager little filly for a romp. But that was before.

"A woman like you is nothing but trouble in a place full of men. I've a mind to send you packing on the next train to Aureus."

Jesus, what would she do in a mining dump? "Listen, I know you're pretty riled up, but there's one thing you haven't thought out. Nor them either, not being used to having to do for themselves." She'd caught his attention. Bedelia pressed her point home. "Who is going to scour the grates and drag the feather beds down for airing? And who's going to sweep the floors and clean the lamps and trim the wicks every day? Not any of those la-de- . . . er, those fine ladies. They wouldn't even know how to go about it."

Grayson was dismayed. She was right. He couldn't

imagine Povey pumping water, then heating cans of water and hauling them up the stairs. Nor could he picture Cassandra beating carpets or blackening the big cast-iron kitchen stove with a homemade mixture of ash, wax, and soot. They were as ill-suited to it as he would be to singing onstage at the San Francisco opera house.

"All right. We'll try it for a month until the next train is scheduled to come into Aureus. I'll pay you a generous wage and you'll have your room and board; in return, you will engage to make yourself useful to the ladies and help Ping in the kitchen. If you prove unsatisfactory or you can't stick it out, I'll take you into Aureus next month to catch the train."

She smiled. She had him now. "That's fine and dandy. But I don't like the idea of being a maid of all work. I would prefer to be called your housekeeper."

Grayson hid his impulse to laugh. She was a bold little minx, and he'd better make sure she knew her place. He pinched her chin between his fingers and thumb.

Bedelia knew better than to blink. She stared up at him, wide-eyed, and took another deep breath to draw attention to her bosom. He pretended not to notice, but she was pleased to see the pulse speed up at his temple. Grayson Howard might be a newlywed, but he was no saint.

"I'll warn you only once," he told her. "Any more of your tricks—or if I catch you trying your wiles on the ranch hands—and I'll bind and gag you and ship you off to the Canadian border in a mail sack. Do you understand me?"

"You needn't pinch so hard." She slid her fingers up his wrist. "You'll be glad you let me stay. I'll prove it to you."

He leaned closer. "You had better, Miss . . . whatever your real name is."

"Bedelia. Bedelia Smith."

"Behave, Bedelia Smith, or I'll make you very sorry."

She pouted prettily. "You didn't tell me how you found out."

Grayson laughed. "You'll know, when you meet Bronco." He released her abruptly and strode away to the barn. She watched him with intense interest. What a man!

From inside the parlor Cassandra watched them both. Povey and Kitty had gone to the kitchen a few minutes earlier but she had witnessed the little scene between her husband and the girl. It had hurt her deeply to see Grayson, who had held and caressed her all night, leaning close to another woman. Lifting her pointed little chin in his hand and staring down into her eyes. Laughing so intimately.

Cassandra pressed her hand against her stomach, to repress a tiny curl of fear.

The party to officially welcome Grayson's new wife was held a week later in the unfinished addition to the main house. The walls and windows were roughed in, awaiting the arrival of the paneling Grayson had ordered from Denver. The ranch hands didn't care: it was still far finer than what they were used to. And as long as there was food, drink, music, and the company of pretty ladies, what else could a man want?

Two of them brought their fiddles to entertain the crowd and provide music for dancing, making the celebration a really roaring success: Beth Leslie, arriving with her escort of ranch hands, claimed the music and laughter could be heard halfway to Aureus.

Swede played bartender, dispensing beer and punch with a lavish hand. There was fresh barbecued beef and chicken and mounds of creamy whipped potatoes and gravy, along with every kind of cake and pie imaginable. This was Cassandra's first opportunity to meet everyone. Povey had struck up a firm friendship with Ping, the Chinese woman who cooked for the main house, and was helping her serve.

Ling Cheung's mother was an ample woman with a wide mouth and shrewd dark eyes. It was plain that she was suspicious of interference in her routines by the new mistress of the Thunder Ranch; but in the inner pocket of her best green robe, she carried her son's letter close to her heart. Ling Cheung had sent many wishes for his mother's continued health and prosperity, and had promised to come home in the spring. He had also asked her to welcome the new bride, for Mrs. Howard was a woman of courage, who had suffered much of late.

Ling Ping reserved judgment. She had traveled halfway across the world to Colorado, leaving two husbands and six children buried in the soil of their ancient home village. Compared to the lot of the other village women, her life was not remarkable. Women ate sorrow with their daily bread. It was their lot in life. Ling Cheung became exasperated when she spoke of such things, so Ping had learned to keep her thoughts on the matter to herself. Her son was young yet, and a male. He could not understand. In all the room, perhaps only Mr. Howard came close. He had never discussed the tragedies in his past, but Ling Ping recognized their mark.

Grayson leaned against the doorway and watched the

festivities. The cowboys were dancing and stomping their feet to a lively jig. They were quite bowled over by Cassandra, but except for a "Howdy, ma'am," they did their worshiping from afar. In a gown of rose silk, with her hair dressed high and a chain of almondine garnets at her neck, she seemed like the heroine of a fairy tale to them.

He kept a sharp eye on Bedelia. From the moment she'd arrived the hands had been casting interested looks her way. A pretty woman, used to bartering her favors, could be a distinct liability among a group of close-knit men. At the moment Swede was gawking at her with his tongue hanging out. If he didn't come to blows with Pete Cane over her before the night was out, it would be a miracle. Grayson wished now that he'd sent her back to San Francisco after she'd ostentatiously written the names on the back of Bronco's family picture. That was when he'd been sure she was an impostor.

Grayson wondered if he'd made a big mistake in letting her stay on.

Nearby, Jaime McFee and a rangy Scot were more interested in Kitty's less obvious charms. She was too shy to notice and too tongue-tied to respond to anyone with more than a yes or a no. Neil MacAlpin admired her gentle ways. He was new to America but he had plans. Once he had a good stake he was going to buy up land in the next valley, bring over his brawny brothers and cousins, and start his own place. It would be nice to have a soft, pretty lass to share it with him. "She's a bonny fair creature, Miss Hamilton."

Jaime drained his pottery mug and held it out for Swede to refill. "Keep away, MacAlpin. She's not for you."

Cookie set his down as well. "You'll no' be trying to crowd me out wi' the wee lass now, would you?"

"You're not even in the competition."

Jaime grinned, but underneath he was serious. He'd seen his father struggle and grow old before his time, chasing a dream that always eluded him. Long ago Jaime had vowed to escape the prison of poverty and he had succeeded, but it was a long, gruesome climb. He'd studied Kitty on the rail journey. She was skittish but sweet and biddable. She'd make some lucky man a good wife—and Jaime intended that man to be himself.

Grayson watched and read his assistant's thoughts quite easily. It wouldn't hurt Kitty to be courted by two handsome young men. She was far too shy and tongue-tied with them, but she'd get over it in time. Neil and Jaime were two very different fellows. He knew which one he'd prefer for Kitty, if it ever came to that.

A set was forming for a reel. Swede, blushing and grinning, asked Cassandra to stand up with him. The fiddlers struck up and the dance began. It had been years since Cassandra had taken part in a country dance. When it ended, amid laughter and merriment, Swede's square face was as pink as country ham and she was breathless.

She looked around for Grayson, who should have led her out for the first dance. Some of her sparkle dimmed when she realized that he was gone. She had noticed earlier how often he had glanced through the crowd as if searching for someone. And how he had stopped whenever he spied Bedelia. Why, oh, why was Grayson so fascinated by that horrid, scheming girl?

Cassandra noticed that Bedelia was missing, also. The next quarter hour passed slowly, but she was relieved to see Bedelia return, followed a scant minute later by Jaime McFee. They had the conscious look of two people who had been together but were pretending they had not. Her liking for Jaime went up another notch.

The pop-pop-pop of exploding firecrackers brought everyone outside. A rocket whistled into the sky and burst into a flower of light. Another followed, greener than emeralds. So this was what Grayson was up to! She relaxed and enjoyed the fireworks display.

Near midnight the party was winding to a close when a lone rider rode up. Everyone who was still sober enough to notice turned to look. A muscular man with a shock of white-blond hair and eyes bluer than Colorado columbines came in, grinning. Shouts and greetings hailed this attractive man in the room. He walked with a cowboy's rolling walk, part swagger and part saunter— not born of arrogance, but years on horseback and from an inborn sense of his own worth. Bedelia wormed her way through the crowd until Grayson stopped her. "Come with me. I'll introduce you."

She was only too willing. The newcomer gave her a radiant smile. There was a look of appreciation in his eyes as Grayson thrust her forward. "Make your bow to the lady."

The blond bear clamped Bedelia's hand between his and bowed low. "I am pleased to make your acquaintance, miss," he said in accented English. I am Stanislaus Bronkowski, at your service. Everyone calls me Bronco."

Bedelia flushed. So that was how Grayson had known she was lying! It had never occurred to her that Bronco wasn't some range-bred American cowboy, and she hadn't realized that Annette's brother would have a different surname—and a Polish one to boot. But she sure knew which side her bread was buttered on. She smiled and dipped a graceful curtsy. "Pleased to meet you, I'm sure."

Cassandra awakened long after sunrise, warm and replete from another night of lovemaking. She reached out for Grayson sleepily, and found only a tangle of linen and his crumpled pillow. His side of the bed was cold and she realized that he had been gone for some time. She glanced at the clock on the mantel. Nine o'clock! She was surely the last one abed.

Suddenly, a series of piercing screams brought Cassandra off the bed and into her robe in a winking. *Povey's voice!* She ran out onto the landing in her bare feet, almost tumbling on her way down the stairs in her haste.

She found Povey in the kitchen, backed against the pine cupboard and shrieking like a banshee. Kitty had taken up a protective stance before her and was wielding a black iron skillet as if it were a mace. The cause of it all was a young Indian in buckskin leggings and moccasins, with a choker of turquoise beads and bird bones about his neck. He seemed amused. He had one of Ping's best knives, and the ham he'd taken from the larder. Keeping an eye on Kitty and her homely weapon, he hacked off a goodly chunk and popped it into his mouth.

Cassandra motioned for the others to leave, but Povey was too paralyzed by fear. She signaled Kitty to slip out and get one of the men, but her niece refused. "I can't leave you in danger!"

"The only danger appears to be to our dinner." Cassandra stepped into the center of the room, with only the table separating her from the intruder. Her heart was pounding so hard she imagined she could see the fabric of her bodice flutter with every beat. "Good morning," she said loudly, to get his attention.

"Good morning," he replied, and put another piece of the succulent meat into his mouth. "Damn good ham." He spoke with a slight, totally unfamiliar accent.

The women were dumbfounded. Cassandra knew she had to do something—but what? Certainly not alarm him. She handed him a plate from the china closet and cleared her throat lightly. "There is plenty of food. If you are hungry, take all you like. But I should like to know what you are doing in my house, if you please."

He turned around, still holding the knife. Povey shrieked again. Cassandra had always heard that Indians had faces of stone, revealing nothing; but the emotions that flickered in the man's dark eyes were easily read: on the surface, pride, disdain, arrogance, still touched with wry amusement. Beneath them a good deal of pain and anger. He froze Povey to silence with a sharp look, then focused his scrutiny upon Cassandra.

"This is the lodge of Gray Wolf. It is not yours."

Gray Wolf. He meant Grayson! The cold from her bare feet seeped upward into her bones. She mustn't let him see that she was afraid. "I am Gray Wolf's wife."

There, she'd startled him. The Indian's eyes narrowed and he examined her from head to toe. She shivered beneath the thin satin robe. The Indian gestured toward the other two, his gaze lingering longer on Kitty's white face. "This other one, is she also his wife?"

"No. She is my niece."

"*Ipewa.*" His face brightened. "She is brave and healthy, and will bear fine sons. I have no woman in my lodge. I will give you many horses in exchange for her."

It was a toss-up as to which of the women were most horrified. Povey found her courage at the threat to her young charge. "How dare you even look at my poor lamb, you heathen savage!"

The Indian eyed Povey solemnly. "I will take you, also."

A ridiculous idea dawned in Cassandra's head, but she concluded finally that it was correct: He was toying with them, playing a game that entertained only himself —and that, bitterly. "You must forgive us," she said smoothly. "We are new here and unused to strangers. We mistook your jest for truth."

He grinned. The light in his eyes grew warmer. "You are not a stupid woman. Perhaps Gray Wolf has not been so foolish as I first imagined." He lifted the top of the apple bin, took one out without looking, and polished it against his legging. "When will he return? I have news for him that will not wait."

Cassandra hesitated only a fraction. He was obviously familiar with the house and where things were kept. This was someone Grayson knew and trusted. "I am not certain. He has probably gone out with his men to check the cattle."

The unorthodox visitor took the ham from the platter and tucked it under his arm. "Tell Gray Wolf that Black Shield has been here. He will know where to find me."

He flashed another look at the other two and pointed at Povey. "I will not take that one," he said, laughter lurking in his eyes. "She is sturdy but her loud shrieks hurt my ear. I will be back for the other one when I get the horses to exchange for her."

He strolled to the back door, opened it, and went out. Cassandra was rooted to the spot for several seconds, then went to the door and flung it open. She saw Ping sitting in the sun, peeling a bucket of turnips, and young Bobby grooming a filly with great diligence. Neither had noticed Black Shield, who had vanished like dew on the morning grass.

It was after moonrise when Grayson returned. He'd ridden out to the rich pasturelands on the lower slopes. The cattle were fat and thriving, the men in high spirits. Tomorrow he'd go back to Silver Creek and inspect the mine. Bronco had made a trip up the mountain under cover of going to Aureus. He reported crumbling along the wall of one tunnel. Grayson didn't like that.

The rock was solid there, except for the thick dark streak of the silver vein. That meant someone was blasting deep inside the rock on the other side of the mountain. Tunneling, under cover of their own claim, straight toward his lode. He'd have to send Neil MacAlpin into Aureus to be his eyes and ears.

He found Cassandra waiting in the rocker for him as the clock struck eleven. There were shadows beneath her eyes. He frowned. "It's late. You should be in bed."

His brusque tone surprised her. She had expected him to be glad that she waited up to greet him. "I was concerned because you're so late."

"A rancher doesn't keep banker's hours."

Cassandra was offended. She hadn't meant it as a rebuke. "I wasn't holding a watch to clock your comings and goings," she said stiffly.

He sat on the edge of the bed and pulled off his boots. "It wouldn't do you any good if you did."

She stared at him. What had happened to the man who had made love to her so passionately only the night before? He seemed to have gone and left a stranger in his place. She turned back to the fire to hide her hurt. "I have a message to deliver. There was an Indian here this morning. I told him you would be back at dusk. He hasn't returned. He called himself Black Shield, and said you knew him."

"Yes. I know Black Shield well. He is my brother-in-law."

Cassandra felt it was a test of some kind. She knew he was watching her. She was so afraid of giving the wrong answer that she didn't say anything at all. Grayson hung up his gunbelt.

"He found me at Beth Leslie's place," he said. "I'll have to go away with him for a few days. Perhaps a week."

"Go where? And why?"

Grayson was taken aback. There was trouble among his people—and he wasn't used to having to answer to anyone for his behavior. "I'll come back as quickly as I can. Meanwhile, Jaime and Bronco will look after things, and Beth has promised to visit as often as she can."

Cassandra pivoted slowly. He was already in bed with the covers pulled up, and his clothes neatly hung on the chair. Her voice rose slightly. "You've already spoken to her about it?"

"Yes." He sensed her sudden indignation and was too tired to deal with it. She'd have to learn to trust him. "Beth and I have known one another for several years. I don't expect our marriage to make any difference in my friendship with her."

The width of the bed separated them. It had never looked so wide. When he closed his eyes, that was the final straw. Beth Leslie was his friend, but she was his wife, and in any question of loyalty his allegiance should be to her. She whirled on her heel and left the room, shutting the door behind her. He was already asleep.

Bedelia had heard the sounds of raised voices, the vehement closing of the door, and Cassandra's rapid footfalls on the stairs. She'd been expecting it, but it had taken a little longer than she'd hoped. She looked in the narrow mirror she'd hung on the wall opposite and inspected her figure in her cammy and petticoat. How she would love to wear Cassandra's silks and satins—and share that big bed with Grayson.

It wasn't unthinkable that it could happen. He was a virile man with strong appetites, and she could match him all the way. She put her hands to her breasts and rubbed them, pretending it was Grayson's bronzed fingers pinching at her nipples. She'd learned a few things from one of the trapeze artists that would surprise the hell out of him . . . and leave him wanting more. Just let her get him alone, first.

A man like Grayson was sure to grow tired of his fine lady and cast his eyes in another direction. By the same token, her high and mighty ladyship might tire of life on an isolated ranch, surrounded by nothing but men. Bedelia laughed. Cassandra wasn't cut out for it, and neither was that mewling scaredy-cat, Kitty. And she intended to do her best to see that they realized it.

It shouldn't be that hard to do. A spider or two under the bedcovers, a dead mouse hidden in the pantry among the flour sacks. Lamp wicks that sputtered when lit, and some unseasoned, sap-rich wood to pop like gunshots in quiet rooms. A pinch of alum in the drinking water, talk of Indians and scalpings, followed by the tap of ghostly branches on the windows. Dozens of possibilities flashed into her mind. Burrs in clothing, mildew on milady's fine gowns. Snakes, if she could catch a big one. After sharing a caravan with Flo for so long, she wasn't afraid of any of them except rattlers. But if she could get hold of a rattler, even a little bitty baby one . . .

Of course, she'd have to set these things up when Grayson wasn't around. And she'd have to watch out for Bronco and Jaime. She'd try her hand at stirring up a little excitement: the rest she'd leave up to nature. When the days shortened and the snows and ice came, the other women would be in for a big shock. Bedelia had lived her early years in Minnesota, and she remembered the hard winters.

Here, surrounded by mountains, it would be ten times worse. Days of howling wind and windows crusted so thick with frost you couldn't see out, even if there'd been something to see besides snow. Times when the cold would seep through the tiniest opening, causing drafts that made a body think she was waist-deep in ice water. When it got into your bones like an ague and you thought you'd never, ever, be warm again. And then, when you finally got close to the fire, you got painful chilblains from being too close. Oh, it wouldn't take long at all. They'd be gone by the first spring thaw, all three of them.

Maybe sooner, if the train plows could keep the mountain passes clear. Bedelia couldn't wait for it to happen. She had it all planned out. She didn't want to be Grayson Howard's maid of all work *or* his housekeeper. She wanted to be his wife.

But, for the time being, she'd have to settle for being his mistress. And that, too, was only a matter of time.

* * *

Later Grayson tried to make amends for his curtness by inviting Cassandra to take a ride about the ranch property with him. He was unused to dealing with the volatile emotions of their new relationship and unable to put his contrition into words. What they needed, he had decided, was time alone, away from the others.

By afternoon they passed a rise and came out between two tilted wedges of stone, striped like a multilayered cake. The ground grew sandy as they went through it into the valley. The land was stony and level as a tabletop. Loose round rocks, looking for all the world like dirty snowballs, were scattered everywhere. They varied from the size of a plum to the size of a small melon.

Grayson broke one open to expose a hollow cavity, lined with tiny colorless crystals, as clear as spring water. Another held deep purple points and made her think of magical fairy caves in the stories Povey had told her long ago. She held it in wonder. More perfect, more precious than any jewels.

A hundred feet later they came out into a sheltered valley. She had wondered where they were heading, sensing a change come over him as the day had worn on. She couldn't know that he was journeying back in time, and bleeding from the heart with every step.

A handful of lodges were set amid the trees and at first they seemed deserted. A string of bony horses were picketed nearby, one with large sores upon its back. Grayson reined in. "I spent most of my youth among these Cheyenne lodges. Then there were over two hundred beside the river when my mother and Logan brought me here."

So, Cassandra realized, the stories were true. What she'd dismissed as speculative gossip had been founded in fact. How silly she had been to think it even mattered. No one challenged their approach. Grayson called out. Black Shield lowered his rifle and came from his place of concealment in the ravine beyond. A second warrior joined them. His eyes were dull with pain. Grayson's rapid questions in Cheyenne were answered with a curt reply. He swore softly and dismounted. Cassandra followed.

The warrior led them inside his lodge, where two children, thin and hollow-eyed, played on a blanket. They crawled over to a heap of buffalo-skin robes lying in one corner. She hadn't realized how large the tipis were nor the translucency of the thin-scraped walls. Light filtered in, warm and golden as honey. There seemed to be a place for everything, stacked or hung efficiently.

The men spoke to one another in Cheyenne. One of the children climbed atop the robes and a low moan of pain frightened him back and away. Cassandra stepped closer. A young Cheyenne woman lay amid the tumbled robes, her lips parched and eyes dark glazed with fever. By the lovely bone structure of her face she had once been very beautiful. Now her limbs were desiccated, her abdomen swollen with disease, and her skin as yellow as a dried lemon peel. "Why this poor woman is desperately ill!"

She would have knelt down but Grayson stopped her. "Don't touch her!"

"But . . ."

"Do nothing. Your help is not wanted here."

Cassandra was upset. "I can't leave her like this. At least let me bathe her face and try to ease her discomfort."

Grayson's eyes were those of a stranger. "She is dying. If you interfere they will blame you for her death."

Black Shield spoke. Cassandra was uncertain. "What is he saying?"

"He warns you to leave her unmolested. He wants no *ve-ho-e* to disturb her peace." She understood his meaning, although not the specific word. With one helpless glance at the sufferer and the two bewildered children, she left the lodge. Grayson followed soon after, and they rode away without speaking. Cassandra had never felt so useless.

They were silent on the way back, both wrapped in their own thoughts. They stopped along a creek in the shade of spreading cottonwoods to eat the last of the food from Ping's picnic basket. Gradually the somber mood lifted. The sun lit fire in Cassandra's hair and her face was flushed and lovely. He wanted to make love to her here and now. The urge was overwhelming.

He drew her into his arms and kissed her. She was warm and willing; but when he pushed her back against the mossy bank and drew her even closer and kissed her, she was suddenly self-conscious. "Grayson, someone might see us."

His hands were at the bodice of her form-fitting habit, undoing the buttons one by one. "There's nothing more natural than a man and a woman making love beneath the trees on such a beautiful afternoon. And I want to make love to you, Cassandra." He pulled down the lace of her camisole and kissed her breasts.

It was something he had done before. She was sure of it. How different they were in every way. It baffled her and filled her with surprising jealousy. As his hands stroked and caressed she was torn between the wild sensations his touch evoked and the habits of a lifetime. When he pressed his mouth against her throat, the soft valley between her breasts and their rosy tips, she was caught up in his passion; but when he pulled her skirts up and she felt the cool breeze over her bare legs, she was yanked back to the reality. He was undressing her out in the open, touching her intimately when, for all she knew, they might be in full sight of any passing cowboy riding out to the range.

Cassandra pushed at his chest. "No! Not here like animals . . . like . . ."

He rolled off her, his face dark with desire and growing anger. "Like what . . . *Indians?* Is that what you were going to say?"

That had been exactly what she had been about to blurt out. "I want to go back to the house," she said, rising. She pulled her bodice together with shaking hands, unable to meet his eyes.

He watched her fumble with the buttons, fighting the primitive heat that coursed through his body with every beat of his heart. He understood her then. "Everything in your life has to be proper and orderly, doesn't it? The dining room is for eating, the kitchen for cooking, and the bedroom is the only place for making love."

Her ways seemed rigid to him, while his, Grayson decided, were savage and uncivilized to Cassandra. "Don't worry, I won't try this again."

Cassandra was confused and angry herself. Why did he make her feel in the wrong? Surely any rational person would see her point of view.

They rode back to the ranch house, separated by mutual feelings of indignation and injured pride. Their time together had started out beautifully and then deteriorated with stunning rapidity.

Bedelia was crossing the yard when they rode to the stables. She noticed their obdurate expression and the way they avoided looking at each other, and smiled her secret, knowing smile.

13

On the third morning of Grayson's absence two cowboys named Zeke and Jed appeared on Cassandra's doorstep, clean-shaven with their hats clutched in their hands. Like their weathered faces and shy courtesy, the wide-brimmed hats, high boots, and gunbelts seemed to be integral parts of them. She had begun to wonder if they slept with them on.

The older of the men rubbed his jaw nervously. "Mr. McFee said as how the addition was ready and as how we weren't doing nothing, would you like us to shift the furniture over for you, ma'am."

She smiled. Jaime had coached them well. "I would be delighted! Please do come in."

She set them to work immediately. With Grayson away, time hung heavily on her hands. In the past she had been chatelaine of a grand mansion, with many responsibilities. Here, Ping and the men took over. With things to do and decisions to make, she was suddenly in her element again. She wanted to surprise Grayson.

The parlor was to become his combination study and ranch office, and the spare bedroom above would be Cassandra's sitting room and double for any guests. Once they'd brought the truckle bed and dresser down to Kitty's new room, she directed them to take her rosewood desk from storage in the hay barn and carry it up. Zeke and Jed willingly shifted bookcases and tables, and just as willingly shifted them to another spot at Cassandra's instructions.

Even Bedelia got into the spirit of things. The barrels and crates were brought out to the porch where the women happily unpacked the things Grayson had shipped along on the train. "Oh, what lovely curtains. They must be for the new parlor. And there is a wonderful turkey rug rolled up in this oilskin!"

Bedelia brought things out faster than Cassandra could find room for them, even with the help of Kitty and Povey. Even Ping joined in. There were dutch ovens and stoneware dishes for the kitchen; a new mantel clock for the bedroom; a quantity of red flannel undervests for the hands had gotten mixed in with the household objects, and looked very funny next to the matched crystal vases and bowls from Cassandra's boudoir at Stoneleigh.

Bedelia unpacked a barrel and found a service of fine china decorated with birds of paradise and fused gold. She touched an eggshell-thin cup reverently. "I've never seen such things!"

"Despite the mess we're making, it is rather fun," Cassandra admitted. "Like opening Christmas gifts."

Bedelia's face closed. "I wouldn't know."

Cassandra heard the bleakness in her tone and felt

guilty for her anger at Bedelia's deception. The girl had had a hard life.

Meanwhile, Kitty was busy unwrapping the items from her aunt's desk. Seeing the familiar silver and crystal inkstand and other items was comforting but they looked out of place in their new setting. She came upon boxes of stationery, some imprinted with "Mrs. Tyler E. Lucton," and surreptitiously buried them in the trash for burning.

The contents of the next case gave her a terrible jolt. It contained her personal belongings from her old bedroom at Stoneleigh. The others were busy seeing the turkey rug properly laid out and no one was paying any heed to her. Kitty was glad of it. Monique, her old china doll, had survived the journey, along with her books, including Mrs. Fortescue's horrible novel, which she'd never returned to Helena. She also found a pair of Staffordshire dogs, which had adorned her mantel, a pillow embroidered by her own hand, a prayer book, and the items from her dressing table, which had been inadvertently packed up with the rest. Without saying anything to her aunt, she repacked them carefully and set the crate aside. She wanted no reminders.

Cassandra made happier discoveries from among the items Grayson had purchased: an exquisite ebony chest inlaid with mother-of-pearl, a damask tablecloth and napkins, and a homely item that Ping identified as a new patent apple peeler. But as she was placing Grayson's items in his study she made the strangest one. Amid the globe of the earth, a silver inkstand, several cigar boxes, and a humidor, she found a plain wooden box. It slipped from her hands and the tiny brass latch swung free.

She knelt to replace the contents: a bit of incised purple shell, threaded with a dried-out leather thong; the society column from a San Francisco newspaper; a clever wooden carving of a nesting bird with tiny tooth-marks on it. There was also a small brass plate about four inches square, and two pieces of glossy tan paper-board. She picked the brass piece up. The design stamped on it showed a spoked wheel with wings and a Gothic letter *F* engraved on the hub. She'd seen it some-where but couldn't place it.

She turned the top pasteboard over and was startled to find the photographic portrait she'd had taken with Kitty at the Ashton studios on her twenty-fifth birthday. The last time she'd seen it, the picture had been in an enameled frame in the drawing room at Stoneleigh. The second was the one of her alone, which Tyler had kept in his study. How peculiar! She wondered what had hap-pened to the frames.

Cassandra studied the newspaper clipping with grow-ing curiosity: *"Mr. Tyler Lucton, owner of the Lucton Shipping Line and president of the Fortuna Investment Company, and his lovely English rose, the gracious and beautiful Lady Cassandra, opened their magnificent mansion to the elite of San Francisco this past Thursday for a glittering extravaganza . . ."* Ah, that explained the brass plate with the wheel emblem: it was the sym-bol of the Fortuna Investment Company, one of Tyler's holdings.

She scanned the guest list: Mr. and Mrs. Alfred Lo-renz, General Ephraim Malone, Mr. Clayton Everett, Mr. and Mrs. Robert St. Claire . . . Names from an-other world. Cassandra skimmed over descriptions of the splendid gowns and jewels of the ladies present, and the food served was described in fulsome detail. *"It is said that the guests supped from silver cups and ate from*

*plates of solid gold, brought forth from the bounteous
depths of the Fortuna Mine . . ."*

She didn't need to look for the by-line. All of San
Francisco knew and recognized the florid style of Sylvanus George. It had been published at least three years
earlier. These must be Tyler's things, and had somehow
been misplaced.

"There you are." Jaime came in looking for Cassandra, and was startled to find her holding the photographs he'd gotten from the parlor maid at Stoneleigh.
He pretended not to notice. "I'm afraid I'll have to leave
you ladies for a day or two. I've got to make a trip to
Aureus. If there's anything you need I'll be glad to bring
it back."

"Thank you. I'll speak with the others and prepare a
list." She put the pictures in the cigar box with the clip-
pings and the brass plaque and set it all in the desk
drawer, promptly forgetting about them. Jaime escaped
to the kitchen with relief.

If Cassandra had questions concerning her discovery
of the photographs, he'd better let Grayson be the one to
answer them.

Jaime wasn't quite off the hook, though. Cassandra's
gaze fell on the picture of Grayson with the Indian couple. He looked so happy. Then she looked closer. The
Indian brave with him was the man called Black Shield.
She wanted to know more about the Cheyenne's connec-
tion with her husband, and followed Jaime into the
kitchen. He was halfway out the door with a slice of
Ping's cinnamon cake in his hand. Cassandra held the
framed photograph out to him. "I found this in the
desk."

Like Bluebeard's wife, Cassandra learned more than
she was ready to know. "That's Grayson's wife and her

brother, Black Shield. I hear he showed up yesterday while I was away," Jaime said. "Harmless fellow."

"*Grayson's wife!*" Cassandra felt as if she'd been struck.

Jaime saw that he had done enough damage. Let Grayson handle this one, too! Swede was calling for him. He ducked out the door and was gone.

Black Shield led Grayson through a rugged pass and out onto a natural terrace of rock. They had an eagle's-eye view of the broad plateau extending east and west, and the green-flanked mountains on the far horizon. The Cheyenne reined in abruptly and shielded his eyes against the glare. Grayson followed his line of sight, then swore and pulled out his collapsible spyglass.

The close-up view sent a shiver down his spine. Approximately sixty men in the remnants of uniforms over civilian clothes were encamped along the banks of Silver Creek. Mercenaries, bands of soldiers for hire, sent out by either the government or land speculators to clear the Indians from their home grounds. He scanned their ranks. Some sported bloody bandages around hands or arms or legs: they had been engaged in combat recently. He passed the spyglass to his companion.

Black Shield surveyed the mercenary camp in grim silence. He knew that red pinto picketed near the water. "Hawk Feather's favorite pony." He handed the glass back. Grayson turned his horse. "I'll go down and talk to them. Keep out of sight."

A flash of impatient anger lit his companion's eyes. "I am not the boy you taught to hunt and ride, Gray Wolf. I am a warrior."

Grayson made a wry face. "You are right, Black

Shield. But you are still my wife's brother and I have great love for you in my heart. I would hate to tell Star Woman that I let you get yourself killed."

The Cheyenne nodded. "Go then. And return quickly. My heart is heavy within me."

Grayson picked his way down to the river, whistling and making enough noise to announce his arrival before some trigger-happy soldier shot first and asked questions later. They saw him coming and watched his descent all the way down from the rim. Their leader was a broad-chested man of middle years, with a sun-scorched face and a major's stripes on his uniform. Grayson raised his eyebrows.

"You've come a long way from your posting, Major. If you're looking for the rim trail, it's up beyond that row of hills."

The man's face darkened. "We're not lost, mister! We're looking for a war party of hostile Injuns."

Grayson's gaze passed over the weary soldiers, some grizzled veterans of the War Between the States, others stripling youths fresh from farms and cities across the Missouri. Half of them bore wounds. "It looks like you've already found them."

The major was incensed. "Get on your way, mister! This doesn't concern you."

"Oh, but it does." Grayson stared him down. "I'm Grayson Howard. This is my land you're trespassing on. I don't want you stirring up things among the peaceful bands and setting them off after my people. So, unless you want me to file a complaint with the territorial governor—who happens to be a good friend of mine— you'll break camp and be off my land before sunset."

The major's hand had crept to his side arm, but when Grayson had said his name the man paused. And when he mentioned the governor, as well, the major removed his fingers from the butt of his gun. "Don't come begging me and my men for help when them hostiles come down on you, burning your place and raping your women. 'Cause, *Mister* Howard, you can just rot in hell."

He barked an order and his men got up and began breaking camp. Grayson waited until the tents were down and packed, the supplies loaded. If he'd turned his back the major might have been tempted to shoot.

When they were on their way he joined Black Shield again. They had planned to stop and rest at Two Foot Rock. "We will press on," Black Shield said.

"Yes," Grayson agreed. "We will press on until we reach your camp." *And find whatever is left of it.*

Jaime set out that afternoon for Aureus, and with Grayson gone, Bronco made it his business to stop by the main house several times a day to make sure there were no problems. Or so he said. He timed his visits to their meals and, of course, was invited to join the ladies.

But each time there seemed to be a little something he'd just happened to have in his pocket—a clear piece of rock crystal for Kitty's glass garden. A loop of string, with which he taught Kitty how to play at cat's cradle, turning and twisting his clever hands to produce yet another intricate design. Another time it was a pink ribbon to tie around Rascal's furry neck in a pretty bow. He treated Kitty with avuncular kindness, talking to the sable kitten more than he talked directly to her. His kindness and gentle strength touched Cassandra. No harm would come to Kitty while Bronco was with her.

In the evening they sat out on the porch in the fading

light. He took a harmonica from his pocket and began to play. Some of the hands wandered out of the bunkhouse to listen. Neil MacAlpin leaned back against the side of the cook house and longed for home, and the bulk of Ben Nevus above the gorse-covered glens.

Bronco knew all the most poignant tunes, and played them with mastery and feeling. Some, like "Shenandoah" and "Aura Lee," were familiar to Cassandra, but most were not. He finished with a haunting melody. The soulful tune brought tears to her eyes. But then she was in a tearful mood.

She had heard it was not uncommon for a trapper or trader to have a wife in his hometown and one or more among the tribes scattered across the plains and mountains. She wanted desperately to know the truth about Grayson's "Indian wife," but she couldn't very well go about questioning his employees on so personal a matter.

Mostly, she was afraid of what she might find out.

When Bronco's song ended there was no sound but the chirrup of the crickets. Kitty's eyes were sparkled with tears. Here was someone who had suffered grievous sorrow. It was as plain to her as if he'd spoken of it aloud. The hands who'd come out to listen stirred and drifted back to the bunkhouse and Bronco sat on the porch steps with his back to them.

Cassandra broke the spell. "That was beautiful. What is the name of the last tune you played?"

" 'O Little Star.' " Bronco looked down at his hands and translated the words as well as he could.

> "Oh, my little star that shone so brightly,
> when I was a child,
> promising to lead me safely

through life's forest wild—
where are you now?
My feet stumble in the darkness.
Without your light I cannot find my way.
Ah, little shining star, where are you now?
Come, guide me once again."

The words lodged in Cassandra's heart. She was lost as
surely as she had been at Stoneleigh after Tyler's funeral.
Somehow she had stumbled off the safe path, into the
wild, dark forest.

Bronco put the harmonica back in his pocket and bid
them good night. Kitty watched after him as he walked
away.

They found the first victim three miles from the Indian
camp, facedown in the grass along the river. Grayson
knew him: an elderly Arapaho named He Seeks Peace,
who had suffered from severe arthritis. He hadn't
walked to the river. He had been tied by the ankles and
dragged behind a horse.

The next was the mutilated body of a young woman.
She had suffered terribly before being stabbed a dozen
times by bayonets. Neither Grayson nor Black Shield
recognized her, but with so many refugees heading for
the mountains that was not unusual. They rode in silence after that, alert to danger and with growing fear
for what might lie ahead. The river took a broad loop
and they cut across through the trees to the other side.

The silence was uncanny. Unnatural. Grayson had
the awful feeling that he had lived through this moment
before. Suddenly he was catapulted back in time to that
terrible day at Bitter Creek. The hair stood up on his

nape. There were no lodge poles silhouetted against the skies as they crested the rise and the air was heavy with the scent of burnt leather and charred flesh. Horror washed over him in a sickening tide.

They picked their way through the ruins of the ten lodges that had been home to a mixed band of Cheyenne, Arapaho, and Comanche. Even five years ago there would have been over a hundred here, in two rows beside the riverbank.

The lodges had been burned to the ground but they found only two bodies, burned beyond recognition. *We will be banished from our hunting grounds and the rivers will run dry. There will be great sorrow in* Tsistsistas *camps, and weeping in the lodges. This, I have seen.*

Black Shield called out. The shadows of the woods stirred and came to life. Women and children came out of hiding along with three or four elderly survivors. Grayson swung down from his horse. "Where are the warriors?"

A tall woman stepped forward. Her face was badly lacerated. "Some are taken captive. Others are dead. The rest have gone after the soldiers." Tears streamed down her face. "They will kill them or be killed themselves."

"Gather what you can. We will take you to a place of safety."

Grayson and Black Shield attended to the dead, wrapping them in the scorched hides that had formed the walls of the lodges. There was no time to build so many scaffolds. They used the poles that had held the tipis, weaving them through the tree branches, and placed the dead upon them with their goods.

"We will no longer call this camp Sweet Water,"

Black Shield said hoarsely. "It shall be called the Place of Fire. Our people shall come here no more."

A crushing weight of anger, sorrow, and guilt pressed down upon Grayson. In the years since the massacre at Bitter Creek, things had steadily worsened for his people, while he had prospered. He had wanted to learn the white man's ways in order to beat the usurpers at their own games. He had learned them well. He had even managed to use his growing influence to divert the railroad away from the sacred hunting grounds, but nothing he did was enough.

Persuading the territorial government that it was in Colorado's best interests to route the railway around the area, and supplying cattle and goods when hunting was poor, were only stopgap measures.

Now the greed for land was growing in leaps and bounds—and the anger of those displaced and dispossessed was growing with it. He saw again the vision that had come to him at Bitter Creek: the wheel emblem of the Fortuna Investment Company rolling west across Cheyenne territory, and blood welling up from the furrow of its passing. But this time it poured out in a crimson tidal wave, engulfing the land.

Cassandra was restless. Grayson's absence had created a void in her life, and she was disquieted by how quickly he had become the focus of her world. She was aware of the vast difference between her attraction to him—sexual and otherwise—and love. Perhaps "falling in love" more properly defined her state: a reckless, giddy, hopeful condition that had her spinning moonbeams out of dust.

She plunged from elation to trepidation and back

again within a span of minutes. It panicked her to know that he had such power over her emotions. Their parting had been strained, and she both longed for and feared his return. Her moonbeams might just turn to dust once more.

She decided to explore the ranch on horseback, and talked Kitty into joining her. Their request for ladies' saddles met an unexpected response.

" 'Sidesaddles'?" Bobby guffawed. "Ain't nothing like that 'round here." He scratched his head. "Which side of the horse do you put them on?"

Swede walked in and gave the boy a good-natured cuff. "On the *top*side, you ignorant young varmint." He eyed their elegant habits. "Young Bobby's right, though. No rigamarole like that at the Thunder Ranch. Might be over to Aureus, with all them fancy English folk—begging your pardon, ma'am. But Mrs. Leslie and some of the other womenfolk around here just sew their skirts up the middle and ride astride. Or I suppose you can just bunch 'em up before and behind."

Cassandra was horrified. "I prefer your first suggestion, Mr. Jansson."

They trooped back to the house and spent an hour sewing a seam up the middle of their skirts. When they returned Swede had saddled up a spirited black mare for Cassandra and a more docile gray for Kitty. He helped them mount and adjusted their stirrups.

Swede had belated qualms about letting them go out alone. Jaime had told him that fine ladies like these always had a groom to accompany them, but if there was one this side of Denver it was more than he expected. He chewed his lip, wondering what Grayson would want him to do.

"I suppose it's all right. Mrs. Leslie rides out alone. But then, she knows how to take care of herself."

That put Cassandra on her mettle. "I assure you that my niece and I are every bit as competent on horseback as Mrs. Leslie!"

"Well, if you say so. Go east along the river," Swede advised them, "and stay out of the hills. That way you won't get into trouble."

Cassandra looped the reins through her gloves. "We're experienced riders. You may rest assured we won't do anything foolish."

"It wasn't you doing something I was speaking of, ma'am. I was thinking more of you being done *to*. There's snakes and coyotes out there. Ravines and rabbit holes. Rustlers and such." He gave her an assessing look from the corner of his eyes. "If you see anything suspicious, you both hightail it on back to the ranch, pronto."

"We'll be sure to do that." Rustlers, indeed! They rode off and she went west and away from the river out of sheer contrariness. They returned three hours later, tired and happy.

Bedelia was envious, and sorry she'd lied to Grayson by saying she was afraid of horses. She finally came up with a solution, and asked Swede to teach her to ride. He took her out every day after their chores were done, and after only two days he was amazed at her rapid progress.

So was Beth Leslie, who saw them as she rode over from the Lazy L one morning to visit. She made the proper admiring noises as she viewed Grayson's study in the former parlor, the new parlor, and the dining room. Cassandra had transformed the old spare bedroom as well. The bed was hidden beneath a counterpane of rose satin, trimmed with matching ribbon and covered with ivory lace. Several pillows, trimmed with the same lace, were plumped against the wall, half covered in rose and half in pale green.

Beth stifled a sigh. She had always imagined this room as a nursery, filled with the children she hoped that she and Grayson would have together. She swallowed her envy and extended an invitation to Sunday dinner. "My cousin is visiting for a few weeks, and I'm sure you will find one another good company."

Cassandra poured out a cup for her guest. "How very kind of you; however, Grayson is away from the ranch. I don't know when he'll return."

"Oh, how disappointing! I was sure he'd be back home by now." She sipped the Earl Grey delicately. "I do hope that Bronco and Jaime are seeing to things satisfactorily in his absence. You must let me know if any problems arise."

Cassandra was torn between amazement at her guest's presumption and the violent urge to slap her pretty face. "Jaime is also away on business," she said stiffly. "However, you needn't concern yourself with the running of the Thunder Ranch. I am sure you have quite enough to do running the Lazy L. And if any problems arise you may be sure that I shall discuss them with my husband upon his return."

Prickly tension filled the parlor. Her guest flushed. "Of course. I am forgetting that things will be . . . quite different here, now that Grayson has taken a wife."

Cassandra wondered exactly how different that might be. Grayson owed her no explanations of his past —yet she wondered if he and Beth had been lovers. The strain remained and the visit ended almost immediately.

As Beth climbed back into her carriage she rescinded her dinner invitation as she mounted. "I'm sure that you'll want to wait until Grayson is back home," she said.

Cassandra watched her ride away, wondering if the brief crossing of swords had caused a serious breach or if, in time, they would overcome their unspoken jealousy of each other and be able to form a friendship.

That night Grayson returned. The others had gone to bed but she was still in the parlor, rereading a favorite novel. She put aside *The Mill on the Floss* when she heard his footsteps on the porch and flew to the door.

He was thinner and he seemed distant and preoccupied. She wanted to ask him about the Indian woman, but was almost afraid to. Although she intended to wait until morning, she found herself holding the photograph and blurting out what had been preying upon her mind. "Jaime said . . . that this is your Indian wife."

Grayson's face set in forbidding lines. "Yes."

"Where . . . where is she?"

"Dead." He went up the stairs to their bedroom without another word. Cassandra heard him shut the door. She saw the pattern of the past repeating itself. Even after the hours of passion and discovery they had shared in each other's arms, he had shut her out from the other parts of his life. He had left without much explanation and returned in the same manner. She was something to be used when needed and then set aside. And she had been an utter fool to think that it would be any different.

She was too agitated to read. She picked up her embroidery frame and jabbed her needle into the linen circle. It was a poor substitute for the music that might have soothed her spirits. How she wanted to pour out her desperate disappointment in furious chords and fierce arpeggios. Instead she was reduced to sewing erratic stitches that would have to be laboriously picked out later when her temper calmed. She set the embroidery aside.

The clock struck midnight as she went upstairs. Grayson was sprawled across the bed in his clothes, sound asleep. She undressed silently and crawled beneath the quilts, shivering. He'd scarcely left her enough room to get in. They stayed like that until the clock struck two, together yet separate.

Suddenly Grayson sat upright. He gave a low moan of anguish that chilled her blood. He fumbled at the table beside the bed and grabbed up the pewter candlestick in his hand, cursing in guttural tones. Cassandra was frightened half out of her mind. His eyes were open and staring at her, yet he seemed to be fast in the grip of a nightmare.

He swung the heavy candlestick at her head. She dodged and cried out in alarm. His blow went wide and he flailed out again at the empty air, growling and cursing. She realized it was not herself, but some imaginary enemy he was fighting. She shook him urgently. "Wake up! You're having a bad dream!"

"Get down!" His face was an anguished mask. This time he seemed to be protecting her from the same invisible foe. "No!" He pushed at her roughly, as if shoving her away from danger. The side of his hand caught her left cheek in a stunning blow. She fell back against the pillows, shielding her numbed face with her arm.

The contact of the blow seemed to free him from the frenzy. He stared down at her groggily. "Cassandra . . . ?" His gaze was unfocused, as if he saw through and beyond her. When she didn't answer he lay down again and closed his eyes. Within seconds he was sound asleep.

Cassandra rocked back and forth, nursing her injured cheek and jaw. She heard footsteps hurrying up the stairs and Povey's agitated voice outside on the landing. She staggered to the door and opened it, hiding her bruised cheek behind the door frame. A cold draft fluttered the hem of her nightshirt. Her maid was in the upper hall with her best pair of shears in her hand like a weapon.

"It's quite all right, Povey," Cassandra whispered. "Mr. Howard was having a bad dream. Please return to your bed before you take a chill."

"If you say so, madam."

Cassandra waited until she knew that Povey was gone, then poured water from the pitcher into the basin and bathed her aching face. She was afraid to go back to bed. And she was more afraid to know what he'd been dreaming about. It was too cold to sit up in the rocker. Finally she went to the spare room and got into bed there. She stared at the dim outline of the window in the darkness, waiting for the dawn.

In the morning, when Grayson awakened, he didn't remember any of it.

Breakfast was a strained affair. Grayson was already at the table with Kitty when Cassandra came down, her face liberally dusted with rice powder. She sat down with her bruised side away from the others and opened her napkin. After two bites of Ping's pancakes she set her fork down again. It hurt too much to chew. Kitty dropped her napkin and when she came up again she had a better view of Cassandra's face. "Oh! You've hurt yourself!"

"It's nothing. I stumbled into the tall chest of drawers in the night."

Cassandra put her hand up to shield the bruise from Grayson's sharp glance. She'd hoped her powder would conceal it, but the discoloration had spread, darkening from light blue to ugly purple. The flesh was puffed and very tender. Povey had said nothing when she'd seen it, but her lips had thinned into a tight, angry line.

Jaime came in through the back door, doffing his hat. "Here's the bad penny, turned up on your doorstep again—or is it supposed to be the black sheep?" He sat across from them. "Speaking of which, you'll never guess who's in town: Mr. Simon Fiddler. I met him while I was skulking around Aureus, trying to get information about his new mine."

Grayson poured another cup of strong black coffee. "I've been expecting him."

"Well, it's a damned small—er, beg your pardon—a doggoned small world, as the saying goes."

He stopped, embarrassed at his slip of the tongue before the ladies. Then he saw the bruise on Cassandra's face. He looked from her to Grayson, accusingly. "You been having those nightmares again?"

"What?" Grayson followed Jaime's gaze to Cassandra. She tried to turn away but he was too quick. He scraped back his chair and went to her side, dusting away the pearly powder with his napkin. "Damn it, you said that you tripped and struck the chest of drawers."

Cassandra winced and pulled away. "You are making far too much of a small episode. I was clumsy and fell. And that is the end of it."

She threw her napkin down on the table and went out

through the parlor and up to her sitting room. Grayson waited until he'd finished his coffee, then followed, his face like a thundercloud. He knew she was lying. With the powder gone he could see the distinct mark of a row of knuckles across her cheekbone. God knows he'd had a few of those himself over the years.

He stopped on the threshold. The room smelled like a warm summer garden full of roses and spiky lavender. Then he noticed she'd set out a bowl of potpourri, made with her special perfume. The Lady Cassandra's bower, he thought.

She was sitting rigidly at the desk with her back to the door when he came in, trying to work on an étude that had been building in her mind for days. It was less a conscious act of composing than a "listening" to her soul, where the music spun out in perfect, golden notes. When Grayson walked in she controlled the impulse to cover the sheets of paper with her arm. He had intruded on her most private thoughts.

"Making up a list of my iniquities?" Grayson asked quietly. "If so, you'll need a much larger sheet of paper."

He came over to her side and touched her injured cheek. The brush of his fingers was so gentle she barely felt it, yet she flinched involuntarily. Grayson's eyes were shadowed with infinite sadness. "Please believe that I would give anything if this had not happened. Does it hurt very badly?"

"Please don't refine on it too much. You were having a bad dream. I understand that."

"Do you?" He let his hand drop. "Few women would so lightly dismiss being awakened from a sound sleep by a fist to the face! Tell me, what else did I do?"

His eyes locked with hers, intense with an emotion

she could not read. She saw that he wouldn't give up. "Very well. You brandished a candlestick about, pushed me down on the mattress—which is when you accidentally struck me—and awakened Povey from a sound sleep! Then you closed your eyes, rolled over, and slept like a baby."

"Is that all?"

Her hand flew up to her throbbing face. "I should think that was quite enough!"

She wished she could have taken the words back immediately. His eyes went dark and opaque, shutting her out. "I never meant to hurt you, Cassandra."

He went out. She could have bitten her tongue. How could they bridge the span of their differing backgrounds when they used the same words to speak a completely different language? When her definition of rudeness met his of frankness, and her definition of social politeness collided with his definition of hypocrisy?

Cassandra went to the window in time to see him ride away with Bronco to check out the north pasture. She desperately wanted this marriage to succeed. To blossom and grow into something fine and wonderful, despite its wretched start. But it was beginning to seem more and more unlikely.

The clock struck eleven and Kitty was unable to sleep. She hadn't realized how much she looked forward to sitting on the porch each evening and listening to Bronco play his harmonica. She had almost screwed up her courage to ask him why his music was so sad, but he'd gone off with Grayson and hadn't returned. She went to the new parlor. Perhaps she would take a book to her room and read by candlelight as she used to do when the rest of the household was deep in slumber. How very long ago that seemed.

There were a few cartons still to be unpacked and she opened the first. Charles Dickens. She was more in the mood for Jane Austen. The second was filled with the music books and notebooks of Cassandra's music. Kitty took an armful out and was carrying them to the small table when Grayson walked in, almost colliding with her. "Oh!" The notebooks teetered and fell, showering loose sheets of paper across the carpet.

Grayson helped her set the books down and then knelt to retrieve the papers. He was surprised to find the curiously lined paper filled with notations, made in Cassandra's graceful hand. Black symbols danced and darted through the lines and spaces like birds in flight. He held one out to Kitty. "What is this?"

"Music. One of Cassandra's own compositions."

"Are you saying that she composed these songs?"

"Why, yes. Some of her work has been published—anonymously, of course. Haven't you heard her play upon the piano? Oh, she is wonderful! Mrs. Lorenz said that she might have made a name for herself upon the concert stage—if she hadn't the misfortune to be born a lady."

"Nicole Farwell has a piano at her home in Aureus. I will hope to hear Cassandra play it one day soon."

He went up to his room thinking of how little he knew about Cassandra. She had been Tyler Lucton's wife and now she was his—but who was she? He knew the smoothness of her naked skin and the way her hair fell down in shimmering waves when it was released from its confining pins. He knew the soft, sensitive place at the nape of her neck and the caresses that drove her to passion. But he didn't know the essential her, the joys and sorrows that had made her the woman she had become.

Cassandra stood at the window, brushing her hair. She had been waiting up for her husband and had almost given up hope that he'd return before morning. She didn't want another night to go by with them at dagger point. The only light came from the hearth and the silvery crescent moon hanging in the night sky. A shadow slid over it and she started to turn. If she hadn't seen Grayson's reflection in the glass, she wouldn't have known he had entered the room.

He made no sound at all as he crossed the floor. He took the brush from her hand without speaking, and pulled it through her shimmering dark hair until it stood out in a glossy cloud. Then he swept it aside and unhooked the chain at her neck.

The gold setting was warm from her skin, but his fingertips were warmer, gliding across her nape. He kissed it, and let the necklace fall. Her gown came next, but this time he was slow and deliberate unbuttoning the long rows, following the elegant column of her spine with his lips. He unhooked her corset and slid it away. Her breasts were free and ripe for his palms. No words were spoken. Or necessary.

Grayson undressed her at the window, watching the shadows caress the curves and hollows of her body. He wanted to make love to her there, to touch and rouse and drive her to sweet insanity. But he knew that she was unused to the luxurious exploration of sensual pleasure. Tyler Lucton had either been impotent or a complete fool, he thought, and pulled her into his arms. His mouth was hot on hers, claiming her for his own. Her body curved against him and her lips were soft and eager for his kisses. God, how he wanted her!

He wanted suddenly to see her naked body glowing in the firelight and watch the patterns of the light caress her skin. What would she do if he put her down across the hearth rug and made love to her there? Probably think he was a madman. He was. Grayson lowered her to the floor and placed her gently on the wooly hearth rug. Then he straddled her and kissed her eyes, her mouth, the peaks of her breasts straining up to him.

Cassandra was shocked at first, but yielded to his gentling. He tore his own clothes off in his haste and her hands moved against his skin, memorizing the width of his shoulders, muscles of his arms, the sculpted planes of his chest. There was little time for more. This was no languorous seduction. This was need, primal and driving.

He cradled her buttocks in his hands, then plunged into her with passionate abandon. She arched against him again and again as he held his body pressed to hers. The sounds of their breathing mingled with the hiss and crackle of the fire. Their lovemaking was quick and hard and satisfying.

He was still inside her when he felt her weeping. The shudders of pleasure that had wracked her were now the tremors of barely suppressed sobs. He cursed himself. She was as innocent as a young bride, and he had gone too fast for her to follow. Her face was buried against his shoulder, bathing it with tears. "Cassandra, did I frighten you? I didn't hurt you?"

She shook her head. Her fingertips had found the deep ridges of scar tissue that striped his flesh. She could see them echoed in the mirror in the bright firelight. There was no mistaking that they had been caused by a metal-tipped whip. "Oh, Grayson! Your back . . . your poor back!"

He jerked away. In the heat of the moment he had forgotten what he'd so carefully concealed from her in the darkness before. But she was bound to have found out sooner or later. He reached for his shirt. "I should have warned you. I know how ugly it looks."

She sat up, her breasts swollen with his kisses and her hair tumbling down like a silken net across her pearly shoulders. "Let me see . . . please."

He turned away wearily. His back was a deep criss-cross of livid scars. Cassandra touched them. Her tears ran down her face and onto her hands. "Who did this to you?"

Grayson shook his head. "Someday I'll tell you about it. Not now. It brings back bad memories."

There was such finality in his tone that she didn't pursue it. She leaned her tear-stained cheek against his back, then pressed her mouth against the scars. Once, twice, a hundred times. Love and compassion flooded through her. She could not imagine the pain he had suffered, or the reason for it. Her lips touched every ridge and puckered furrow of scar tissue.

When Grayson turned back to her, she thought she saw a gleam of teardrops in his own eyes, but perhaps it was only a trick of the moonlight. He held her in his arms, kissing her gently, tenderly. Then more ardently. He pushed her back against the rug and covered her with kisses. Then they came together again in a communion that needed no words, and soothed their souls with a balm as old as time.

In the middle of the night Grayson dreamed again. The nightmare was more terrible than before. The life of the village depended upon his strength and bravery. If only he knew what to do, he could protect them, avert the bloody massacre. But the enemy advanced, faceless in the black night. Grayson heard the terrified whimpers of She Laughs and Two Bears and threw himself at the invisible foe. He caught an enemy warrior by the throat and tightened his fingers, squeezing . . . squeezing . . .

A knee to the groin cut off his breath and he fell back, but he recovered quickly and launched himself again. Fabric ripped as the enemy warrior escaped. Grayson cursed and scrambled after him, over the spongy ground. A wave of cold water slapped across his face . . .

Grayson tore free of the dream's clinging webs. He was not at Bitter Creek. He was in his own bedroom, dripping wet. Cassandra had grabbed the water pitcher from the washstand and dashed its contents in his face. She held the heavy china pitcher at shoulder height, ready to throw that as well.

It stopped him where he stood. "Cassandra?"

"You were having another nightmare. I didn't know what else to do!"

The shadow of a smile touched his mouth and was gone. "It was very effective."

She handed him a towel and lit her candle. He wiped the water streaming down his face and chest, unconscious of the graceful strength of his every movement. She rubbed her aching throat. Grayson threw the towel down and pulled the collar of her nightgown away. Cassandra flinched and his hand recoiled as if burned. The red marks from his fingers stood out against her pale skin.

Grayson couldn't deny the evidence of his eyes—or the painful ache in his groin. If she hadn't kneed him and gotten away he would have killed her. Jaime was right. He was mad.

"It's all right," she told him hoarsely. "You were dreaming."

"Forgive me." He took her hand and kissed it, then cradled it to his cheek. "You are a remarkable woman, Cassandra." And unlucky in your choice of husbands. But then, he reminded himself, she had not chosen him —he hadn't given her any real choice at all.

He took the spare quilt from the wardrobe. "I'll go down to the study for the rest of the night."

She watched him go, her heart beating erratically. She would be a fool to admit she hadn't been afraid. No, it was more than that. She had been terrified. Cassandra got back into bed, but left the candle burning, and wondered what it was that tormented him so.

Bedelia had sharp ears. She heard someone on the stairs and peeked out through the kitchen door. Grayson went toward his study, naked except for the blanket he'd wrapped around himself. His physique had been honed by years of hard work and the sight of him took her breath away. How long had it been since she'd had a man? Too long, evidently, because she felt hot and sweaty just looking at him. She'd heard him making love to his wife overhead night after night. She grinned in the darkness. He was a passionate man, with a lot of endurance.

Which made her wonder all the more why he was sleeping alone in his study tonight. Well, well, well. Just when she'd been afraid she'd mistaken the situation, her first impression turned out to be right after all. He and Cassandra were quarreling again.

Bedelia stared at the closed door, fantasizing about him. She tiptoed to the study and opened the door. The curtains were open to the moonlight. Grayson was sprawled on the sofa with the quilt half on the floor. His dark hair was tousled and his bronzed body was every bit as magnificent as she'd expected it to be. What a chest! And those arms! He looked like a picture of one of those Greek statues she had seen on public buildings in her travels. And here he was, all alone when she had a nice warm bed she was eager to share.

She grinned and shook her head. Cassandra was not just a prissy little blue blood, she was a dyed-in-the-wool fool, turning a man like that out of her bed. Because, sure as she was standing here, there was nothing wrong with him . . .

She leaned down, catching the clean, masculine scent of his body. Her fingers traced a pattern over his chest and her mouth found his. He was more than half asleep but his arms wound around her and his strong fingers twined in her hair, pressing her lips against his. He was hard as a rock already. She stretched out atop him and he tugged at her nightgown, pulling it up over her thighs. Bedelia ground herself against him and laughed low in her throat. It was a fatal mistake.

Grayson had been dreaming of Cassandra. They were in Deer Meadow, lying on a bed of soft leaves and watching the otters play along the stream. At first he'd thought it was her touch that had wakened him. But when he heard Bedelia's husky laugh and saw her avid face he was completely, violently awake. He grabbed her arms bruisingly and pushed her away.

"What the hell . . . Bedelia! You little whore, what do you think you're doing!"

"You sure seemed to know!"

He sat up, pinning her against the back of the sofa, so angry that he could have throttled her on the spot. "By God, I warned you!" He shook her, hard. "You'll be on the next train out of Aureus!"

She smiled saucily. "Sure you really want to get rid of me?" He hadn't lost his erection.

For a moment she thought he was going to hit her. A door opened somewhere and he released her, perhaps not quickly enough. Bedelia jumped up and danced away. He opened the door and she went out, grinning like a Cheshire cat when she heard the bolt rattle shut. She'd won the first round. She might leave the ranch, or she might not. She hadn't really decided. But Bedelia was sure he wouldn't try to send her away as he'd threatened. He wouldn't admit, even to himself, that in those first seconds when he'd realized her identity, he'd responded like a man. A real man.

She went back to her room, still grinning.

Povey shut the door to her room and went back to bed, shaking with anger. She was gravely disappointed with Grayson and filled with sorrow for Cassandra. Povey had watched her grow to womanhood through one tragedy after another. She had thought her mistress was finally safe now.

Poor lamb, she thought sadly. Poor deceived little lamb.

14

"*There's Aureus,*" *Neil* MacAlpin said as the wagon came around a wing of the rugged hill and began a rather steep descent.

Bedelia didn't answer. She was wedged in between Bronco and MacAlpin, with her trunk in the back, and she'd sulked the entire ride in. Damn it! She hadn't really thought that Grayson would make good his threat.

Especially now, when she knew for a fact that he and his wife weren't sleeping together anymore. Cassandra had moved all her things into her "sitting room" ten days ago, and Grayson was gone from dawn to dusk. Another week or so and he'd have come around. At least he hadn't humiliated her in front of the others by telling them the real reason she was leaving. Grayson had merely said that Bedelia found she wasn't suited for ranch life and was going to Denver.

The others had gone on ahead in the carriage but she

was going straight to the depot. Or so they thought. But she'd heard that the fellows in town all had their pockets lined with gold and silver, and she decided to see what the gents of Aureus had to offer a lively lady like herself. If it looked good, she could trade in her ticket to Denver and use the grub stake Grayson had given her to set up a little business on the side. Gambling, maybe. She knew fifty ways to cheat at euchre, and a dozen more at faro. Or if that didn't work out—

A roar of sound shook the valley. The team whinnied and plunged, but Bronco kept control of them. "Blasting somewhere close," he said.

"Too close," MacAlpin answered. "That's Thunder land. Who the hell would be blasting up there?"

Bedelia looked up in time to get an eyeful of dust as pellets of debris rained down. The horses were still spooked and she was glad to get away from the hills and into the valley. She wiped her watery eyes with the edge of her sleeve and cursed so long and hard the two men were awed.

Meanwhile Grayson's carriage had reached the main street. Kitty hadn't really wanted to go into town but Bronco had persuaded her. Cassandra was glad to be away from the ranch. Perhaps a change of scene would do them all good. Aureus was not at all what she had pictured, after seeing it from the top of the valley. The scenery was pure Colorado. The houses were wood, not stone, and their roofs were covered with wooden shingles instead of thatch or slate tiles—but otherwise Cassandra might have imagined herself in a strange little English town.

There was St. John's, a wooden house of worship vaguely based on a Norman church, with an arched, stained-glass window and a small churchyard fenced with wrought iron. The one-storied houses along a section of the main street were really shops, disguised with shutters and window boxes to look like cottages. Two taverns were complete with latticed windows and the hanging signs she knew so well. One was The Rose and Crown, the other The Jester's Arms.

The other streets were unpaved and ringed with narrow three-story houses, each painted in at least three contrasting colors. Leaded glass panes shone like dark jewels in the sunlight, at odds with the craggy landscape beyond. In direct contradiction to the attempt at gentility in the valley, the gray sheds and chutes of the mines rose on the heights against the backdrop of the more distant mountains. It was all bewildering.

A small but elegant theater was plastered with bills promising lectures, dance troupes, "French artistes," and "visiting experts of every subject known to mankind." The Silver Palace Hotel was four balconied floors built around a central courtyard, and most of the ground floor was given over to a restaurant.

Kitty was dismayed. "I didn't expect to find anything so grand out here in the middle of nowhere." Cassandra squeezed her hand reassuringly.

Grayson handed them down from the carriage. "Don't be fooled. Except for a few rituals, this town is as wild and wooly as Abilene. The cowboys and miners have to have someplace to spend their hard-earned gold. Then Crispin Farwell decided that the money would burn holes in their pockets once they got to Denver or Central City, so he figured it was just as well they spent it in Aureus."

Cassandra had noticed the ornate building at the opposite end of town and inquired if it were the opera house. Grayson laughed for the first time in many days.

"You won't hear grand opera sung there. That's Buffalo Mary's. The bottom floor houses the most notorious saloon and dance hall this side of Denver. And that, my dear, is all any lady should know of it."

Grayson registered his party at the Silver Palace and escorted them to their suite to freshen up. When he returned a short time later Cassandra was just waiting for him in their gold and white parlor. He handed her a small revolver. The grip was inlaid with mother-of-pearl. "Here," he said, handing it to her. "I bought this for you."

Cassandra stared at it with loathing. She never wanted to touch a gun again. "Your taste in gifts runs to the unusual."

"Diamonds and rubies might be more beautiful, but you'll find a gun much more useful out here," he said shortly. "Keep it with you when you're riding out alone. You already know how to shoot. I'm sure you know how to load and clean it."

At his insistence she tucked it into her reticule. "Get used to carrying it with you."

They lunched with Nicole Farwell and her brother Crispin, who owned the hotel. The dining room was as elegant as any in San Francisco, with mirrored panels and white wainscoting on three walls and bow windows on the fourth. The Farwells were English, both tall with very fair hair and strikingly blue eyes.

The resemblance ended there. Nicole had a quick, mercurial charm and flitted from subject to subject without pausing for breath; Crispin had a slow, indolent manner that belied a quick intelligence and a droll sense of humor. Both were full of wry comments, news of the world, and tidbits of gossip from the life Cassandra had left behind. Nicole eyed Grayson admiringly and leaned close to Cassandra's ear. "A rough and tumble place, but you must admit that men like your husband more than compensate for the lack of amenities."

In the midst of the conversation there was another blast of sound that shook the floor and walls and set the lusters in the chandeliers tinkling. A veil of fine white particles drifted down from the plaster ceiling, coating them all with a layer of bitter dust. Nicole ran her finger over the tabletop and held it out, laughing.

"Really, Crispin, you must speak to the miners. Threaten to water their whiskey or short sheet the beds." She shrugged an elegant shoulder at Cassandra. "Tit for tat: it's the only thing those poor fellows understand."

Grayson stood a little apart from the rest, gazing out the window. Like Neil MacAlpin, he realized that the blasting was on his property. Whoever the claim jumpers were, they were grossly careless. A plume of smoke feathered the air high in the hills above Aureus. Any closer and they would bring the side of the cliff down in a landslide. Even as he thought it, a section of the upper hillside folded in upon itself in an ominous brown cloud.

Grayson frowned. "I'll get my men and take a ride up there."

Crispin frowned. "I'd accompany you, but the next train is bringing in some dignitaries. Lady Fergusson and her granddaughter are visiting from Edinburgh, and Glenn Hilliard is aboard also. I'm sure you met him in San Francisco. He's president of the Empire Bank. Charming man. They were due in this morning, but I fear the train has been delayed."

"There are probably buffalo on the track," Nicole

offered with a roll of her pretty eyes. "A problem we never faced in England!"

After the men left, Kitty and Povey went to their adjoining rooms while Nicole took Cassandra up to her own suite. "I've been dying to meet you," she confided. "I wanted to meet the woman who put Beth Leslie's nose out of joint."

Cassandra wasn't sure how to reply. There was no need: Nicole proved to be a source of unending—and disconcerting—information. She gestured for her guest to take a seat on one side of the curved sofa and took the other. "Oh, dear. Perhaps I shouldn't have said that, Cassandra. You don't mind if I call you by your given name, do you? After all, we are both Englishwomen in exile. Do you mind that Beth hates you? *I* shouldn't if I were you. Grayson never intended to marry her."

Cassandra blinked. "Does she hate me?"

"Of course." Nicole's blue eyes flashed with genuine amusement. "Why, if I hadn't got my eye on another fish entirely, I would have hated you, too. After all, you came along out of nowhere and stole the best catch in the Colorado Territory from under our very noses!"

Her assessment of the situation appalled Cassandra. "It wasn't quite like that."

"Oh, dear. I've let my tongue run off with me again." Nicole cocked her head like a curious bird. "Do you know, you are exactly the wife I told Grayson he must have if he intends to become governor when the territory is granted statehood. He's widely known and well thought of, but there *are* those rumors that he has Cheyenne blood."

She smiled at Cassandra ingeniously. "If not for that, Beth might have been suitable enough, although she lacks a certain something, wouldn't you say? You, however, will make a perfect political wife. Why, if the Indian question is ever put to rest, Grayson could even run for the presidency."

Cassandra's head was reeling. Grayson had never spoken of any political ambitions. But then, they hadn't done much discussing of anything of late. She grasped at the only comment that seemed safe. "Why," she asked faintly, "do you think I would make a good wife for a politician."

"My dear Cassandra, you have the three B's—beauty, birth, and breeding. Americans, for all their speeches of equality, are quite snobbish about such things."

"I don't suppose that brains would count?"

Nicole clapped her hands. "How clever of you! You see, you are indeed perfect. Grayson knew exactly what he was doing when he married you. And when you are the wife of the governor, I expect you to invite me to all your soirees and find me a husband who is either wealthy and distinguished or young and handsome. I would prefer a combination of both, if possible."

She wasn't speaking facetiously. Her frankness stunned Cassandra. "You mentioned earlier that there was another . . . fish . . . I believe you said?"

The merriment left Nicole's face. "Yes. I've been madly in love with Beth's cousin—he's the real owner of the Lazy L, you know—for the past year, but only from the framed photograph she has at the ranch. I met him for the first time yesterday, and I must say that he's even better in the flesh. Quite the handsomest man I've ever seen, except perhaps for Grayson. Positively the face of an angel."

"Perhaps he isn't as angelic as his picture seems."

Nicole smiled. "I certainly hope not. I like a man with a dangerous edge. And from what Crispin tells me of his

reputation, I am sure that Mr. Simon Fiddler has more
of the Devil in him."

It was three hours on horseback to the site where the
explosion had occurred. Grayson left Jaime to hide the
horses and follow, then directed Bronco and Neil Mac-
Alpin to split up and circle up toward the ridge.
Buzzards were already circling overhead. That saved a
lot of searching. An army could hide amid the crests and
troughs and wind-worn boulders.

MacAlpin scanned the rock. "Whoever it is, they
don't know a damn thing about mining. This is the
wrong kind of rock to carry a silver vein."

"Exactly what I've been thinking." Grayson sent him
on and swung himself up a shelf of jutting stone and
around the bend.

The mountain dipped beyond the ledge, then fell
away sharply on either side for half a mile. He kept a
sharp eye due north. The shaft he was looking for
wouldn't be dug in the search for silver: it would be a
tunnel hidden by rock and scrub that bored straight
back through the crest of rock for several miles and into
his own claim, right to the heart of the Thunder lode.

He jumped down and picked his way carefully, looking for signs of digging. Instead he found the back end of
a smashed wagon covered in dust. The rest of it was
buried forever beneath tons of rubble. A hundred yards
farther he found a gravely injured man on his back in a
welter of dirt and blood. Half the victim's face was
bruised and bloodied and his body was twisted at an
improbable angle.

Grayson knelt beside the dying man. It was Joe Crawford, who'd worked at the Thunder Mine for two years,

before quitting without notice a week ago. Joe was an inveterate gambler, losing most of his wages at the Wagon Wheel Saloon in Aureus every Saturday night. He recognized Grayson and grasped at his shirt.

"Kill me," Crawford moaned. A thread of red spittle bubbled at the corner of his mouth and ran down his chin. "Kill me, Mr. Howard, for the love of God!"

Grayson felt sick. Joe would die before he ever got him off the mountain, that was certain. And heeding his desperate request would bring the other half of the hill down upon them. He knelt beside the miner. "Are there others in there?"

"Two." The man's breathing grew more irregular. "All dead. Told him it wasn't safe . . ."

Grayson wet his kerchief from his canteen and wiped the man's parched lips. He held the bloodied hand in his. "Who's behind this? Tell me and then you can go in peace."

The little tableau held for less than half a minute. The man gasped out something Grayson couldn't hear, and died.

Grayson wiped the drying blood from his fingers. He felt bad for Joe Crawford. Someone had lured him away to work at this illicit digging, with high wages for keeping his mouth shut. And he intended to find out just who that was, if he had to search the records for the name of every landholder and investor from here to Denver.

But it wasn't the claim jumpers who'd set off the blast. Grayson frowned. There was only one reason to set one off where that last one had exploded. He spied MacAlpin ahead and waved him down. The brawny Scot helped him carry Joe's body down to where the horses were hidden. "By God," MacAlpin said, "someone will pay for this."

"Don't go off half-cocked. I have a plan in place—"

Grayson caught a flash of metal from the corner of his eye and drew his gun. "Look out!"

There were two shots, almost simultaneously. Mac-Alpin went down. A bullet slammed into Grayson's shoulder and the impact sent him reeling backward. The ground beneath his feet had been loosened from the earlier blasts and it crumbled and slid away beneath him. His shot went wild and he went over the edge of the high ridge and into sheer, blue nothingness.

Cassandra was worried. It was past sunset and Grayson and his men hadn't returned. She had dressed for the dinner party the Farwells were giving in their honor with growing unease. Nicole tapped on the parlor door and entered, dripping with sapphires and pearls.

She took in Cassandra's off-the-shoulder gown of black lace over satin with a measuring glance. "How beautiful you look! And what a stunning dress." She cocked her head in that curious birdlike manner. "And how clever of you to wear a simple black ribbon about your throat instead of mere jewels. I've a mind to do the same—but then, I do want to impress Simon Fiddler, so I suppose I'll have to make do the best I can."

Kitty had pleaded tiredness from the journey and Cassandra left her in Povey's charge. She went down with Nicole, wondering what on earth could be keeping Grayson.

The Farwells' private apartments were in a wing adjoining the main hotel. "We have tried to re-create the atmosphere of our country home in Essex."

The dark paneling was exquisite and hung with hunt scenes. A fire burned merrily in the hearth and the chimney breast was carved with the Farwell coat of arms. The two uniformed maids and the dignified butler blended in perfectly. With the windows covered with thick velvet draperies to hide the Colorado night, Cassandra might have imagined herself back in England.

Crispin was already there by the fire, drinking champagne with Simon Fiddler and Beth Leslie. Simon rose, eyes twinkling with malicious laughter, and bowed over Cassandra's hand. "Charmed, Mrs. Lucton. Oh, forgive me. Mrs. Howard. I'm afraid it will take a little getting used to—I haven't had time to adjust to the change."

Simon's rudeness was unexpected. Cassandra was stunned by his attack. Beth was shocked and sent her cousin a look of displeasure, but Nicole's eyes danced with eager curiosity. She knew it had been no slip of the tongue on Simon's part. "I didn't realize that you were acquainted."

Simon smiled. "Alas, I am sure that Mrs., er, Howard, had quite forgotten the matter. Do you know, I once sent her every golden rose to be had in San Francisco?"

"How romantic!" Nicole murmured.

"I had hoped so." Simon's mouth twisted into a self-deprecating half smile. "Unfortunately they did not please the lady. She had them taken off to wilt in the gloom of hospitals and churches and God knows where."

Beth broke in with a question about the length of his stay in Aureus and started the conversation on a new track. Cassandra was grateful for her intervention.

While the others were engaged, Simon turned to Cassandra once more. His voice was silky and pitched so that only she could hear.

"When I learned of your hasty marriage I understood, of course, why you had disdained my poor roses." He smiled his beautiful smile. "You had already set your cap in another direction."

His crude insinuations infuriated her. "I scarcely knew Grayson when we married."

"Ah, but I'm sure you cannot say the same thing now. He seems like a lusty fellow."

But before Cassandra could even reply a portly old gentleman with a guardsman's mustache entered the room, and Nicole hailed him. "Here is our last guest," she said as the man came toward them. "Lady Fergusson and her party were invited but she is worn out by the journey. Mr. Hilliard is still joining us, however."

The newcomer was already acquainted with Simon. "The world of finance is small," he said, smiling. "Rather like a private club, don't you know. And with so many of us investing in the expansion of the western territories, it's no wonder that we bump into one another everywhere we go."

Nicole introduced him to Beth and Cassandra. He bowed over their hands. "There is nothing that does an old man's heart as much good as a fine dinner in the company of beautiful women."

They took their assigned seats. Cassandra found herself placed between her host and jolly Mr. Hilliard. "Howard," he said ruminatively. "There was a man named Howard who came to San Francisco a few months back. Bought up every share he could in the Fortuna Investment Company and lost it all when that Lucton fellow put a bullet through his head. Didn't seem to mind, though."

Beth's fork clattered against the edge of her dish. Cassandra was frozen in place, aware that everyone but the banker was looking at her in fascinated horror at the man's unknowing gaffe. "I wondered afterward," he added, concentrating on cutting his succulent beefsteak, "if ruining Lucton had been his plan from the start."

Cassandra's voice rang out in the sudden stillness. "You are wrong. My husband would never have done such a scurrilous thing."

Simon's voice was soft but carried with awful clarity. "Ah, but he did, my dear Mrs. Howard. Your present husband loaned money to your, er, *late* husband, encouraging him to overextend himself with the promise of further loans. And right to the end he might have saved Tyler Lucton from ruin—but at the last minute Grayson Howard refused to give the loan he'd promised—and Lucton's house of cards fell to pieces."

Cassandra went pale as ash. Beth rose and went to her side. "That's enough, Simon!" she cried.

Crispin rose hurriedly, glass in hand. "A toast!" he announced loudly. "To small worlds and to beautiful women!"

No one was listening. Cassandra pushed back her chair and ran to the door. Beth shot a furious glance at her cousin and hurried after her. The hall was deserted but a knot of people had gathered at the foot of the stairs. Cassandra heard Jaime's agitated voice and Grayson's name.

Jaime leaned against the wall. His face was scraped raw and bloody on one side and there was a bullet hole through his hat. ". . . ambushed up by the notch. Three or four of them, at least. MacAlpin's dead. Shot in the back."

She ran to his side. "What has happened? Where is Grayson?"

Jaime paused. "You must be brave, Cassandra. I'm so sorry to be the one to tell you—Grayson is dead."

* * *

Cassandra watched from the window of her suite as the search party assembled to recover the bodies of Grayson, Bronco, and Neil MacAlpin. The men had assembled before dawn and it was barely light enough to see. She felt as gray inside as the sky over Aureus. She couldn't believe that Grayson was dead. Wouldn't believe it until she saw his corpse with her own eyes.

She blocked out everything that had been said at dinner. She would not pass judgment on Grayson unless she had proof. Not on a stranger's casual remarks, and certainly not on anything that Simon Fiddler might say.

Jaime stood awkwardly, turning the brim of his hat between his fingers as he tried to prepare her. "We might never find him," he said sadly. "The area is riddled with ravines and gullies."

She turned back to him, her eyes bright with unshed tears. "You must. You must find him and bring him back—one way or another."

"I'll try, ma'am."

He went out into the hallway. Kitty had heard voices. She peeked out from the rooms she shared with Povey. "Is something wrong?"

He hesitated. Cassandra might need her, but if Kitty went into hysterics it would be even worse. She had Beth with her if she required the company of another woman. "No," he said softly. "Go back to sleep."

Jaime went out into the street where his horse was saddled and waiting. Crispin Farwell shook his head. "Do you really think you're up to the ride?"

"You'll never find the spot without me." A look of utter misery clouded Jaime's face. "And he was my friend." There were no more suggestions that he stay behind.

They started off in the predawn light with the slow and steady pace of a funeral cortege. The sun had been up for two hours before they found the first body. They loaded Joe Crawford's corpse across one of the spare horses. His limbs were still stiff and stuck out at awkward angles.

It took longer to find Neil MacAlpin. He was facedown in a gully. He'd been shot once through the spine and once through the head. The second had been fired at close range. "Jesus H. Christ!" someone whispered. Crispin turned away and vomited.

The slim hope for Grayson all but vanished. "He was somewhere near that ridge," Jaime said. He'd grown tenser with every passing hour. They finally divided into four parties, to quarter the ground as closely as possible. Jaime drew Simon for a partner. Simon wanted to investigate the ravine to the right. "You're wasting time," Jaime warned. "If he's alive—which I doubt—every minute counts."

"Have you perhaps made a study of geometry, Mr. McFee?" Simon raised his eyebrow condescendingly. "No? I thought not. Then let us not dispute the angle and trajectory of falling bodies. You may look atop the ledge, but I shall continue my search in the ravine."

He made his way through the rocks and the thickets that lined the ravine, trying not to mourn the ruin of his best riding jacket on the brambles. One must suffer to be a hero, he supposed. His sacrifice was rewarded twenty minutes later when he saw the heel of a boot beneath a thick growth of shrub. He ducked beneath and found Grayson. He was stark white, as if all the blood had drained from his body through the gaping shoulder wound. Simon lost color himself when he realized that the object protruding from Grayson's thigh was a piece of bone.

He thrashed his way forward and touched the wounded man's arm. He was rewarded with a groan. "By Jove, he's alive!"

Grayson moaned again and opened his eyes. When his vision cleared he blinked slowly, unable to quite believe what he saw. His throat was dry as sand and his voice was little more than a rasp. "You're the . . . last person I expected . . . to owe gratitude . . ."

Simon laughed. "But, my dear fellow, you did me a very good turn when you burned down my warehouse. Oh, yes! I knew you were responsible. I was aware of your relationship with Ling Cheung, you see. And I can't think of another man who would put his life in danger for a few unknown women."

Grayson grimaced against the pain. "Good turn? You're a . . . strange man, Fiddler."

"I don't think—I know. You see, a plum of an opportunity had come my way via New York, but I'd dreadfully overextended myself between dabbling in mining stock and building my new hotel. I needed a goodly amount of cash that wouldn't have to be repaid—hence my attempt to lure the upstanding citizens of the city into a blackmailable escapade. But insurance is such a lovely thing, isn't it? Much cleaner than arson or blackmail.

"Of course, I'd already thought of fire—such an easy thing to accomplish, and who would question it in a place like San Francisco, where burning down the city seems to be the chief entertainment of the common class?"

And, Simon thought, smiling to himself, he had already sewn seeds of dissension in Cassandra's mind. If Grayson survived his injuries, he would himself reap the bounty of their destroyed marriage.

Grayson wasn't listening. He tried to struggle up. "Broke my goddamned leg. Crawled halfway up . . . couldn't go any farther. The others . . . they're dead, aren't they?"

"All but Mr. McFee. He organized the search party."

"Did he?" Grayson tried to shift his weight. "My damned gun is digging into my other leg. Feel pretty naked out here without having it . . . handy. Can't . . . reach it, or I would have f-fired a shot . . . when I heard voices earlier."

"Save your breath." Simon assisted him. His hands came away bloody. He started to say something soothing and saw that Grayson had passed out. Simon cupped his hands to call out to the others. He was stopped by an ominous click, and knew that someone was behind him with a cocked revolver. He turned to find Jaime behind him, pointing a gun right at his head.

"I told you not to come down here," Jaime said. "You should have listened to me."

Grayson stirred behind Simon. The voices had roused him and the danger of the moment gave him renewed strength. "You can't shoot us all, Jaime," he said hoarsely. "If you litter the landscape with bodies . . . someone's sure to figure it out."

The gun wavered in Jaime's hand. Tears streamed down his face. "Jesus! I'm sorry, Grayson. I had to do it. I didn't want you to find out what I'd done."

"To MacNeil and Bronco . . . or do you mean that business with the Morning Star Mine?"

Simon listened intently, edging almost imperceptibly to the left, but never taking his eyes off the man with the gun. Jaime's tears glistened in the dim light of the ravine. "You don't understand. I thought you were dead in the warehouse fire! And you never cared about the money anyway. All you cared about was your goddamned revenge!"

His words were like dagger wounds to Grayson's heart. "So you took my power of attorney . . . put the Morning Star stock in your name . . . and ruined Tyler Lucton."

Jaime swallowed. "Isn't that what you intended to do?"

Grayson curled his fingers around the butt of his gun. He was losing blood fast but he had to keep Jaime distracted until Simon was in position. It took an effort of supreme will for Grayson to keep from sliding down into unconsciousness. "You said I was mad, Jaime . . . and I was. But I came to my senses in time. I wish to God that you had."

Now Jaime's tears flowed even faster. "It would have been all right if that goddamned banker hadn't come to town. You believed me when I said that I pledged the stock against one of Lucton's loans and that it was forfeited when he failed to repay the money."

Now it was Simon's turn to divert Jaime's notice for a few crucial seconds. He cleared his throat. "But what has Mr. Hilliard to do with all of this?"

Jaime scowled. "Hilliard is on the board of the Empire Bank, where I deposited the money from the sale. Once he recognized me it would all come out. I knew it was over."

"I see," Simon replied. "And that's why you had Crawford set the charge to go off so close, knowing that Grayson would come up here to investigate."

The gun wavered in Jaime's hand. "Jesus, I'm sorry. I

never meant to let it end like this. But to see all that money within my reach . . . you don't know what it's like to face that kind of temptation. And now you've left me no choice." He looked from Simon to Grayson and back again.

Jaime's face twisted with pain. "You were my hero, Gray! You had everything I wanted, and you were everything I wanted to be. I couldn't face you. I didn't want to see your face when you found out what I was. That I could never measure up to your standards."

"I already knew. I was waiting for you . . . to come to me and admit it," Grayson said softly. "We've been friends for a long time . . ."

His mind was fogging. He took a ragged breath and used his last bit of strength to find the trigger. "It's over, Jaime. I've got my revolver aimed at your heart. You can only get one of us."

Jaime choked back a sob. "Good-bye, Gray!"

Two shots echoed like thunder through the ravine. Jaime crumpled and fell in a bloody heap. Grayson's aim had gone wide. It was the bullet from Jaime's gun, turned upon himself, that had shattered his temple on entrance, and exploded out the other side of his head on its exit.

Simon looked down at his trousers and found a hole near the crotch where Grayson's bullet had passed through them. "You took a terrible risk, old fellow. You might have shot off a very important part of my anatomy!"

But Grayson didn't answer. The final effort had been too much for his dwindling strength, and he had lapsed once more into merciful unconsciousness.

15

Cassandra kept watch by Grayson's bed. The curtains were open, letting in a view of Aureus and the distant hills where so much tragedy had occurred. Kitty crossed the road from the apothecary shop, arm in arm with Bronco. The cut on his head was bandaged, but otherwise he seemed no worse the wear for a night down an abandoned mine shaft. It was a miracle he'd only sprained his leg instead of breaking it.

She saw her niece move away from Bronco the moment they stepped up on the wooden sidewalk. She had wanted a brilliant match for Kitty, but one that was also a love match. Now, she would gladly settle for the latter. Although she enjoyed his company, Kitty might never trust any man enough to give him the gift of her love.

The door opened and Simon came in with a decanter. "Give him some of this if he awakens—and it wouldn't hurt for you to have some brandy. You are looking positively peaked."

She did look rather on the edge, he thought, experiencing a brief but real pang. Beauty in distress was something that had never appealed to him in the past, but there was something about the fair Cassandra that brought out the best in him.

Not, Simon thought hurriedly, that he was ready to don a halo yet. He could have easily alleviated some of her distress by telling her of Jaime's confession and letting her know that Grayson had not brought Tyler Lucton to ruin. Could but wouldn't. At least, not yet.

Simon was the only one who knew the true story. If Grayson should succumb to his wounds—which seemed highly likely—his lovely widow would need a shoulder to weep on. The chance of comforting her was far greater if Cassandra thought that Grayson had been the villain in her domestic tragedy.

He poured her a drink. She stared at the glass without seeing it. Simon set it down on the side table.

Cassandra's hands were clasped so tightly before her that her knuckles blanched. "Do you think he will survive?"

"My dear Cassandra, I am not a physician. Nor am I very good at attendance in sick rooms. If you'll excuse me, I shall retire to the billiard room in search of our genial host."

As he reached the door Bedelia came in with a pile of clean bandages torn from linen sheets. After intentionally missing the train to Denver she had learned of the shootings and come to the hotel, where Kitty had pressed her into helping. She froze on the doorstep, wary and ready to bolt. Simon looked her over from head to toe and smiled. "I believe we've met."

Cassandra heard something in his tone that she didn't like. She went to Bedelia's side. "I sincerely doubt that. Miss Smith is my housekeeper."

His smile widened to take in Cassandra. "Is that so? Then I see that I am mistaken. Good day, Miss . . . Smith!"

He went out. Bedelia waited a good while before scurrying back to join Kitty in her rooms. That had been a close one. She owed Cassandra something for that. Maybe she'd go back to the ranch with them to help out —and feather her nest at the same time. It was sure as hell a lot safer there than here in Aureus, with Simon Fiddler on the loose.

When Bedelia left Cassandra noticed the decanter on the dresser. Brandy had helped her get through the trying days after Kitty's rape and Tyler's death. It might help now. She poured a finger of brandy into the glass, then splashed in more. It burned its way down and sent out immediate tendrils of warmth. She had a little more. Anything to shake off the cold that had settled in her soul with Simon's cruel revelations.

Until she'd met Grayson her world had been a limbo of white and black and infinite shades of gray. He had brought her to life in a new world where everything was sharper, clearer, and bursting with color. Anger, hatred, grief, tenderness—they were a thousand times brighter now. And she wished that she could return to the numbing safety of that dim netherworld where emotions were felt distantly, if at all.

The doctor came in at noon, pursing his lips and shaking his head. "Will he recover?" Cassandra asked.

"My dear Mrs. Howard," the doctor replied, "I am not God."

Cassandra was ready to pull her hair out: first Simon,

and now Dr. Bean. "Can you not at least give me some idea of what I might expect?"

The physician cleared his throat. "He could come around any moment, or he could succumb to his injuries. Or he may remain like this through the length of his natural lifespan."

"I see." She didn't really. Grayson was too alive and vital to be reduced to this. She stared down at his still form, covered with bandages and with his leg splinted from thigh to ankle. "Then I should like to take him home to the ranch—unless that would cause him to come to harm."

Dr. Bean removed his spectacles and polished them carefully with his linen handkerchief. "At this point I don't see that it will make any difference."

Within a week of their return Bronco and the others were coming to Cassandra for decisions that had formerly been made by Grayson. She had two responses for most: "What course of action do you recommend I take?" and "What would Grayson do?" They served her well in nearly all situations.

She had no experience of ranching, but she did know horses and the fine points of breeding. Her years of dealing with committees, of running a big household and delegating appropriately, stood her in good stead. She liked keeping busy. It kept her mind off Grayson, lying so quietly in the big bed upstairs. If he recovered—she corrected herself—*when* he recovered, she would be on the next train out of Aureus. Until then she divided her time between caring for him and overseeing the ranch with Bronco's help.

He came to her one afternoon while she was sitting in

the kitchen, helping Ping peel apples for a cobbler. His hair was meticulously brushed, at odds with the look of a man who had just ridden in a few minutes earlier. Cassandra smiled to herself.

Bronco sent Ping and Kitty a nod of acknowledgment as he addressed Cassandra. "Mrs. Leslie has a stallion— black with a white blaze, and swift as the wind. She is looking for a buyer and the price seems fair. I think he would be a good stud for our mares."

"That's good news. I'll ride over to the Lazy L this afternoon. I've been getting lazy myself, sitting inside all day."

Kitty smiled. "You don't sit enough. Every time I turn around you are upstairs with Grayson or out in the barn or riding up to the north pasture."

Cassandra set aside the last cored and sliced apple. "And thank God for it! I don't know what I'd do with myself if I couldn't keep busy. If that's all, Ping, I think I'll ride over to see that stallion."

The cook nodded. She'd been wrong about the new mistress at the start, but she had proved her mettle. She had strength and courage. And she only wept at night, when she thought no one could hear. Ping understood.

As Cassandra went up to check on Grayson, she was aware that Bronco lingered behind. It was difficult to carry on an unspoken courtship under the eyes of the entire population of the Thunder Ranch.

Except for one person, she amended. Grayson rarely opened his eyes, and when he did they seemed focused on some inner world. She wondered if he heard her when she spoke to him. "I'm going out to the Lazy L," she told Povey, who was sitting with him. "I'll be back in time for supper."

The brisk ride helped clear the cobwebs from her

mind. For the first time in her life she felt real. Not a toy or a pet. Not a prop or a mute character in someone else's play. All her life she had been treated as a thing. A pawn in her mother's financial schemes, a feather of success in Tyler's cap, marking his ascendance from the ranks of the merchant class to that of the privileged. Something to possess, a decorative object with no use beyond the purely ornamental—other than being a dupe in Tyler's affair with Margaret.

She was surprised to find that the pain of it had ebbed considerably. Perhaps because the pain of Grayson's betrayal was so much worse now.

When she reached the birch grove she was supposed to turn right and head for the gap in the low hill ahead. It was the quickest way to Beth Leslie's place. As she neared the grove, however, Cassandra heard rifle shots and cattle lowing in distress. "Get up, Ajax!" She set her mount to a gallop and headed for the direction of the shots.

She found herself at the head of a shallow valley and reined in sharply. A yearling bawled over the body of its mother. Two Indians were already flaying the hide from the carcass while a third cut the bloody meat into chunks and threw them on a hide blanket. They looked up when they saw her and the tallest reached for his rifle.

She was frightened until she saw that they were, too. When her heart started beating again she realized that two of them were only boys—and that all of them were gaunt with starvation. "You are welcome to the cow," she called out to them. "Are you Black Shield's people?"

They spoke among themselves and the youngest ran away into the valley. The others, seeing that she meant them no harm, continued with their task. Cassandra wondered if she should ride away. Then the hair prickled at her nape and she knew someone was behind her. As she turned in the saddle Black Shield came up from behind a rock and caught her bridle.

"Greetings, wife of Gray Wolf."

She returned his salutation. "That is my cow they are butchering. However, they appear to have more need of it at the moment than I."

His face hardened. "Where is Gray Wolf. He has not come in answer to my messages."

"Messages?"

"For two weeks now I have left pebbles by your doorstep and made the partridge call. Gray Wolf has not come."

She explained the accident, haltingly. The Cheyenne grew somber. "Does he not move or speak at all?"

"Sometimes he mumbles in his sleep, or shifts in bed as much as he is able."

"Good. His *tasoom* is not gone." Black Shield scratched his chin. "I will send a medicine woman to him tomorrow. Her husband and her brother were doctors among my people and her power is strong. She will cure him."

He broke off suddenly. Cassandra heard it, too. Many horses traveling toward them. Black Shield sent her a piercing look. "Horse soldiers. They will slay us as they did our people before Gray Wolf and I found them."

She drew herself up. "Not on the Thunder Ranch, they won't! This is private property." Nudging Ajax gently, she wheeled him around and rode up to the top of the valley and beyond. Black Shield watched her ride off, then gestured to the rest. They ran off among the rocks and vanished from view.

Cassandra walked her horse across the meadow. A double column of men in ragtag uniforms made their way up the hill toward her. Major Barnett tipped his campaign hat. He kept an eye on the valley ahead as he talked. "Afternoon, ma'am. You oughtn't to be riding out all alone hereabouts."

She lifted her chin with the air of gracious hauteur she'd seen her great-grandmother use. It carried with it the unyielding air of authority born of generations of command. Major Barnett's face reddened and he wished he'd washed his uniform recently. "There's hostile renegades on the rampage in this area," he added. "We heard gunshots a few minutes ago."

Cassandra smiled coolly. "Your concern is unwarranted, Major. There is nothing but Thunder Ranch cattle from here to the river. As for the gunshots"—she pulled her revolver from her pocket, praying he wouldn't wrest it away from her and smell the barrel—it hadn't been fired since she'd gotten it—"I saw a rattlesnake and fired at it. Unfortunately, I missed. Do be careful when you go through that rocky section on your way back."

The steel in her voice struck a spark from his flinty impatience. "I have no intention of turning back now, ma'am. We're going to cut through that valley."

"I am afraid that is not possible. Your horses would trample the grass to ribbons and I cannot allow it."

"Just who the . . . who do you think you are?"

"I am Mrs. Grayson Howard," she replied sweetly. "And you are trespassing on my property."

Barnett gritted his teeth. He should have known. She was as hoity-toity as her husband. He'd already gotten a reprimand for ridding the place of those women and children up at Smokey Point a few weeks back. He wasn't about to get another. If there was one thing his employer had stressed, it was keeping on the right side of the people with power.

He doffed his hat and swept her a bow. "Then I'll wish you a good day, ma'am." He signaled his men and they wheeled about and marched back across the meadow. She sat stiffly in her saddle until they were gone from sight.

The next morning she was awakened by Povey tapping on her door. "There's another of those heathens at the kitchen door," her maid said in stern disapproval. "A woman, this time. Shall I send for one of the men?"

Cassandra threw on her robe. "No! Please offer her something to eat—she will likely be hungry. And then bring her straight up to my husband's room." Not that she believed in such things, but at this point she was ready to try anything.

The woman was old and wrinkled but her eyes were young and filled with light. She ignored Cassandra until she finished examining Grayson. "It is his spirit that sickens, not his body. It has been festering a long time."

She made smoke of dried leaves and offered it to the four directions, then blew it across Grayson's body three times. Next she made a salve of butter from Ping's pantry and a pinch of herbs from her medicine bag. She applied it to his head and his feet, then took out a rattle of snakeskin and shook it over him from head to toe. All the while she chanted beneath her breath. It had a mesmerizing quality. Cassandra felt very sleepy.

"No!" the woman said sharply. "You must not sleep. I have used a powerful medicine. Hold his hand. Do not let go until the evil is drawn out, or he will slip away."

Cassandra did as she was bade. "How will I know when I can safely let go?"

The medicine woman smiled. "You will know." She did up her bundle of herbs and left. Cassandra held Grayson's hand. It was limp. A few minutes passed. This is silly, she told herself. I have things to do. But she held on. A few more minutes and she saw a change. Where he had been still before, he was now restless, moving his head from side to side. His grip suddenly tightened on her hand. She cried out in pain. Her fingers had gone numb and the pain jagged up her arm. She wanted desperately to let go but didn't dare. And after a while she couldn't have, his grasp was so strong. Her arm was numb to the shoulder.

Grayson dreamed. He rode up the ridge toward the camp at Bitter Creek. Dread ate at him. Any moment now the silence would descend upon him. Then he would smell the blood . . . see the bodies . . .

But when he crested the rise there was only a wide meadow and the song of birds. He dismounted and walked toward the center. Cassandra sat on a fallen log, waiting patiently. He kept waiting for the dream to change. When his feet began sinking into the spongy ground he knew that this was another nightmare. He just didn't know what form it would take next.

Every step made him sink farther into the quagmire. It was past his ankles, past his knees. He held his hand out to Cassandra imploringly. She didn't seem to see. Now the muck was up to his waist, drawing him deeper and deeper. Another minute and it would close over his head, forever. He almost didn't care. At least this time it was only him . . .

Suddenly Cassandra looked up and saw him. At the

last moment possible she reached out her hand. He grasped it and held on. If he let go he would be lost.

Povey came to the door to ask her something. Suddenly Cassandra felt buffeted by a brisk wind. The hairs stood up on her arms and at the nape of her neck. The wind tried to tear her away but she clung to Grayson's fingers with all her might. The wind gusted and then died away completely. Grayson released her hand.

Cassandra pushed back a lock of hair from her face. She was totally drained. She looked at Povey. "What was *that!*"

Povey stared at her. "What was what, madam?"

Cassandra looked back at her husband. He was sleeping peacefully and his color was the best it had been since the accident. She collapsed in the chair, rubbing her hand to restore the circulation and still wondering what she had witnessed.

Grayson improved greatly after the medicine woman's visit. That evening he opened his eyes for the first time. He expected to find himself in the ravine with Simon and Jaime. If not for the splint on his leg and his bandaged shoulder, he would have thought that he imagined it all. Dr. Bean rode out and told him he was a damned lucky young man. He removed Grayson's splint and announced that the invalid could get out of bed and into a chair for short periods with the aid of a stout crutch.

"Starting tomorrow. Don't push yourself too hard," he warned. "You'll take a fever if you don't watch out. There's influenza in Aureus."

Black Shield also paid a visit and revealed how Cassandra had turned back the mercenaries. "But they will come again and again," he said bitterly. "There is too much gold and silver in our hunting grounds and the greed of the white men is too great. We must leave before the snow comes. It will be early this year, and the winter will be long and hard."

"You'll join the southern band?"

"No. We will go north with the Kiowa-Comanche to a place the Blackfeet have told us of. Up to Canada, where the horse soldiers will not follow. There we will raise our small warriors in peace, so that we may come back again one day and drive the *ve-ho-e* from this land. It must be so, Gray Wolf. Our paths divided long ago, but ran the same way. Now they will take us in another direction. But we shall always meet as kin. As *Tsistsistas*."

Grayson bade him a sad farewell, and was restive after Black Shield left. A part of him wanted to head north with the remnants of the Cheyenne band; another part told him he could help them most by using his influence with the landowners and government officials. It seemed that another lonely road had opened up before him. Thank God he had Cassandra.

But as he recuperated he realized that something had changed in their relationship. There was a wall between them, invisible but very real. She was locked away from him inside herself, and he had no idea why it was so. He brooded over it and finally brought it out in the open one morning when she brought his breakfast tray in. "What is it, Cassandra? It's plain that something is wrong."

She was silent, gathering her thoughts. Since the tragedy she'd been concerned with its aftermath—and with

Grayson's very survival. Now that he was healing she had to face some hard facts and deal with them.

She set the tray down. His hair was tousled from raking his hand through it and his face was all shadows and planes. He was so masculinely beautiful that it brought a catch to her breath. She turned her head and gazed out the window. The sky was cobalt-blue and the aspens had lost their leaves. How quickly the seasons changed here. As quickly as Grayson did from one minute to the next. Did the man she had loved even exist, or was he something she had conjured up out of her loneliness and need? She might not like the answer, but she had to know the truth.

"Tell me, Grayson, is it true that you planned and executed Tyler's ruin? That you encouraged him to borrow great sums from you so that he would overextend himself financially and end up hopelessly in debt?"

He pushed himself up on his elbows. "Where the hell did you hear that?"

Her stomach sank. "You don't deny it?"

"Goddammit, Cassandra!"

He broke off. Anger would only make things worse.

Grayson struggled to hold in his temper, realizing his fury was directed at himself—and that the real cause of it was cold fear of losing her. "Yes," he said quietly. "That was my original intention. But I didn't go through with it."

Cassandra stared at him blindly. She had expected— no, *hoped*—that he would deny the ugly accusations. Instead he had confirmed them.

Grayson had never seen her eyes so green and stormy. He saw he was making no headway. "Damn it, if anything, I kept Lucton Enterprises afloat longer than I should have, by throwing good money after bad, in a futile attempt to bail him out. When Lucton Enterprises failed, I lost a small fortune. I had to sell off some of my holdings."

Her face was stiff and pale. "I want to believe you, Grayson, but how can I, when you admit that you set out to cause his ruin?" She couldn't meet his eyes. "I don't think I really know you at all."

She went out, almost colliding with Bedelia, who'd been listening outside the door. "I brought up the clean sheets," Bedelia said hurriedly. Cassandra thanked her and went into her sitting room like a sleepwalker.

Bedelia put the sheets away in the linen cupboard and went to her own room, as excited as a forty-niner who'd unexpectedly struck the mother lode. She pulled several papers from underneath her bureau drawer and read through them again. They would change her luck for the better. And all because Povey had set her to packing up Jaime's things after he'd died.

She went back upstairs and knocked on Cassandra's door before entering. There was something sly and significant in her expression but Cassandra was too upset to really notice. "What is it, Bedelia?"

"I didn't know what you wanted me to do with these. I found them when I was packing up Mr. McFee's things."

"Thank you." Cassandra accepted the papers and scanned them with growing distress. It was sad to think that an entire life was summed up in a handful of documents. She stopped when she saw the name of Tyler Lucton on a letter mixed in with receipts and a copy of Jaime's birth record. It was a letter from the president of the California Investment Bank notifying Grayson that since he'd reneged on his proposal of putting up the Morning Star Mine to back Tyler Lucton's loans, they had no choice but to cancel the transaction. Both were dated shortly before Tyler's suicide.

Cassandra was sick at heart. Instead of proof of Grayson's innocence she'd found proof of his perfidy. He was as false to her as Tyler had been, his words nothing but a mockery. Lies, and more lies. She couldn't even bear to be under the same roof with him.

She went out to the stables and had Bobby saddle her mare. "Don't go too far," he warned. "Weather's mighty changeable this time of year."

Cassandra scarcely heard him. She mounted and set out on a hard ride across the valley, trying to clear her head and sort out what to do. The only thing she was sure of was that she couldn't stay with Grayson any longer. She urged her mare into a wild gallop.

Bedelia stood at the kitchen window, scraping turnips, and watched her ride off. She gloated over her good fortune. Jesus, she'd been lucky to find that bill of sale and the letter. Who said it didn't pay to snoop and pry?

She'd thought of using the letter from the bank to stir things up between Grayson and his lah-de-dah wife, but this was beyond anything she had hoped for. Their marriage was as good as dead—and Cassandra would be gone when the next train came through Silver Creek in two weeks.

Bedelia smiled like a cat at a mouse hole. Grayson was recovering rapidly, and he was a hot-blooded man. His kind always needed a woman. And when a man like that couldn't have what he wanted, he'd reach for what was near at hand. She intended to stay very near.

Meanwhile, she wasn't content to sit idly by if there was something she could do to set things in motion. An hour later Povey found Bedelia ironing Cassandra's laundry. "I did that up myself only yesterday," the older woman sniffed.

Bedelia slipped the wooden handle in the iron shoe and lifted it off the hot stove gingerly. "I spilled something on it. I didn't want you to have to wash and iron it just because I was clumsy."

That surprised Povey very much. Perhaps she'd misjudged Bedelia.

Cassandra was quiet that evening. She let Povey spell her at Grayson's side after supper and went up to her room, pleading a headache. Kitty met her at the foot of the stairs.

"It's snowing! Lovely, fluffy little flakes dancing in the air like moths." Her face was lit by a rare and touching eagerness. "I know that it's months away yet, but shall we have a Christmas tree? Bronco has offered to show me how to make snowflakes and other ornaments from straw, to trim the tree, like they do in Poland."

A weak smile trembled on Cassandra's lips. "Christmas! Why, I can't even think that far ahead yet." By Christmas they might be in Denver or Sacramento or God only knew where.

As she was brushing her hair out Grayson hobbled into her room. The startled look on her face pained him. "You needn't be afraid. I won't touch you."

Cassandra flushed. "You're not supposed to be walking about."

"And we're not supposed to be talking like two strangers. We're man and wife, Cassandra."

She didn't reply and Grayson knew he had lost her. He could hardly blame her for condemning his original intentions to bring Tyler Lucton to ruin. He understood her anger and disillusion. He even understood that she couldn't forgive him; after all, anger and vengeance had been his creed for more years than he cared to count. A marriage based on such a foundation was doomed to disaster.

A draft stirred the sheer lace at the window. The lower corners of each pane were etched with frost. He placed his palm on one of the icy panes, holding it there until the cold burned through his skin. Five years ago he'd stood on this same spot, buffeted by the wind, and had envisioned this house, this ranch. He'd accomplished it and more, yet his cup was empty. Some men were meant to be alone.

He turned from the window. He was hard gray rock, arising from the stony soil of the Colorado Territory like the distant, moonlit mountains. Cassandra was an exquisite hothouse flower. Meant to be carefully tended and sheltered. He didn't like her world, but he could survive in it. She was withering away in his.

"The Silver Spur will come through Thursday at noon. There will be snow in the Sierras but the plow trains will keep the passes clear. You can make it back to Sacramento before the rails are closed down."

"You're sending me away?" Cassandra was surprised to feel more distressed than relieved.

His eyes reflected the lamplight. "Don't worry, my dear, I'll give you a generous allowance. You and Kitty can set yourselves up in style wherever you choose."

Cassandra's throat was drier than sand. She couldn't utter a word. So this was the end of her fine hopes and dreams.

Grayson stood there, watching her. How cool and composed she was, as if he'd made a comment about the weather instead of admitting that he couldn't continue the farce. Couldn't bear to know that she slept a few yards away from his own bed, and that it might as well have been a million miles.

I should have never married you.

She gasped, as if he'd struck her, and Grayson realized he'd spoken his thought aloud. He turned and made his way out again.

Grayson sprawled on his bed. The banked fire was his only source of illumination. He squinted at the embers, pretending he was back in a Cheyenne lodge. It didn't work.

The wind sang and howled around the eaves. During the height of his fever he had fought against the infection, against the warm red darkness that pulled him down, down, down. It would have been so easy to let go. But he had fought like a madman . . . for *this*. To lie alone in the night and know that he would always be alone. It was his curse.

The firelight winked on the facets of the crystal decanter Cassandra had left there after Dr. Bean's visit. Tiny lights of brilliant red and green and blue. He reached for it and poured himself a drink. He wanted to get so damned drunk that he didn't care. Didn't feel.

The case clock chimed the hours: one, two, three, four o'clock in the morning. He experienced a violent urge to smash the beveled glass doors, yank out the weights and pendulum, and rip the brass hands from its painted face. Instead he poured himself another drink.

If he could have turned back time he would have done so willingly. He'd been swept along by folly, blinded by his need to seek revenge. Dazzled by a pair of changeable sea-green eyes. He'd come back to the Thunder Ranch with the hope that he could heal himself and put the past behind him forever. So much for new beginnings.

Cassandra! Despite his anger and the brandy, he wanted her so fiercely it was a physical ache. He lowered himself to the bed gingerly. To know she was awake beneath the same roof was torture. To know that—no matter what he did or said—she would never really be his, was worse.

The brandy muzzied his thinking and sheer exhaustion caught up with him at last. Grayson drifted until he realized that the door had opened and closed softly. Dull light filtered through the closed draperies. Almost dawn. He reached for his revolver and stopped. This was no enemy intruder. A rustle of silk, a waft of Cassandra's lavender and rose perfume, his name whispered softly, set his blood stirring. He felt the silk and lace of her favorite peignoir brush against his naked skin. Then her hands touched his shoulder, caressed his chest, cradled his face as she rained kisses on him. Her gestures told him more than mere words. The cold ache of loneliness fell away before the heat of his need for her. Everything was going to be all right. They would work it out, together.

"Cassandra . . . Cassandra . . ." He drew her into his arms and his mouth found hers, warm and yielding. When she moved away he let her go, fighting the elemental need to conquer and possess. He didn't want to frighten her away this time.

Silk whispered to the floor. All his fine resolve vanished as she moved back into his arms, naked and warm. He pulled her hard against him. The brush of her bare skin against his had them both gasping. Their kisses were hot and wild. Her fingers dug into his shoulders and raked across his chest.

He was on fire with the need to bind Cassandra to him, if not through love, then through this physical melding. The heat of it was blinding.

But the light had another source. Grayson heard a gasp and opened his eyes—and thought that he had tumbled into one of his nightmares. Cassandra was still locked in his embrace, yet Cassandra stood in the connecting doorway between their rooms with a kerosene lamp in her hand. The truth slammed into him with sickening force.

Cassandra stood rigid and white in the yellow glow. She had been lying awake, wrestling with regrets. The soft cries had alerted her and she'd hurried down, thinking that Grayson was having one of his nightmares. But now the circle of lamplight fell on the bed. On Grayson, his bronzed body naked beneath a sheen of sweat. On Bedelia, pinned beneath him.

The terrible tableau was frozen in place until Bedelia laughed low in her throat. "Why, Mrs. Howard," she said sweetly, "we didn't mean to wake you!"

Cassandra didn't move or speak. She was incapable of either. Grayson turned on Bedelia in a rage such as she'd never seen before. She thought he was going to kill her then and there. She slipped sideways off the bed, snatching up the discarded peignoir, and rushed past Cassandra, knocking her into the doorjamb. The lamp fell with a crash at Cassandra's feet.

The puddle of kerosene spread across the floor. Before she could jump clear the flames licked their way toward her, igniting the hem of her nightgown. She didn't feel their heat or hear Bedelia's shouts of alarm. She didn't see fire eating holes in the silk or the charred cloth in its path. The image of her husband and Bedelia, locked in the throes of passion, blotted everything else from her mind.

Grayson sprang forward and beat at the flames with his bare hands. There was no time for explanations. Cassandra tried to run from the room and the flames leapt higher. He tackled her to the floor and rolled on top of her to extinguish the burning gown. She struck wildly at him, in her daze. Grayson held her fast. "It's all right, Cassandra. The fire is out."

Bedelia ran downstairs. Jesus! The fat was really in the fire. It had been going so beautifully until that little fool had to come in and ruin everything. She threw things into a leather valise any which way. She thought of putting the back of the straight chair under the handle but decided not to waste the time. Grayson was the kind of man who'd come through it if he wanted to. She had to be out and away before the sun came up, which didn't give her much time. In five minutes she was packed and ready to flee with a change of warm clothes and whatever jewelry she had filched from Cassandra over the past few days.

Grayson was too concerned for Cassandra to bother with Bedelia. She broke away from him, weeping and cursing. By the time he ran after her she'd locked the sitting-room door from inside. He pounded on the door and called to her but she refused to answer. By now the entire household was awake. He heard Kitty calling as she hurried through from the back wing.

Grayson put on his trousers and leaned over the railing. He saw their faces turned up to him, white and alarmed. He went down the steps. "Go back to bed."

Kitty looked stricken. He went down to her. "Did the shouting frighten you?" She was shaking badly. Grayson put his arm around her shoulders and led her back to the new wing, with Povey trailing. Somewhere a door opened and shut. "I would never harm a hair of Cassandra's head. You know that, don't you?"

She searched his eyes for the truth, then nodded. "Yes, I do."

Povey took her arm and they went through toward their bedrooms. Grayson uttered an oath beneath his breath. It was true that he would never willingly harm Cassandra, but this night's work had destroyed any hopes of salvaging their marriage.

Grayson shook with reaction and anger. He wanted to go after Bedelia but didn't dare. He'd kill her. With his bare hands.

He sat in the darkened parlor for a while with his head in his hands. He might be able to make Cassandra understand, but he doubted it. And he could never make her forgive what was, after all, unforgivable. This time he went up the stairs more slowly. He felt a hundred years old. A light flickered inside the bedroom. "Cassandra?"

He went in, hoping to find her there. The room was empty and the light was a thread of flame that had charred through a strip of the rug and was hungrily licking its way up the edge of the draperies. As he dashed forward to tear them down the fire whoomped and blazed up the undercurtains. They moved lazily with the breeze of the heated air and twisted into bizarre shapes before his eyes. In the same split second burning shreds fell to the bed, igniting the sheets and quilt. The entire room exploded in an inferno and the air turned thick and black.

He fought his way out and shut the door to contain the blaze, shouting the house down. Cassandra's door was open, the room empty. Smoke hazed the ceiling of the hall, growing thicker. "Fire!" he called out as he stumbled down the stairs. "Everyone outside! Wake up the men!"

Kitty and Povey rushed past with Ping behind them. The fire spread with stunning speed. The wallpaper peeled away in a shower of sparks, and flames licked along the ceiling. Grayson heard the triangle clanging furiously and the alarmed cries of his men. There was nothing he could do inside, and he went out shouting to form a bucket brigade.

Bronco brought a ladder and got a second crew to pass buckets to him on the roof. It was too late to stop the blaze. The heat of the flames drove them back and the thick black smoke had them choking and coughing. Nothing could save the old wing, so they bent their efforts to saving the new section. "Get the women in the bunkhouse," Grayson shouted to Swede over the whoosh and crackle of the flames.

The wind was against them, but it brought the damp smell of impending snow. A few scattered flakes drifted down, melting almost immediately; but within a quarter hour the wind changed and came out of the north, bringing an arctic blast of air and gusts of snow so thick and fast that they could hardly see.

The upper story fell in with a roar and a blaze of sparks mingled with the snow. When the gusts blew strongly they caught glimpses of the front wing shell. It was nothing but a mass of blackened, smoking timbers. The rest of the house appeared to be intact. The dividing wall between the kitchen and study had once been part of the exterior, and thick wet plaster covered the logs. It had prevented the flames from feeding on it. The heavy snow and the water-bucket brigade took care of the rest.

The dawn broke, gray and cold, but the new wing was saved, except for a layer of oily soot. They searched the wreckage for smoldering, but the fire had been conquered by the fast-falling snow. Grayson pushed his hair back from his forehead. His face was singed and soot-streaked, like his skin and trousers, and his leg hurt like hell. It was a mess, but he'd built it before, and he could build it again.

Grayson began the damage count. "Was anyone hurt?"

"Bobby singed his eyebrows but he's fine. Bronco got his hands blistered going in for that damned kitten." Swede grinned. "It must've been worth it. Kitty's got him in the bunkhouse, doctoring his hands with a wet poultice and smiles. He'll live."

"Where are the other women?"

"In the bunkhouse, warming up."

Grayson set off across the snow. His boots were soaked and his toes were numb. He needed dry clothes and a cup of hot coffee, but he needed to sort things out with Cassandra even more. If he could only get her to listen to him. God only knew what she must be thinking.

He walked to the bunkhouse through drifts that were knee-high. The bunkhouse was warm and smelled of sweat and men and horses. Kitty looked up from bandaging Bronco's hands. The sable kitten slept at his feet. Povey and Ping were heating coffee on the potbellied stove and Bedelia sat huddled in a blanket on one of the bunks, her eyes red from smoke or weeping.

Grayson stood over her, threateningly. "I'll deal with you later. Where's my wife?"

"I don't know. I haven't seen her."

Kitty stopped her work. "We thought she was with you!"

Fear gripped Grayson. "Stay here!" He ran back out into the snowstorm. *"Cassandra!"*

He ran back to the ruins of the front wing. No, she couldn't have been inside. They would have found her by now. He stumbled through the main room and library. The rooms and their contents were totally black, covered with a layer of oily soot. The fear grew. He rallied the men, sick at heart.

The next half hour was grim, as they picked their way through the debris, expecting to discover her body beneath a fallen beam or the wreckage of the staircase. As he shifted a burned table he heard one of the men shout. "God damn, will you look at that!"

Grayson pushed his way to the man, who was standing amid the collapsed section of bedroom floor. "Over there," the cowboy said, pointing. "Pair of andirons from the missus's bedroom. Melted like wax candles."

Relief poured through Grayson in a torrent. The snow hampered their efforts, but at the end of an intensive search there was still no clue to her whereabouts. Had she holed up in one of the other buildings? The sun should have been up the past half hour, but the clouds were so thick and the snow so blinding that the world was wrapped in icy twilight. "Check the barns. I'll look in the stables."

The horses were whinnying in fear. Grayson had no time to spare for them. One quick glance and his blood ran cold.

Cassandra's horse and saddle were gone.

16

 Cassandra rode blindly across the dawn landscape, trying to outrun the images in her mind. She gave Ajax his head and didn't pay any attention to her surroundings for a long while. When she finally slowed him to a trot the sky was gray and forbidding. Wind whipped at her hair. She should have taken her hat, but when she'd ridden out her only goal had been to ride as hard and fast as she could. To put as much distance as possible between herself and the end of her dreams.

She was a failure as a wife and a woman. Tears tracked down her face, drying in the icy wind. What was there about her that drove men away—and into other women's arms?

It was a long time before the cold seeped into her bones. She realized that the sun should have been up before this, but it was getting darker by the minute. The sky was clotted with thick gray clouds in every direction and it was beginning to snow. She had better get her bearings soon.

She rode to the top of the hill ahead. The wind was stronger, tearing at her hair and whipping her skirts against her legs. Her long cloak was warm but didn't provide enough protection as the temperature plummeted. Cassandra scanned the landscape with growing apprehension. There was nothing familiar to mark her location: not a rock or a grove or a dwelling she could recognize.

The air thickened around her, turning white with stinging snow as the north wind loosed its full fury. In less than a minute Cassandra couldn't see past the end of Ajax's nose and she had long lost her way. And she knew in her bones that this storm would not blow over quickly. She had to find shelter soon, or they'd both perish.

They made their way haltingly toward the few trees she'd noticed before the snow had obliterated them from view. Ajax began sidling and tossing his head. He didn't want to go on. Cassandra dug her heels in and forced him forward. The horse balked. "Go on, you stupid creature!"

Suddenly he stumbled and she almost pitched over his head. When her fright was under control she realized that he had stepped into a small stream. He reared and edged away. She bit her lip in chagrin. The horse knew more than she did! Cassandra had no choice. She let Ajax pick his way through the slanting snow, trusting his instincts more than herself.

She had never imagined such a storm. Nothing in her experience had prepared her for the suddenness of its onslaught or its violence. Soon she was beyond cold, beyond terror. Her eyelashes stuck together and her hands were unfeeling lumps, barely able to hold on to the reins. She ducked to keep her face from freezing, and clung to the horse's neck.

The roan had great heart and stamina. He went steadily into the blasting wind, snorting and whinnying. He seemed to know where he was heading. She crouched low and tried to offer encouragement when he faltered. "Good Ajax. Wonderful Ajax! Keep going!" The wind tore her words away.

Her woolen shawl and the collar of her coat were rimed with frost from her breath. There was no sensation in her toes and she feared that her hands and feet were frostbitten. There was nothing she could do about it now; but she tried to keep her hands from freezing, alternately slipping one or the other inside her cloak and beneath her arm for warmth.

The wind stabbed through her and she knew that soon she wouldn't be able to hold the reins. Suddenly Ajax stumbled and went down. She clung to him as they slid headfirst down an embankment. At the last minute she managed to throw herself far enough to avoid being pinned beneath him. He gave a great scream of pain and his forelegs flailed wildly. Then he went still and didn't move again.

"Ajax!" She felt his neck. It was twisted terribly. His noble neck had been broken in the fall. Cassandra put her face against him and wept. It was her fault that he was dead—and if she didn't do something she would be next. The temptation to stay where she was, sheltered from the wind and comforted by his warm but rapidly cooling body, almost overwhelmed her; but the urge to live was still strong.

She climbed up the embankment. He had been heading this way for a definite reason. There was help somewhere ahead. The wind almost knocked her down and the cold brought tears to her eyes. She tried to force them back because they froze and stuck her lashes together. After a while she no longer cared. The cold was replaced by lassitude and a spreading warmth.

Just a little bit farther. If she didn't see or hear anything she would go back to Ajax, curl up against him, and let go. But first, just a little bit farther. There must be something ahead. Every step was harder than the one before. She wanted to drop where she was and let the snow fall over her like a featherbed. Cassandra fought the seductive urge. She had to find shelter . . . had to find shelter . . . had to find shelter . . .

She tripped and went sprawling. Coarse grains of snow filled her mouth and froze her throat, but her hand had struck something. Cassandra reached out. Her fingers were unresponsive, her hand a block of wood. But she made out a shape. A log. *A wall!*

Afraid that she was hallucinating, she forced herself to her knees. It felt real enough. Then she wanted to weep in disappointment. She'd tripped on the edge of a woodpile. She sat down in the snow while it piled all around, her brain too slow to think properly. Then she realized that where there was a woodpile, there was bound to be some sort of shelter. She crawled through the drifts, one hand on the woodpile, afraid she would lose it in the whiteout. Her knee hit a flat stone. A threshold? Then she pushed against the door and fell inside.

She lay rolled up in a ball, too tired and cold to move. So drowsy. I'll just close my eyes for a minute, she thought. A small, furry creature scampered across her and she jolted awake. She had to move. Movement was life.

Gradually she made out her surroundings. It was very dark. She was in a small one-room cabin, with a puncheon floor and a rude stone fireplace on one wall. It was furnished with a table, two stools—one made from a tree stump—and a bed. And, Blessed God, there was a blanket on it. She wrapped it around her shivering body. Her feet were stiff. She couldn't feel them at all. Somehow she must build a fire.

Although the place had an abandoned air there was kindling in a basket and two logs in the fireplace. Someone had lived here recently, or perhaps it was a hunting cabin. The three sulfur matches sealed in an oilskin packet atop the mantel were like a miracle. Cassandra shook even more with relief. She rasped them clumsily against the strike plate as she had seen Povey do. They wouldn't light. The damp had gotten into them. It was a crushing blow. She sank down on the stool with her face buried in her hands and realized she had no sensation in them at all. It was as if they were missing. The cabin that had seemed like her salvation would be her tomb.

There must be something . . . *something!* She rose and searched the cabin. A pair of boots, a metal pot, a stone knife set in a wood haft, a hoelike tool, and a small metal box. She reached for the latter and opened it, afraid that her hopes would be dashed once more. It was a tinder box. She'd seen one used as a young girl, but had never tried it herself. It took a long time and an abundance of curses, which she hadn't even realized that she knew, before the small spark caught.

Blowing softly, she finally managed to get the kindling alight. A yellow flame blazed, sputtered, and caught. Cassandra held her hands over it and something crashed down through the chimney. Some*things*. A nest of snakes. She jumped back, falling against the table as they wriggled out across the floor in all directions. She didn't know if they were poisonous or not.

Grabbing up the hoe, she flailed at the darting, sinuous bodies. She put all her dread and fear of dying into the task, hacking until they were dismembered. The wind howled and shrieked as she opened the door to throw the remains outside. The snow had drifted halfway up the door. She changed her mind.

When she had discovered Grayson with Bedelia, she had wanted to die. But the instincts of survival were too strong. Cassandra stared at the hacked-up remains of the snakes and evaluated the situation. With the heavy accumulation of ice and snow it might be days before they found her, but her predicament wasn't too dire. There was plenty of firewood for warmth and there was snow to melt for drinking water.

And now she had something to eat.

A pall of gloom settled over the Thunder Ranch. Ping, Povey, and the ranch hands had given Cassandra up for dead, and mourned her deeply. Kitty refused to believe it and was comforted by Bronco. "But why would she ride out at a time like that?"

He had no real answer, but they all knew that Cassandra and Grayson had quarreled just before the fire broke out, although they didn't know why. Bedelia did. The fire and Cassandra's flight into the storm were her fault. Jesus! She hadn't meant it! She remembered that Cassandra had been kind to her and how she had stepped in when Simon Fiddler had recognized her.

It was a wonder that Grayson hadn't killed her.

He was half mad with grief. He spent all his waking

hours by the window, praying and waiting for the storm to break. No one could come near him without feeling the wrath of his temper. Except for Kitty. He knew that her grief was as real as his. And although Bedelia had been the agent of cause, he blamed himself for everything. He had started it all by going after Tyler Lucton, and this was where it had led.

The moment the wind and snow abated he was out with his men, searching the frozen land on horseback despite the strict orders Dr. Bean had left him. The land was white and alien as a moonscape. The winds had piled drifts higher than the rooftops in some places and scoured the frozen ground bare in others. They carried long poles to prod the drifts. Cassandra could be anywhere.

They widened the search day by day for over a week. Grayson's instincts pulled him one way but logic pulled him the other. If she'd headed west the snow would have been in her face. It made more sense for her to have gone the other way. He drew inside himself and listened to his inner voice, as he had learned to do so long ago. "We'll go west," he said firmly.

It was three more days before he stumbled on the embankment and found the stiff body of Cassandra's horse. The wind had blown the snow from Ajax's carcass. Grayson dismounted and knelt down, placing his hand against the gallant beast. He knew now where Ajax had been heading.

Bronco and Zeke swung down from their own mounts a few yards away. Their horses didn't react at all. There was no smell of death here yet, only the puzzling stillness of their comrade's fallen body. The Pole crossed himself and whispered a prayer for the dead.

"God damn!" Zeke muttered. "How the hell did she get this far in that shit?"

Grayson climbed out of the ravine, his face wet with tears. His companions were afraid to meet each other's eyes. Or his.

But Grayson's tears mingled joy with grief. He knew. He *knew!* Climbing back on his black gelding, he started off over the melting snow. He knew every inch of this ground—just as Ajax had. The gelding caught his excitement. Together they flew up the crest of the embankment, gouts of snow flying from the great hooves. There was a cabin just ahead.

The day was overcast and visibility poor due to blowing snow, but suddenly the sun broke through the clouds. A wisp of smoke came from the chimney, a gauzy gray veil against the shimmer of blue sky. Grayson jumped down by the diminished woodpile and pushed the door open. Cassandra lay on the bed at an angle, her eyes closed and so shadowed they looked bruised. He crossed the floor to her side. "Cassandra! Thank God!"

She didn't stir at his voice. Grayson's heart contracted painfully. How long had she been like this? He brushed the hair back from her forehead. Her skin was hot and dry. She was so thin, her face sharp angles and hollows. He swept her up in his arms and felt the terrible heat radiating from her frail body, the rasping shudder of her ragged breaths. Fear swept through him like a cold wind. It would be unforgivingly cruel of fate to let him find her here, only to lose her to the ravages of fever.

He gave a shout and the others came running.

*   *   *

Voices, low and concerned.

". . . double pneumonia and pleurisy. The crisis will come sometime tonight."

A woman's sob, a man's rough curse, and then the same voice continued. "You're her maid—Povey, is it? How far along was she?"

"Not two months, if that, sir."

"Well, even if she pulls through, she'll probably lose the child. You never can tell, though. That's one thing I've learned in my years as a physician. You never can tell."

Strange words to Cassandra, floating in even stranger dreams. What child? Whose child? She pictured a small shape, stumbling toward her through the snowscape of her dreams. Then it vanished. Oh, oh, oh! I have lost the child in the snow. Poor, poor thing. How angry everyone will be . . .

Then snow and child faded away. She was in the cabin, hearing Kitty give orders with quiet authority; but when Cassandra turned she was alone except for the snakes twisting and writhing across the floor. Later she dreamed that Povey bathed her heated brow and brushed her hair, but her wrinkled face shifted and melted into Kitty's tearful one. Later, she drifted to the surface and saw Grayson—but was he real or only a dream image, wavering in the soft lamplight?

Cassandra was desperately tired. She closed her eyes. Why wouldn't they all go away and leave her alone? She wanted to sleep forever. But the pain kept rousing her. Pain and fire. In her feet and hands, in her chest with every struggling breath.

Pain in her heart.

People came and went. She heard them murmuring to one another—or were they speaking to her? She neither knew nor cared. Eons passed while she hovered in a shadowy limbo. Cassandra heard weeping. She struggled up from nothingness to find herself in a fog-filled room. It was crowded with people, some solid and substantial, others as shadowy as herself. A balding man with spectacles looked down at her sadly and shook his head. Dr. Bean. Or was it the medicine woman? Shapes shifted and blurred, shadows dancing. Grayson took their place.

Cassandra stared at her husband. How stern he looked. How pale. It frightened her, and she let go of her moorings and sailed away on a warm tide of nothingness. Away from the pain and toward the glow of distant light.

Something snagged at her like the weight of an anchor. Caught and held her, although she struggled to be free. It took great effort to open her eyes. No anchor after all, she saw in surprise, only Grayson's hands clasping hers. "Breathe," he commanded. *"Breathe, goddammit!"*

She did. Oh, God! It hurt so badly. Please, she thought, please don't ask me to do it again. But Grayson's voice and touch were there, urging her to fight the deadly apathy and accept the pain of living. His hands held hers and would not let them go.

Slowly, slowly, he pulled her back to him. Infusing her with the will to live. Grayson became, not her anchor, but her lifeline. Cassandra knew that she could still drift away if she really wished to, but she didn't want to let go of him. Now the voices soothed her. As long as there were voices she didn't have to think. Or feel.

The sound of Grayson's voice pierced her through the layers of lethargy that cocooned her. "I should have never brought her here. I knew it from the start. When the first train comes through, Cassandra . . ."

"No," she mumbled. "I won't go."

Her voice was rusty and the effort exhausted her. Before she sank into a deep and dreamless sleep, Cassandra realized that her face was wet with tears that were not her own. Perhaps it was a dream. But Grayson lay beside her, his arm across her protectively. He smiled and whispered her name. Cassandra smiled back. Just another dream, she thought, and closed her eyes, sinking gratefully into slumber.

Grayson stroked her hair and listened to her soft breathing, and wept to know his prayers had been answered.

Sunshine, warm and golden. Cassandra felt it through her closed eyelids. She opened them, suddenly awake and aware. She was in bed, in an unfamiliar room. The rich light poured in through the new parlor windows, pooling on the polished wood floor and turning the colors of the small turkey carpet into stained-glass patterns. Cassandra realized her bed was set up in the new parlor. How very odd.

Her fingers felt numb and stiff. She wiggled them a few times. They responded woodenly. How long had she been lying in this bed? She turned her head. There was an evergreen tree in the corner, trimmed with paper chains and red ribbons and hung with straw ornaments and jagged snowflakes snipped from tin. They flashed with sunlight, bright as mirrors. And Grayson was sleeping in the rocker beside the bed with a colorful quilt thrown over him.

His face was thinner and lined with fatigue. A rush of

love and sorrow brought tears to her eyes. Cassandra understood the first emotion but the heavy sadness baffled her. She tried to search her memory but her thoughts were still thick and cobwebby. The last thing she could recall was sitting in the kitchen with Ping, peeling apples for the pies. And the more she tried to force remembrance, the more it eluded her.

She sighed, and the soft sound awakened Grayson. He threw off the quilt and jumped up in alarm just as Kitty entered the room. Her niece flew to her side. "Oh, you're awake at last! We have been so worried."

Cassandra looked from her niece to Grayson. For a few seconds his face had shone with the same light that illuminated Kitty's. Now it was quenched, as if it had never been. Dreams tangled with reality. She had lost a child somewhere in the snow. Had they found it in time?

Cassandra cleared her throat. "The child . . ."

Kitty waited for Grayson to respond, but he was silent. She took Cassandra's hand in hers. "The child is fine. Dr. Bean says there is no reason you should not deliver a healthy baby near the end of June."

Surprisingly, Cassandra remembered that. Waiting, counting the days, fearing that she was only late. Praying that, after years of barrenness, she carried a new life within her womb. Anticipating Grayson's reaction.

"I am so glad," she whispered. "At first I couldn't believe the signs. I had been barren so long."

She held out her hand to her husband and he took it in his clasp. His face was so grave. "I didn't want to tell you until I knew for certain. I wanted so much to give you a child, born of our love."

He raised her hand to his lips and kissed her fingers, one by one. His joy was tempered with worry. Cassandra had survived her illness, yet he still might lose her. It was apparent that she remembered nothing of the incident that had caused her to flee the house—at least for the time being. But when memory returned . . . Grayson shuddered and held her close.

Kitty smiled. Her presence was considerably de trop. She slipped quietly out of the room to spread the good news. Povey was still asleep and Ping had gone into the pantry for the buckwheat flour. The first person Kitty saw was Bronco. He came in the kitchen door, knocking the snow from his boots on the mat. When he saw her his blue eyes took on a warm glow. Over the past weeks they'd had little time together and she realized how terribly she had missed his company. No, missed *him*.

She hurried toward him. "Bronco!" was all she managed to say before bursting into tears.

He immediately thought the worst. Forgetting everything except that Kitty was in distress, he pulled her into his arms and held her against his chest. "Kitty, *moja kohana*!"

She turned her tear-streaked face up to his and he saw joy there. "Cassandra is awake," she said, her voice choked with emotion. "She's going to be all right."

Bronco knew the right thing would be to release Kitty. Knew it and ignored it. He'd wanted to take her in his arms a hundred times, a thousand times before. She was skittish as a new foal and he'd handled her as gently; but he was a man, holding the woman he loved. Flesh and blood could only stand so much. He lowered his head and kissed her tenderly.

When his arms tightened around her Kitty grew rigid, but then a feeling of love and protection surrounded her. This was right and good. This was Bronco. This was where she belonged.

She melted against him, turning her face up for another kiss, knowing that she loved him deeply, and that her love was returned in full measure.

Ping came out of the pantry just in time to witness the second kiss. The sack of flour dropped from her hands. Neither Kitty nor Bronco noticed.

The parlor became a combination of bedroom and keeping room, and the house revolved around it. By day it was the ladies' territory and after supper Grayson, and occasionally Bronco or Swede, sat with them. Cassandra noticed that Bedelia kept to herself as much as possible. One morning as Bedelia went out of the room with a tray of tea things, she ran into Grayson. Their voices, although low, carried clearly to Cassandra's ears. First Grayson: "I told you to stay out of my wife's room, and out of my sight. I won't rest easy until you're on that train bound for Denver and out of our lives for good."

Bedelia's reply was terse. "Why, are you afraid she'll remember?"

They moved away toward the kitchen. Cassandra bit her lower lip. Remember what? What was this terrible thing that they all tiptoed around? This thing that affected them all, yet was never mentioned. A flare lit her memory. Flames. Flames and burning cold and . . . snakes? No, she was mixing her dreams up with reality again. But something dark stirred in the back of her mind, filling her with great unease.

She supposed it had something to do with the time she'd been snowbound in the cabin, for her slumber was disturbed almost nightly by dreams that vanished with the morning light. She had no intention of opening Pandora's box by accosting her husband or Bedelia on the matter. Whatever the reason, she hoped the memory would stay lost to her forever.

She forgot about it in the excitement of plans for the approaching holiday. On Christmas Eve Cassandra dressed in her finest gown of red silk for the occasion, with her wedding ring, a pair of garnet earbobs, and her mother's gold locket as her only jewelry. The activity tired her and she sat in the armchair by the fire to marshal her energy. They planned to exchange gifts tonight and sing carols. The house smelled of Ping's wonderful pies—mincemeat and apple and caramel custard—and of Povey's gingerbread cookies.

Grayson stopped on the threshold when he saw her. "You are more beautiful than ever," he told her.

"And you, sir, are even more gallant."

He noted the signs of fatigue in her face. "Ping has tea and refreshments set out in the dining room. Are you up to a walk?"

She pushed herself up out of the chair. "Of course, I'm not an invalid."

But she was. Everyone thought so except Cassandra, and she was determined to prove them wrong.

Her stamina had improved daily and she made up her mind that she would be as fit as ever when she delivered her baby. She entered the dining room on her husband's arm. The doors and windows had been decked with evergreen bows. Instead of the usual oil lamps, two branches of silver candlesticks stood on the polished table. Ping and Kitty exchanged glances. Even Bedelia, who rarely spoke to anyone unless addressed directly, seemed in on a great secret.

Kitty looked young and heartwrenchingly beautiful in a gown of primrose satin trimmed with rows of delicate French lace. Povey had dignified the occasion with her best outfit of olive merino and Ping had put aside her apron for once and dressed in the colorful silks of her homeland.

Grayson helped Cassandra to the rocker beside the big cast-iron stove. She felt the quiet strength flowing from him to her. His touch was welcome but infrequent. As if there were an invisible wall between them that he rarely breached. She wondered if it had to do with her folly in riding out that day and into the storm. Perhaps it was because she'd endangered their child so recklessly. If so, the wall would surely crumble come spring, after the baby's birth. She wanted so much to be a wife to Grayson. In every way.

He settled her in the rocker. "Not too close? Good. I'll be right back."

"And," Kitty admonished, "no peeking."

They went back to the parlor and closed the door.

Cassandra strained her ears to discover what was going on. There was much thumping and bumping from the sitting room. Zeke cursed and Bronco laughed aloud. Cassandra sipped her cup of tea with candied orange peel and honey, and waited.

The door opened at last. "All right. You can come in."

Grayson helped her back to the parlor. Her dresser had been moved to the far wall. In its place, between the two windows, was an upright piano. Carvings of oak leaves and acorns decorated the top panels and twined around the front legs. Grayson smiled. "Merry Christmas."

Cassandra burst into tears.

"Grayson bought it from Beth," Kitty told her. "We prayed the weather would hold so we could bring it over from the Lazy L by sleigh. Mr. Hanks is coming out from Aureus to tune it as soon as the road clears."

"It's beautiful!" Cassandra sat on the cushioned piano stool and beamed. It didn't matter that the instrument would be out of tune from the journey and the cold. "It's the most splendid Christmas gift in the world."

She sat down and tried to run the scales. Her fingers faltered, then gradually picked up speed. A shadow crossed her face, so quickly only Grayson noticed: she could still play, but not as she had done before. Her touch was off from the frostbite she'd sustained. It felt as if she were wearing a thick pair of woolen gloves. Perhaps one day she would be able to make music again with her former skill. Until then she still had the music in her head and in her heart.

The baby moved inside her and her heart leapt for joy. After refreshments they sang Christmas carols. Kitty and Grayson took the melody, while Cassandra and Povey sang the harmony, with Bronco and his harmonica joining the piano. Cassandra hadn't had such a Christmas celebration, filled with love and song, since her childhood.

Later Bronco taught them carols of his homeland. Soon Kitty was picking them out on the piano keys. Grayson watched them from beside the fireplace. He wished that he and Cassandra had met as simply as Kitty and her swain, that they had gone as easily from friendship to love. He wished that they had started out as innocently, with no shadows between them.

Cursing himself for a coward, he turned and gazed at the fire. He was living in a fool's paradise. If Cassandra's memory ever returned, he prayed that it would be years from now, when they had built up a strong relationship. So strong that not even the truth could destroy it.

He nudged a log with the toe of his boot. A bright shower of sparks cascaded into the ashes. He wished like hell that Bedelia was already gone. He couldn't stand the sight of her. Not a day went by that he didn't want to wring her neck until the bones snapped. His fingers curled at the thought of it.

Bedelia saw his face reflected in the mirror and read his thoughts. Grayson was the only one who knew what she had done, and he hated her for it. The others would if they knew, too. Funny that the one man she'd wanted to love her now loathed the very sight of her.

Kitty began handing out gifts, wrapped in silver tissue paper. There were two for Bedelia. She stammered her thanks for the satin collar from Kitty and the silver chain and pendant from Cassandra. At the first possible moment she slipped away. Jesus Christ, talk about rubbing salt in wounds! Or was that heaping stones or something upon her head? She never could get that Bible stuff straight.

Cassandra saw her leave the room. Poor girl, she thought. We are all happy together and she is alone, without family at the Christmas season. It must be very difficult for her at such a time.

It wasn't the lack of family that had upset Bedelia, it was seeing Grayson watching Cassandra, his eyes filled with love. She threw herself down on the narrow bed, dropping the collar and pendant on the patchwork quilt. She'd been stupid to think he would ever feel that way about her. All she had to offer was her body and the tricks she'd learned in her wanderings. What Grayson and Cassandra had was something far deeper, far stronger than that. If she hadn't been so blind herself she would have realized it from the start.

Maybe that was why she'd gone after him. Wanting to belong to someone. To be a part of something greater than herself. She'd never really wanted to hurt Cassandra and her baby. Jesus, she hadn't even known that Cassandra was pregnant at the time, or she wouldn't have made a play for Grayson that terrible night.

Bedelia rolled over and brushed a single tear from her eye. She hadn't cried since her mother had left her at the orphanage. Not when Miss Lane had accused her unjustly of stealing from the schoolmarm's desk. Not when her best friend, Fanny Newton, had died.

She sat up, rubbing her eyes. And not now, by God. Bedelia was ashamed of herself, sniveling and sniffling like a snot-nosed kid. She was also scared. For the first time in her life she really cared what other people thought of her. She didn't want Cassandra and Kitty to turn away from her as if she had some vile disease, the way that Grayson did.

After bathing her face with water from the basin she changed into her nightshift. A tap sounded at her door. She opened it to find Cassandra waiting.

"May I come in? I couldn't help but notice that you left the room so suddenly." Cassandra's face was very serious. "I think I know the reason for it."

Bedelia's face went pasty white. She knew beyond all doubt that she didn't want this conversation to take place. Should she deny everything? Lie and say it was Grayson who tried to seduce her? No, that wouldn't do. Cassandra would believe her husband. And, strangely enough, Bedelia realized that she couldn't lie to Cassandra. Not anymore.

"Oh, God! I'm so sorry," she blurted. "It wasn't his

fault. I want you to know that. Grayson thought I was you. I wore your perfume and that fancy white thing of yours when I went to him that night and . . . he thought I was you."

At first Cassandra had no idea of what Bedelia was talking about. Then images of what had sent her riding off into the gray dawn tumbled into her mind. She blanched whiter than Bedelia. The emotions were as real to her now as they had been when they occurred. They hit her like a roundhouse punch, dazing her senses and filling her with pain. Shock. Betrayal. Raw anguish and overwhelming anger.

Cassandra stumbled to the bed and sat abruptly, as if her legs had no strength to hold her upright. Her ears rang and she felt dizzy. The room was blotted out by the scene in her mind's eye. As she struggled for composure she saw now what she had been too stunned to notice when it happened: the startlement in Grayson's face when he saw her at the door with her lamp, and the recoil and revulsion when he realized that it was Bedelia in his arms.

Cassandra closed her eyes. She should have known that Grayson wouldn't have taken another woman beneath their own roof, no matter what the provocation. He wasn't that kind of man. He wasn't Tyler.

Bedelia's frightened voice seemed to come from far away. "I'll get help."

"No!" Cassandra's hand shot out to grasp Bedelia's wrist. She recovered her composure. In the past months she had suffered worse shocks and survived them. She would survive this as well. "We took you in and gave you a home, even after Grayson uncovered your deception. We treated you kindly. What did I—or any of us—

ever do to you, Bedelia, that you would hurt us so and come so close to destroying our happiness?"

Bedelia hung her head. "Because I was jealous of everything you had. I'm not a good person. I've been nothing but trouble to anyone from the day that I was born. Even my own mother abandoned me."

Cassandra took the other woman's measure. This time she was seeing a very different Bedelia from the clever, confident, and sharp-tongued one she knew. This person was awkward, vulnerable, and tragically touching. Cassandra very well remembered what it was like to be alone and friendless. "Tell me everything," she said with quiet authority. "From the beginning."

Bedelia poured out her story—the truth, this time. It came between sniffles and sobs, which made her tale all the more believable, because it was quite plain that she disdained tears as a weakness. Cassandra listened to the end. Afterward she sat staring at her hands, sorting out her thoughts. There were things she could have told Bedelia: that Kitty had been raped, too; that she, herself, had killed a man. They had a lot in common, despite the outward differences. She came to a decision.

"You've had a hard life, Bedelia. I won't sit in judgment on you. But when the tracks are clear I will expect you to be on the first train out of Silver Creek or Aureus."

Grayson had already told Bedelia that. His initial fury had been so great she wouldn't have been surprised if he'd left her out in the snow. Only his anxiety to find Cassandra had saved Bedelia from his immediate wrath. She twisted the fringe on her blue gown. She had never had a female friend or confidante. Not the kind you could really talk to. She realized that Cassandra might have been that friend. Now she would never know. Bedelia felt a bewildering sense of loss.

"You have no reason to believe me," she said huskily. "I didn't think of anything but myself but . . . but I'm different now. And if there is ever any way I can make it up to you, I will."

Neither of them thought that very likely.

By New Year's Eve Cassandra felt her strength return in good measure. With it came a longing to be held in Grayson's arms again. To be made love to, and to touch and kiss and love in return. That night she wanted to move her bed back up to the new bedrooms that had been added overhead. "It's too crowded in here," she told them. "And I have hogged the parlor far too long. It's time to put it to its normal use. I can manage the stairs now. The exercise will be good for me."

Bronco and Grayson dismantled her bed and took it up. But when Grayson helped her up the steps that evening she didn't go to the new sitting room that had been added on next to the bedroom. "I've been treated like a fragile piece of china too long. I don't want to sleep alone tonight, Grayson. I want to sleep in the same bed with my husband."

He hesitated, but for an instant there had been a flash of hunger in his eyes. Then she realized that he was afraid to touch her. "I love you, Grayson. I want to start our new year together on the right note. I want to be a wife to you in every way. I want you to make love to me."

He tilted her chin up with his hand and gazed into her eyes. He wanted her so badly it was a physical ache. But the incident with Bedelia and its consequences to Cassandra weighed heavily on his soul. He let his hand drop. If he made love to her the way he wanted to, what would happen when her memory returned? She would surely hate him for deceiving her, and it would destroy her trust in him forever.

She saw sorrow and doubt in the lines of his face, mingled with great longing. Without him saying a single word she knew that the incident with Bedelia was a barrier. "I know everything," she said quietly. "My memory returned on Christmas Eve. Bedelia and I had a long talk. I feel so foolish. If I hadn't run out of the room, dropping the lamp, things would never have come to such a sorry pass."

Cassandra held out her arms to him. Grayson had no need for mere words. He crushed her against his wide chest, pressing kisses on her hair, her temples, her ripe and willing mouth. Then he swept her into his arms and carried her to bed.

All the pain and loneliness of the past months were banished when they were alone in the big, comfortable bed. Firelight gleamed on their naked bodies. He lavished kisses on her breasts, sensitive and full with her advancing pregnancy. She touched the deep ridges of scars upon his back and washed them again with her tears. They made love with great tenderness and an urgency born of long denial. Afterward they slept in each other's arms.

Cassandra fell into a deep sleep cradled against his shoulder. Grayson stayed awake for hours just to savor the sheer delight of holding her again. When he slept at last his dreams were untroubled. The nightmares that had haunted him for years had finally been vanquished.

When Cassandra opened her eyes again it was just after dawn. Grayson was standing beside the bed, fully dressed. He touched her arm and put a finger to his lips. "Shhh. We have a visitor."

She pulled the sheet up over her nakedness. Black Shield was asleep in the armchair by the fireplace. At least she thought it was him, but the man's face was so lined and gaunt she couldn't be sure. A sick feeling came over her, almost like a premonition of danger.

The Cheyenne warrior opened his eyes. They seemed weary and ancient beyond belief. They absorbed the light rather than reflecting it. Grayson spoke with him while Cassandra huddled in the bed. Grayson went down to the kitchen and brought back a plate of ham and roast beef from the larder. Black Shield tried to eat but couldn't. His stomach was so unused to food that he retched repeatedly.

Cassandra forgot about modesty. She got up, wrapped in the sheet, and slipped behind the screen to put on her robe. She went downstairs in search of tea and soup. Black Shield was able to take a few mouthfuls. Grayson provided him with a blanket. Black Shield rolled up on the hearth rug and fell asleep immediately. Cassandra stared at his thin figure, little more than bones beneath the covering. "What is wrong? He seems very ill."

Grayson's hands formed into tight fists of helpless anger. "Not physically. At least not yet. But he is sick to death in his soul. His people are starving. Some are already dead." Sweet Medicine's prophesies echoed in Grayson's mind. *The white man will come and we will go.*

He went to the wardrobe and took out his long, sheepskin-lined coat. "I'm going to take two men and drive some cattle down to the Cheyenne camp. They're holed up in a box canyon on the other side of Aureus, near that rock formation called Half Mountain. I'll be gone a week or two."

"No!" The cry was wrung from her and she was shamed by it. She got a grip on herself quickly. Cassandra took a deep breath. "I was thinking selfishly. Of course you must go. Is there anything I can do to help?"

"Warm garments would be useful and any blankets you can spare. And one of Ping's iron kettles."

"I'll gather them up."

Within the hour Grayson was ready to depart, with Zeke and a gnarled half-breed named Duncan Keedy. Grayson took his leave of Cassandra with regret. "I hate to leave you here."

She kissed him lingeringly. "Do what you must," she said, "and hurry home to me again."

There was so much love in his eyes when he looked at her that it made her heart turn over. She bit her lip and kept her uneasiness to herself.

He returned in two weeks, quiet and indrawn for several days. Cassandra talked of the baby and showed him the cradle that Bronco had made for them out of clear pine. The weather warmed gradually. Snow slithered from the roof and crashed to the ground, taking the glittering icicles from the eaves with it.

Grayson made two more trips to the Cheyenne camp at Half Mountain. News of Black Shield's plans filtered to others of the scattered Northern Cheyenne and they joined his band, which put an added strain on their meager resources. He kept the news from Cassandra that the mercenaries were abroad again and looking not just for Black Shield but for anyone aiding him and his band. The territorial committee had made that a hanging offense. Tempers were high and hatred was smoldering, fueled by the greed for land and the minerals it contained.

If he wasn't damned careful he'd get caught in the middle of it.

17

Cassandra, safe and content at the Thunder Ranch, was unaware of the growing sentiment against the Cheyenne or the danger to Grayson. She had grown heavy with child and was increasingly wrapped up in her preparations for the birth. Ping had served as midwife to her fellow villagers in China, and Dr. Bean would be less than an hour's ride away.

Kitty was thrilled with the coming baby and Ping made sacques and jackets out of flannel and padded silk, saying she had done the same for her own children. She would make him—Ping was sure the child was a boy, having consulted her oracles—a tiny cap and jacket with a dragon on the back to protect him from evil spirits.

Grayson swallowed a smile at the thought of the grave Ling Cheung in such tiny garments, richly embroidered with plum blossoms and peaches and hares. And he was glad that the coming baby took Cassandra's mind off his visits to Half Mountain. He left again one promising morning, when the only reminders of winter were the patches of snow in the lee of rocks and a lingering bite to the wind.

Cassandra laughed at her own attempts at crocheting under Povey's tutelage, but Kitty and Bedelia proved adept. A layette was taking shape and not a moment too soon. Before they knew it, it would be spring. And sometime in late April or early May, her baby would be born. Hers and Grayson's.

Kitty brought her another skein of wool. Cassandra kissed her niece's cheek. "You're such a comfort to me, dearest. I'll hate to lose you."

"Nonsense." Kitty blushed and blinked away a sheen of tears. "You won't be rid of us so easily. Bronco and I intend to stay here when we're married, until we can build a house down by the creek."

Cassandra smiled. During her illness Kitty had assumed the responsibilities of the woman of the house. She could see her in the kitchen now, a blue gingham apron on over her morning dress as she rolled her sleeves up and took a turn at cranking the big over-and-under churn. Bedelia blackened the cast-iron stove with a mixture of soot and Mrs. Cutter's Blacking Compound. Ping was a stern taskmaster. The stove must be scoured and blackened every Wednesday and the butter must be prepared just so.

They treated Bedelia with meticulous but distant courtesy. She was still amazed that Grayson hadn't killed her. And that Cassandra hadn't had her thrown out into the cold. That was Bedelia's severest penance. Being understood by the persons you had wronged was a hard cross to bear. She'd be gone on the first train— and they'd all be relieved to see her go.

Ping stood beside Kitty, watching her closely. Too little salt or washing of the butter, or too much air in the finished product, would turn it rancid. Kitty applied herself and it was no time at all before the butter was washed, salted, and ready to be pressed into decorative wooden molds. "Very good," Ping told her when all was finished. "Now you know how to make butter, from milkpail to molds. I will teach you everything a good wife needs to know."

Kitty glowed with the pride of accomplishment. She had taken on an unfamiliar task and triumphed at it. "Perhaps the next time you will show me how to milk the cow as well."

Ping cast her hands up in horror. "That is not something I know how to do—nor wish to know!"

Cassandra laughed and they all turned to smile at her. It was a sound that had been remarkably absent of late. She had realized, too late, that by giving Kitty every material advantage, she had unwittingly deprived her of something vital: the freedom and magic of an unstructured childhood. In her own youth she had roamed the grounds of Castle Fayne alone or with her sister, liberated from lessons and the oppressive rules of adult etiquette. On wet days they had explored the crumbling ruins of Castle Fayne or haunted the kitchens in hopes of getting jam tarts fresh from the huge oven.

On warm afternoons they had taken bread and cheese and gone off for an entire day, to watch the swans or hunt for bluebells or play at Robin Hood and his Merry Men. How wonderful it had been to lie in the grass and watch the cloud patterns overhead, with not a worry or care or timetable!

Kitty had never known those delights. Instead she had passed her days in the way of American girls of her class, with endless lessons in deportment and dancing, riding and embroidery, in learning watercolor painting and Italian and the pianoforte. Warm summer days, made for exploring the world, for learning self-reliance and to be comfortable with her own company, had been spent in the schoolroom or with tutors, or in endless fittings for dresses and habits and shirtwaists. Kitty had never had the time to be a child. She had been a miniature adult.

Another thing to feel guilty about, Cassandra mused. But that was in the past. Over the past weeks Kitty had matured and blossomed. A new happiness had settled over her, masking the shadow of the past, but it had not been banished. It would take Bronco's love and tenderness to heal that deep-seated scar. It took a good deal of strength for a man to be so patient and gentle. To build up Kitty's trust with friendship. And that was how real love came, Cassandra realized now. Not suddenly, like infatuation's thunderclap, but with nurturing from deep within, like a tree growing and stretching upward toward the sun. Like her love for Grayson.

The complacency of pregnancy came over her and she no longer worried when Grayson took supplies to the Cheyenne camp. Her life was whole and perfect. Lulled and content, Cassandra mistakenly thought the halcyon days would go on forever. Two days later her peace was shattered once again.

Grayson was gone longer than the two weeks. He cut several head of cattle from the herd and went north with them to where Black Shield's people were holed up. Zeke and Swede went with him and Black Shield rode ahead. Bedelia came galloping across the meadow, after delivering a bolt of cloth to Beth Leslie at the Lazy L. She came over a rise and saw them.

Swede rode up to her. Bedelia shaded her eyes. "Where are they going with that Indian and those cows?"

"Ain't cows," Swede replied. "Those're steers."

"Steers, then. But where are they going?"

He eyed her gravely. "Bedelia, I want you to forget you saw them. No cows. No Indian."

Bedelia shrugged. "Sure. It's nothing to me."

A few days later Major Barnett came to the ranch with an escort of ten men. "I'm looking for Grayson Howard," he said shortly.

Cassandra felt the hairs rise at the nape of her neck. "He's gone to Aureus for a few days. If you have any business with my husband, you may discuss it with me."

"Aureus, eh? Well I've a report that he was seen taking twenty head of cattle across the hills north of Little Branch. And that's off your ranch, isn't it?"

"Your informant was mistaken. In any event, however, I can't see that it is any of your business if my husband takes his steers over our boundaries to graze."

Barnett took a paper from out of his tunic. "This makes it my business. There's some that don't approve of giving aid to the enemy. Selling cattle to hostiles comes under that category. Them Cheyenne and Sioux and Kiowa have been on the warpath again, raiding outlying settlements. Someone's selling them beef on the hoof up by Buffalo Creek. I aim to stop 'em."

He unfolded the document and held it out to her. "And, as you can see for yourself, this here paper give me the authority to arrest any man found conducting such illegal business—and hang him from the nearest tree."

Cassandra scanned the lines quickly. She had seen enough official papers to know it was real. She willed her hands not to shake. "Very interesting, Major Barnett. But, as I said, my husband is in Aureus or up in the hills at the mine. I shall inform him of your visit."

Barnett grinned. She was scared. He could tell by the way her pupils widened and by the stiff way she held her head. He'd come out to the ranch on a suspicion. Now he was damned sure that Grayson Howard was somewhere past Little Branch with the renegades. "Well," he said tauntingly, "then I'll just mosey on in to Aureus and speak to him myself. And if he's not there, well, I'll see that he's found and taken into custody. Can't have any redskin-lovers running loose, now can we?"

Cassandra was aware of Bedelia and Kitty standing behind her. She prayed that neither one would give her away. The major waited a few seconds, then tipped his hat. "Good day, ladies."

He rode off, whistling.

They watched him ride away with his men. Cassandra gnawed on her finger. The hands were up in the north pasture and the women were alone at the house.

"If only Bronco or Swede were here! One of them could ride out and warn Grayson to turn off and go straight in to Aureus. He should be on his way back from Black Shield's camp by now. If he rode hard he might make it in by sundown."

"Don't worry," Bedelia said without hesitation. "I'll go. I know where the camp is, and I'll take that stallion you bought from Mrs. Leslie. He looks like a prime goer."

Cassandra was horrified. "Why, you would be killed! That stallion is only half-broken."

"Hell, I can handle him. I was just pretending that I couldn't ride. I can ride anything but a tiger—and I'd try that if I could." Bedelia grinned. "I used to be a trick rider with the circus. And if I cut across the river and over the ridge, I can head Grayson off. He could be in Aureus by sunset, like you said."

Cassandra didn't know what to say. She couldn't go herself. She was far too clumsy with her ripening belly. There was no time to fetch a man from the north pasture. Bedelia put her hand out imploringly.

"Trust me. I won't let you down. And it's the only way to save Grayson. That bastard will really string him up on the spot if he catches him. And I can ride faster than the wind."

"You're taking a terrible risk."

"I promised I'd repay your kindness one day." And, her eyes said sadly, I love Grayson, too.

Cassandra clasped Bedelia's hand in hers. "I will be eternally grateful. Godspeed!"

Bedelia borrowed trousers and a shirt from Bobby, saddled the stallion with his help, and streaked off across the countryside. The boy tipped back his hat. "God damn, that girl can ride!"

Bedelia rode the stallion half into the ground. It hurt her to use it so hard, but Grayson's life and the happiness of everyone at the ranch was at stake. She was out of practice and her arms and back ached. But she'd find Grayson and warn him if it killed her.

He was coming up from the end of the valley when she intercepted them. His first reaction was fear that something had happened to Cassandra. "She's fine," Bedelia said, wiping strands of sweaty hair back from her forehead. "It's you that's in trouble."

She poured out the news of the major's plan and was dismayed when Grayson turned his bay back the way he'd come. "Where the hell are you going? Cassandra told him you were in Aureus."

"I've got to warn Black Shield before they track me here."

Bedelia was tired and sore. Jesus Christ. She never thought she'd have to throw herself on the Indian side of things. "You get yourself over to Aureus. I'll warn Black Shield."

It was a way out of the trap. But Bedelia had lied and deceived her way through life. He couldn't trust her.

She saw the look in his eye. "Please," she begged. "I swear on my own head that I'm telling the truth. And if anything happens to you, what will Cassandra do with the baby coming and all?"

He frowned at the ring of sincerity in her voice. And she'd taken a real risk herself, riding that hellion all the way here. Grayson held out his hand to her. "Thank you. I'll see that you're rewarded for this when the dust settles down."

Bedelia put her hand in his and shook it solemnly. She didn't want any reward. She wanted him, and knew that she would never have him. A simple handshake would have to suffice. "I'll see you back at Thunder," she said, and wheeled the stallion. Putting the spurs to him, she streaked off toward Black Shield's camp, while Grayson rode hell for leather toward Aureus.

That evening Major Barnett was startled to see Grayson ride down the rugged road from the mining camp. He narrowed his eyes. Son of a bitch! There was no way the man could have gotten back to the Thunder Ranch from Little Branch and then on to Aureus so quickly.

Sweat broke out on the major's forehead. Shit! He'd already been warned about overstepping his bounds after the incident with that pretty little squaw, and Grayson Howard had friends in high places. If he complained that he was being harassed, there'd be the very devil to pay. He rode over to Buffalo Mary's and consoled himself with several whiskeys and a pock-faced whore who'd do anything a man asked if he paid enough for it. In advance.

Grayson returned home on Saturday. Cassandra hurried to the door when he rode into the stableyard. He swung down from his horse and took her into his arms. She was trembling. "Everything is fine, Cassandra. Black Shield and his people are on their way to join the Northern Cheyenne along the Powder River in Wyoming. They'll go on from there when they've gathered their strength."

Time passed and the earth sprang to life in the warmth and sunshine. Blue columbines poked their graceful heads up toward the sun and yellow mountain daisies dotted the meadows. On a golden day in early June her son was born, red and furious that he'd been forced from his cozy home and into the loud, bright world. He came so quickly there was no time to notify Dr. Bean.

Ping and Kitty assisted the infant into the world while Bedelia kept the household running. Her heroic ride had wiped the slate clean, and Grayson had settled a sum of money on her. She was free to stay on now, but as she looked at her arms, plunged into soapy washwater, Bedelia shook her head. This domestic stuff was catchy, like the chicken pox. Already she was thinking of how nice it would be to settle down and have a family one day. If she was wise she'd be on her way soon.

Grayson and Cassandra smiled down at this small miracle in wonderment and awe. There was no word that either knew that could describe the joy they felt at seeing their healthy young son. They named him Micah.

Bronco and Kitty stood as his godparents for his baptism at the church in Aureus one bright August morning. Beth gave the baby a blanket she had crocheted herself, and Simon presented Micah with a silver cup. The ungrateful infant curled his tiny fingers around the handle and whacked Simon in the face. "An excellent judge of character," he said, rubbing his nose.

As they loaded up the carriages for the ride back to the ranch, Bedelia announced that she was staying behind. "Swede's cousin has a horse-breeding operation south of the border. I think I'll try my hand at breaking horses awhile. Circus riding is too tame, after what we've been through in the past year."

Cassandra embraced Bedelia. She had saved Grayson, and that had balanced the scales. "Mexico is a long way away. I'd feel better if there was someone going with you."

Swede shifted from one foot to the other. "Well, there you go. I've been thinking the same thing. You'd have to keep a sharp eye out for trouble, Bedelia. Seems," he said, brushing his hair back with his fingers, "that four eyes would be better than two. I've always had a hankering to go down to Mexico. A man can only take so much snow in his life, and I reckon I've had more than my share."

Bedelia eyed him admiringly. "A riding partner would be right welcome."

It was a fair imitation of Swede's voice, right down to the inflection. Grayson had to smile. They'd make an odd pair, but Grayson had an uncanny feeling that they might stick together. He shook Swede's hand.

"I knew I'd never keep you here long. Five years was a pretty good run." He handed him a wallet of banknotes. "Half of this is Bedelia's, come what may.

It'll be a little more inconspicuous on a big fellow like you. And there's more if you ever need it."

Swede glanced at the contents and whistled. "I think this will do just fine."

They left together shortly after, with him wondering how Bedelia would look in a red silk dress, and Bedelia wondering if there was enough money to start a little business. If the horse-breaking didn't turn out—well, she wondered if they liked circuses in Mexico. You could do a lot with six horses, a tent, and a wooden chariot.

Cassandra and Grayson spent a few days with their friends and on the way home he took a detour. They went cross-country in his specially sprung carriage, through the golden light of high summer, across the winding river at a shallow ford, and then up into the pine slopes. When they broke out of the trees they were on a stony ledge above a beautiful valley. Most of it was covered with wild grasses, but one area was denuded. Cassandra had never seen anything like it before.

Grayson led them down a trail so faint it was invisible to her eyes. She was surprised when they came out behind a fall of rock and she saw a small log cabin in a clearing. The memory of her ordeal assaulted her. She went pale as death and Grayson reached across to take her hand. "Is this the place?" she asked in a low voice. He nodded. Cassandra shook her head. "I never asked how you ever found me."

The answer was so simple. Grayson's eyes shone with that curious silver light. "This is where I was born."

She understood then why Ajax had been trying to carry her to it. He'd been here before with Grayson, many times. "I can't go in," she said. "Not yet."

"I understand."

He nudged his black gelding and they started off. She left the cabin behind without regret, and yet there was a great peace about the place, as if it stood alone above the flood of human suffering, safe unto itself.

They skirted the western edge of the valley where Grayson's cattle grazed, then doubling back to a break in the lowest rank of hills. The scenery was breathtaking, from the small flowers growing wild along the riverbanks to the panorama of the endless, snowy peaks floating like a mirage in the sky. Grayson's love for the land was unmistakable.

He showed her the fox dens and the tracks of the bobcat, the dark spots that were the nests of eagles perched on the most inaccessible ledges. They saw deer and elk and the remains of a beaver dam, half swept away in the spring floods. He pulled smooth lumps of jasper and broken pieces of banded agate from the river's shallows, and showed her how to find the tiny purple flowers hiding in the grass. Cassandra was enchanted. Micah slept cradled against her breast, smiling in his sleep.

A hundred feet later they came out into a sheltered valley. To her it was like a descent into a savage level of Dante's hell. She had wondered where they were heading, sensing a change come over Grayson. She couldn't know that he was journeying back in time, and bleeding from the heart with every step.

Fir trees terraced the slopes and the blue-gray mountains rose beyond them, cold and aloof beneath their tasseled caps of snow; but there was something about this place that made her skin crawl. Even the birds and small animals seemed to avoid it.

A river had once wound through it but the bed was dry now. Rocks and stones littered its former course.

Grayson dismounted and hunkered down, examining it. Cassandra had never seen a rock so oddly shaped. It looked like—it couldn't be—an arm bone?

It was. Now that her eyes were trained to look for them, she saw that the place was full of broken pottery and grisly relics. Her voice came out in a hoarse whisper. "What is this place?"

"You told me once that you wanted to know about me." Grayson walked slowly toward her, his face grave and shadowed with memories. "Earlier I showed you where I was born." He looked out across the silent plain. "To know me you must know this place also. This is where I died."

She went to him and put her head against his shoulder. Grayson's arms went around her like a vise. "You've given me new life, Cassandra. You and Micah have saved me from what I might have become, bitter and twisted as the scars on my back."

The memories had been locked up so deep inside him that it was like lancing an abscess. He told her his tragic story. Of his wife, and their young son. Of how he'd gone off to the trading post and returned to find them slaughtered along with the rest of the village. Slaughtered by men who wanted the land for the gold and silver hidden in it.

She was afraid to ask. Intuition told her that she wouldn't like the answer. "Who were they . . . these killers?"

Grayson almost didn't tell her. But it was time to tear down all remnants of the wall that had separated them. "They were hired guns, like Major Barnett, enlisted in a private army to clear us off our hunting grounds—by a group of wealthy white men." He went on reluctantly. "Hired by the Fortuna Investment Company."

Cassandra thought she was going to be sick to her stomach. Tyler had been more than an investor in that company, he had been its leader. "I . . . I saw the piece of metal in your desk. I thought that it belonged to Tyler. But I see now . . ." She gazed at the ground. "You found it here."

"Yes. Covered with my son's blood. I went after them and took my vengeance but I was captured. You've seen the scars of what they did to me. But in the end it was the mercenaries who died, while I lived."

He looked around the clearing. His eyes were haunted again. "I couldn't forgive myself for being away during the massacre. If I had been here I might have saved them."

"If you had been here you would have died with them."

"I wanted to. It was my punishment to live and avenge them."

She touched his face gently, and he felt the love radiating from her. "Don't look back, Grayson. Look ahead, to our future."

He knew she was right. It was time to finally bury his pain and begin anew.

He looked at her steadily and the haunted look gradually faded and was gone. "Yes. I spent a part of my life working with only one aim: to destroy the man responsible. Then I met you and Kitty and I knew I couldn't go through with it. There had already been too much blood and death."

Cassandra nodded. "In the end Tyler destroyed himself—and with Jaime's help. He was many things, but this is beyond him. He didn't know . . . I'm sure of it."

"Perhaps not until afterward. But he was as responsible as if he'd murdered them himself. A man can't excuse his actions by closing his eyes to the consequences."

Cassandra swallowed the bile in her throat. There was something wrong. She frowned. "When did the massacre take place?"

"Ten years ago next month."

She closed her eyes in relief. "Ten years ago Tyler was on his way to California from England with me. He hadn't heard of the Fortuna Investment Company, much less been its guiding partner. He bought into the company that fall. I remember, because he said it was a lucky day and the name struck him."

Cassandra was glad that whatever Tyler had been, he had not been a part of this. It would have always been there between herself and Grayson.

Grayson began to laugh at the irony. He had gone seeking vengeance and instead had been given his greatest blessing. He took the beaded medallion from around his neck. Odd, how light it seemed now. It had weighted him down like a chain. He said a prayer and put it on the ground. He was free of the past now. Old loves and old griefs were laid to rest.

Cassandra watched him bury his ghosts. When he rose she went to him. Grayson drew her close and kissed her passionately. Later they would go away from this place of memories. First he wanted to make love to her out in this wild land where he'd been born amid storms and thunder. The sun was out, warm on their faces. He looked down into her eyes. The frost was gone from his. "I want you, Cassandra. Will you lie with me?"

She smiled up at him, recognizing the same words he had spoken on their wedding night, and again when they'd first arrived at the ranch. Remembering the time beneath the cottonwoods when she'd been so horrified by his suggestion. She stood on tiptoe and pressed her mouth on his in answer. "Yes," she breathed against his lips. "Here."

His indrawn breath sent her pulse racing, and her last inhibitions fell away with their clothes. While Micah slept they made love in the clearing with the warm sun burnishing their bodies. Cassandra didn't care. She was with her beloved husband in a sheltered, private world; and she was, minute by minute, falling more in love with him. She hadn't even imagined that that was possible.

There was the same love in his face as he looked at her, but being a woman, she wanted him to say it. She tickled him beneath his chin. "You do love me, Grayson, don't you?"

He laughed suddenly, a sound of pure joy. It was a strange sound in the quiet valley. The birds flew into the branches of the trees and a squirrel ran down the hill toward it, instead of away. "I love you, Cassandra."

He wound his fingers in her hair and kissed her until she was breathless. "I love you more than I dreamed was humanly possible. More than life or reason. My God, woman, how I love you!"

Grayson pulled her into his arms again, and the sun rose overhead, chasing the last of the shadows away.

COMING NEXT MONTH

TAPESTRY by Maura Seger

A spellbinding tale of love and intrigue in the Middle Ages. Renard is her enemy, but beautiful Aveline knows that beneath the exterior of this foe beats the heart of a caring man. As panic and fear engulf London, the passion between Renard and Aveline explodes. "Sweeping in concept, fascinating in scope, triumphant in its final achievement."—Kathryn Lynn Davis, author of *Too Deep For Tears*.

UNFORGETTABLE by Leigh Riker

Recently divorced, Jessica Pearce Simon returns to her childhood home. Nick Granby, the love of her youth, has come home too. Now a successful architect and still single, Nick is just as intriguing as she remembers him to be. But can she trust him this time?

THE HIGHWAYMAN by Doreen Owens Malek

Love and adventure in 17th century England. When Lady Alexandra Cummings stows away on a ship bound for Ireland, she doesn't consider the consequences of her actions. Once in Ireland, Alexandra is kidnapped by Kevin Burke, the Irish rebel her uncle considers his archenemy.

WILD ROSE by Sharon Ihle

A lively historical romance set in San Diego's rancho period. Maxine McCain thinks she's been through it all—until her father loses her in a bet. As a result, she becomes indentured to Dane del Cordobes, a handsome aristocrat betrothed to his brother's widow.

SOMETHING'S COOKING by Joanne Pence

When a bomb is delivered to her door. Angelina Amalfi can't imagine why anyone would want to hurt her, an innocent food columnist. But to tall, dark, and handsome police inspector Paavo Smith, Angelina is not so innocent.

BILLY BOB WALKER GOT MARRIED by Lisa G. Brown

A spicy contemporary romance. Shiloh Pennington knows that Billy Bob Walker is no good. But how can she ignore the fire that courses in her veins at the thought of Billy's kisses?

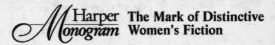 **Harper Monogram** The Mark of Distinctive Women's Fiction

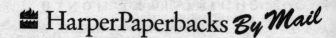
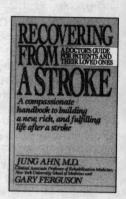